Lian Hearn's beloved Tales of the Otori series, set in an imagined feudal Japan, has sold more than four million copies worldwide and has been translated into nearly forty languages. It is comprised of five volumes: *Across the Nightingale Floor, Grass for His Pillow, Brilliance of the Moon, The Harsh Cry of the Heron* and *Heaven's Net is Wide*. The series was followed by two standalone novels, *Blossoms and Shadows* and *The Storyteller and His Three Daughters*, also set in Japan. Lian's new series, The Tale of Shikanoko, is made up of two books: *Emperor of the Eight Islands* and *Lord of the Darkwood*.

Lian has made many trips to Japan and has studied Japanese. She read Modern Languages at Oxford and worked as an editor and film critic in England before emigrating to Australia.

www.lianhearn.com
🐦 @LianHearn
📘 LianHearnAuthor
📷 LIAN_HEARN

Praise for *Heaven's Net is Wide*

Also by Lian Hearn

TALES OF THE OTORI

HEAVEN'S
NET IS WIDE

TALES OF THE OTORI

LIAN HEARN

hachette
AUSTRALIA

hachette
AUSTRALIA

First published in Australia and New Zealand in 2007
by Hachette Australia
(an imprint of Hachette Australia Pty Limited)
Level 17, 207 Kent Street, Sydney NSW 2000
www.hachette.com.au

Second edition published in 2008
Reprinted 2010

This edition published in 2016

10 9 8 7 6 5 4 3 2 1

National Library of Australia
Cataloguing-in-Publication data:

Hearn, Lian.
Heaven's net is wide / Lian Hearn.

ISBN: 978 0 7336 3521 2 (paperback)

Tales of the Otori ; book 5
Fantasy fiction.
Adventure stories.
Japan – History – Fiction.

A823.4

Cover design by KI229 Design
Text design by Ellie Exarchos and Simon Paterson (Bookhouse)
Calligraphy by Sugiyama Eiichi
Map by Xiangyi Mo
Clan symbol designed by Claire Aher
Digital production by Bookhouse, Sydney
Printed and bound in Australia by McPhersons Printing Group

Asialink

Visit www.lianhearn.com

For R

天網恢恢

疎にして漏らさず

鐡宝

Heaven's net is wide, but its mesh is fine.
tenmou kaikai so ni shite morasazu

LAO TSU

THE THREE COUNTRIES

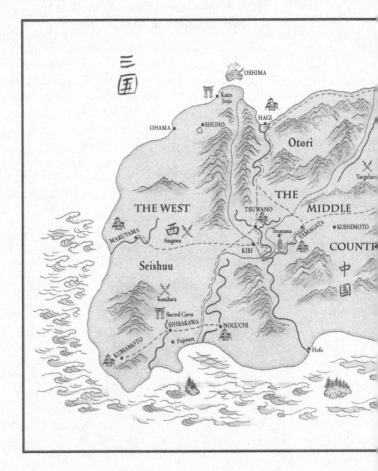

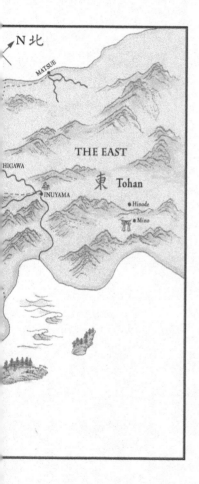

N 北

MATSUE

THE EAST

HIGAWA

東 Tohan

INUYAMA

● Hinode

Mino

───── *fief boundaries*

.... *fief boundaries before Yaegahara*

----- *high road*

 battlefields

castletown

shrine

temple

CHARACTERS

THE CLANS

The Otori
(Middle Country; castle town: Hagi)

Otori Shigeru . . . . heir to the Otori clan

Otori Takeshi . . . . his younger brother

Otori Shigemori . . . . his father, lord of the clan

Otori Masako . . . . his mother

Otori Shoichi . . . . his uncle

Otori Masahiro . . . . his uncle

Otori Ichiro . . . . Shigeru's teacher

Chiyo . . . . head maid of Lady Otori's household

Otori Eijiro . . . . head of a branch family

Otori Eriko . . . . his wife

Otori Danjo . . . . his son

Harada . . . . one of Shigeru's retainers

Komori. . . a Chigawa man, 'the Underground Emperor'

Haruna. . . . . owner of the House of the Camellias
Akane . . . . a famous courtesan, daughter of
the stonemason
Hayato . . . . her lover
Yanagi Moe . . . . Shigeru's wife

Mori Yusuke . . . . the Otori horsebreaker
Mori Yuta. . . . . his oldest son
Mori Kiyoshige . . . his second son, Shigeru's best friend
Mori Hiroki. . . . . . . his third son, who becomes a priest

Miyoshi Satoru . . . . an elder of the clan
Miyoshi Kahei . . . . his older son, Takeshi's friend
Miyoshi Gemba. . . . . his younger son
Irie Masahide . . . . . . sword instructor to the Otori boys
Kitano Tadakazu . . . . . lord of Tsuwano: an Otori vassal
Kitano Tadao. . . . . his oldest son
Kitano Masaji. . . . . his second son
Noguchi Masayoshi . . . . an Otori vassal
Nagai Tadayoshi . . . . the senior retainer at Yamagata
Endo Chikara . . . . the senior retainer at Hagi
Terada Fumimasa . . . . head of the Hagi fishing fleet
Terada Fumio . . . . his son
Matsuda Shingen . . . . a former warrior, now a priest,
later the Abbot of Terayama

The Seishuu
(An alliance of several ancient families in the West;
main castle towns: Kumamoto and Maruyama)

Maruyama Naomi . . . . head of the Maruyama clan
Maruyama Mariko . . . . her daughter
Sugita Sachie . . . . . . her companion, Otori Eriko's sister
Sugita Haruki . . . . senior retainer to the Maruyama,
Sachie's brother
Arai Daiichi . . . . heir to the Arai clan at Kumamoto

The Tohan
(The East; castle town: Inuyama)

Iida Sadayoshi . . . . lord of the Tohan clan
Iida Sadamu . . . . his son, heir to the clan

Miura Naomichi . . . . a Tohan sword instructor
Inaba Atsushi . . . . his retainer

THE TRIBE

Muto Shizuka . . . . Arai's mistress
Muto Zenko }
Muto Taku } . . . . their sons

Muto Kenji . . Shizuka's uncle, head of the Muto family,
friend to Shigeru
Muto Seiko . . . . his wife
Muto Yuki . . . . his daughter

Kikuta Kotaro............Shizuka's uncle, head of the
                                    Kikuta family
Kikuta Isamu............his cousin, one of the Tribe
Bunta ....a groom

THE HIDDEN

Sara ....Isamu's wife
Tomasu ....their son
Shimon.....................Sara's second husband
Maruta ....their older daughter
Madaren ....their younger daughter
Nesutoro ....an itinerant priest
Mari ....his niece

HORSES

Karasu..............................Shigeru's black
Kamome..............Kiyoshige's black-maned grey
Raku ....Takeshi's black-maned grey
Kyu ....Shigeru's second black
Kuri...............................a very clever bay

CHAPTER ONE

The footfall was light, barely discernible among all the myriad noises of the autumn forest: the rustle of leaves scattering in the northwesterly wind, the distant beating of wings as geese flew southwards, the echoing sounds of the village far below, yet Isamu heard it and recognized it.

He put the digging tool down on the damp grass, along with the roots he had been collecting, and moved away from it. Its sharp blade spoke to him and he did not want to be tempted by any tool or weapon. He turned in the direction of his cousin's approach and waited.

Kotaro came into the clearing invisible, in the way of the Tribe, but Isamu did not bother concealing himself in the same fashion. He knew all his cousin's skills: they were almost the same age, Kotaro less than a year younger; they had trained together, striving always to outdo each other; they had been friends, of a sort, and rivals their entire life.

Isamu had thought he had escaped here in this remote village on the eastern borders of the Three Countries, far from the great cities where the Tribe preferred to live and work, selling their supernatural skills to whoever paid them highest and finding plenty of employment in these times of intrigue and strife among the warriors. But no one escapes the Tribe forever.

How many times had he heard this warning as a child? How many times had he repeated it to himself, with the dark pleasure that the old skills induce, as he delivered the silent knife thrust, the twist of the garrotte or, his own preferred method, the poison that fell drop by drop into a sleeping mouth or an unprotected eye.

He did not doubt that it echoed through Kotaro's mind now as his cousin's shape came shimmering into sight.

For a moment they stared at each other without speaking. The forest itself seemed to fall quiet and in that silence Isamu thought he could hear his wife's voice, far below. If he could hear her, then Kotaro could too, for both cousins had the Kikuta gift of far-hearing, just as they both bore the straight line of the Kikuta that divided the palm of the hand.

'It took me a long time to find you,' Kotaro said finally.

'That was my intention,' Isamu replied. Compassion was still unfamiliar to him and he shrank from the pain it awakened in his newborn heart. He thought with regret of the girl's kindness, her high spirits, her goodness; he wished he could save her from grief; he wondered if their

brief marriage had already planted new life in her and
what she would do after his death. She would find comfort
from her people, from the Secret One. She would be
sustained by her inner strength. She would weep for him
and pray for him; no one in the Tribe would do either.

Following a barely understood instinct, like the birds
in this wild place that he had come to know and love, he
decided he would delay his death and lead Kotaro far
away into the forest; maybe neither of them would return
from its vastness.

He split his image and sent his second self towards
his cousin, while he ran swiftly and completely silently,
his feet hardly touching the ground, between the slender
trunks of the young cedars, leaping over boulders that had
tumbled from the crags above, skimming across slippery
black rocks below waterfalls, vanishing and reappearing
in the spray. He was aware of everything around him: the
grey sky and damp air of the tenth month, the chill wind
that heralded winter, reminding him that he would never
see snow again, the distant throaty bellow of a stag, the
whirr of wings and the harsh calls as his flight disturbed
a flock of crows. So he ran, and Kotaro followed him,
until hours later and miles from the village he had made
his home, Isamu allowed his pace to slow and his cousin
to catch up with him.

He had come further into the forest than ever before;
there was no sun. He had no idea where he was; he hoped
Kotaro would be as lost. He hoped his cousin would die
here in the mountains on this lonely slope above a deep
ravine. But he would not kill him. He, who had killed so

many times, would never kill anyone again, not even to save his own life. He had made that vow and he knew he was not going to break it.

The wind had shifted to the east and it had become much colder, but the pursuit had made Kotaro sweat; Isamu could see the gleaming drops as his cousin approached him. Neither of them breathed hard, despite their exertions. Beneath their deceptive slight build lay iron-hard muscles and years of training.

Kotaro stopped and drew a twig from within his jacket. He held it out, saying, 'It's nothing personal, cousin. I want to make that clear. The decision was made by the Kikuta family. We drew lots and I got the short piece. But whatever possessed you to try and leave the Tribe?'

When Isamu made no reply Kotaro went on, 'I assume that's what you are trying to do. It's the conclusion the whole family came to when we heard nothing from you, for over a year, when you did not return to Inuyama or to the Middle Country, when you failed to carry out tasks assigned to you, commissioned – and paid for, I might add – by Iida Sadayoshi himself. Some argued that you were dead, but no one had reported it and I found it hard to believe. Who could kill you, Isamu? No one could get near enough to do it with knife or sword or garrotte. You never fall asleep; you never get drunk. You have made yourself immune to all poisons; your body heals itself from all sickness. There's never been an assassin like you in the history of the Tribe: even I admit your superiority, though it sticks in my gullet to say it. Now I find you here, very much alive, a very long way from where you are supposed to be. I have to accept that you have absconded from the Tribe, for which there is only one punishment.'

Isamu smiled slightly but still said nothing. Kotaro replaced the twig inside the front fold of his jacket. 'I don't want to kill you,' he said quietly. 'That's the judgement of the Kikuta family, unless you return with me. As I said, we drew lots.'

All the while his stance was alert, his eyes restless, his whole body tense in expectation of the coming fight.

Isamu said, 'I don't want to kill you either. But I will not return with you. You are right to say I have left the Tribe. I have left it forever. I will never go back.'

'Then I am under orders to execute you,' Kotaro said, speaking more formally as one who delivers a sentence of justice. 'For disobedience to your family and to the Tribe.'

'I understand,' Isamu replied, equally formally.

Neither of them moved. Kotaro was still sweating profusely despite the cold wind. Their eyes met and Isamu felt the power of his cousin's gaze. Both of them possessed the ability to induce sleep in an opponent; both were equally adept at withstanding it. The silent struggle continued between them for many moments before Kotaro brought an end to it by pulling out his knife. His movements were clumsy and fumbling, with none of his usual dexterity.

'You must do what you have to do,' Isamu said. 'I forgive you and I pray Heaven will too.'

His words seemed to unnerve Kotaro even further. 'You forgive me? What sort of language is this? Who in the Tribe ever forgives anyone? There is either total obedience or punishment. If you have forgotten this you have turned stupid or mad – in any case the only cure is death!'

'I know all this as well as you. Just as I know I cannot escape you or this judgement. So carry it out, knowing that I absolve you from any guilt. I leave no one to avenge me. You will have been obedient to the Tribe and I . . . to my lord.'

'You will not defend yourself? You will not even try to fight me?' Kotaro demanded.

'If I try to fight you I will almost certainly succeed in killing you. I think we both know that.' Isamu laughed. In all the years that he and Kotaro had striven with each other he had never felt such power over the other man. He held his arms wide, his chest open and undefended. He was still laughing when the knife entered his heart; the pain flooded through him, the sky darkened, his lips formed the words of parting. He began the journey on which he in his time had sent so many others. His last thought was of the girl and for the warm body in which, though he did not know it, he had left a part of himself.

CHAPTER TWO

These were the years when the warlord Iida Sadayoshi, who employed so many members of the Tribe, including Kikuta Kotaro, was engaged in unifying the East of the Three Countries and compelling minor families and clans to submit to the triple oak leaf of the Tohan. The Middle Country had been held for hundreds of years by the Otori, and the current head of the clan, Lord Shigemori, had two young sons, Shigeru and Takeshi, and two discontented and ambitious half-brothers, Shoichi and Masahiro.

Takeshi had been born the year Lady Otori turned thirty-two; many women were already holding their grand-children by that age. She had been married to Shigemori when she was seventeen and he twenty-five. She had conceived a child almost immediately, giving great hope for a swift guarantee of succession, but the child, a boy, had been still-born, and the next, a girl, lived only a few hours after birth. Several miscarriages followed, all water-children consigned to the care of Jizo: it seemed her womb was too unstable to carry a living child to full term. Doctors, then priests, were consulted, and finally a shaman from the mountains. The doctors prescribed foods to strengthen the womb: sticky rice, eggs and fermented soybeans; they advised against eating eel, or any other lively fish, and brewed teas that were reputed to have calming properties. The priests chanted prayers, and filled the house with incense and talismans from distant shrines; the shaman tied a straw cord round her belly to hold the child in, and forbade her from looking on the colour red, lest she revive the womb's desire to bleed. Lord Shigemori was privately advised by his senior retainers to take a concubine – or several – but his half-brothers Shoichi and Masahiro were inclined to oppose this idea, arguing that the Otori succession had always been through legitimate heirs. Other clans might arrange their affairs differently, but the Otori, after all, were descended from the imperial family, and it would surely be an insult to the Emperor to create an illegitimate heir. The child could of course have been adopted and so legitimized, but Shoichi and Masahiro were not so loyal to their older brother that they did not harbour their own ideas about inheritance.

Chiyo, the senior maid in Lady Otori's household, who had been her wet nurse and had brought her up, went secretly into the mountains to a shrine sacred to Kannon, and brought back a talisman woven from horse hair and strands of paper as light as gossamer and holding within it a spell, which she stitched into the hem of her lady's night robe, saying nothing about it to anyone. When the child was conceived Chiyo made sure her own regime for a safe pregnancy was followed: rest, good food, and no excitement, no doctors, priests or shamans. Depressed by her many lost babies, Lady Otori held little hope for the life of this one; indeed, hardly anyone dared hope for a live child. When the child was born, and it was a boy and furthermore showed every sign of intending to survive, Lord Shigemori's joy and relief were extreme. Convinced it was born only to be taken from her, Lady Otori could not nurse the child herself. Chiyo's daughter, who had just given birth to her second son, became his wet nurse. At two years old the child was named Shigeru.

Two more water-children were consigned to the care of Jizo before Chiyo made another pilgrimage to the mountains. This time she took the living baby's navel cord as an offering to the goddess, and returned with another woven talisman.

Shigeru was four when his brother was born. The second son was named Takeshi – the Otori favoured names with Shige and Take in them, reminding their sons of the importance of both the land and the sword, the blessings of peace as well as the delights of war.

The legitimate succession was thus secured to the great relief of everyone except possibly Shoichi and Masahiro, who hid their disappointment with all the fortitude expected of the warrior class. Shigeru was brought up in the strict, disciplined way of the Otori, who valued courage and physical skill, keen intelligence, mental alertness, self-control and courtesy in grown men and obedience in children. He was taught horsemanship; the use of sword, bow and spear; the art and strategy of war; the government and history of the clan; and the administration and taxation of its lands.

These lands comprised the whole of the Middle Country from the northern to the southern sea. In the north, the port of Hagi was the Otori castle town. Trade with the mainland and fishing the rich northern seas made it prosperous. Craftsmen from Silla on the mainland settled there and introduced many small industries, most noteworthy the beautiful pottery: the local clay had a particularly pleasing colour, which gave a flesh-like lustre to the pale glazes. Yamagata, in the centre of the country, was their second most important city, while trade was also conducted in the south from the port of Hofu. Out of the Three Countries, the Middle Country was the most prosperous, which meant its neighbours were always eyeing it covetously.

In the fourth month of the year after Kikuta Isamu's death, the twelve-year-old Otori Shigeru came to visit his mother, as he had done once a week since he had left the house he had been raised in and gone to live in the castle as his father's heir. The house was built on a small point near the conjunction of the twin rivers that encircled the town of Hagi. The farms and forests on the opposite bank belonged to his mother's family. The house was built of wood, with verandas all around it, covered by deep eaves.

The oldest part of it was thatched, but his grandfather had had a new wing constructed with a second floor and a roof of bark shingles, an upstairs room and a staircase made out of polished oak. Though Shigeru was still a few years off his coming-of-age day, he wore a short sword in the belt of his robe. This day, since his visit to his mother was considered an occasion of some formality, he wore appropriate clothes, with the Otori heron crest on the back of the large-sleeved jacket and divided wide trousers under the long robe. He was carried in a palanquin, black lacquered with sides of woven reeds and oiled silk curtains, which he always raised. He would have preferred to ride – he loved horses – but as the heir to the clan certain formalities were expected of him, and he obeyed without question.

He was accompanied in a second palanquin by his teacher Ichiro, a distant cousin of his father's, who had been in charge of his studies since he was four years old and had begun his formal education in reading, writing with the brush, history, the classics and poetry. The palanquin-bearers jogged through the gates. The guards all came forward, and fell to their knees as the box was set down and Shigeru stepped out. He acknowledged their bows with a slight inclination of his head, and then waited respectfully for Ichiro to extricate himself from his palanquin. The teacher was a sedentary man and was already smitten by pains in the joints that made bending difficult. The old man and the boy stood for a moment, looking at the garden, both affected by the same sudden gladness. The azaleas were on the point of flowering and the bushes were brushed with a red gleam. Around the pools, irises bloomed white and purple, and the leaves of the fruit trees were a bright fresh new green. A stream flowed through the garden and red-gold carp flickered below its surface. From the far end came the sound of the river at low tide, a gentle lapping – and the familiar smell, beneath the scent of flowers, of mud and fish.

There was an arch in the wall, a conduit through which the stream flowed into the river beyond. A grille of bamboo rails lashed together usually stood against the opening to prevent stray dogs entering the garden – Shigeru noticed it had been pulled to one side and he smiled inwardly, remembering how he used to go out onto the riverbank the same way. Takeshi was probably playing outside, engaged in a stone battle, no doubt, and his mother would be fretting about him. Takeshi would be scolded later for not being ready, dressed in his best clothes, to greet his older brother, but both mother and brother would be quick to forgive him. Shigeru felt a slight quickening of pleasure at the thought of seeing his brother.

Chiyo called a welcome from the veranda, and he turned to see one of the maids kneeling beside her on the boards with a bowl of water ready to wash their feet. Ichiro gave a deep sigh of satisfaction and, smiling broadly in a way he never did at the castle, walked towards the house – but before Shigeru could follow him there was a shout from beyond the garden wall, and Endo Akira came splashing through the water. He was covered in mud and bleeding from cuts on his forehead and neck.

'Shigeru! Your brother! He fell in the river!'

Not so long ago, Shigeru had engaged in similar battles, and Akira had been one of his junior officers. The Otori boys, along with Akira and Takeshi's best friend Miyoshi Kahei, had an ongoing feud with the sons of the Mori family who lived on the opposite bank and considered the fish weir their own private bridge. The boys fought their battles with round black stones, prised from the silt at low tide. They had all fallen in the river at one time or another, and had learned to deal with it in all its treacherous moods. He hesitated, reluctant to plunge into the water, disinclined to dirty his clothes and insult his mother by making her wait for him.

'My younger brother can swim!'

'No. He hasn't come up!'

A lick of fear ran round his mouth, drying it.

'Show me.' He leaped into the stream and Akira came after him. From the veranda he heard Ichiro call in outrage, 'Lord Shigeru! This is no time for playing! Your mother is waiting for you.'

He noticed how low he had to bend to go beneath the arch. He could hear the different notes of the water, the cascade from the garden, the splash of the stream as it flowed through the conduit onto the beach by the river. He dropped onto the mud, felt it close malodorously over his sandals, tore them off, and his jacket, and his robe, dropping them in the mud, hardly noticing, aware only of the green empty surface of the river. Downstream to his right he saw the first column of the unfinished stone bridge rising from the water, the incoming tide swirling between its footings, and one boat, carried by the same tide, steered by a young girl. In the instant his eyes flashed over her he saw she was aware of the accident, was rising and stripping off her outer robe, preparing to dive. Then he looked upstream to the fish weir where the two younger Mori boys were kneeling, peering into the water.

'Mori Yuta fell in too,' Akira said.

At that moment there was a splashing disturbance in the water and Miyoshi Kahei surfaced, gasping for breath, his face pale green, his eyes bulging. He took two or three deep breaths, then dived again.

'That's where they are,' Akira said.

'Go and get the guards,' Shigeru said, but he knew there was no time to wait for anyone else. He ran forward and plunged into the river. A few paces from the bank it deepened rapidly, and the tide was flowing back strongly, pushing him towards the fish weir. Kahei surfaced again a little in front of him, coughing and spitting water.

'Shigeru!' he screamed. 'They're stuck under the weir!'

Shigeru thought of nothing now except that he could not let Takeshi die in the river. He dived down into the murky water, feeling the strengthening power of the tide. He saw the cloudy figures like shadows, their pale limbs entwined together as though they were still fighting. Yuta, older and heavier, was on the outer side. Pushed against the wooden structure of the weir, in his panic he had forced Takeshi further between the piles. His loincloth seemed to be snagged on a jagged piece of wood.

Shigeru was counting under his breath to keep himself calm. The blood was beginning to pound in his ears as his lungs demanded air. He pulled at the sodden cloth but it would not come free. He could not get Yuta out of the way to reach Takeshi. He felt a movement in the water next to him and realized he was not alone. He thought it was Kahei but saw the pale outline of a girl's breast against the darkened wood and the green weed. She grasped Yuta and jerked at him. The cloth broke free. The boy's mouth was open: no bubbles came from it. He looked already dead – Shigeru could save one but not both, and at that moment he could think of no one but Takeshi. He dived further in and grabbed his brother's arms.

His lungs were bursting, his vision red. Takeshi's limbs seemed to move, but it was only the river's current rocking them. He seemed extraordinarily heavy: too heavy for an eight-year-old, far too heavy for Shigeru to lift. But he would not let go. He would die in the river with his brother before he left him alone in it. The girl was alongside him, dragging at Takeshi, lifting them both upwards. He could just make out her eyes dark and intense with effort. She swam like a cormorant, better than he did.

The light above was tantalizingly near. He could see its fractured surface but he could not reach it. He opened his mouth involuntarily – maybe to breathe, maybe to call for help – and took in a mouthful of water. His lungs seemed to scream in pain. The river had become a prison, its water no longer fluid and soft but a solid membrane closing round him, choking him.

Swim up. Swim up. It was as if she had spoken to him. Without knowing how, he found a tiny amount of strength left. The light brightened dazzlingly, and then his head broke through the surface and he was gulping air. The river relaxed its serpent grip and held him up, and held Takeshi up in his arms.

His brother's eyes were closed and he did not seem to be breathing. Treading water, shivering, Shigeru placed his mouth over his brother's and gave him his breath, calling on all the gods and spirits to help him, rebuking the river god, rebuking death itself, refusing to let them take Takeshi down into their dark world.

Guards from the house had appeared on the riverbank and were splashing into the water. One of them took Takeshi and swam strongly back to the shore. Another plucked Kahei up and helped him swim back. A third tried to help Shigeru, but he pushed him away.

'Mori Yuta is still down there. Bring him up.'

The man's face blanched and he dived immediately.

Shigeru could hear the youngest Mori boy sobbing on the weir. Somewhere in the distance a woman was screaming, a high sound like a curlew. As he swam to the shore and staggered from the water, Shigeru was aware of the ordinary peacefulness of the late afternoon, the warmth of the sun, the smells of blossom and mud, the soft touch of the south wind.

The guard had laid Takeshi face down on the beach and was kneeling beside him, pushing gently on his back to empty the water from his lungs. The man's face was shocked and sombre, and he kept shaking his head.

'Takeshi!' Shigeru called. 'Wake up! Takeshi!'

'Lord Shigeru,' the guard began, his voice trembling. He could not speak the terrible fear, and in his emotion pressed more strongly on the child's shoulders.

Takeshi's eyes flickered and he coughed violently. Water streamed from his mouth, and he choked, cried out and retched. Shigeru raised him, wiped his face and held him as the boy retched again. He felt his eyes grow hot, and thought Takeshi might weep from relief or shock, but the boy struggled to his feet, pushing Shigeru away.

'Where's Yuta? Did I beat him? That'll teach him to come on our bridge!'

Takeshi's loincloth and sleeves were full of stones. The guard tipped them out, laughing.

'Your weapons nearly killed you! Not so clever, was it!'

'Yuta pushed me in!' Takeshi cried.

Despite Takeshi's protests, the man carried him back to the house. News of the accident had travelled fast; the maids from the household had come running into the street and were crowded on the bank.

Shigeru gathered up his clothes from the mud and put them on. He wondered if he should bathe and change before he saw his mother. He looked back at the river. The girl had climbed back into her boat and dressed herself again. She did not look towards him but began to row downstream against the tide. Men were still diving repeatedly for Yuta. Shigeru remembered the clinging, stifling embrace of the river and shivered, despite the warmth of the sun. He bent again and picked up one of the smallest stones – a round black pebble, water-smoothed.

'Lord Shigeru!' Chiyo was calling to him. 'Come,' she said. 'I'll find you fresh clothes.'

'You must apologize to my mother for me,' he said as he vaulted up onto the bank. 'I am sorry to keep her waiting.'

'I don't believe she will be angry,' Chiyo said, smiling. She took a quick look at Shigeru's face. 'She will be proud of you, and your father too. Don't be sad, don't fret over it. You saved your brother's life.'

He was weakened by relief. The enormity of what might have happened was still too close. If he had not been in the garden; if Akira had not found him; if he had called the guards first; if the girl had not dived down after him... He had been brought up to have no fear of death, nor to grieve excessively over the deaths of others, but he had not yet lost anyone close to him, and he had not realized how fierce was his love for his brother. Grief came close to him with its grey numbing breath and its array of insidious weapons to flay the heart and torment the mind. He saw how grief was an enemy to be feared far more than any warrior; he realized he would have no armour against its assault. And he knew that the rest of his life would be a struggle to hold grief at bay by keeping Takeshi alive.

CHAPTER THREE

The following day, Mori Yuta's body was washed up on the opposite bank, a little downstream from his family home. Whatever their own grief might have been, his parents hid it in their shame and remorse for nearly drowning the son of the lord of the clan. Yuta was twelve; almost a man. He should not have been indulging in childish games, causing danger to an eight-year-old. After the funeral, his father sought and was granted an audience with Lord Otori.

Shigemori and his younger brothers were seated in the main hall of the Otori residence, which lay within the castle grounds, surrounded by gardens leading down to the great stone walls that rose directly from the sea. The senior retainers were also in the room: Endo Chikara, Miyoshi Satoru and Irie Masahide. The sound of the waves and the smell of salt washed through the open doors. As summer progressed, every day became warmer and more humid, but here the air was cooled by the sea, as well as by the dense forest that covered the small hill behind the castle. At the top of the hill was a shrine to the sea god where a huge bronze-cast bell hung, said to have been made by a giant; it was struck if foreign ships were sighted or a whale stranded on the beach.

The three Otori lords were dressed in formal robes and wore small black hats, and each held a fan in his hand. Shigeru knelt to one side. He also wore formal robes – not the ones that had been mud- and water-stained; they had been carefully washed and then presented to the small shrine near his mother's house where the river god was worshipped, along with many other gifts of rice wine and silver, in the hope that the spirit would be placated. Many in the town murmured that the god was offended by the building of the new bridge and had seized the boys in anger – it was a warning: the construction should be stopped at once. The stonemason was spat upon, and threats made to his family. But Lord Shigemori had set his heart on the bridge, and would not be dissuaded from it. The footings for the arches were in place and the first arch already rising from them.

All these thoughts flashed through Shigeru's mind as Mori Yusuke prostrated himself before the three Otori brothers. He was a horseman, and taught Shigeru and the other warriors' sons. He bred and broke the Otori horses, who were said to be fathered by the river spirit; now the river had taken his son in return. His family were middle rank, but wealthy. Their own ability and their water meadows had brought them prosperity. Shigemori favoured Yusuke to the extent of entrusting his son's education to him.

Yusuke was pale but composed. He raised his head on Shigemori's command, and spoke in a low, clear voice.

'Lord Otori, I deeply regret the pain I have caused you. I have come to offer you my life. I ask only that you will permit me to kill myself after the fashion of a warrior.'

Shigemori said nothing for a few moments. Yusuke lowered his head again. Shigeru saw his father's indecisiveness: he knew its causes. The clan could not afford to lose a man of Yusuke's competence, but the affront had to be addressed or his father would lose face and be perceived as weak. He thought he saw impatience in his uncles' expressions, and Endo was frowning deeply too.

Shoichi cleared his throat. 'May I speak, brother?'

'I would like to hear your opinion,' Lord Otori said.

'The insult and grievance to the family are unpardonable in my view. It is almost too much of an honour to allow this person to take his own life. The lives of his whole family should also be required, and the confiscation of his lands and property.'

Shigemori blinked rapidly. 'This seems somewhat excessive,' he said. 'Masahiro, what are your thoughts?'

'I must agree with my brother.' Masahiro ran his tongue over his lips. 'Your beloved son Lord Takeshi nearly died. Lord Shigeru was also endangered. Our shock and grief were extreme. The Mori family must pay for this.'

Shigeru did not know his uncles well. He had barely seen them when he lived at his mother's house. They were both considerably younger than his father, born of a second wife who still lived with her oldest son, Shoichi; he knew they had young children of their own, still toddlers or infants, but he had never set eyes on them. Now he saw his uncles' faces and heard their words as he would a stranger's. The expressions were those of loyalty to their older brother and devotion to the family, but he thought he discerned something deeper and more self-serving behind the soft-spoken phrases. And his father was right: the punishment demanded was far too harsh; there was no reason to ask for the lives of the family – he recalled the boy sobbing on the weir and the other brother; the woman who had screamed like a curlew on the bank – unless his uncles coveted what they had: Yusuke's fertile land and crops, and above all his horses.

His father broke into his thoughts. 'Lord Shigeru, you were the most immediately affected by these unfortunate events. What would be, in your opinion, a punishment both just and sufficient?'

It was the first time he had ever been asked to speak during an audience, though he had been present at many.

'I am sure my uncles are prompted only by devotion to my father,' he said, and bowed deeply. Sitting up, he went on: 'But I think Lord Otori's judgement is correct. Lord Mori must not take his own life: rather he must continue to serve the clan, which benefits highly from his loyal service and his skills. He has lost his oldest son and has therefore already been punished by Heaven. Let him make recompense by dedicating one of his other sons to the river god, to serve at the shrine, and by donating horses to the shrine also.'

Shoichi said, 'Lord Shigeru displays wisdom beyond his years. Yet I do not believe this deals with the insult to the family.'

'The insult was not so great,' Shigeru said. 'It was an accident that happened during a boys' game. Other families' sons were involved. Are their fathers to be held responsible too?'

All the fathers involved were present in the room – Endo, Miyoshi, Mori and his own... Something sparked anger in him, and he burst out, 'We should not kill our own. Our enemies are eager enough to do that.'

His argument sounded hopelessly childish in his own ears and he fell silent. He thought he saw scorn in Masahiro's expression.

Lord Otori said, 'I agree with my son's judgement. It will be as he suggests. With one addition. Mori: you have two surviving sons, I believe. Let the younger go to the shrine, and send the older one here. He will enter Shigeru's service and be educated with him.'

'The honour is too great,' Mori began to protest, but Shigemori held up a hand.

'This is my decision.'

Shigeru was aware of his uncles' hidden annoyance at his father's judgement, and it puzzled him. They had all the advantages of rank and sufficient wealth yet they were not satisfied. They had desired Mori's death not for the sake of honour but for darker reasons of their own – greed, cruelty, envy. He did not feel able to voice this to

23

his father or to the senior retainers – it seemed too disloyal to the family – but from that day on, he watched them carefully without seeming to, and he lost all trust in them.

CHAPTER FOUR

Mori Kiyoshige became Shigeru's closest companion. While his younger brother had been sobbing on the weir, Kiyoshige had run to his home to fetch help. He had not cried then or later: it was said of him that he never shed tears. His mother had been prepared for her husband's death and the family's ruin; when Yusuke returned home alive, and with the news that Kiyoshige was to go to the castle, she wept in relief and joy.

Kiyoshige was small in stature, but already immensely strong for his age. Like his father he had a great love of horses, and great skill with them. He was self-confident almost to the point of brashness and, once he had got over his shyness, treated Shigeru in the same way as he'd treated Yuta, arguing with him, teasing him, even occasionally scrapping with him. His teachers found him irrepressible – Ichiro in particular found his patience stretched to the limit – but Kiyoshige's good humour, cheerfulness, physical courage and skills at horsemanship endeared him to his elders as much as he irritated them, and his loyalty to Shigeru was complete.

Despite their relative prosperity, the family had been brought up with great frugality and a disciplined way of life. Kiyoshige was used to rising before sunrise and helping his father with the horses; then working in the fields before the morning's lessons. At night, while his mother and sisters did sewing work, he and his brothers were expected to study, if they were not engaged in more practical tasks like making sandals from straw while their father read to them from the classics, or discussed theories of horse breeding.

The Otori valued two sorts of horses above all others: blacks, and pale greys with black manes and tails. Mori bred both sorts and ran them in the water meadows. Occasionally a grey would be so pale as to be almost white, with white mane and tail. When the horses galloped together, they were like a storm cloud of black and white. The year Kiyoshige went to the castle, his father gave a young black colt to Shigeru, a black-maned grey the same age to his son, and presented a pure white horse to the shrine along with his youngest son, Hiroki. The white horse became a sort of god itself. Every day it was led to a stall in the shrine grounds, where people brought it carrots, grain and other offerings. It became very fat and rather greedy. The shrine was not far from Shigeru's mother's house, and occasionally he and his brother were taken to festivals there. Shigeru felt sorry for the horse that could not run free with the others, but it seemed perfectly content with its new divine status.

'Father chose this one because of its placid nature,' Kiyoshige confided in Shigeru one day that summer, as they hung over the poles at the front of the horse's stall. 'It would never make a warhorse, he said.'

'The god should have the best horse,' Takeshi said.

'It is the best-looking.' Kiyoshige patted the snowy-white neck. The horse nuzzled him, looking for treats, and when it found none drew back its pink lips and nipped the boy on the arm.

Kiyoshige smacked it; one of the priests who had been sweeping the entrance to the shrine came hurrying over, scolding the boys. 'Leave that holy horse alone!'

'It's still just a horse,' Kiyoshige said quietly. 'It shouldn't be allowed to get away with bad manners!'

Hiroki, his younger brother, trailed after the priest, carrying two straw brooms that were taller than he was.

'Poor Hiroki! Does he mind having to be the priest's servant?' Takeshi said. 'I'd hate it!'

'He doesn't mind,' Kiyoshige whispered confidentially. 'Father said that too – Hiroki is not a warrior by nature. Did you know that, Shigeru? When you gave your opinion?'

'I saw him dance the heron dance last year,' Shigeru said. 'It seemed to move him deeply. And he cried when your older brother drowned, while you did not.'

Kiyoshige's face hardened and he said nothing for a few moments. Finally he laughed and gave Takeshi a punch on the shoulder. 'You have already killed – and you are only eight. You've outstripped both of us!'

No one else had dared say this aloud, but it had occurred to Shigeru too, and he knew others thought it.

'It was an accident,' he said. 'Takeshi did not mean to kill Yuta.'

'Maybe I did,' Takeshi muttered, his face fierce. 'But he was trying to kill me!'

They dawdled under the shade of the curved eaves of the shrine building. 'Father can't help putting the horse first,' Kiyoshige said. 'Even if it's a question of an offering to the gods. The horse has to have the right nature to be an offering – most of the horses would be miserable standing in a stall all day, never having the chance to gallop.'

'Or to go to war,' Takeshi said longingly.

To go to war. The boys' heads were full of it. They trained for hours with the sword and the bow, studied the history and the art of war, and at night listened to the older men tell stories of the ancient heroes and their campaigns: they heard of Otori Takeyoshi, who had first received the legendary sword Jato – the Snake – from the Emperor himself hundreds of years earlier, and who had slain a tribe of giants single-handed with the same sword. And all the other Otori heroes right down to Matsuda Shingen, the greatest swordsman of the present era, who had taught their fathers the use of the sword, who had rescued Shigemori when he had been ambushed by the Tohan clan, five men against forty on the border with the

East, and who had been called by the Enlightened One and now served him at the temple at Terayama.

Now Jato had been passed down to Shigeru's father, and one day it would be his.

Above their heads hung carvings of the long-nosed goblins that lived in the mountain. Glancing up at them, Kiyoshige said, 'Matsuda Shingen was taught the use of the sword by goblins. That's why no one else came near him.'

'I wish I could be taught by goblins!' Takeshi said.

'Lord Irie is a goblin,' Kiyoshige replied, laughing – their sword instructor did have an abnormally long nose.

'But the goblins could teach you all sorts of things Irie doesn't know,' Takeshi said. 'Like making yourself invisible.'

There were many stories about men with strange powers: a tribe of sorcerers. The boys discussed them endlessly with a certain amount of envy, for their own skills emerged slowly and painfully out of rigorous training. They would have loved to be able to escape their teachers through invisibility or other magic skills.

'Can people really do that?' Shigeru questioned. 'Or is it just that they can move so fast it's as if they were invisible. Like Lord Irie's pole when it hits you!'

'If it's in the stories, someone at some time must have been able to,' Takeshi said.

Kiyoshige argued with him. They talked in whispers, for the sorcerers from the Tribe could both hear and see from afar. The other world of goblins, ghosts and in-human powers lay alongside their own; occasionally the membrane between the two worlds thinned and one rolled into the other. There were stories too of people who strayed into the other world and then came back to find a hundred years had passed in a single night. Or of beings that came from the moon or the sky and seemed like women, and made men fall in love with them. There was a road leading towards the south where a beautiful woman with a long neck like a snake enticed young men into the forest and fed on their flesh.

'Hiroki used to cry about the goblins,' Kiyoshige said. 'And now he's living here among them!'

'He cries at everything,' Takeshi said scornfully.

CHAPTER FIVE

Isamu's body was buried first by falling leaves and then by snow, and lay undiscovered until the following spring when the village boys began to search the mountains for mushrooms and birds' eggs. By that time his murderer, his cousin Kotaro, was long back in Inuyama, the clan capital of Iida Sadayoshi and the Tohan, where he ran a business making soybean products, lent money and behaved much like any other merchant of the city. Kotaro told no one of the precise details, only that the execution had been carried out and Isamu was dead, and he tried to put the whole affair out of his mind with his customary callousness, but at night Isamu's face floated before his eyes and he was often woken by his cousin's fearless and incomprehensible laughter. He was tormented by the fact that Isamu had refused to defend himself, had spoken of forgiveness and obedience to some lord. Death had not removed his rival, the traitor; it had made him more powerful; indeed, invincible.

Kotaro had at his command a network of spies, for the Tribe operated throughout the Three Countries, working at this time mainly for the Iida family as they tightened their grip on the East and began to consider how they might expand into the Middle Country and beyond. The Iida family kept a close watch on the Otori, whom they correctly judged to be their main rivals; the clans in the West were less warlike, more prepared to make alliances through marriage. The Middle Country, moreover, was rich, had many silver mines and controlled fishing and trade in the northern and southern seas. The Otori would not relinquish it lightly.

Kotaro began to make enquiries about the villages that might lie near where he had tracked Isamu down. None was recorded on any map, nor counted as a source of taxation by any domain. There were many places like this throughout the Three Countries; the Tribe had a few themselves. Two things made Kotaro uneasy. The lingering fear that Isamu might have left a child, and the gradual uncovering of something he had known little about: a secret sect who lived unrecognized among the poorest – peasants, outcasts, prostitutes – where people had too hard a struggle of their own to concern themselves overmuch about their neighbours; for this reason sect members were known as the Hidden.

Kotaro began to gather fragments of information about them, information he was careful to pass on to his contacts among Iida's warriors, in particular a man called Ando, whose lineage was obscure but who had come to be one of Sadayoshi's most trusted retainers on account of his cruel tastes and brutal skill with the sword. The two main facts that emerged about the Hidden – that they would take no life, including their own, and that they paid allegiance to an unseen god, greater than any lord – were both serious affronts to the warrior class. It was not hard, through Ando, to inspire Sadayoshi's son, Sadamu, with hatred for this sect and to initiate the drive to eradicate them.

Kotaro never found the village but he trusted that sooner or later Iida Sadamu and his warriors would, and any children Isamu might have left behind would be dealt with.

CHAPTER SIX

The colts grew and at three years old were broken in by Lord Mori with Kiyoshige's help. The routine of study and training continued. Shigeru and Kiyoshige were joined by the two sons of Kitano Tadakazu, Tadao and Masaji. Tadakazu was the lord of Tsuwano, a small castle town three days' journey to the south of Hagi, in the shadow of the main mountain range that divided the Middle Country. It was an important stopping place on the high road to Yamagata, the second city of the Otori clan, and had many inns and eating places. The Kitano family had a residence in Hagi, where the boys lived while pursuing their education with the others of their generation. They became a close-knit group, encouraged by their teachers not to compete with each other but to form strong ties of loyalty and comradeship that would be the basis of the future stability of the clan. Their different abilities were recognized and fostered: Shigeru with the sword, Tadao with the bow, Kiyoshige with horses, Masaji with the spear.

As they began to grow to their adult stature, they also experienced together the first urgencies of desire. Shigeru dreamed often of the girl in the river, though he never saw her again, and found himself gazing with longing at the form of a maid kneeling in the doorway, the white nape of her neck, the curve of her body beneath the soft robe; Kiyoshige, although a year younger, was precocious in development and equally stirred. In the way of close friends they turned to each other, discovering the pleasures of the body, sealing the bonds between them with passion. One day one of the maids, a year or two older than Shigeru, came into the room, surprising them – she apologized deeply, but her breathing quickened and a flush rose in her cheeks; she loosened her robe and joined in with great willingness. Shigeru was enthralled by her for two weeks – he was enchanted by the feel of her skin and by her silky pelt, the scent that emanated from her body and the way her desire matched his without shame – until she disappeared suddenly and his father summoned him.

To his surprise they were alone in the room – the first time he could remember ever being in his father's presence without the senior retainers or his uncles there. Lord Otori beckoned to him to come closer, and when they sat knee to knee his father scrutinized his face.

'You are nearly a man, it seems, and you must learn how to behave with women. They are among the great pleasures of life and enjoyment of them is entirely natural.

But your position means that you cannot indulge yourself as freely as your friends might. It is a question of inheritance and legitimacy. The woman in question has been sent away; if she has conceived a child it could cause problems, particularly if we do not know if the father is you or Kiyoshige. At the right time I will provide you with a concubine, who will be yours alone. It will be best not to have children with her. Children should only be born to your legitimate wife. A marriage will be arranged, of course, but at the moment you are too young, and there is no suitable alliance.'

His voice changed slightly. He leaned forward and spoke more quietly. 'I must also counsel you to resist becoming infatuated. There is nothing more contemptible than a man who is distracted from his duty, turned from his purpose or weakened in some other way because of love for a woman. You are young and the young are very susceptible. Be on your guard. Many women are not what they seem. I am going to tell you of my own experience: I hope it will prevent you from making the mistake I did – one that has haunted me all my life.'

Shigeru found he also leaned forward to catch every word.

'I was about your age – fifteen – when I started to notice a girl who worked here: a maid. She was not beautiful, but there was something about her that I found immensely attractive, irresistible. She was full of life, very graceful and seemed very self-contained. She was always perfectly respectful and her ways of service were irreproachable, yet something lurked in her expression, as if she were laughing – at men in general, at the lords of the castle, myself included. She knew how I felt – she was very quick-witted and observant: you felt she could hear your thoughts, and she came to me one night when I was alone and gave herself to me. We were each other's first lovers; I became obsessed with her and she told me often that she loved me. My own father had spoken to me as I have to you, about the dangers of sleeping with maids and the folly of falling in love, but I did not seem able to combat the way I felt. It was truly stronger than I was.'

He paused, sunk in memories of his remote youth. 'Anyway, she came to me one day unexpectedly, saying she had to talk to me. It was the hour of study; I was waiting for one of my teachers and tried to send her away. But at the same time I could not resist taking her in my arms. My teacher came to the door. I asked him to wait, saying I felt unwell. I tried to hide her – but there was no need. She heard him coming long before I did; it was as if she had disappeared. There was no sign of her in the room. When the man had left she was there again. One moment she was nowhere, the next she stood in front of me. All the strange things I knew about her ran through my mind: her unnaturally acute hearing, the curious lines on her palms which seemed to cut her hand in half. I thought I understood my infatuation: clearly she had bewitched me. I thought she must be some kind of sorceress. I realized with a sort of sick dread the risks I had been taking. She told me then who she was: one of the Tribe.'

He paused and looked questioningly at Shigeru. 'Do you know what that means?'

'I have heard of the name,' Shigeru replied. 'Sometimes the boys talk about them.' He paused, then added: 'People seem afraid of them.'

'With good reason. The Tribe are a collection of families, four or five maybe, who claim to retain skills from the past – skills that the warrior class have lost. I have seen some of these skills first hand, so I know they are real: I have seen a person disappear and come back from invisibility. The Tribe are used, in particular by the Tohan, as spies and assassins. They are invariably extremely effective.'

'Do the Otori use them?' Shigeru asked.

'Occasionally: but not to the same extent.' He sighed. 'This woman told me she was from the Kikuta – the lines on the palms were characteristic of that family. She said she had indeed been sent as a spy, from Inuyama; she admitted it all very calmly, as though it were not by any means the most important thing she wanted to tell me. I was silent in shock. It was as though a spirit from beyond the sky or a shape-shifter had captivated me. She took my hand and made me sit in front of her. She said that she would have to leave me; we would never see each other again – but that she loved me, and that within her she carried the proof of our love: my child. I was never to tell anyone: if the truth were ever known, both she and the child would die. She made me swear it to her. I had nearly lost my senses through shock and grief. I tried to seize her in my arms, gripping her roughly: maybe the thought was in my mind that I would kill her rather than lose her. She seemed to dissolve at my touch. I held her: then my arms were empty. I embraced air. She was gone. I never saw her again.

'It is over thirty years ago, and I have never been free of longing for her. She is almost certainly dead by now – and our child, if it lived, is middle-aged. I often dream of him – I am sure it was a son. I am filled with fear that one day he will appear and claim me as his father; and I am filled with grief knowing that that day will never come. It has been like a chronic illness that I despise myself for. I delayed marriage for as long as I could – if I could not have her I did not want any woman. I have never told anyone of this weakness and I am trusting you never to reveal it. When I married your mother I thought I might recover, but the many dead children and your mother's grief, her desire to conceive and her fear of failing to bear a live child did not bring contentment between us. I simply longed more for my one living child, forever lost to me.

'Of course, your birth and Takeshi's have consoled me,' he added, but there was a hollowness behind the words. Shigeru felt he should speak into the silence that followed, but he could think of nothing to say. He had never been on intimate terms with his father; he had no words to use, no patterns to follow.

'It only takes one mistake to poison a life,' Lord Otori said bitterly. 'Men are at their most foolish and most vulnerable when they are ruled by their infatuations. I am telling you all this in the hope that you will avoid the trap into which I fell. I am sending you to Matsuda at Terayama. You will find no women there. The discipline of temple life and Matsuda's instruction will train you to control your desires. When you return we will find you a safe woman, with whom you will not fall in love, and after that a suitable wife – provided we are not by then at war with the Tohan. In that case we will have to put away our personal gratification and concentrate on the art of war.'

CHAPTER SEVEN

A few days later, the preparations for the journey were completed and Shigeru left for Terayama with Irie Masahide, to arrive before the plum rains made travel unpleasant with their sticky warmth. Horses and men were ferried across the river in large flat boats. The stone bridge had three of its four arches completed. It will be finished when I return, Shigeru thought.

The journey to Tsuwano would take two or three days; the road followed the river valley between the ranges, but after Tsuwano, where the land became much more mountainous, it circled the slopes and then curved back through two or three steep passes to Yamagata. Here Shigeru would spend some time reacquainting himself with the city before the short journey through the mountains to the temple.

Kiyoshige was not to accompany him: he returned to his family house; his father was raised to a higher rank and given an increased stipend. It could hardly be considered a punishment, yet to Shigeru it felt like it. He missed the cheerful, high-spirited Kiyoshige, his irreverence and his jokes. As he rode on the black, Karasu, he missed seeing Kiyoshige's grey, Kamome, alongside him with its black mane. But he kept his feelings to himself. The Kitano brothers went with him, summoned by their father to Tsuwano. The boys were puzzled by the sudden command. They had expected to remain in Hagi or go with Shigeru to Terayama. They envied him the opportunity to be taught by Matsuda Shingen and wondered why their father would not permit them to take advantage of these circumstances.

'It would be better to stay in Hagi,' Tadao said for the fourth or fifth time. 'We have no teachers in Tsuwano like Lord Irie or Lord Miyoshi. Father is a great warrior, but he is so old-fashioned.'

The spring planting was completed and the clear green of the young seedlings shone against the mirror surface of the rice fields, in which the blue sky and the high white clouds were reflected. On some of the banks around the fields, beans had been planted, their white and purple flowers attracting many bees. Frogs croaked and the summer's cicadas were beginning to drone. Shigeru would have liked to be able to look more closely at the land, talk to the farmers about their crops and methods. The last two years had been good for harvests – no infestations of insects, no great storm damage – which made everyone cheerful, but he couldn't help wondering about their lives.

He knew them only as figures from the clan records of what their fields should produce and what proportion they should pay in taxes.

The secrets his father had told him hung in his mind. The idea that he should have a brother, so many years older, tormented and fascinated him. And the boy's mother, the woman from the Tribe. The sorceress and shape-shifter. His father had met such a woman, had lain with her. The idea both horrified and aroused him. He reflected deeply on his father's life, and saw his weaknesses more clearly. He also wondered how many of the grooms who accompanied them now on the road, or the servants at the inns, might be Tribe members, spies or assassins. He did not share these thoughts with anyone, but resolved to question Matsuda Shingen during his stay at Terayama. He did not want to listen to the other boys' gossip and complaints; he had too much to think about. But he forced himself to joke lightly with them, masking his preoccupations, finding he could be two people: the ordinary fifteen-year-old, and an inner ageless man, more watchful and more guarded, the emerging adult self.

On the afternoon of the second day, they descended through the pass into a fertile valley which belonged to one of the Otori branch families, distant cousins of Shigeru's. Though of extremely high rank, this family had always farmed their own land, rather than exacting taxes from tenants. Shigeru was enchanted by their residence, which combined the restrained elegance of the warrior class with a rustic informality, and impressed by the head of the household, Otori Eijiro, who seemed endlessly knowledgeable about the nature of the land and its crops. His family was large and boisterous, though somewhat subdued on this occasion by the status of their guest and his companions.

After the visitors had washed the dust of the journey from their feet and hands, they sat in the main room, all the doors open to catch the soft breeze from the south. Eijiro's wife and three daughters brought tea and sweet bean-paste cakes. His sons put on a display of horsemanship in the grassy meadow to the south of the house, then they all competed with the bow, shooting both on horseback and on foot; Tadao was declared the winner and Eijiro gave him a quiver made from deerskin. The two older girls also competed and were equal to their brothers in skill. When Shigeru commented on this – for though most Otori girls learned to ride he had never seen women taught the arts of war – Eijiro gave his usual loud laugh. 'My wife is from the Seishuu. In the West they teach their girls to fight like men. It is the influence of the Maruyama, of course. But why not? It keeps the girls healthy and strong, and they seem to love it.'

'Tell me about Maruyama,' Shigeru said.

'It's the last of the great Western domains to be inherited through the female line. The present ruler is Naomi; she's seventeen and recently married. Her husband is a much older man closely connected to the Iida family. It seemed a strange alliance; there's no doubt the Tohan hope to acquire the domain by marriage, stealth or war.'

'Have you been there?' The West lay at least a week's journey beyond Yamagata.

'Yes, I have. I spent some time with my wife's parents two or three years ago. The domain is rich: they trade with the mainland and mine copper and silver. They get two crops of rice a year – we are considered too far north for that but I intend to try it myself. It was a pleasure to be there. I learned many new things, new ideas and methods.'

'Did you meet Lady Naomi?' For some reason his interest was aroused in this girl, not much older than himself, who ruled and fought like a man.

'Yes, indeed. My wife is from the Sugita family; her cousin Sugita Haruki is Lady Naomi's senior retainer. My wife is the same age as Naomi's mother and has known Naomi since she was born. In fact, my wife's sister is Naomi's closest companion. Lady Naomi is a remarkable young woman, intelligent and with great charm. I think my wife modelled our girls' education on hers.'

'They have benefited greatly from it,' Shigeru replied.

'Well, they are only a pale copy of Lady Naomi, and many in the Middle Country think that I am a fool.' Eijiro tried to look modest, but his pride in his children could not be completely disguised. Shigeru liked him even more for it.

That night they ate venison – mountain whale, Eijiro laughingly called it – for many country people added meat to their diet by hunting, though the teachings of the Enlightened One, followed by the warrior class, forbade the killing of four-footed animals for food.

Shigeru was also given gifts: a small steel-bladed dagger, home-woven indigo garments, and barrels of rice wine to present to the temple.

The following day, wanting to know his host better, he rose early and accompanied Eijiro on his morning inspection of the rice fields and vegetable gardens. He noticed how the older man spoke to the peasants, asking their advice and occasionally praising them. He noticed the exchange of respect between them.

This is the way to treat men, he thought. They are bound to Eijiro by more than custom and rules. Attention and respect ensure their loyalty.

He asked many questions about Eijiro's methods, intrigued by the interlocking systems of fertilizing and cropping, observing how they followed the cycle of the seasons and enhanced the natural fertility of the land. Not an inch was wasted, yet the earth was always being replenished. The villagers he saw looked well fed; their children were healthy and happy.

'Heaven must approve of your ways,' he said, back at the residence.

Eijiro laughed. 'Heaven sends many challenges: droughts, insects, floods, storms. But we know the land, we understand it... I think we are blessed by Earth as much as by Heaven. This has always been the Otori way,' he added quietly, glancing at Shigeru. 'If Lord Shigeru wishes to know more about it, I have written a little on the subject...'

His oldest son, Danjo, said, 'A little! Father is too modest. Lord Shigeru could read for a year and not come to the end of Father's writings.'

'I would very much like to read them,' Shigeru replied. 'But I fear I will have no time; we must ride on today.'

'You must take some with you. You may be able to add them to your studies while you are at the temple. You are the heir to the clan: it is fitting that you know about the land.'

Eijiro said no more, but he was frowning and his usually bluff, open expression was clouded. Shigeru imagined he heard the unspoken thoughts: that his father had no such interests; indeed the castle lands around Hagi were left entirely to officials to run. They were productive enough, he knew, but they did not look like Eijiro's. Overmindful of his own position, introspective by nature, indulging in private grief and regret, his father had allowed himself to be cut off from the land that gave him that position. A fief is like a farm, Shigeru thought: everyone in it has their place and their purpose, and all work together for the good of the whole. When the head of the farm is just and competent like Eijiro, everyone flourishes.

He thought of his farm, the fief of the Middle Country, and felt pride and joy flood into his belly: it was his and he would cherish and protect it, like this beautiful valley. He would fight for it, not only with the sword in the way of the warrior, but with Eijiro's tools.

Several scrolls of Eijiro's writings were added to the boxes of gifts. Tadao and Masaji teased Shigeru about them.

'You have the luck to study the sword with Shingen and you'd rather spend time reading about onions!' Masaji mocked.

'Lord Eijiro can have my shit for his mulberry trees and pumpkins,' Tadao said. 'But he's not getting my brain too.'

'His sons are skilful warriors as well as being farmers,' Shigeru said.

'Skilful! They wield the bow more like a hoe. They fought like girls. It was so easy to beat them!' Tadao replied with arrogance.

'Maybe because they train with their sisters,' Masaji added scornfully. 'If all the Otori fight like them, we deserve to be overrun by the Tohan.'

Shigeru thought this was no more than a careless remark and he did not comment on it. However, it returned to him later, when they reached Tsuwano and were welcomed in the castle by the boys' father, Lord Kitano. The contrast between the two families could hardly have been greater. Eijiro, being related to the clan lord's family, was of higher rank than Kitano, but Kitano maintained a small castle and, like Shigeru's father, delegated the running of his estates to officials. He was passionate about war, its conduct and strategy, and the appropriate training and upbringing for young men.

The Kitano lived an austere, soldierly life. The food was simple, the living rooms uncomfortable, the mattresses thin. Despite the season of early summer, the castle interior was gloomy, the lower rooms dank, the upper rooms stiflingly hot in the middle of the day.

Lord Kitano treated Shigeru with all the necessary deference, but the young man found his manner patronizing, his opinions rigid and old-fashioned. His sons, who had been so outspoken and lively in Hagi and on the journey, became silent, speaking only to agree with their father, or to repeat to him some tenet they had learned from Ichiro or Endo.

Lord Irie said very little, and drank sparingly, his attention mainly on Shigeru and his needs. There was another guest present: an Otori vassal from the south of the Middle Country, Noguchi Masayoshi. During the evening's conversation it transpired that Noguchi would accompany Kitano's sons to Inuyama. Neither of the lords revealed much more about this plan, and the boys hid their surprise. Nothing had been said about it in Hagi, and Shigeru was sure his father had not known about it.

'At Inuyama my sons will learn the art of real warfare,' Kitano said. 'Iida Sadamu is gaining the reputation of being the greatest warrior of his generation.' He drank, and glanced from under his heavy eyebrows at Irie. 'Such knowledge can only benefit the clan.'

'Presumably Lord Otori has been informed,' Irie said, though he must have known the contrary.

'Letters have been sent,' Kitano said, a vague note creeping into his voice. Shigeru read his evasiveness, and suspected he could not be trusted. He wondered about Noguchi Masayoshi too. Noguchi was in his early thirties, the eldest son of an Otori vassal family whose southern domain included the port of Hofu. It was in the south that the Otori were most vulnerable – less protected by mountains, the south lay between the ambitious Iida family in Inuyama and the rich lands of the Seishuu in the West. It would be hard for Kitano to resist the Tohan if his sons were in Inuyama. They might as well be hostages. Shigeru felt anger beginning to simmer in his belly. If the man was not a traitor, he was a fool. Was it up to him to forbid expressly such a rash decision? If he advised against it, and Kitano disobeyed him, it would bring out into the open divisions that could only lead to strife within the clan – maybe even to civil war. He had been surrounded all his life by loyalty: it underpinned the whole structure of the warrior class – the Otori prided themselves on the unswerving loyalty that bound all the ranks to each other and to the head of their clan. He had been aware of his father's weaknesses, but had not realized how these were viewed by men such as Kitano and Noguchi, who had their own ambitions.

He tried to find an opportunity to speak to Irie about his misgivings. It was not easy, as they were always accompanied by Kitano or his retainers. Before they retired, he said he would like to walk outside for a while, to enjoy the night air and the waxing moon, and asked Irie to accompany him. They were led from the castle to the battlements, huge stone walls that rose from the moat where the moon's silver disc was reflected in the black, still water. Occasionally there was a splash as a fish surfaced or a water rat dived. Guards were stationed at each right-angled turn of the walls and above the bridge that led from the castle to the town, but they were relaxed – Tsuwano had been at peace for years; there was no threat of invasion or attack. The idle chat of the guards, the tranquil night, the moon above the sleeping town, did not allay Shigeru's fears. He duly admired the moon and the battlements, but there was no way of seeking his teacher's advice discreetly. When they retired, Shigeru told the servants to leave them alone, and sent Irie to make sure no one lingered outside to eavesdrop: no maids, servants or guards. He remembered his father's words. If Kitano were in contact with the Tohan, might he not use the same spies from the Tribe?

When Irie returned and he felt safe, he said quietly, 'Should I prevent them going to Inuyama?'

'I believe you should,' Irie replied, equally softly. 'And strongly. There must be no doubt about your wishes. I do not believe Kitano will defy you openly. If there is any treachery smouldering, we will contain it early. You must speak to him in the morning.'

'Should I have spoken at once?'

'You were right to ask advice first,' Irie responded. 'It is usually better to proceed slowly and with patience. But there are times when one has to act decisively: wisdom is knowing which course to pursue, and when.'

'My instincts were to forbid it at once,' Shigeru murmured. 'I must confess, I was astonished.'

'I was, too,' Irie said. 'I am sure your father does not know.'

Shigeru slept restlessly and woke angry with Kitano, with the boys he had thought were friends, and with himself for not acting immediately.

His anger grew when his request to speak to Lord Kitano was delayed. By the time the lord's arrival was announced, he felt insulted and deceived. He cut short the customary courtesies by saying abruptly, 'Your sons must not go to Inuyama. It cannot be in the best interest of the clan.'

He saw Kitano's eyes harden and realized the temper of the man he was dealing with: ambitious, strong-willed, deceitful.

'Forgive me, Lord Shigeru, they have already left.'

'Then send horsemen after them and bring them back.'

'They set out last night, with Lord Noguchi,' Kitano said blandly. 'Since the rains will commence any day now, it was thought –'

'You sent them out because you knew I would forbid it,' Shigeru said angrily. 'How dare you spy on me?'

'What can Lord Shigeru be talking about? There was no spying. It was a longstanding arrangement, to take advantage of the waxing moon. If your lordship had objections, you should have made them known last night.'

'I will not forget this,' Shigeru said, fighting to master his rage.

'You are young, Lord Shigeru, and – forgive me – inexperienced. You are yet to learn the art of statecraft.'

His rage exploded. 'Better to be young and inexperienced than old and treacherous! And why has Noguchi gone to Inuyama? What are you plotting between you with the Iida?'

'You accuse me, in my own castle, of plotting?' Kitano let his rage rise in response, but Shigeru was not intimidated.

'Do I need to remind you that I am the heir to the clan?' he replied. 'You will send messengers to Inuyama to demand the return of your sons, and you will not conduct any negotiations or other dealings with the Tohan without the knowledge and consent of my father and myself. You may give the same message to Noguchi. I will leave at once for

Terayama. Lord Irie will return to Hagi as soon as possible after my arrival there and my father will be informed. But first I expect you to reaffirm your pledges of loyalty to myself and to the Otori clan. I am displeased, affronted by your behaviour. I think my father would be too. I expect your complete loyalty from now on. If my wishes are not complied with, if there are any further such lapses, you and your family will face punishment.'

His words sounded weak in his own ears. If Kitano or Noguchi defected to the Tohan, they could not be stopped except by resorting to war. He could see that the rebuke had struck home: Kitano's eyes were smouldering.

I have made an enemy, Shigeru thought as the older man prostrated himself, swearing loyalty and obedience, and asking forgiveness. All this is a deception. Both his penitence and his loyalty are feigned.

'How did Kitano know my decision?' he asked Irie as they left Tsuwano an hour later.

'He may have guessed it; he may have set spies on us last night.'

'How dare he!' Shigeru felt the rage rise in him again. 'He should be forced to slit his belly; his lands should be seized. But you yourself checked that we were not overheard.' The thought came to him fleetingly that Irie also was not to be trusted, but glancing at the warrior's honest face, he put it from him. He did not believe Irie Masahide would ever entertain even the slightest thought of treachery against his clan. Most of the Otori would be like him, surely? But I must not be too trusting, he told himself. Even though I am inexperienced.

'He may use Tribe spies with their acute hearing,' Irie said.

'No one could have heard us –'

'No one normal,' Irie said. 'But the Tribe have powers that go beyond normal.'

'Then what defence do we have against them?'

'It is cowardly to use them,' Irie said bitterly. 'No true warrior would stoop to such methods. We should trust in our strength, in the horse and the sword. This is the way of the Otori!'

But if our enemies use them, what alternative do we have? Shigeru wondered.

CHAPTER EIGHT

Proving that Kitano's fears about the onset of the plum rains were fabricated, the weather stayed fine and mild; Shigeru put aside his anger and unease to enjoy the pleasures of the journey. It only took three days to reach Yamagata, where he was received rapturously. He knew the town and its castle well, having often stayed there with his father. Every year, in the autumn, the seat of government was moved from Hagi to Yamagata for three months, returning to winter in Hagi. Yamagata lay on the high road to Inuyama: it was as important for trade as it was for defence and it was within easy reach of the most sacred place in the Middle Country: the temple at Terayama, where the worship of the Enlightened One took place alongside an ancient shrine where the older gods of the forest and mountain were honoured. Here were the tombs of Shigeru's ancestors: almost all of them were buried here, the rare exceptions lying at the temple of Daishoin in Hagi.

The Otori loved Hagi for the beauty of its setting, for the islands that surrounded it, for its twin rivers; but they loved Yamagata for its closeness to Terayama and, more mundanely, for its inns and drinking places, its hot springs and its beautiful women.

Not that Shigeru had any dealings with the women, though his eye was drawn to them constantly. Irie was somewhat ascetic by nature, believing in discipline and self-restraint, and Shigeru was influenced sufficiently by this and by his father's disclosures to try to master his own desires.

They spent three weeks in the mountain town, during which time Shigeru met with the senior retainer, Nagai Tadayoshi, and the clan officials, and heard their reports on military and administrative matters. There had been one or two skirmishes on the Eastern borders with Tohan warriors – nothing serious; the Tohan had been driven back with little loss of Otori lives, but these small straws might show the direction of the coming wind. And there were a number of people fleeing from the East, it was rumoured, though it was hard to know how many since they slipped across the border by mountain paths, now the snows had melted.

'There is talk of a religious sect,' Nagai Tadayoshi told Shigeru. 'They call themselves the Hidden. They are extremely secretive and live alongside ordinary villagers with no one knowing the difference. It explains how they survive here: existing families that we know nothing about must take them in.'

'What kind of religion – one of the differing forms of worship of the Enlightened One?'

'Possibly. I have not been able to find out. But the Tohan seem to dislike them intensely and seek to eradicate them.'

'We should try to find out more about them,' Shigeru said. 'They have no connection with the Tribe?'

'It does not seem so. There are very few Tribe families in Yamagata and the surrounding districts.'

How can you be so sure? Shigeru wondered, but did not speak the thought aloud.

Still impressed by Eijiro's ideas on farming, Shigeru asked Nagai to accompany him into the countryside, to see for himself the methods used by the farmers, and their way of life.

'It is quite unnecessary.' Nagai was taken aback. 'Lord Shigeru can be shown the records and the figures.'

'I want to see what the records cannot show me: I want to see living people,' he replied. Despite the usual excuses and delaying tactics he found he was able to get his own way by stubborn insistence. He realized that in the end everyone had to defer to him. He had of course known this in theory, since he was the heir to the clan, but up until this time he had been bound by the ties of obligation and respect to his teachers and elders: they had influenced and moulded his character. Now as he approached adulthood he became aware of the full extent of his power, and how it might be wielded. The older men might resist him, might argue with him and delay him, but they had to submit to his wishes no matter what their opinion of them. The knowledge of this power was sometimes exhilarating, but more often sobering. His decisions had to be the right ones, not for himself but for the clan. He was aware of his shortcomings in both wisdom and experience, but he trusted in his instincts and in the vision he had had of his fief as a farm.

'There is no need to arrange a formal procession,' Shigeru said when Nagai eventually gave in. He had had enough of ceremony. 'I will ride with Irie, yourself and a couple of guards.'

'Lord Otori.' Nagai bowed, his lips pressed tightly together.

Shigeru went out into the villages, saw the flooded rice fields being weeded, learned how the dikes were constructed and the water managed, climbed into airy lofts and heard the silkworms munching their short lives away, and finally overcame the reluctance of his companions and the shyness of the farmers and spoke to them, learning from their own mouths about their skills and customs, from their hands about their farming implements; heard the drums of the summer festivals held in local shrines high in the hills, as the rice god was celebrated with straw ropes and paper figures, rice wine and dancing; saw fireflies above clear rivers in the velvet dusk; realized the hardships and rewards of this life, its eternal cycles, its indestructibility. He put on travelling clothes, unmarked by the clan symbol, relishing the feeling of anonymity, but he could not remain unrecognized for long. People stopped work to look at him, and he was aware of their gaze, conscious that he was becoming a symbol to them, transcending his own self and his human limitations, turning into the embodiment of the Otori clan. He was there for three weeks only, but it was a visit that was never forgotten, forming the foundation of the love and reverence the people of Yamagata held for Otori Shigeru.

He also rode or more often walked through the town, noting its shops and small businesses, soybean processing and wine fermenting, swordsmiths, potters, lacquer artists, carpenters, mat-makers, painters and draughtsmen, peddlers and street sellers; he had map-makers come to the castle to show him their charts of the town and he pored over them, memorizing each house, each shop and temple, resolving he would do the same in Hagi when he returned.

Nagai was an austere and meticulous man. The records of the Otori clan at Yamagata were scrupulously kept. Shigeru grasped how easy it was to find information among the scrolls, which were kept in paulownia and camphor wood boxes, rue leaves placed inside. They were stored in logical order, by year, district and family, and written clearly and legibly, even the oldest ones. It was reassuring to see the history of his people recorded in such detail. Realizing that the records interested Shigeru as much as the farmers and townspeople, Nagai softened towards him. By the end of his visit, the two had formed a close bond of respect and affection, and like Shigeru's teachers in Hagi – Irie, Miyoshi and Endo – Nagai was relieved that the son showed none of his father's shortcomings of indecisiveness and introspection.

•

Shigeru would have stayed longer – there was so much to learn – but the imminent arrival of the plum rains demanded his departure. However, Yamagata was close enough to the temple to allow frequent visits, he hoped, during the year he was to spend with Matsuda Shingen.

As they rode slowly past the rice fields, where dragonflies skimmed and hovered, and into the bamboo groves, his thoughts turned to the man who would be his teacher. Everyone spoke with awe of Matsuda, of his supreme skill with the sword, his unequalled knowledge of the art of war, his complete mastery of mind and body, and now his devoted service to the Enlightened One.

Like all his class, Shigeru had been raised in the teachings of the saint, brought from the mainland centuries before but adapted somewhat to the philosophy of the warrior. Self-control, domination of the passions, awareness of the fleeting nature of existence and the insignificance of life and death were all instilled from childhood, though to the fifteen-year-old, life seemed not at all insignificant but something immeasurably rich and beautiful, to be enjoyed with all the senses, and his own death so remote as to be almost inconceivable. Yet he knew death could happen at any moment – a fall from a horse, an infected scratch, a sudden fever – as easily as on the battlefield, and at this time more probably. He had no fear of his own death – the only death he still feared was Takeshi's.

The saint, a young man like himself, a ruler with all the material blessings life can offer, had been moved by pity for men and women trapped in the never-ending cycle of birth, death and suffering, and had studied, travelled and finally sat in meditation until he came to the Enlightenment that freed him and all those who followed him. Many hundreds of years later the warrior Matsuda Shingen had become one of the most devoted of his disciples, had given up the practice of war and was now a simple monk, rising at midnight to pray and meditate, often fasting, developing skills of mind and body that most men did not even dream of.

So Shigeru had heard from his companions in Hagi, but what he remembered most clearly from his previous visits was the older man's bright eyes and serene expression, filled with wisdom and humour.

Here, deep in the forest, cicadas droned incessantly. The horses' necks turned dark with sweat as the climb grew steeper. The air beneath the huge trees was humid and still. By the time they reached the inn at the foot of the steps to the temple, it was almost midday. Here they dismounted and washed hands and feet, drank tea and ate a little. Shigeru changed his clothes and put on more formal attire. It was almost unbearably sultry; the day had darkened and clouds were massing in the west. Irie was anxious about returning to Yamagata. Shigeru told him to leave at once.

Several of the men stayed at the inn with their horses. They would remain there for the entire year in case Shigeru needed them. The rest returned with Irie, first to Yamagata, then, when the weather allowed it, to Hagi. There was no time for long farewells – rain was already threatening.

Two monks had come from the temple to greet Shigeru. He gave one final look at Irie and his men as they rode back down the mountain path, one of them leading Karasu, the banners with the Otori heron floating above the last horse, and then followed the monks as they began to climb the steep stone steps. Servants trailed after him with baskets and boxes, his other clothes, presents for the temple, Eijiro's writings and scrolls from Yamagata.

The monks did not speak to him. He was alone with his thoughts, a mixture of anticipation at this new stage of his life and apprehension, knowing that the training and discipline would be immensely demanding, fearing it would be too hard, that he would fall short or fail, conscious – overconscious, maybe – of who he was, not wanting to disgrace his father and his own name. He had no intention of sharing these misgivings with anyone, but when he came through the temple gates where Matsuda was waiting for him in the first courtyard, he felt the older man's penetrating eyes could see through his chest and read the records of his heart.

'Welcome, Lord Shigeru. I consider it a great honour that your father has entrusted you to my care. I will take you to meet our Abbot and show you your room.'

As they stepped out of their sandals onto the boards of the cloister, Matsuda added, 'You are to lead the life of a novice, apart from studying with me. Therefore you will sleep and eat with the monks and join them in meditation and prayer. You will have no special privileges while you are here. If you are to be trained in self-mastery, the more humble your spirit the better.'

Shigeru said nothing, not sure how this humbleness would sit with his awareness of his position as heir. He was not used to thinking of others as superior, or even as his equals. His rank had been instilled into him in many subtle ways since he was born. He hoped he was not arrogant – he knew he was not humble.

They walked past the main hall, where lamps glowed around the golden figure of the Enlightened One. Incense filled the air, and Shigeru was conscious of many half-hidden monks in the dimness: he felt the power of their concentration, and something within him lifted in response, as if his spirit had been touched and wakened.

'Yes, your father judged it right. You are ready,' Matsuda murmured, and Shigeru felt his apprehension fall away.

The Abbot was a tiny, wizened man – Shigeru had never seen anyone so old. He must have been at least eighty. Men were considered adults at sixteen, women at fifteen; age twenty-five to thirty was the prime of life, forty already approaching old age. Few lived beyond sixty years; Matsuda must be close to fifty, the same age as his father – and next to the Abbot he looked like a young man.

The old man was supported by arm rests, but he still sat erect, legs folded beneath him. Like Matsuda, he wore a plain monk's robe, woven from hemp and dyed brown. His head was shaved. Round his neck was a string of ivory prayer beads, from which hung a silver amulet with a strange engraving on it, holding inside a prayer written in some distant temple on the mainland – in Tenjiku itself, possibly. Shigeru bowed to the floor before him. The old man did not speak, but exhaled deeply.

'Sit up,' Matsuda murmured. 'The Lord Abbot wishes to see your face.'

Shigeru raised himself, his own eyes carefully cast down, while the other's bright black eyes studied him. Still the old man did not speak.

Glancing up, Shigeru saw him nod twice. Then the eyes slowly closed.

Matsuda touched Shigeru on the shoulder and they both lowered their foreheads to the floor. A strange fragrance emanated from the old man, not the sour smell of age that might have been expected, but a sweet rich scent that hinted at everlasting life. Yet the old man seemed only a breath away from death.

Matsuda confirmed this as they left. 'The Lord Abbot will depart from us shortly. He has been awaiting your arrival. He wanted to advise on your studies. Once that is done, he will be free to leave us.'

'Does he ever speak?' Shigeru asked.

'Very rarely now, but those of us who have served him for many years have an understanding with him.'

'I suppose Lord Matsuda will become Abbot in his place?'

'If the temple and the clan desire me to, I cannot refuse,' Matsuda replied. 'But for now I am a humble monk, one among many, no different from any other, except I have the honour to be your teacher.' He smiled radiantly when he said this. 'I am looking forward to it! This is where you will sleep.'

The room was huge and empty, the thin mats that the monks slept on folded and put away in the closets behind sliding doors. On the floor lay a pile of clothes.

'Your own things will be stored away for you,' Matsuda said. Shigeru had dressed in his most formal clothes in honour of the Abbot and the temple. Now he took off the plum-coloured silk garment, woven with a deeper pattern of purple, the Otori heron in silver on the back; it was carefully folded and put away, along with his other clothes. In its place he put on the simple brown robe like the monks' – the only difference between him and them now was that his hair was not cut. The material, clean but not new, was rough, unlike the silk he was used to; it chafed his skin and had an unusual smell.

There was a clap of thunder overhead, and a few moments later the sound of rain pouring in torrents onto the roofs and cascading from the eaves.

CHAPTER NINE

The rain continued without let-up for a week. Every day Shigeru expected his lessons with Matsuda to start but he did not see the older man, nor did anyone speak to him other than to instruct him, with the other novices, in the teachings of the Enlightened One. The monks rose at midnight, prayed and meditated until daybreak, ate the first meal of the day – a little boiled rice mixed with barley – and devoted themselves to the daily chores of the temple: sweeping, washing, tending the gardens and the vegetable plots; though these outdoor activities were curtailed by the rain. The novices spent three hours studying, reading sacred texts and listening to their teachers' exposition. They ate again at the first half of the Hour of the Horse, then returned to the main hall of the temple to pray and meditate.

Later in the afternoon they performed exercises designed to train them in the control of the life force and to make the body and limbs strong and supple. The exercises, Shigeru could see, bore some relation to swordplay – in the stance, the shape of the movements, though not their speed. But the boys never held a sword in their hands. The older men practised with wooden swords at this time, the clash of the poles and their sudden shouts breaking the silence of the temple, setting the doves into flight.

Shigeru overheard one of the novices whisper that they would be allowed to use poles one day, and he found himself longing for it. He practised the exercises as diligently as anyone, but he could not see how they were enhancing what he assumed he already knew. When the physical training was over, they ate again – vegetables and a little soup – then retired at dusk to sleep for a few hours until midnight.

The other boys, aged from eleven upwards, seemed in awe of him. They sometimes whispered to each other, risking a reprimand from their stern-faced teachers, but none of them spoke to him. Their heads were already shaved; unless they ran away, as novices occasionally did, the temple would be their home for the rest of their lives. Where would anyone who ran away go? They could hardly return to their families, bringing disgrace and dishonour to them; nor, being cut off from their relatives and clan, could they enter the service of any other. They would become at best masterless, at worst bandits or beggars. The boys seemed quite content with their lot: they studied hard and did not complain. Some of them entered into close friendships with older monks, performed small services for them, possibly shared their beds, certainly formed ties of affection and loyalty.

Shigeru wondered how they could bear to live without women. He had not realized how much time he had spent watching the girls in Hagi castle, always aware of their quiet presence, their soft footsteps, their scent as they knelt with trays of food, bowls of tea, flasks of wine, always offering something. Then his thoughts strayed to the girl who had offered herself to him, until he thought he would be driven out of his mind by longing for her. He slept badly at night, unaccustomed to the strict routine and always hungry. He also missed Kiyoshige, and he worried about Takeshi – who would keep his brother from killing himself if he were not around?

All the boys suffered from tiredness, their growing bodies craving sleep. The worst time was after the midday meal. They sat cross-legged, heads nodding, eyes closing, on hard black cushions in the dim hall, which was airless and heavy with the smell of incense, wax and oil. Often the priest leading the meditation would walk quietly among the seated figures, his hand descending with sudden force against an ear or a neck. Then the guilty boy would jerk awake, eyes stinging, cheeks flushing.

Shigeru dreaded being struck, not from fear of pain, but from the ignominy. He could never forget that he was the heir to the Otori clan: his role and his position had been impressed upon his nature before he could even talk. At his mother's house he had been beaten in punishment for various childish misdemeanours, but since he had lived in the castle no one had raised a hand against him. No one would have dared, even if there had been a need.

He had suffered the usual mishaps of growing up: concussion from a fall from a horse; a fractured cheekbone from a blow in practice, which turned one side of his face purple; bruises and other scars – from all these he had learned to ignore pain. When finally he could keep his eyelids up no longer and felt his whole body plunge towards sleep, the cuff from the priest was not hard, just enough to wake him; it did not hurt but it enraged him, sending such a wave of fury from his belly he thought he would faint if he did not immediately hurt someone in return. He clenched his fists and his jaw, struggling to control it, trying to submit his emotions to the calm dispassionate words of the sutras, seeking to let go of all striving, all desires . . .

But it was impossible: though he sat motionless, his heart smouldered in rage. He was full of desire and passion, full of energy. Why was he squandering all that in this dreary, lifeless place? He did not have to remain: he was wasting his time. He was not even receiving the teaching he had been so eagerly looking forward to. Matsuda was treating him with scorn; so was everyone in the temple. He could leave, no one could stop him: he was the heir to the clan. He could do what he wanted. He did not have to master his desires: he could have them all gratified – he had the power to command whoever he wanted. It was on his father's wishes that he was here, but he saw his father with a sudden flash of clarity as a weak, self-indulgent, wavering man who did not merit obedience. I would lead the clan better than he. I would not tolerate my uncles' greed; I would act at once to deal with the Tohan. The Kitano boys would not now be in Inuyama. Then he began to imagine that his uncles had had a say in sending him away: that their influence over his father was greater when he was not there, that even now they were scheming their takeover of the clan while he mouldered away here in the gloom and the rain. The idea was intolerable.

Not only was it possible for him to leave; it was his duty.

These thoughts occupied him for the rest of the day; he lay awake that night despite his tiredness, imagining the women he would have brought to him when he got to Yamagata, the hot baths he would take, the food he would eat. He would leave in the morning, walk down to the inn where his men waited for him, and ride away. No one would dare stop him.

When the bell sounded at midnight the rain had ceased, though it was still intensely humid. Shigeru felt sticky with sweat; his eyes scratched, his whole body was restless and uncomfortable. Mosquitoes whined around him as he hurried back from the privy. Owls hooted, and stars appeared overhead as the clouds broke up. Dawn was still several hours away. If it was not raining, perhaps they would work outside today – but it did not matter to him. He was not going to sneak away like a thief, but would simply leave.

After meditation, he wanted to change into his own clothes, but they had been stored away. He thought of sending for them, but decided against it. He went into the study hall, intending to inform the novice master of his intentions. The other boys were preparing their inkstones for writing practice.

Before he could speak, the older man said, 'Don't sit down, Lord Shigeru. You are to go to Matsuda today.'

'What for?' Shigeru said, somewhat impolitely, confused by this sudden obstacle to his plans, and by its timing.

'He will tell you.' The old man smiled at him and took up the scroll for dictation.

'Begin writing,' he said to the other novices. 'The causes of human suffering are manifold...'

'Where will I find him?' Shigeru asked.

'He is waiting for you in his room, across the cloister: the third on the left. Wakefulness is the way to life; the fool sleeps as if he were already dead.' One of the boys stifled a groan.

As Shigeru left the room he could hear the teacher's voice continue: 'But the master is awake, and he lives forever.'

'Ah, Lord Shigeru.' Matsuda was on his feet, dressed as if he were going on a journey. 'The rain has stopped. We can set out today.'

'Sir, where are we going?'

'To study the art of the sword. Isn't that why your father sent you?' Without waiting for an answer, he indicated two wooden swords lying on the floor. 'Pick those up.'

As Shigeru followed him back around the cloister into the entrance, Matsuda said over his shoulder, 'But perhaps you have decided to leave us.'

They both paused on the edge of the boards to step into sandals. Matsuda hitched up his robe and tied it into his sash, leaving his legs bare.

'You'd better do the same,' he said. 'Otherwise you'll get your clothes soaked. Skin dries quicker than cloth.'

Puddles dotted the gravel of the courtyard and the earth smelled of mud and rain. Beyond the gate, the moss of the further courtyard was a brilliant green. Water still dripped from the heavy thatch of the older roofs, but the sky between the scudding grey and white clouds was a deep summer blue.

'Well?' the old man prompted, looking up into Shigeru's face.

'I would not leave without consulting you.'

'You are the heir to the clan, Lord Otori. You can do what you want. There is no need for you to consult an old fool like me.'

Shigeru felt the blood tingle in his neck and cheeks. There was nothing he could say. The only choices were to grow angry and leave or to follow Matsuda docilely. He swallowed his rage, feeling as if it burnt his gullet.

'You have done me a great honour by agreeing to teach me,' he said. 'I think I am a far greater fool than you have ever been.'

'Possibly, possibly,' the old man grunted, smiling to himself. 'But then, we're all fools at fifteen.' He called out, and one of the monks came across the courtyard from the kitchens, carrying two bundles on a carrying pole, fire in a small iron pot and a bamboo basket.

'Carry these,' Matsuda said, indicating the bundles. He picked up the iron pot and basket himself, sniffing appreciatively.

Shigeru lifted the pole and put it across one shoulder, the two wooden swords across the other. The monk returned with two conical straw hats, which he placed on the others' heads.

He might be the heir to the clan, but with bare legs, a pole across his shoulders, face hidden under a deep hat, he looked and felt like a servant. He swallowed again, the irritation abrading him inside.

'Goodbye.' Matsuda nodded briefly to the monk.

'When shall we expect you?' he replied.

'Oh, sometime. Whenever.' Matsuda waved vaguely. 'You'd better send some more supplies if we're not back in a month.'

The smell from the basket was already making Shigeru's stomach ache with hunger, but it seemed a depressingly small amount of food for a month.

The deep shade of the outer gate was pleasant; beyond, the sun seemed hotter and the air stickier. They did not take the stepped path that led down to the inn at the foot of the mountain, but instead went upwards, following a small stream that cascaded down the slope.

The bundles were not heavy, but it was awkward carrying them through the heavy undergrowth, and the footing was slippery. Insects whined around his head, and horseflies bit. Matsuda went at a swift pace, clambering upwards as agilely as a monkey, while Shigeru scrambled behind him. Before long he was dripping, soaked as much by the wet grasses and bushes as by his own sweat.

After two hours or so, the path turned away from the stream, towards the north-west. They stopped here to rest for a few moments, drank from the cool water and splashed it on hands and face.

'I'm glad you decided not to leave,' Matsuda said airily, taking off his hat and wiping his face on his sleeve. 'Had you done so I might have felt obliged to accept Iida Sadayoshi's invitation to visit him at Inuyama.'

'Inuyama?' Shigeru repeated, astonished. 'Why would you go there?'

'Sadayoshi seems to think his son would benefit from my teaching. He would not risk sending him into the Middle Country; he hopes I will go to him.'

'And you would have gone?'

'Well, I don't like Inuyama. It's too hot in the summer and freezing in winter. But the Iida are not a family to be lightly insulted,' Matsuda replied. 'And Sadamu has a growing reputation as a mighty warrior.'

'But you have become a monk: you have given up that life.'

'I've learned I am a teacher above all. A teacher is nothing without worthy pupils who value and appreciate his teaching. I don't know how much Iida's son could learn from me, to be honest. He is already in his twenties: habits good or bad are usually set irrevocably by then.'

'You will not teach Iida Sadamu or anyone else from the Tohan,' Shigeru said furiously. 'I forbid it and my father would too!'

Matsuda said, 'If there are any worthy among the Otori I do not need to look elsewhere.'

Shigeru remembered his thoughts from the previous night; all those desires now seemed shallow and frivolous. Yet to open his mouth and plead his own case seemed equally contemptible. He stood and picked up the carrying pole and the wooden swords, saying nothing, determined to master his anger and his pride.

They walked mostly through forest, though sometimes this cleared into grassy slopes dotted with flowers: clover, buttercups, pink vetch. Twice, startled deer leaped away, and once a cock pheasant rose whirring almost under their feet. Kites mewed overhead, their dark pinions outlined against the blue sky. The clouds were clearing, the breeze came from the south.

Around midday Matsuda halted on the edge of one of these clearings and sat down on the grass in the shade of a huge oak. He opened the basket and lifted out one of the containers. Six small rice cakes lay on a bed of perilla leaves. Matsuda took one and held out the wicker tray to Shigeru.

Shigeru put his hands together and bowed in thanks; inside his mouth the rice cake seemed even smaller, and by the time it hit his belly it was no more than a grain. The second one disappeared as quickly and made as little impression on his hunger.

Matsuda made up the fire, adding dry grass and twigs to the glowing charcoal. He seemed in no hurry to continue. He lay back, saying, 'There's not many pleasures that can compare to this!'

Shigeru leaned against the oak's trunk, hands behind his head. Matsuda was right, he thought; it was pleasant to be outside, unknown to anyone, unbothered by retainers and attendants, free to be oneself, to know who one really was. After a while the old man fell asleep. Shigeru's eyes were heavy, but he did not think he should sleep: he did not want to be taken by surprise and killed by bandits. He gazed up into the branches of the oak. They spread above his head, seeming to touch the sky. The tree had a majesty about it that was almost sacred. Staring up at it lifted his own spirit skyward, made him imagine a world unknown to him that existed all around him and that he had never noticed. Spiders' webs stretched between the twigs, catching the sun as the south wind stirred them. Insects hummed around the tree, and birds chirped and fluttered among its leaves... And always the drone of the cicadas, the constant sound of summer. It was an entire world to these creatures, giving them food and shelter.

He fell into a sort of waking dream, lulled by the warm afternoon and its myriad sounds. The sun glinted through the dappling leaves; when he closed his eyes he could still see the patterns black against the red.

He heard a loud and unfamiliar bird call in the branches above, and opened his eyes. Perched just above him was a bird he had only ever seen in pictures, but he knew it at once: it was the houou, the sacred bird that appears when the country is at peace, under a just rule. For the Otori it had special meaning, for they wrote their name with the same character, and had done ever since the Emperor had decreed it, at the same time as the sword Jato had been given to Takeyoshi and he had married one of the Emperor's concubines. Shigeru saw its red chest, the flowing pinion of its wings, its bright golden eyes.

It gazed at him with these bright eyes, opened its yellow beak and called again. All other sounds ceased. Shigeru sat transfixed, hardly daring to breathe.

A ripple of wind set the leaves dancing; a ray of sunlight struck his eyes, dazzling him. When he moved his head to look again, the bird was gone.

He jumped to his feet, peering up into the dense foliage, waking Matsuda.

'What is it?' the old man said.

'I thought I saw... I must have been dreaming.' Shigeru was half ashamed, thinking he had fallen asleep after all, despite his good intentions. But the dream had been so vivid – and a visitation even in a dream was not to be discounted.

Matsuda stood and bent down to pick up something from the ground. He held out his hand to Shigeru. On his palm lay a single feather, a white plume, its edges tipped red as though it had been dipped in blood. 'A houou has been here,' he said quietly. He nodded two or three times and made a grunt of satisfaction. 'The right time, the right person,' he said, but did not explain more. He put the feather carefully away in the sleeve of his robe.

'I saw it,' Shigeru said excitedly. 'Right in front of me; it looked directly at me. Was it real? I thought it was just a myth, something from the past.'

'The past is all around us,' Matsuda replied. 'And the future ... Sometimes we allow ourselves to see into both. Some places seem to act as crossroads: this tree has often proved to be one of them.'

Shigeru was silent. He wanted to ask the older man what it meant, but the words he had spoken had already diminished the memory and he did not want to weaken it further.

'The houou is special to the Otori,' Matsuda said, 'but it's a long time since one has been seen in the Three Countries. Certainly not in my lifetime. There is one feather at the temple, but it is almost decayed from age, so fragile it is no longer exposed to the air; it would fall apart at once. I will keep this. It is a message for your future: that it is you who will bring peace and justice to the Three Countries.'

He added quietly, 'But the white feather is red-stained. Your death will be in the cause of justice.'

'My death?' Shigeru could not imagine it; he had never felt more alive.

Matsuda laughed. 'At your age we all think we will live forever. But each of us has only one death. We should make it count. Make sure when you die that it is the right time, that your death is important. We all hope our lives have meaning; for our deaths to be significant is a rarer blessing. Value your life: don't cling to it, but don't discard it trivially.'

'Do I have that choice?' Shigeru wondered aloud.

'The warrior must create that choice,' Matsuda replied. 'Moment by moment he must be aware of the paths that lead to life or death – his own, his followers', his family's, his enemies'. He must decide with a clear mind and unclouded judgement which path each must take. To develop this clarity is one goal while you are here.' He paused for a moment as if to let his words sink in. When he spoke again his voice had lightened. 'Now we must get moving again, or we'll be spending the night in the forest.'

Shigeru picked up the wooden swords and the bundles and slung them over his shoulders. His impatience and rebelliousness of the previous day had disappeared. He pondered Matsuda's words as he followed the teacher up the steep mountain path. He would strive to follow them and choose his own death, strive always to be conscious of the right path – but may it be many years ahead, he prayed.

CHAPTER TEN

The sun had slipped behind the mountain peaks and a blue dusk was descending when they came to a hut at a fork in the path. It was small, its roof thatch; a lean-to along one side sheltered a pile of neatly stacked logs. It had one door, a heavy wooden one, and no screens. They paused to wash their hands and drink from the nearby spring. An animal scampered under the veranda at their approach. Matsuda heaved at the door, slid it open and peered inside. He chuckled. 'It's withstood winter well. No one's been here since last summer.'

'No one but rats,' Shigeru said, looking at the droppings on the floor.

Shigeru had placed the bundles on the wooden step – hardly a veranda, though it served the same purpose. Matsuda knelt to untie one and took out a handful of wood shavings. He put the embers from the iron pot in a small brazier, added the shavings and blew gently on them. When they began to smoke he stood again and took up a broom.

'I'll do that,' Shigeru said.

'We'll share these simple chores. You go and find kindling.'

Mosquitoes whined around his head as he searched for dry wood in the gathering darkness. The forest here was beech and oak, with one alder by the pool where the spring overflowed. Here and there were white mountain lilies and arum, and near the stream kingcups gleamed. The first stars were appearing through the heavy foliage above.

He breathed out deeply.

The fallen branches on the ground were still sodden after the rain, but there was enough dead wood on the lower limbs and trunks of the trees to gather an armful of kindling. He could smell the pine shavings from the hut, a friendly human smell in the lonely forest. When he returned, a frog was calling from the pool. Another answered it.

He broke the kindling into small pieces and carried them inside. The floor was clean and Matsuda had lit a small lamp and spread out the thin hemp bedding and quilts in order to air them. The tiny room was filled with smoke.

An iron hook suspended from the ceiling held a small pot, which was starting to steam. With the extra wood it was soon boiling. Matsuda took dried mushrooms and bean paste from a container in the bamboo basket and added them to the water. After a few minutes he took the pot from the hook and poured the soup into two wooden bowls. He performed all these movements with dexterity and great skill, as though he had done them many times before, and Shigeru guessed the master had been to this hut on many occasions, alone or with other pupils, during the years he had served the Enlightened One at Terayama.

They drank the soup and followed it with the last two rice cakes from the container. Shigeru wondered what they would eat the next day; maybe they were to fast. Matsuda told him to take the pot to the spring, rinse it and refill it: he would make tea.

It was completely dark by now, the stars visible through the swaying branches, the moon a faint glow in the east behind the peaks. A vixen screamed in the distance, an inhuman sound that made him think of goblins – and suddenly of Takeshi, who had wanted to be taught the art of the sword by the goblins of the mountain, like Matsuda himself. Maybe it had been in this very place: maybe Shigeru would see the same goblins, be taught by them, become the best swordsman in the Three Countries, far better than Iida Sadamu ... He resolved not to waste a moment of this time with Matsuda, whether it involved fasting, fetching wood, sweeping the floor: he would carry out all the tasks of the disciple in order to learn from his master.

Behind the hut was a small clearing, level and smooth-grassed. Rabbits, hares, deer and other forest creatures came to graze here before sunrise. It made a perfect natural training ground, and Shigeru was eager to begin. Yet Matsuda seemed in no hurry. He roused Shigeru while it was still dark, the silent darkness that precedes dawn when the sounds of night, even the frogs, are muffled. The moon had already set, and the stars were dimmed by mist rising from the damp earth. The embers of the fire still glowed, a tiny light against the darkness of mountain and forest that lay around them.

After they had relieved themselves, washed their faces and hands in the spring and drunk from the water, Matsuda said, 'We will sit for a while. If you are to learn, it must be with an empty mind. Watch your breath; that is all you need to do.'

The old man sat down, legs crossed on the small wooden step. Shigeru could not see his face, though he was barely a pace away. He also sat, on the ground, legs crossed, hands on his knees, the first finger lightly touching the thumb.

He breathed in and out, feeling the breath as it filled his chest and flowed out through his nostrils. The inbreath was strong, the outbreath weak: the inbreath full of life, the other somehow suggestive of death. Always the strong breath followed it, the body possessed of its own desire to live, but one day that outbreath would be the last. The air would no longer go in and out of him. This body, which was so familiar to him, indeed so loved by him, would decay and rot: eventually even the bones would crumble. But his spirit? What happened to that? Would it be reborn into the endless cycle of life and death? Or into the hell reserved for the wicked, as some sects taught? Or would it reside in some remote shrine, like this one, as the country people believed, or at Terayama, where his descendants would revere him and honour him?

His descendants: he would be married; he would have children . . . he brought his thoughts back from that direction. He would not start dwelling on women. He opened his eyes and glanced guiltily at Matsuda. The old man's eyes were closed but he said quietly: 'Watch the breath.'

The breath went in and out. Thoughts circled around it like goblins or demons, clamouring for his attention.

As the fletcher whittles arrows, as the horseman tames horses, so you must direct and control your straying thoughts.

But the horses made him think of Kiyoshige, and of the black colt he had left behind. He thought he could see through the horse's eyes, taste the summer grass in the water meadows; he longed to feel the animal beneath him, the springy, controlled tension, the excitement in the curve of neck and back, the pleasure in controlling a creature so much larger and more powerful than himself. And the arrows: he felt his hands change out of their meditative pose into a longing to shape themselves around the bow, the rein, the sword.

He breathed in and out.

If you cannot quieten yourself, what will you ever learn?

The words fell into his hearing: he knew it was Matsuda who had spoken them, yet they seemed to come from some other source, some place of truth within himself. He repeated them under his breath. If you cannot quieten yourself. They became the breath. For a few brief moments his mind emptied. However, almost immediately the clamorous thoughts returned. So that's what my teacher meant! I did it. Now maybe I can start using the sword.

Impatience set its ant bite on him. As if in response, his body began to complain about its discomfort. His legs were cramped, his belly empty, his throat dry. Yet Matsuda, over three times his age, did not move at all, merely breathed calmly, in and out.

I will be like him, Shigeru thought. I will. He tried to discern the master's breathing and follow it. He watched himself breathe. In. Out.

Birds were starting to call from the trees. A thrush burst into song. He opened his eyes briefly and realized it was lighter. He could make out the shape of the hut, the trees beyond Matsuda's figure sitting above him. He could not help thinking of the morning meal: his mouth filled suddenly with water. In Hagi, at this moment, the kitchens would be coming to life, the fires stoked, the soup boiling, the cooks slicing vegetables, the maids preparing tea: the whole army of servants that maintained the life he led would be awake, working, deftly, silently. All his life he had been able to command them: even in times of famine, after natural disasters such as typhoons, droughts or earthquakes when many in the Middle Country had starved, he had not gone hungry. Now he had given all that away: he had become like one of them: dependent entirely on the will of another. He trusted Matsuda: he believed the old man could teach him many things he needed to know. He submitted his reluctant will to the master's, let the thoughts of food float into his mind and float out again, breathed in: breathed out. His mind stilled, like a green horse that finally accepts that all its bucking and rearing will not unseat the rider. He saw how all desires, all longings, can either be indulged or allowed to dissipate. He grasped what the master meant about choice. In the stillness came a sense of his spirit, a wave on the surface of the ocean; calm flooded over him, together with compassion for all beings, compassion for himself, reverence and love for Matsuda.

A sudden warmth struck him as the sun cleared the high peaks around them. Shigeru opened his eyes involuntarily, and saw that Matsuda was looking at him.

'Fine,' the old man said. 'Now we will eat.'

Shigeru stood, ignoring his cramped legs, and went into the hut. He took the pot to the spring and filled it with water, fetched wood and built up the fire. When the smoke had dissipated – like desire, he thought – and the flame glowed strong and clear, he set the water above it to boil. He took the bedding and spread it in the sun to air, trying to copy Matsuda's way of doing such things, his deftness and economy of movement. Something of the hours of meditation coloured his actions, giving him single-mindedness and concentration.

Matsuda stepped into his sandals, and beckoned to Shigeru. 'We'll see what the forest has for us this morning!'

He took a small basket and a digging tool, a sharp blade set into a curved wooden handle, and they walked up the path towards the west, the sun warm on their backs. The track curved between huge rocks for a while, and the climb was steep, but eventually the ground levelled again, and a clearing opened up in front of them. Here grew cedars, cypress and spruce; but on the edges of the clearing, ferns were starting to push through the forest floor, their heads curved in snail-like spirals. Matsuda showed Shigeru how to cut the tenderest ones; then they walked through the forest until they came to a small upland pool. It was full of birds, heron, duck and teal that took off at their approach with harsh cries. Round the edge grew wild lotus and burdock. Matsuda pulled the lotus from the water for its succulent roots, and dug the burdock from the soft ground. Its roots were long and thin, the flesh white beneath the dark, fibrous skin.

It was too early in the year for mushrooms or yams, but on their way back they found fresh sorrel leaves and the new green foliage of hawthorn bushes. Matsuda ate this as they walked and Shigeru copied him; the taste vividly recalled his childhood.

The burdock they peeled and left to soak, but the rest of the harvest formed the morning meal, boiled in soup; Matsuda poured dry rice grains into the remains of the soup and put it aside to swell. Then he told Shigeru to practise the warm-up exercises he had been studying at the temple. 'With an empty mind,' he added.

The food and the sun's warmth had brought the sleep-demon closer. Shigeru strove to drive it away as he went through the routine, thinking of the other boys at the temple, wondering if they were doing the same exercises at that moment with minds far emptier than his. But there was something about the exercises, he realized, that worked with the meditation, that enhanced it. In the same way that exercising the muscles of his mind had shown him how to control his thoughts, so using the body's muscles brought control of mind and body together. Tiredness disappeared; in its place came anticipation, and an alert calmness.

He had been moving at the measured pace he had been taught at the temple, each exercise recalled almost unconsciously as one movement followed another; he found that here in the lonely forest the impatience he had felt at the temple disappeared. He thought he had practised diligently before, but he could see now how far he had fallen short, how divided and weak his attention had been, how his own self-pride had slowed and blinded him. He watched his breath flow in and out as each exercise was executed, and felt how the sun, the air, the ground beneath his feet seemed to follow the breath and flow through him. The world around him was ready to share its power with him: its energy, lightness, steadiness. He simply had to accept the gifts and draw on them.

'Good,' Matsuda said. 'The teachers at the temple were worried that you lacked concentration – your father's greatest weakness, I'm afraid – but I think we will prove them wrong. Tie up your robe – we are going to move a little faster now.'

'Shall I bring the poles?' Shigeru started to ask, but Matsuda held up one hand.

'When you're ready for the poles, I'll tell you to bring them.'

His own robe hitched up, the old man stood in front of Shigeru, his feet planted firmly on the sandy ground.

'Watch carefully.'

The movement was so swift Shigeru could barely follow it. He saw the form of the old man, but through the lean frame, the sinewy limbs, flashed something ageless, a force that transformed his teacher. He was open-mouthed.

Matsuda saw the expression on his face and laughed. 'It's nothing magical, no sorcery or anything like that about it. Anyone can do it. You just have to work hard and empty your mind. You prepare your body for the life force to enter it, and then you use it with an undivided heart. All it takes is training: training and practice. You are not patient now, but you will be.'

Shigeru set himself to copy his teacher's movements, amazed that a man over three times his age could move so much faster. But by the end of the session, when the sun was at its highest point in the sky, he'd come to realize that the exercises he had learned gave his body the pattern in which to move. His muscles had been readied for this.

'It's a question of stages,' he said to Matsuda as they wiped the sweat from their faces. 'You build one thing on another.'

'Yes, like most things worth doing,' the old man said. 'Hard work, infinite patience, learning from those who have gone ahead.'

He seemed in a very good mood; Shigeru dared to say, 'People say that you learned from goblins!'

Matsuda laughed. 'I was taught by a holy man who lived in the mountains. Some thought he was a spirit – a goblin or even an ogre – but he was a human being, though a rare kind. I sought him out and served him as a disciple, just as you now serve me. But he was a harsher taskmaster than I am. I spent a year fetching his firewood and cleaning his dishes before he even acknowledged my existence. I was after all only a humble warrior: my time was my own. Your case has a greater urgency. We do not have forever.'

When they returned to the hut, someone had come silently and left offerings of millet cakes and dried mushrooms, two tiny salted plums and fresh bamboo shoots. Matsuda bowed in thanks.

'Who was it?' Shigeru said, looking around. 'Who knows we are here?'

'There is a small hamlet no more than two hours' walk away. They often come to leave offerings for the god who provides the water for their fields. They are sharing what they have with him and us.'

Shigeru also bowed in thanks, grateful to the unknown farmers who gave so generously.

'My brother Takeshi wants to be taught by goblins,' he said, when the food was finished.

'How old is he now? About ten?'

'He's four years younger than me; he turned eleven last year.'

'Ah, time goes by fast,' Matsuda said. 'I hope he will also come to Terayama.'

'He will be a better fighter than I am. He has no fear. He killed a boy older than himself when he was eight.' After a pause Shigeru admitted, 'I have never killed anyone.'

'In times of peace there is no need,' Matsuda said quietly. 'All your training may seem to be a preparation for war, but we hope it will also be its prevention. There are many ways to prevent war – alliances, marriages – but the best way is to be strong enough to make your enemy think twice about attacking you, yet not so aggressive that he feels threatened. Keep your sword sheathed as long as you can, but once it is unsheathed, use it without hesitation.'

'Are the Otori strong enough to prevent war with the Tohan?' Shigeru said, remembering the Kitano boys in Inuyama.

'The Iida family are very ambitious. Once a man has set his foot upon that path to power, little will stop him save his own death. He will always strive to be the greatest, and he lives in constant fear that somewhere another is greater than him and will topple him. And of course this will happen, because everything that has a beginning has an ending.'

Just beyond the shade from the eaves, an army of ants was milling over a dead dragonfly, tugging at the body with their tiny jaws.

'The dragonfly soars above the earth,' Matsuda said, 'yet its body becomes food for ants. All creatures are born; all must die.'

'You gave up the desires of the world to follow the teachings of the Enlightened One,' Shigeru said. 'You have compassion for all living beings. The Holy One taught his disciples to harm nothing. Yet you are my teacher in the art of war. It's not possible for me to follow you, even if I wanted to. I have duties to my family, my clan, my country. I cannot renounce that.'

'I would never expect you to. Your path is in this world. But it is possible to live in this world yet not be a slave to it. If I can teach you that I'll be happy.' Matsuda added, 'Along with swordsmanship and the art of war, naturally, for to answer your question clearly: yes, the Otori will have to fight the Tohan. Within the next five years is my guess. Either in the south or on the eastern borders.'

'Lord Kitano at Tsuwano has sent his sons to Inuyama,' Shigeru said. 'It suggested disloyalty to me.'

'Noguchi also has been making friendly advances to the Iida family. These are the straws that show the direction of the wind. Both these men are highly pragmatic; Noguchi is a coward and an opportunist. They expect war and they do not expect the Otori to win.'

'They are traitors,' Shigeru said furiously, his former sense of patience completely destroyed. 'I should be back in Hagi.'

'Your father is still the head of the clan; he must know how things stand. It's up to him and his advisors to deal with the situation.'

'My father...' Shigeru began; then fell silent, not wanting to sound disloyal himself.

'It's one of the lessons of adulthood,' Matsuda said. 'To see our parents clearly and recognize their strengths and their weaknesses, yet still honour them as our parents.'

'My father has many weaknesses,' Shigeru said with pain. 'If the Otori are defeated by the Tohan, it will be because of them.'

Matsuda said, 'We hope the onset of war will be delayed long enough for you to take a greater part in the leadership of the clan. And we hope that you have escaped the same weaknesses,' he added dryly.

'You must already know what they are,' Shigeru replied, feeling the blood mount to his cheeks. 'And they are many!'

'The usual Otori failings, no doubt. Over-hasty temper, lack of patience, a tendency towards easy infatuation. These are minor defects that you will master.'

'I will make every effort to,' Shigeru promised.

CHAPTER ELEVEN

The days fell into a regular pattern of meditation and exercise, like the recurring motifs in a woven cloth. In the middle of the day or after the evening meal, Matsuda often talked about the history and politics of the clan and the strategies of war. He questioned the young man about his previous teaching: Shigeru was expected to retain everything in his mind. Matsuda's memory was astonishing and Shigeru could feel his own becoming sharper as he absorbed all that the older man could tell him.

After two weeks of following his teacher's movements daily, and practising on his own, Matsuda told him one morning to bring the poles to the training ground. Shigeru was amazed at how his muscles and coordination had improved. He had been considered a talented pupil in Hagi, but that boy had been clumsy and slow compared to what he had become. Now the pole became what the sword would be, an extension of his own arm and brain. It would move as fast as thought with all his strength behind the blow. And in its return it would be as flexible as his own muscles, as swiftly and easily manipulated as his own hand. Breathe in, breathe out. The emptiness of mind that he achieved in meditation he now entered into effortlessly. He did not think about who he was in combat with; he forgot Matsuda was his teacher, was an illustrious warrior; he even put aside his overwhelming desire to outwit, outfight his opponent: he saw only the movements of the attack and his response in defence and counter-attack.

In the late afternoons he explored the mountain paths, finding whatever wild food he could. Sometimes he thought he heard human movements, or felt he was being watched, and once he came upon signs that someone had been digging up aconite, arum root and bugloss. However, he saw no one in the forest, though every now and then a farmer or a village woman came from the hamlet with offerings of food. If they met, Matsuda would give them a blessing and urge them to drink from the spring, while Shigeru questioned them about their farms and crops, their weather predictions, their folk tales and remedies. At first they were silenced by shyness, but as the weeks went by they began to open up to him.

Matsuda teased him about it, saying he must have been a farmer in a former life.

'If we are only warriors we would all starve,' Shigeru replied. 'We should never forget who feeds us.'

'Already wiser than most warriors in Hagi,' Matsuda said as if to himself.

'If there is to be war, I must be a warrior,' Shigeru said lightly. 'But if peace prevails I will be a farmer, and no one will go hungry in the entire Middle Country.'

The summer solstice came, and then the days of the Great Festivals, but Matsuda gave no indication that they would return to the temple. A few days before the Festival of the Dead, two monks came from Terayama, bringing food, bags of rice and dried vegetables, a cask of pickles and one of salted fish. It seemed like a feast after the meagre diet of the past weeks. They also brought news from Hagi of the good health of the Otori family, and a letter from Takeshi.

'He asks if I have met any goblins,' Shigeru said, reading it eagerly. 'He had a fall from Karasu, my black horse, and saw double for a day.' He felt the old anxiety threaten to rise and swallowed, willing it away. 'I told him not to ride the black: he is barely broken and too strong for a child. I hope he is not hurt worse than he allows.'

They had brought no writing materials with them, so he could not write a reply, but the monks promised they would send messengers to Hagi to seek more news. They talked a little during the evening meal: events in the temple, the Abbot's good health and spirits, the progress of the novices. The two visitors stayed the night and sat in silent meditation with Matsuda and Shigeru. The hut was too small for four, so Shigeru slept outside under the stars.

It was a sultry night and he slept lightly, his sleep broken by the hooting of owls, the croaking of frogs, whining mosquitoes; once a wolf howled in the distance, and just before dawn something padded past his head on soft paws: he opened his eyes to see a tanuki staring at him. When he moved, it slipped quickly under the hut.

He rose then, and saw the three men were already awake – and must have been for some time, for they already sat in meditation. He joined them, drawing strength from the fading night and the growing daylight. He turned his thoughts to Takeshi and prayed his brother had recovered completely, though he wondered if any sort of prayer worked backwards like that. Then he stilled his thoughts and concentrated on his breath.

When it was full daylight, Shigeru fetched water, blew gently on the embers of the fire and built it up, preparing the meal as he now did daily for Matsuda. With his plain hemp robe hitched into his belt, Shigeru looked no different from the monks, apart from his hair; he felt he could be one of them: the youngest, hence the servant. The visitors made little sign that they were astonished by the heir to the clan waiting humbly on them, though the younger one thanked him effusively and the older one shot one quick look at Matsuda, who smiled slightly in response. The two monks left immediately afterwards, wasting no time, walking swiftly away down the path. It was already very hot, and thunder rolled in the distance where black clouds massed over the furthest ranges. The sky above was a deep purple-blue, the sun's light bronze-tinged.

'Start your exercises now,' Matsuda said. 'There will be storms before midday.'

He had thought himself tired, but the fatigue slipped away as he went through the familiar routine. Matsuda continued to meditate, but after about an hour had passed he stood, hitched up his robe and picked up the poles. Shigeru bowed to his teacher and took one of the poles, feeling the usual pleasure at its balanced weight and smoothness.

Thunder rolled again, closer this time. The air was charged with intensity, like lightning.

During the previous weeks, Matsuda's attack had grown daily more aggressive. His control over the pole was so great Shigeru had no fear of being injured by him, but he had had enough slight blows and bruises to take each combat seriously. This day his teacher seemed even more ferocious. Twice the force of the onslaught drove Shigeru to the edge of the training ground. He felt the master was seeking something more from him, pushing him to his limits to get at some unawakened power. He could feel anger rising in him: a blow to the side of his neck smarted; the sun's harsh light made his head ache and sweat was pouring from him, stinging his eyes.

The third bout was even more intense. Shigeru had thought up till now that he trusted Matsuda not to hurt him, but suddenly the older man's hostility seemed real. It shook his confidence as much as anything else. His trust in his teacher wavered, and once weakened began to dissolve; previous tiny misgivings all joined together. He intends to kill me, Shigeru thought. He said he would go to Inuyama: he is in contact with the Iida. He will kill me here as if by accident, and join Kitano and Noguchi in their treachery. The Otori will be overthrown, the Middle Country lost.

A fury rose in him such as he had never experienced before, so intense it wiped everything from his mind. And into the emptiness flowed the power he had not known he possessed until the moment when he realized that he was fighting for his life and everything he valued.

All reverence for Matsuda evaporated; any awe he might have felt for the older man disappeared. He attacked with single-mindedness. Matsuda parried the first stroke, but its force unbalanced him slightly. He turned it into a feint to regain his footing, but in that instant Shigeru circled so his teacher was on the downhill slope, the sun now in his eyes. He remembered the world's power and saw how he could use it. He struck with all his strength and speed into the opening, hitting Matsuda on the side of the head with a crack as loud as thunder.

The old man grunted involuntarily and staggered. Shigeru dropped his pole, appalled at what he had done. 'Master!'

Matsuda said, 'I'm all right. Don't worry.' Then his face went pale. Sweat stood out on his forehead. 'I'd better sit down.'

Shigeru helped him to the veranda and lowered him down in the shade, fetching the quilts for him to lie on, bringing water to sponge the bruise, already swelling and black.

'Shouldn't sleep,' Matsuda muttered. 'Don't let me go to sleep,' and promptly closed his eyes and started snoring.

Shigeru shook him. 'Master, wake up! Don't sleep!' But he could not rouse him.

He is going to die! I've killed him! His immediate thought was to get help. The monks had been gone for over an hour – but maybe if he ran... and shouted... they would hear him and return. They would know what to do. But should he leave Matsuda here alone? He had to decide at once, and to act seemed preferable to doing nothing. He turned the old man on his side, put a pile of clothes under his head and covered him with a quilt. He filled a cup of water at the spring, wetted Matsuda's lips and left the cup near him.

Then he began to run down the mountain track, calling as he went. 'Hey! Can anyone hear me? Come back! Come back!'

He had run blindly for about two miles before he realized it was useless. The monks had too long a start on him; he would never catch up with them. The sun shone with one last dazzling burst and then was swallowed up by the thunderclouds. Lightning flashed briefly, and afterwards the world seemed to plunge into darkness. Thunder cracked overhead and almost immediately rain came pouring down.

Within moments he was soaked. Just as Matsuda had said, storms before midday. Shigeru now became even more worried about leaving the old man. He felt he must return to him. But as he turned to go back he was no longer sure of where he was: the rain disoriented him and it was several moments before he realized he had taken a wrong turn in his blind rush down the mountain. He tried to retrace his steps, but the track he had come down on was already running with water, and with no sun to guide him he could not be sure of the direction.

There was a tremendous crack ahead of him as lightning struck the top of a cedar. The tree lit up, crackling with fire, steaming as the rain doused the sparks. He halted for a moment, fearing the cedar might topple, but though split it did not fall. However, in the moment he stopped, he thought he saw through the rain a figure ahead, a man, sheltering beneath the overhang of a rock.

He called out, 'Hey, help me please, I've lost my way.'

The man turned his head in Shigeru's direction. Their eyes met. The man vanished.

He hadn't moved, or run away. He had disappeared. One moment he was there: the next he was not.

I've seen a goblin, Shigeru thought, but at that moment he would take help even from one of hell's demons. He ran on towards the rock, calling out as he went.

'Don't go away! I need your help. My teacher is injured. I've lost my way and must get back to him.'

The rain fell in solid sheets from the lip of the rock; he stood for a moment in the shelter and wiped the water from his eyes. The noise of the storm drowned all other sounds, but he felt suddenly there was another person close to him. He reached out, and could not help crying out in shock as he touched living flesh, and the flesh began to make itself seen, shimmering into being in the dim light.

It did not look like a goblin, with staring eyes and a long nose, but it had to be something supernatural, some mountain spirit, or a restless ghost, murdered in this place and unavenged. He saw a young man, perhaps seven or eight years older than himself, with a pale, mobile face and strange opaque eyes, which held both mockery and curiosity. Apart from the eyes, there was nothing exceptional about him: he wore ordinary clothes, a short jacket over a loincloth, his legs were bare, and a head cloth hid his hair; he did not seem to be armed, but Shigeru saw the right hand move closer to the chest and guessed there was a weapon hidden there.

He himself was completely unarmed in his sudden rush from the hut. But what weapons would be effective against this spirit of the mountain who could appear and disappear at will?

He forced himself to speak. 'Whoever or whatever you are, please help me. My master is injured: I went to get help and am now lost. He is in the hut near the spring, where the shrine is.'

'Your master? Who is he?'

'Matsuda Shingen, from Terayama.'

'And who are you?'

'Just one of his novices. I beg you, show me the path.'

The man smiled slightly, but made no response. He took a step backwards and rain cascaded over him; he vanished again.

Shigeru fought back a cry of disappointment and stepped out into the rain, determined to retrace his steps and discover where he had gone wrong. However, a little way ahead of him he saw the dark figure reappear. It turned and beckoned to him.

'Follow me,' the man called.

They went straight up the slope along a narrow fox track, occasionally dropping to all fours to clamber over rocks or through the undergrowth. The man kept well ahead, vanishing if Shigeru came too close but always reappearing again. It was like being led by a fox – and Shigeru wondered if he had indeed been enthralled by a fox spirit and was being led into the spirit world. The pelting rain, the greenish light, the crack and roll of thunder, the silver-blue streaks of lightning, all seemed to come from some other domain where the normal rules of life were broken and magic prevailed. His reality had been jolted, and it made him feel sick and dizzy, as if he had received a blow to the head. And what of Matsuda? What if he were already dead? He had not only injured his teacher; he had utterly failed to bring help to him.

They crossed a small ridge and began to descend, and suddenly Shigeru knew where he was. Not penetrating deeper and deeper into the spirit world, but coming down towards the hut on a track he had often used before. He began to run, not knowing if he passed the spirit-man or not, only thinking, with bursting chest, of Matsuda.

The rain streamed from the eaves of the hut, churning the ground beneath, running in muddy eddies towards the pool. Matsuda lay on his side, exactly as Shigeru had left him, still asleep but no longer snoring.

Shigeru knelt beside him: the quilts were already wet and the old man's skin felt clammy.

'Sir! Lord Matsuda!' He shook him gently. To his relief Matsuda's eyes flickered, but he did not waken.

There was a slight change in the pattern of the rainfall and Shigeru's guide stepped onto the veranda. Also kneeling, he felt for the pulse in the neck.

'What happened?'

'I hit him; we were practising: he is teaching me the sword.'

'You hit Matsuda? What kind of a novice are you? You look like one of the Otori.'

'I am Otori Shigeru. I have been sent to Terayama for a year; it's part of my education.'

'Lord Shigeru: I'm honoured to meet you,' the man said, with a hint of irony. He did not offer his own name. Bending over Matsuda again, he opened the old man's eyelids and peered into his eyes. Then he gently felt the contusion on the temple.

'I don't think you broke the skull. You just knocked him out. He'll wake up soon. I've got some herbs here – dried vervain and willow bark, and other things. Make a tea from them: it will stop the pain and the nausea. Make sure you stay with him. The danger is not so much from the blow as from choking afterwards.' He took out a small bag and handed it to Shigeru.

'Thank you,' Shigeru said. 'I am extremely grateful to you. Come to me when I return to Hagi and you will be rewarded.'

His voice trailed away; he felt foolish, for what reward could he offer a fox spirit? Yet when the man was there he seemed so real, human and ordinary.

'Maybe one day I will come to Hagi.'

'You will always be welcome. Tell me your name.'

'I have many names. Sometimes people call me the Fox.' He laughed at Shigeru's expression. 'Take care of your teacher.' He bowed deeply, saying, 'Lord Otori,' his tone both respectful and mocking. He vanished.

Shigeru carried Matsuda into the hut and set him down on the mattress, built up the fire and fetched fresh water. He was soaked to the skin. He took off his clothes to dry them and sat naked by the fire until the water boiled. It was not cold; when the rain eased at the end of the afternoon the heat returned, even more sultry than before.

Just before nightfall Matsuda began to stir. He seemed to be in some pain. Shigeru quickly brewed the tea and helped the old man sit up and drink it. Matsuda did not speak, but patted Shigeru's hand as if to reassure him. Then he lay down again. The herbs took effect quickly. The old man slept deeply and calmly until dawn.

Shigeru dozed a little, but mostly stayed awake thinking about the extraordinary events of the day. He no longer believed the stranger to be a supernatural being. Now he was thinking more calmly it was all too clear who the man was: he could only be from the Tribe. He had vanished and reappeared just as his father had described when speaking of the woman he had loved. What an amazing skill to have: how useful it would be; no wonder warlords like the Iida family used such men as spies. How vulnerable his own clan seemed. What defence could there be against such people? The encounter had ignited an intense curiosity in him to find out more about them, to discover how he could protect himself and his people against the Tribe – even if he might use them himself.

He hardly allowed himself to think about the most extraordinary event of all: that he had overcome his teacher in combat; he had knocked out Matsuda Shingen. It seemed even more impossible than the man who could go invisible.

The heat eased a little, a slight breeze sprang up and birds began to herald the dawn. Shigeru sat cross-legged and began the morning meditation. When he opened his eyes it was fully light, and Matsuda was awake.

'I need to piss,' the old man said. 'Help me outside.'

He walked a little unsteadily but otherwise seemed to have recovered. After relieving himself he went to the spring and rinsed his mouth with water.

'Does your head hurt?' Shigeru said, helping him back to the hut.

'Not much now. Whatever it was you gave me last night worked.'

'I'm so sorry,' Shigeru began.

Matsuda said, 'Don't be sorry. Be proud of yourself. It's quite an achievement. No one's done that to me for a long time. Of course, I'm not as young as I used to be.'

'It was a fluke,' Shigeru said.

'I don't think so. But who was here with you?'

'I met a man in the forest. I ran after the monks and took a wrong turn... There was a huge storm...'

'You were panicking, in other words,' Matsuda said. 'I thought I'd killed you!'

'If you had, it would only have served me right.' Matsuda laughed. 'Nothing to panic about. Who was it, one of the villagers? I must get the ingredients of that tea.'

'I'd never seen him before. I wasn't even sure he was human. He seemed more like a spirit. Then afterwards I realized he must have been from the Tribe.'

'In Heaven's name,' Matsuda said. 'You gave me tea made by one of the Tribe? I'm lucky to be still alive.'

Shigeru thought of poison: thought of the signs he himself had seen of someone searching for aconite and arum, this man or someone like him.

'I'm a fool,' he said. 'For some reason I thought I could trust him.'

'You are too quick to trust,' Matsuda rejoined. 'Still, it seems on this occasion no harm was done. That brew is a very effective painkiller. I'd like to know what's in it.'

'He knew your name.'

'I don't want to boast; a lot of people know my name. I am not popular with the Tribe. I've tried to keep them out of the temple. I don't like spies. Did he use invisibility?'

Shigeru nodded. 'How is it done?'

'It's a trick, a way of moving that fools the eyes of the watcher. You can't teach it – it's inborn, like most of their skills. Training enhances them: from what I've heard a lot of it is like meditation, emptying the mind and concentrating, though the Tribe use cruelty as a teaching tool to silence the conscience and eradicate compassion. They say that the Iida family use some of these methods with their sons, and that Sadamu in particular has benefited from them.'

'The Sadamu that also hoped to learn from you!' Shigeru said.

'Ah, I would never have gone to Inuyama. I don't like the climate. Anyway, I don't have to now: I am content with my Otori pupil. In fact, I'm very proud of you.'

'Even though I did everything wrong afterwards! In the moment I overcame you, I saw you as a traitor,' Shigeru confessed. 'I thought you were part of a conspiracy... It's too stupid to think about.'

'I was pushing you as hard as I could. I knew there was more in you than you had allowed me to see till now. You have a trusting nature, Lord Shigeru: it's a virtue, but only up to a point. Now you know how to unleash your true power, through suspicion of betrayal, and the pure rage that came from it. You can practise on your own today. You have to summon up by will what you discovered through emotion. I am going to rest.'

'We should return to the temple,' Shigeru said, looking at his teacher's pale face, and the growing bruise. 'They can take care of you there.'

'It's not time yet,' Matsuda replied. 'I'll rest for a couple of days; we will spend the Festival of the Dead here and return to the temple before the autumn storms, unless I am summoned earlier. Our Abbot's health is fragile, as you know. If he should die, I would have to return at once.

'Now we have talked for far too long. We will spend the rest of the day in silence. You can prepare a little soup and then begin your exercises.'

There were many things Shigeru longed to talk about:
his thoughts were chasing each other round his mind. He
realized he craved praise, reassurance, and knew that
Matsuda had already given him as much as he was going
to. He opened his mouth to say, 'Just one more question,'
but Matsuda silenced him. 'I suggest meditation first, to
still your thoughts.'

While he meditated, he looked dispassionately at his
actions, seeking to learn from them. He recognized the
ability that lay behind his swordplay, as clearly as he saw
the immaturity of character than had led to his panic and
confusion. Gradually his thoughts calmed; his mind
emptied.

In the evening he went out to collect mushrooms for
the meal, half-hoping to see the man from the Tribe again
– the Fox, he thought, smiling. So the Fox roamed these
mountains, collecting herbs for medicine and poison. His
curiosity had been aroused as much by the man himself
as by the mysteries of the Tribe.

I'll know him if I see him again, he told himself, and
felt they would meet again, as if there were some bond
between them from a former life. I must find out more
about the Tribe: maybe even use them, as the Tohan do.

However, he did not see the Fox again; nor were there
any signs of the man's presence. Matsuda recovered and
resumed their daily combats. Shigeru learned to use his
new-found strength with greater accuracy: he frequently
dominated his teacher, but never again struck him so hard.

They spent the days of the Festival of the Dead in
fasting and meditation. It was the first time Shigeru had

spent this solemn festival away from his family. His father alternated visits to the temples of Tokoji and Daishoin in Hagi and to Yamagata and Terayama. This year he would stay in Hagi. Shigeru pictured his brother and their friends setting lanterns adrift in paper boats on the river, watching the tide take them far out to sea. He saw the view of the bay, the islands rising jagged from the water, lanterns casting their gold light in the blue haze, and felt a pang of homesickness for the place he loved so much.

The forest around him was no less beautiful: he had come to love it too as he explored it more, knowing it better; but it was lonely, empty of humankind, and on the nights when the dead revisit the living it seemed even more solitary.

Lights glimmered in the distance where the villagers lit huge fires to show their dead the way home. Shigeru also made a fire outside the hut, but he did not expect to see his ancestors. They would be where their graves were, in Hagi or at Terayama. Not even the dead would visit them here.

He and Matsuda had hardly spoken for days: combat, exercise, meditation and the daily chores had all been conducted in silence. So on the second night of the festival Shigeru was surprised when, instead of sleeping immediately after the evening meal, Matsuda told him to light the lamp and make fresh tea.

'We will talk for a while.'

They moved outside onto the small veranda. It was a clear night: the Bear and the Hunter blazed above their heads. Shigeru fetched fresh water and lit an oil lamp with a wood shaving from the fire. He served his teacher and then sat cross-legged on the floor, waiting to hear what Matsuda had to say to him.

'You had many questions before,' Matsuda said. 'You may ask them now.'

'I have been thinking about the dead,' Shigeru said. 'Are they reborn immediately or do their spirits live on? They revisit us each year; where do they dwell in between? When we worship our ancestors, do they see and hear us?'

'We revere our ancestors as if they still lived,' Matsuda replied. 'And we treat all living things with compassion, for into them our own ancestors might have been reborn. The fate from our past lives influences our present life, just as this life will influence our future. We can escape the cycle of birth and death by following the teachings of the Enlightened One. But you are called to another path: you will be the head of an ancient and powerful clan. The safety and well-being of many will lie in your hands. You have to live in the world with all its deceptions and dangers.

'It is no small thing to be born Otori. Your family are the most illustrious in the Three Countries, whatever the Iida may think of themselves. Your lineage is the most ancient: you share the blood of the imperial family. The strengths of your family are courage, compassion, warmth of feeling, fair-mindedness; their weaknesses are reckless-ness, soft-heartedness, infatuation and indecision.'

'Each weakness is the shadow of each strength,' Shigeru said quietly.

'Yes, indeed. You must see how your father's sense of justice too often leads him into indecisiveness. He sees everyone's point of view, and wants to appear fair to them all. Possibly he cares too much about what people think of him. He desires his brothers' good opinion – in return they despise him.'

'Are they also traitors?'

'I believe they would be if they had more courage.'

'If the Tohan are preparing for war, how can we protect the Middle Country?'

'By defeating them. There is no other way. Your father does not want to fight; your uncles are in favour of making concessions in return for peace.'

'What sort of concessions?'

'Ceding territory, for example.'

'Giving up parts of the Middle Country to the Tohan? It's unthinkable.'

'Many are already thinking it. It's up to you to persuade them otherwise.'

'I should return to Hagi at once.'

Matsuda chuckled. 'Now you are going to have to learn patience.'

Shigeru took a deep breath. His temper had been rising throughout the conversation. Disloyalty, treachery, seemed to him the greatest of crimes, and the suspicion that they flourished within his own family made his gullet burn with rage. 'If you tell me I must, I will,' he conceded reluctantly.

'Stay as planned through the winter. When you return you will be sixteen: you will have your coming-of-age ceremony and become an adult. You will have more influence then on the elders and your father.'

'Can the elders be trusted?'

'Irie, Mori, Nagai – I would stake my life on their loyalty. Endo and Miyoshi are pragmatists: their loyalty is first to the clan, so they will support whoever leads it. When you do return, you must be on your guard. If you advise war with the Tohan, the opposite faction will be tempted to eliminate you, and they will have the backing of the Tohan. Be careful who you trust. And try not to let anyone from the Tribe into your life.'

'It must be almost impossible to recognize them,' Shigeru said, smiling ruefully.

'They are human. Despite their almost supernatural skills they die like any other man. I believe they can be identified and overcome.'

'My enemy is double: an aggressive, ambitious clan, and a tribe of assassins.'

'But you meet them with double weapons: your own character and the love and loyalty of your people.'

'Will these be enough to prevail?'

Matsuda laughed again. 'I cannot see into the future. I only know these are enough to start with. You may sleep if you wish, now. I will sit for a while in the company of the dead.'

Shigeru was not tired, and wanted to keep his teacher talking. 'I know nothing of your life, your family,' he said. 'Do you have sons; did you ever marry?'

'Of course I married, when I was a young man. My wife died many years ago. We had several children but none survived childhood. And as far as I know I have no living offspring: my children are my pupils, the monks who are in my care. I hope I will die and be buried at Terayama.'

'And what made you give up your life as a warrior when you were the greatest fighter the Three Countries has ever known?'

'No one is the greatest,' Matsuda said. 'There will always be another greater than you, or with greater potential. All my energy and years of my life had gone into one thing: to become an expert in the art of death. It is a terrible thing to imagine oneself the greatest: it gives rise to pride in oneself, envy in others. Young men sought me out to challenge me. I became tired of their foolishness and their courage.' He fell silent. The night insects droned loudly; frogs croaked.

'I killed once too often. I did not want to feel that regret again. I came to Terayama ten years ago, at this same time of year. I never left. I did not want to live in the world any longer. But the world does not leave us alone. It is always calling at the door; only the Enlightened One led a life free of error. The rest of us make mistakes and then have to live with them. Now, go to bed.'

'I will sit with you and keep you and the dead company,' Shigeru said. 'If you will permit it.'

Matsuda smiled and nodded, then dowsed the lamp. They sat silently without moving as the vast starry heaven wheeled above them.

CHAPTER TWELVE

A fter these conversations, in the days following, master and pupil resumed their silent routine. It was the time of the greatest heat, but Shigeru learned to ignore the sticky discomfort of the body just as Matsuda did. The spring ran cool throughout the hottest days, and he often stripped off his clothes at the end of the day and bathed in the pool. He had grown during the summer and had reached his full height, well above average, and the constant exercise and discipline had built up his muscles and burnt away the last vestiges of childhood. He knew he had become a man, and was often impatient to return to the world, especially when his thoughts turned to the tensions between the clans and the untrustworthiness of his uncles, but he accepted that he still had the lessons of patience and self-control to learn.

A vixen sometimes trotted through the clearing at dusk, and once Shigeru surprised the cubs playing in a hollow. Deer and rabbits occasionally came to graze on the summer grass. Apart from the villagers, who returned when the Festival of the Dead was over with offerings of cucumbers, apricots and summer vegetables, they saw no human being.

However, one day at sunset, when they had taken advantage of the cool of the evening to fight a bout with the wooden poles, they heard the unusual sound of horses coming up the track. Matsuda made a sign to Shigeru to halt; they both turned to see two men on horseback cantering up to the hut.

Shigeru had not seen a horse since he had left his own to walk to the temple. There was something astonishing about the two snorting creatures with warriors on their backs. They were both dark bay, with black legs, manes and tails. The riders wore chest armour laced with black and gold, and on their backs the triple oak leaf of the Tohan.

The leader reined his horse in and called out a greeting. Matsuda returned it calmly. Shigeru, knowing his teacher's moods so well, saw him tense slightly: his feet balanced themselves on the ground, and his grasp on the pole tightened.

'I am Miura Naomichi,' the man continued, 'from the Tohan at Inuyama. My companion is Inaba Atsushi. I am looking for Matsuda Shingen.'

'You have found him,' Matsuda said evenly. 'Dismount and tell me your business.'

Miura did so, leaping agilely down; his companion also dismounted, and took the reins of both horses while Miura stepped forward and bowed slightly.

'Lord Matsuda. I am glad to have found you engaged in instruction. We were led to believe in Inuyama that you had given up teaching. There seemed no other explanation when Lord Iida, head of the Tohan, expressly commanded you to come to teach his son.'

'I am grateful for Lord Iida's opinion of my ability, but I am under no obligation to obey any command from him: it is well known that my allegiance has always been to the Otori. Besides, Lord Sadamu is a little old for my instruction, and I am sure has already benefited from Inuyama's greatest swordsmen, such as Lord Miura himself.'

'I am flattered that you know me. But you must also know that my reputation is nothing in the Three Countries compared to your own.'

Shigeru heard arrogance behind false humility. *He does not believe what he says. He believes himself to be better than Matsuda; he feels slighted because Iida approached Matsuda... He has come here to challenge him. There can be no other reason.*

'Well, it's a pleasure to meet you,' Matsuda said, apparently affably. 'We live very simply here, but you are welcome to share whatever we have...'

Miura interrupted him. 'I have not come all this way to drink tea and compose poems. I have come to challenge you: first because you insult the Tohan clan by refusing my master's invitation, and second because if I defeat you

117

Lord Iida will know he does not have to look for teachers among the Otori.'

'I am no longer a warrior,' Matsuda said. 'Just a monk who does not fight any more. I have no weapon here, apart from the training poles. No insult was intended.'

'Take my sword, and I will fight with Inaba's: that will make us equal.' Miura unsheathed the sword and took a step forward. 'Either we fight or I cut you down now, you and your pupil. Fight me and whatever the outcome I will spare him.'

It was clear the warrior was not going to be dissuaded. Shigeru felt his heartbeat pick up: he tightened his grip on the pole and moved his feet slightly so the setting sun fell over his shoulder.

Matsuda said, 'Since you show such consideration for my pupil, you may fight him.'

Miura sneered. 'I don't challenge boys or novices.'

Matsuda addressed Shigeru formally. 'Lord Otori, take Lord Miura's sword.'

Shigeru bowed equally formally, handed the pole to his teacher and stepped forward. There was a moment when he felt his own complete vulnerability, unarmed before Miura's sword. He masked it by gazing calmly at the warrior, assessing him.

Miura was a little shorter than he was, ten or fifteen years older and much broader in the shoulders. His arms and legs were solid with muscle. Shigeru guessed his technique would be grounded in power rather than speed. His reach would be limited. His strength would be greater, but he had not been taught by Matsuda Shingen.

'Lord Otori?' Miura said, taken aback. 'The oldest son? Shigeru?'

'Lord Otori is the only man who has ever bested me,' Matsuda said calmly.

And there was another advantage. Miura was disconcerted by the situation that now presented itself, into which his own blustering had led him. To challenge Matsuda and kill him was one thing: to kill the heir to the Otori clan was quite another. It might be Sadayoshi and Sadamu's secret desire: it could never be condoned by them publicly or forgiven by the Otori. It would plunge the Three Countries into immediate war. Miura's life and the lives of his family would be forfeit.

Good, Shigeru thought. The sooner we fight the Tohan, the more likely we are to defeat them. My father has another son. It seemed suddenly, in that moment, a good death, and he chose it steadfastly, neither looking at the future nor dwelling on the past.

'Give me your sword,' he said.

'You will let a boy fight in your place?' Miura attempted to browbeat Matsuda.

'As I said, Lord Otori is my better. Defeat him and you defeat me. You may then take my life, worthless as it is. All the insults you imagine will be wiped out. And I certainly will not have to go to Inuyama. Give your sword to Lord Otori as you suggest. It seems quite fair to me, unless you often practise with your companion's sword.'

'I have never held it in my hands till now,' Miura replied.

The exchange of swords was made. Shigeru took Miura's in both hands and, stepping to one side, looked at it carefully: the cutting edge was unblemished, the curved steel perfectly honed. It was a little heavier than his own, suiting Miura's greater bulk, but its balance was good and it responded to his grip. He made a couple of swift passes through the air and heard the steel sing as the sword came to life. He deliberately chose simple, basic exercises, knowing Miura would be watching him, hoping to maintain the disconcertion, hoping to lull him into overconfidence.

He felt his teacher's trust, and had the same confidence in him, knowing Matsuda would never put his life at risk, would have fought Miura himself rather than do that.

They faced each other on the sandy ground. Inaba took the horses a little distance away and stood between them. Matsuda was on the opposite side of the clearing. He said nothing, but gazed steadily at Shigeru.

It was over quickly. Miura made a conventional attack, not unlike the sort of thing Shigeru had learned from his sword teacher in Hagi, Irie Masahide. He was strong but slow, and less than wholehearted, as Shigeru had suspected. Shigeru's upbringing and training had prepared him for this moment: he had known it would come and he was ready for it. He had not longed for it, but neither did he flinch from it. He feinted against the attack, making it look as if he would repeat the elementary exercise he had just practised, and as Miura's sword responded, he moved the other way and found the unprotected area between chest and groin.

He was amazed at how easily the blade slid through clothing and flesh, how swiftly it whipped back and cut again, this time into the top of the neck as Miura fell forwards. Shigeru was filled with a terrible sense of anguish as the blood spurted from the neck and foamed from the belly, anguish and sorrow at the fragility of flesh and bone, and of the life they held together. It seemed an appalling thing that a man should travel so swiftly from life to death, the abrupt journey from which there was no return. He wished he could turn time back to a world in which Miura and Inaba never came at sunset to the lonely shrine, yet he knew he had to accept that Miura had come there to meet the death decreed for him at Shigeru's hands.

'Lord Miura!' Inaba cried, dropping the horses' reins and running forward. The horses reared at the smell of blood and trotted off across the clearing, one of them whinnying loudly, eyes rolling.

Miura died without speaking.

I have killed, Shigeru thought with neither pleasure nor elation, but rather with a sense of dread and heaviness, as though he had lost the lightness of boyhood and taken on adulthood, with all its burdens.

Matsuda picked up Inaba's sword from where it had fallen. 'Lord Shigeru, catch the horses before they wander off. Inaba, take your master's head and carry it back to Inuyama. I expect you to give an accurate account of his death, which was not without honour.'

Shigeru, persuading the horses to allow themselves to be captured, heard the blow that separated the head from the body. Matsuda brought water from the spring and washed the blood from the face, wrapping it in a cloth from the hut, apologizing for the poor quality of the fabric.

Inaba's eyes were bright with emotion, but he said nothing. He took a container from the saddle bow of his horse and placed the head reverently inside. Then he undid the scabbard from Miura's belt, wiped the sword, checked the blade, then returned it to the scabbard.

'Lord Otori.' He bowed to Shigeru and laid the sword on the ground before him.

'You may take the body to Terayama,' Matsuda said. 'They will arrange for burial there.'

'No!' Inaba said. 'Lord Miura must not lie among the Otori. I will take him back to the East. When I have performed this last service for him, I will join him in death.'

'As you wish,' Matsuda said, and helped the other man strap the body onto the horse while Shigeru held the animal steady, soothing it as it trembled.

Inaba mounted and rode slowly down the slope. After a few minutes the sound of the hoof beats died away. The sun had set completely, but it was not yet dark.

'Go and cleanse yourself,' Matsuda told Shigeru. 'We will pray for the dead.'

As the light faded and the stars began to gleam, the old man chanted the sutra for the dead, the ancient words acting as a ligament between Earth and Heaven, this world and the next.

Later Matsuda said, 'I knew you were in no danger.'

'You would never allow me to be,' Shigeru replied. 'It gave me confidence.'

'You did well. Miura has been an excellent fighter and a good teacher. Sadayoshi should not have slighted him.'

'It seemed almost as though you might have contrived it,' Shigeru ventured.

Matsuda replied, 'I would not contrive anyone's death – I don't need to, for fate brings all of us to that final encounter. But if I had wanted to, I could not have set up anything better.'

The next day was even hotter; the sunlight had the same bronzed tinge and the air was oppressively heavy and still, as though Heaven held its breath. The cicadas' drone continued mercilessly, but all birds seemed silenced by the heat.

After the morning exercises, which left even Matsuda soaked in sweat, they spent the rest of the day in silent meditation. In the evening, Matsuda said, 'I think we will return to the temple. Our work here seems to be completed, and I have the feeling I am needed. And you must take up your studies again before you forget how to write.'

They packed up their few belongings, and Shigeru swept out the hut for the last time. They rose before dawn. The tanuki was sitting on the veranda, watching them with round, wary eyes. Matsuda bowed to it.

'Goodbye, old friend. Thank you for sharing your home with us. It's yours again.'

The moon had set, but Matsuda strode along the path as if it were clearly lit by the sun. Shigeru carried the fighting poles and the bundles as he had on their outward journey. He was sorry to leave the remote hut where he had learned so much, but he too knew that the work they had come to do had been achieved.

Day was dawning as they passed beneath the great oak where Shigeru had seen the houou, and he looked for it again in the arching canopy. Matsuda had put the feather away and now carried it in the breast of his robe. But there was no sign of the sacred bird. I will see it again, he thought; I will create a place where it can dwell. It will return to the Middle Country.

They reached the temple before midday; as soon as they entered the first courtyard, Shigeru realized something untoward had happened. A solemn hush lay over the whole place, quite different from its daily atmosphere, broken only by a monotonous chanting from the main hall. He recognized the words of one of the sutras for the dead.

'It's as I thought,' Matsuda said quietly. 'Our Abbot has passed away.'

After this Shigeru saw very little of Matsuda. The Abbot's funeral was held, and after the mourning period Matsuda became the new Abbot as had been expected. Shigeru took his place again among the other novices, and followed the same routine as before but with greater diligence and self-discipline. He had the same anxieties about events in the world beyond Terayama – the activities of the Tohan, his own clan's response – but he laid them to one side and devoted himself to meditation, exercise and study. He took out the scrolls he had brought from Eijiro and from Yamagata and applied himself to learning them by heart. He saw that the work that lay ahead of him would be immense, and that he would need all his energy, intelligence and strength to grapple with it. He worked, with the help of his teachers, on developing his natural abilities and curbing his weaknesses. He learned to control his body's needs for sleep and food, to master his temper and his thoughts.

The heat of summer gave way to the onset of autumn. Then came the equinox; autumn lilies blossomed round the rice fields. The storms of late summer abated; the leaves turned red and gold; chestnuts ripened in the forest and persimmons in the gardens. Work in the fields seemed endless to bring in the harvest of rice, beans and vegetables that would feed them through the winter. The air echoed with the sounds of flails as the grains were separated from the husk, the dull chopping of the bean straw and shelling of the pods, beans falling into baskets and buckets with a patter like hail.

One day, suddenly it seemed, the work was finished; the fields were bare and brown. Mist hung around the mountains, and the first frosts stiffened the bamboo grass and turned it white. The airy rooms of the temple that had been cool in summer became freezing as the autumn wind chilled. The year turned and snow fell, closing off the temple from the outside world.

CHAPTER THIRTEEN

The last stone was slipped into place, and Akane could no longer see her father's face. The stone slid perfectly in, its carefully hewn edges fitting seamlessly into the stones on either side. She stood at the northern end of the bridge. There was a huge crowd behind her, yet they left a space around her, people pressing to see but no one wanting to approach her in her grief – or, possibly, come close enough to catch the contagion of the curse that must surely lie on her family.

There was a gasp from the crowd, a collective drawing of breath. The men who lifted the stone – Wataru, the stonemason's right-hand man, and Naizo the apprentice – stood with white faces and rigid jaws; Wataru's eyes were bright with tears; Akane could see muscles in Naizo's neck twitching from the strain, his face contorted in a grin of fear and pity. The masons moved backwards until they no longer stood on the bridge. Her father was alone on it: the only living thing, entombed in stone.

The stone would never be removed. Her father was behind it, in the dark. He would never see daylight again, never feel the spring breeze on his face, nor see the cherry blossom drift down onto the green waters of the river, never hear the river's changing song as it ebbed and flowed with the tide. Would he sit with the same calm that he had displayed till now, while the air was slowly exhausted? Or would he panic now that there was no one to see his shame and despair?

She had lived by the river all her life. Mori Yuta was not the first person she had seen drowned; she knew how hands grasped and clung and scrabbled for life. Were her father's hands scrabbling like that now? Looking for chinks in the stones he knew fitted perfectly, his strong flexible hands where his gift was contained: the hands she knew so well and had watched so often, holding adze and chisel, or curved round a tea bowl at night, the stone dust still embedded in the lines around the joints of knuckle and wrist, and across the palms. He smelled of dust and sometimes came back at night looking as if he had been hewn from stone, grey from head to foot. He had been admired and respected, had built wonderful constructions, but the obsession with the bridge had undone all that. He neglected his family. His wife bore no more children – the neighbours joked maliciously that she would have needed a body of stone to attract her husband. Their only daughter ran wild, a thin, strange child who could swim like a cormorant and handle a boat like a man. When she turned fourteen, not a single family would consider her for marriage to their sons, even though the sons themselves were not averse to her lithe body, slender neck and wrists and beautifully shaped eyes. But the family was obviously deeply unlucky, if not actually cursed, and Akane had a bold look about her that drove away future mothers-in-law. It was obvious to everyone except her father that the girl would become a prostitute: even as a child she'd had that look, they said knowingly.

And browbeaten girls, not much older than Akane and already married, envied her silently, for they could imagine no life worse than their own drudgery.

Akane had overheard plans for her future being discussed by her father and the brothel owner: her father was shocked by the man's suggestion; Akane was more shocked by how low a price was being offered. She went immediately to a rival establishment, run by a widow, and bargained for over twice the sum, half of which she gave to her parents and half she kept for herself. Her parents were moved by her decisiveness and filial devotion, and relieved that she would not become a burden to them but on the contrary would be able to support them in their old age – particularly her mother, since her father's obsession seemed all too likely to lead to penury. And her mother hoped eventually Akane would attract a long-term protector who might even want to have children with her.

For the lack of grandchildren was their greatest disappointment in Akane's new arrangement. All her attentions and dutiful behaviour could not make up for the fact that there were no grandchildren. The stonemason's line would die out: he had no sons or nephews, and now no grandsons to tend his grave and pray for his spirit.

He did not know then that his grave would be both public and anonymous: that hundreds would walk past it every day, that his stone would declaim the Otori challenge to those who entered their city, and that his voice would be heard forever, as he talked endlessly with the river.

Akane was barely fifteen when she moved to the widow Haruna's establishment and worked as a maid to the girls there. Men came to drink wine and eat Aunt Haruna's legendary fried octopus and sea urchin. The girls sat with them, their company as highly valued as the other services they provided, and Akane learned how a quick wit was as attractive as a shapely body, long silky hair or a flawless nape. Some of the girls sang; they danced like children and often played childhood games with an added sexual edge. Aunt Haruna's establishment was fairly exclusive, visited by richer merchants and even the sons of the warrior class.

In an attempt to control prostitution, Lord Shigemori had decreed that all brothels should be confined to one district, in the new town across the river from the port. It was on the opposite side to the stone bridge: at the back of Haruna's place was a natural hot spring, and behind it rose a small volcano on whose slopes grew a variety of shrubs and flowers warmed by the mountain itself – camellias, azaleas and other more exotic plants that grew nowhere else in the Middle Country. The priest who served at the shrine of the god of the mountain loved plants more than people, it was said. He hardly spoke to pilgrims to the shrine – the mountain was supposed to protect and increase the virility of men – but spent most of his time tending and talking to his plants.

The southern slope of the volcano, then, was a fine place for a pleasure house. Haruna's was named the House of the Camellias, and she was in her way an artist – of pleasure; Akane, who had grown up absorbing the elements of beauty and design from her father, found herself responding with her whole being to her surroundings. She was spoiled and petted by the older women and became a favourite with the men, though Haruna did not allow any of them to take her with them into the private rooms. She guarded Akane jealously, and Akane did not resist it; the rooms were called private but with their flimsy walls and fragile screens they were hardly that. Akane grew accustomed to the sounds and smells of desire. She was interested in men's enslavement, as it seemed to her, to the pleasures of the flesh, how desperately they sought release within the body of a woman. She found their need, their desire, both pitiable and arousing – it seemed so easy to satisfy them, and so pleasurable – and so much more comprehensible than her father's desperate obsession with the unforgiving stone.

She had a way of thinking that was all her own – the same characteristic that had made her seem bold and uncontrollable as a child. She studied the world around her with detachment, even irony; Haruna perceived this, and admired it, for it drove men wild. Akane, she thought, liked men but would never fall in love with one. She would be safe from the infatuations that destroyed so many women when they fancied themselves passionately in love with her clients. The men were flattered at first, but usually quickly tired of the demands and the jealousy. But women like Akane, whom they knew they could never own, drew them back, got under their skin and made them itch, made them offer any price to be allowed to be her only lover, after which they drove themselves mad with jealousy. Women like Akane were all too rare. Haruna would choose her clients herself, and make sure they paid a good price for her. She had high ambitions for Akane – maybe even the highest, a plan that would ensure her influence and prosperity in her old age – but she shared these with no one.

She delayed Akane's deflowerment until the girl was almost seventeen, not wanting to have her damaged physically or emotionally, and she chose one of her favourite clients: Hayato, younger son of a middle-rank warrior family, a good-looking man, not too old, who adored women but was not possessive and was adept in the art of love. Others had offered more money for Akane's virginity but Haruna disqualified them for various reasons: too old, too selfish; drank too much; could often not perform.

Akane enjoyed sex as much as she had thought she would. She had other clients beside Hayato, though he remained her favourite and she was grateful to him for all he taught her, but she regarded them all with the same amused detachment, and, as Haruna predicted, it made her all the more desirable. By the time she was nineteen, her fame had spread throughout the city. People came to the house on the side of the mountain hoping for a glimpse of her. Haruna had to employ extra guards to dissuade rowdy hopefuls who turned up drunk and amorous. Akane rarely went outside, other than to walk in the shrine garden and look out over the bay with its steep-cliffed islands fringed with white in the indigo sea. From the top of the volcano, where sulphurous steam issued from the old crater, she could see the whole city, the castle rising opposite from the sheer sea wall that her grandfather had built, its white walls gleaming against the dark forest behind it, the huddle of houses in the narrow streets, the roofs glistening after rain in the morning sun, the fishing boats at the port, the canals and the rivers. She could even see the stone bridge rising from between its bristles of scaffolding.

The bridge was finished in the spring, just as new green leaves were bursting from willow and alder by the river, beech and maple on the mountain, poplar and ginkgo in the temple gardens. Akane had gone with Hayato to look at the cherry blossom around the shrine, and when they returned, Haruna drew the man aside and whispered to him.

Akane walked slowly ahead to her room and called to the maid to bring wine, feeling the anticipation of pleasure that Hayato always aroused in her. He made her laugh; his mind and tongue were as quick as hers. The air was soft and warm, full of the sounds and scents of spring. She gazed at the white arch of her foot and could already feel his tongue there. They would spend the rest of the afternoon together and then bathe in the hot spring, and she would see no one else after him, but eat and sleep alone.

However, when Hayato came into the room, his face was sombre and full of pity.

'What is it?' she said at once. 'What's happened?'

'Akane.' He sat down next to her. 'Your father is to be sealed within the stones of his bridge. Lord Otori has ordered it.' He did not attempt to allay or soften the news, but told her carefully and clearly. Yet she still did not understand.

'Sealed? His body?'

He took her hands then. 'He is to be buried alive.'

Shock closed her eyes and momentarily wiped all thoughts from her mind; a bush warbler called piercingly from the mountain. In another room someone was singing of love. A fleeting regret came for the pleasures she had expected, which now had to be laid aside, which would be smothered by grief.

'When?'

'The ceremony will be held in three days' time,' Hayato replied.

'I must go to my parents,' she said.

'Of course. Ask Haruna to order a palanquin. Let my men escort you.'

He touched her gently on the side of her face, meaning only to comfort her, but his sympathy and the feel of his hand combined to ignite her passion. She pulled at his clothes, feeling for his skin, needing his closeness. Normally their lovemaking was slow, controlled and restrained, but the collision with grief had stripped her of everything but the blind need for him. She wanted him to cover her, to obliterate her, to reduce her to the basic drive of life in the face of brutality and death. Her urgency fuelled his, and he responded with a new roughness which was just what her body craved.

Afterwards she wept with long gasping sobs while he held her, wiped her face and held the wine bowl to her lips so she could drink. The depths of her grief, the ferocity of the passion and his tenderness all undermined her. She felt on the verge of wanting to cling to him forever.

'Akane,' he said. 'I love you. I will speak to Haruna about you. I will buy your freedom from her. I want you to be my own. I will do anything for you. We will have children together.'

She allowed herself to reflect, once, How pleasant that would be, while at the same time she thought coldly, That will never happen, but she did not reply.

When she finally spoke, it was to say, 'I want to be alone now. I must go to my mother before the end of the day.'

'I will arrange the escort.'

'No,' she said. 'You are very kind but I prefer to go alone.'

Everyone would recognize whose men were with her. It would be as good as announcing she was his mistress already. Haruna had not been consulted, and anyway she would not let any man own her. She would not fall in love with Hayato, though she knew she had been on the edge of love earlier, when her body had known such gratitude for the intensity of both his passion and his tenderness. She drew back from the crater, where love's fires burned and steamed; she would never allow herself to plunge into it.

Akane stood without moving; she would not weep. Her mother was doing all the weeping at home, had been prostrate with grief for days.

'Don't make it harder than it has to be,' her father had said, just once, and Akane had resolved then that she would save her tears for when he was dead, when he would be beyond all suffering and fear and would not be weakened or shamed by her sorrow.

The priest was shaking a white tasselled stick over the parapet that had become a tomb. The stone bridge, completed after six years, was festooned with new straw ropes and white streamers tied to fresh young willow wands. Chanting rose from the crowd, and drums were beating sonorously and rhythmically. From the far side of the bridge, the young boys who served at the shrine to the river god came, dancing the heron dance.

They were dressed in yellow and white, with tassels like feathers bound round wrists and ankles. Each held a talisman in his right hand, with a design made of bronze metal that reminded her of a heron's skull – the small brain pan and the huge beak, the empty eye sockets.

Did he hear the drums and the chanting? Did any sound penetrate into his grave? Did he regret the obsession that had driven him to build this beautiful thing that now spanned the river with its four perfect arches and had brought him to this end, sacrificed to placate the river god and to prevent him ever building anything to rival it?

People said it was built by sorcery. Many still poled across the river in ferry boats rather than use it. It changed the song of the river. More than fifteen workers had died during its construction, as though the river had already extracted payment for the arrogance and effrontery of man. Yet the head of the clan, Lord Otori himself, had ordered its building; and the same Lord Otori had ordered her father's death to quieten the fears and suspicions of the people, and maybe also to placate the river god who had so nearly taken his younger son, Takeshi, and had taken Mori Yuta, the oldest son of the horsebreaker.

The dancers came from the southern end of the bridge, their feet almost soundless on the smooth stone. On the northern side, a small wooden platform had been erected, matted like an outdoor room, the sides swathed in silk cloth, the roof a canopy. On either side, banners rippled in the soft breeze, so the Otori heron seemed to fly.

Lord Otori sat in the centre of the platform, flanked by his brothers on his right, and his two sons, Shigeru and Takeshi, on his left.

Akane remembered how she had helped one brother pull the other from the water and she wondered if they knew who she was. Yuta's little brother had been given to the shrine: he would become a priest, but now he was still a child, and danced the heron dance with the other boys crossing the bridge, passing by her father's tomb.

Was he dead yet?

The silence of the crowd, the insistent pulse of the drums, the graceful movements of the dancers, full of controlled energy and power, ancient beyond words, moved her unbearably. Despite herself, a cry of emotion forced itself from her throat, a cry like a seabird's that pierced the souls of those who heard it.

Her father did not hear it, and would never hear anything again.

The Otori lords were escorted away and the crowd mainly dispersed, though a handful of people remained, Wataru and Naizo among them. There was nothing they could do for their master, but they could not bring themselves to leave him either. It was unthinkable that they would return to their homes, to their ordinary lives, while he, no longer alive but not yet dead, crouched in the dark among the stones.

Akane had not thought her legs would obey her, but they did, taking her with hesitant steps towards the centre of the bridge. Here she knelt and prayed for her father's swift death, for his soul's safe passage.

Wataru came and knelt beside her. He was like an uncle to her: she had known him all her life.

'He made it perfectly,' he said quietly. 'There will be no air. It will be quick.'

She did not dare to ask how long.

They stayed there all day, until the sky faded to grey, the haze rose from the sea, and one by one, stars appeared. It was a warm night, and a rain frog was croaking from the reed beds, echoed by the tinkling bell frog. At one point Wataru spoke to Naizo and the boy disappeared for a while and came back with a flask of wine and two bowls. Wataru poured a little into one of the bowls and set it before the stone. Then the three of them drank in turn from the other. As Akane lifted the bowl to her lips, she heard a new sound in the voice of the river.

'I can hear him,' she whispered, and swallowed the wine in a gulp.

'No, he is long dead,' Wataru replied. 'Don't torment yourself.'

'Listen,' Naizo said, and then all three of them heard it, a sort of low keening beneath the flow of the river. It was her father's voice, transmuted into water. He had become one with the river.

CHAPTER FOURTEEN

Shigeru heard the girl's cry and glanced towards her. He could not see her face – her head was covered with a wide cloth – and he did not recognize her, but the way she stood straight and calm impressed him. The stone-mason's death troubled him, though he had said nothing against his father's decision, feeling his loyalty was more important than his conscience.

He had returned from Terayama as soon as the snows melted and the roads were open. Winter might call an end to skirmishes and campaigns, but intrigue was not smothered by the snow. He had intended to stop in Tsuwano and insist again that Kitano's sons be recalled from Inuyama, but messengers had come saying that spring had brought an outburst of smallpox and Lord Shigeru was on no account to risk endangering his life: he should return directly to Hagi. It was impossible to know if this

was a lie or not. Shigeru himself was determined to go to
Tsuwano and prove it was, but Irie, who had come to the
temple to escort him home, advised against it.

The new year had seen him turn sixteen. He was now
fully a man: his coming-of-age ceremony was held in the
third month with great solemnity and rejoicing. He was
glad to be back in Hagi, though he missed Matsuda's
advice and support, and relieved that his brother had
survived the fall from his horse, a slight inflammation of
the lungs during the coldest days of winter, and numerous
blows from wooden swords in practice. For Takeshi now
lived in the castle with his father and trained with the other
boys of the Otori clan.

The brothers were delighted to be together, their separation having strengthened the bonds of affection between
them. Moving away from home and his mother's over-
loving influence had made Takeshi grow up. He was tall
and strong for his age, still as self-confident as ever, perhaps
rather to excess, as he tended to be boastful, but his teachers
assured Shigeru that this was being tempered by discipline
and training, and in any case Lord Takeshi had a lot to
be boastful about. He excelled at all the warrior's arts, his
mind was quick, his memory retentive. Shigeru was pleased
to see that the Otori characteristics that could so easily
become defects, as Matsuda had told him, were still strong
– though Takeshi had lost none of his recklessness.

After his conversations with Matsuda, Shigeru watched
his uncles more closely, alert to any hint of treachery. He
told his father of Kitano's decision to send his sons to
Inuyama. At first Shigemori was inclined to agree with

Shigeru and Matsuda that they should act swiftly to put an end to such disloyalty, but he consulted his brothers, who advised against it, saying it seemed unwise to provoke the Tohan and insult the Iida family further.

'The unfortunate incident with Miura has already enraged Lord Iida and his son,' his father's older half-brother said pointedly. 'It was reported – of course we know there is no truth in it – that you insisted on challenging Lord Miura but were overcome by him, and Matsuda struck him from behind to save your life.'

'Who dares to spread such lies?' Shigeru said, in fury. 'I fought Miura alone. Inaba was there as a witness.'

'It does not suit the Tohan to see one of their warriors bested by an Otori,' Shigemori said. 'Especially not by you, the heir to the clan.'

'They will seize on any pretext to be insulted,' Shigeru replied. 'They think they can intimidate us by threatening war. We should give them war, now, before they subvert our allies and become even stronger.'

But his uncles' counsel of appeasement prevailed. Apologies for Miura's death were sent to Inuyama, together with gifts in compensation. Many in the clan were as outraged as Shigeru, and, in the Otori way, songs and stories began to circulate about what really happened in the forest encounter when the fifteen-year-old Otori heir defeated the best swordsman the Tohan had ever produced. Shigeru deplored this exaggeration as much as the Tohan's distortion, but there was nothing he could do about either.

He tried many times to speak to his father, but though Shigemori listened to him and praised his opinions, the head of the clan seemed unable to take action or even make decisions. He consulted endlessly – with his brothers, with the elders, and more disturbingly with priests, shamans and soothsayers, who all came forward with conflicting ideas and beliefs about which gods were offended and how to placate them. During Shigeru's absence, Shigemori had become increasingly religious. Ever since Takeshi's near-drowning, he had been apprehensive about the stone bridge he had commanded to be built, and as it neared completion he feared some other act of retaliation from the affronted river god. The offering, he thought, would also allay the fears of the townspeople, who still viewed the bridge as a kind of sorcery.

Shigeru had spent the last year absorbing the austere teachings of Terayama, emptying his mind of illusions, vain desires and fantasies; he did not believe either prayers or spells had any effect or would move any being in the cosmos in any way. If religious belief had any role to play in human life, he thought, it was to strengthen the character and the will so that a man might be ruled by justice and compassion, and might face death without fear. He was impatient with his father's preoccupation with auspicious days, dreams, amulets and prayers, a preoccupation that led to vacillation and inaction. And he was angered by the unnecessary sacrifice of the stonemason, both for its cruelty and its waste of talent. The bridge was a marvel: there was surely nothing like it in the Three Countries. He could see no reason for its creator to be put to death in such a fashion, entombed alive.

He said nothing about these feelings, and watched the proceedings impassively, but the single sharp cry from the stonemason's daughter moved him. Kiyoshige, the son of Mori the horsebreaker, had returned to his service; the two young men had resumed their close friendship. Mori Kiyoshige was lively and irrepressible by nature, and as he matured he used this exterior to mask an extremely astute mind. If his brother had not died, he might have turned into a typically irresponsible second son, but Yuta's death had tempered and strengthened him. During Shigeru's absence, he had kept an eye on Takeshi and had become a close friend to the younger boy. They were similar enough in character to enjoy many escapades, and Kiyoshige's good sense kept the more headstrong Takeshi out of trouble. The circumstances of their childhood, Kiyoshige's older brother's death, their shared love of horses, formed strong bonds between them. It was under Kiyoshige's supervision that Takeshi rode Shigeru's black stallion, and it was Kiyoshige who carried the boy home concussed after falling. But Takeshi learned to ride the black, and indeed to master any horse, and when Shigeru returned another colt was presented to the castle to be Takeshi's own.

Kiyoshige was precocious and popular, had many friends and acquaintances from all walks of life, and drank a great deal more than a boy of his age should, but he always remained far less drunk than he appeared, and never forgot what was said to him. His position as the horsebreaker's son and friend to Lord Otori's sons, and his own taste for low life, meant he moved freely through many different levels of the city's society. He talked to people and, more importantly, listened to them, and had a whole range of informants – nothing to do with the official spy system maintained by the castle, or with the sporadic attempts of Tohan spies to infiltrate the Otori – by whom he was kept aware of everything that went on in Hagi.

Kiyoshige knew all the gossip of the city, and that evening when they were alone together Shigeru asked him about the woman.

'The family should receive some compensation – they must not become destitute. Arrange something for them, but let no one know about it.'

Kiyoshige smiled. 'You have been away. You don't know who she is?'

Shigeru shook his head.

'Her name is Akane: she is a woman of pleasure – perhaps the most famous in Hagi at the moment.'

'Where does she work?'

'The place on the slopes of Fire Mountain: the House of the Camellias. It's owned by a woman called Haruna.' Kiyoshige laughed and said slyly, 'Do you want to visit her?'

'Of course not! I was only concerned for the family's well-being.' But he could not help remembering how he had felt at Terayama, how he had longed to escape to Yamagata and have women sent to him. His father had said a concubine would be arranged, but so far the matter had not been attended to.

He had thought he had mastered his desires during the long, cold winter, but now the thought of Akane in the house of pleasure on the mountain reminded him that he was sixteen years old, that it was spring...

'Just make enquiries discreetly,' he said. 'If she needs a dowry, to get married, it could be supplied.'

'Of course,' Kiyoshige agreed gravely.

CHAPTER FIFTEEN

The stonemason's ghost had an effect on the towns-people that was both disturbing and consoling. Hearing the sound of his disembodied voice at night sobered drunks and silenced children, but on the other hand people were proud of him – for his marvellous creation, his stoic and moving death, and the strength of his spirit that chose to remain with his obsession. Lord Shigeru gave orders for a boulder to be erected above the parapet where the body was sealed, and himself chose the words to be carved into it.

The Otori clan welcomes the just and the loyal.

Let the unjust and the disloyal beware.

Akane was pleased by the inscription and deeply grateful to the young Otori heir who had arranged it. Now she had to make decisions about her own future. On the night of her father's death, she had allowed Wataru to see her back to Fire Mountain. There she kept to her room for three days, seeing no one, not even Hayato, and hardly eating. After that, she went to her mother. Hayato wrote to her daily, urging her to accept his offer, declaring his love for her. Her mother quickly became aware of the situation and it comforted her considerably; she also urged Akane to accept, and began to make her own plans for her daughter's future life. However, four weeks after the stonemason's death, and a week after the carved stone had been erected, Haruna came to visit her.

'I am very sorry,' Akane apologized. Her mother was serving tea to them both: the fragrance filled the room. Haruna was dressed in a simple but formal robe; she had come by palanquin. Their fans fluttered in the still, humid air. 'I have neglected you and my work. After all you have done for me there is really no excuse. I will return very soon. My mother is almost well enough to do without me.'

'But our guest must know about Lord Hayato,' her mother exclaimed. 'Akane must accept him; Haruna, persuade her yourself.'

'I would like to speak to your daughter alone,' Haruna replied, in her usual tone that allowed no argument, and Akane's mother bowed to her and left.

'Come closer,' Haruna said. 'This is for your ears only. I had intended to advise you to accept Hayato: of course, he has offered me a great deal of money for you, but apart from that I believe he would make you happy. He is not likely to tire of you, and he will always support you and any children you might have together. I am very fond of you, Akane, and I have known Hayato for a long time. It would be a very satisfactory arrangement.'

'But?' Akane questioned when the older woman fell silent.

'A few days ago I was summoned to the house of Lord Mori Yusuke, the horsebreaker. His son, as you may know, is a close friend of Lord Otori's sons, especially close to Lord Shigeru. It seems there is a certain interest in you in that quarter.'

'Kiyoshige is only a boy,' Akane said, smiling.

'Not Kiyoshige: Shigeru.'

'Lord Shigeru does not know me. Has he ever even seen me?' He would not remember the girl in the river.

'Apparently he has. He saw you on the recent tragic occasion, and gave instructions that you and your family were to be looked after: there is money available for you. Kiyoshige will deliver it to me.'

Akane was silent for a few moments. Then she said lightly, 'It is an act of kindness, no more. Lord Shigeru has always had a reputation for compassion.'

'Lord Mori and his son seemed to think it could be more than that. Shigeru is a man now: there are no plans yet for his marriage. He will be provided with a concubine. Why should it not be you?'

'The honour is far too great for me,' Akane said, fanning herself more vigorously, for the suggestion had made her pulse beat quickly and brought a flush of heat to her skin. As a child the clan lords had seemed almost like gods to her, completely removed from people of her class. They lived in an elevated world, occasionally glimpsed at ceremonies, barely even gossiped about. The encounter in the river no longer seemed real to her. She could hardly even bring herself to consider being in the same room as the Otori heir, let alone lying with him, skin against skin.

'To tell you the truth, it's an ambition I've sometimes dreamed of for you,' Haruna replied. 'But Hayato's offer made me think again. I had decided to lay aside my ambitions for the sake of your happiness, until the suggestion came from their side. The Otori situation, great honour though it is, has many drawbacks. Your life would necessarily be more secluded, you would have to put up with all the intrigue of the castle, and of course they would not allow any children.'

'This is my mother's main reason for supporting Hayato's case,' Akane said. 'She longs for grandchildren. But I have no desire for children. Why bring them into this world just to suffer?' After a moment she added, 'Anyway, do I have a choice? Surely Lord Shigeru's wishes cannot be refused?'

'His wishes have not yet been voiced as such: the Mori family were simply sounding things out, as it were. However, I had the feeling they were advising against any other precipitous decisions that you might make.'

'Hayato has hardly been discreet,' Akane said.

'It's true. Everyone knows he is pursuing you.'

'I suppose he will be "advised" as well.'

'Almost certainly.'

'So I am supposed to refuse Hayato and do nothing until Lord Shigeru voices his wishes,' Akane said with a flash of anger.

'You only need do what you have been doing: stay here with your mother and continue not to see Hayato. As I said, money has already been provided for you. You do not need to work.'

'It's not only money I work for,' Akane said. 'How long do I have to live without a man?' She was already missing her favourite lover, longing to feel again the intensity of the passion that had momentarily numbed her grief.

'Not long,' Haruna promised. 'Shall I take a favourable response back to the Mori?'

Akane sat in silence. She could hear her mother in the kitchen, the sounds of the street and the river. She stood suddenly, as if seized by anger, and walked to the door and back again. 'What other response can there be?'

After Haruna had left, Akane ignored her mother's eager questioning and went to sit in her father's workshop, among the piles of half-carved stones. It was empty and silent; she missed its constant noise, the tap of iron on iron and the sigh of iron on stone. Wataru had returned to his own village, saying he was too old to serve anyone else, and Naizo had been taken on by another mason who had already offered to buy her father's store of stone. Soon the oxcarts would come and carry them away. The air was full of dust, and the sun's rays seemed almost solidified by the motes, as if they themselves were about to become stone. She let her gaze linger over all the different shades of grey that lay between white and near-black: rocks brought from mountainside, riverbed and seashore, hewn, hauled and lifted by men's strength.

How strange were the workings of fate, she mused. Lord Shigemori had ordered her father's death; if that had not taken place she would never have come to the attention of his son. If she went to him, she would be raised to a position her family could never have dreamed of – but she would have no children.

Yet, she thought, my father has no use of grandchildren. He will not be like other spirits. He will stay forever with his bridge – many will bring him offerings and gifts, almost as if he were a god himself.

She rose then and took flowers and wine to place before the stone. It had rained and the sky was overcast, the bridge, the streets, the river's surface all as grey as the stones.

As she had expected, there were other offerings there. Her father had worshippers now, and always would have. He did not need grandchildren. She prayed to his spirit and told him what she was going to become. There seemed a certain balance in place: she also would be a sacrifice – to the river god, to the Otori – though she thought her sacrifice would not be unpleasurable.

Weeks went past without any further word from the horse-breaker or from the castle. Akane was disappointed.

'They have changed their minds,' she said to Haruna, who called on her regularly to keep her spirits up and bring money to her mother.

'These things take time to arrange,' Haruna said. 'You must be patient.'

'I have been persuaded to give up a good man for the sake of an empty dream. You had better take me back!'

'Be patient,' Haruna whispered.

Akane's patience was wearing thin, and she became even more annoyed when one morning, when she woke early and could not sleep, rose at dawn and went to the bridge to take food and drink to her father, she saw a group of horsemen riding towards her. She recognized Mori Kiyoshige on his grey horse with the black mane and tail, Irie Masahide, the sword instructor, and Lord Shigeru himself, along with a large number of retainers. She and the others in the crowd on the bridge dropped to their knees and watched with bowed heads until the horsemen had passed, the horses' feet padding over the stones.

'Lord Shigeru is leaving the city?' she said to the man next to her, as they both stood.

'Looks like it. Going to deal with the Tohan, I hope. It's time someone taught them a lesson.'

They will be away all summer, she thought. Am I expected to do nothing till the typhoons come and drive them home?

She watched the group as they trotted off the bridge and along the riverbank. The young man on the black horse turned his head and looked back. It was too far away to tell if he was looking at her, but she felt he had seen her standing by her father's grave. She continued to stare after them until they disappeared from sight. She sighed. I may as well wait, she thought.

CHAPTER SIXTEEN

Shigeru had allowed his thoughts to stray to the stone-mason's daughter once or twice, but he did not know about Kiyoshige's negotiations, and he had very little time to pursue any of his own in that direction – for shortly after the entombment messengers arrived from Chigawa, a small town on the high road between Yamagata and the coast, right on the Eastern border of the Middle Country. The reports were that the Tohan were carrying out some sort of campaign against their own peasantry to root out an obscure sect known as the Hidden – Shigeru remembered Nagai talking about the same sect at Yamagata. The persecuted were fleeing over the border into the Middle Country: Tohan warriors were pursuing them, torturing them and killing them, along with any Otori peasants that might have given them shelter. It was this that outraged Shigeru when he heard it. The Tohan were entitled to do what they liked within their own borders, and Shigeru did not care one way or the other about the sect: there were a lot of religious movements that sprang up and withered away, and most of them seemed harmless, presenting no threat to the stable order of society. But if the Tohan started believing they could come and go as they liked into Otori lands, sooner or later they would come and stay. A further complication was that the border incursions all took place around Chigawa, an area rich in silver and copper. Such aggressive provocation had to be met with equal boldness and decisiveness: it was the only way to stop it.

As always, and to Shigeru's displeasure, his uncles were present at the meeting Lord Shigemori called to discuss what the Otori reaction should be. He felt that now he was an adult and could advise his father, there was no need for his uncles to be present. It seemed to him to indicate confusion about who actually led the clan, and to say that Shigemori dared do nothing without his brothers' agreement. Again, Shigeru's uncles advised appeasement, reiterating their thoughts on the strength of the Tohan and the dangers of insulting the Iida again so soon after Miura's unfortunate death. In his turn, Shigeru voiced his opinion forcefully, and was supported by the senior retainers, Irie and Miyoshi.

But the arguments went on. He saw how skilfully his uncles played his father, seeming always to defer to him, flattering him, wearing him down with their persistent reasoning. They claimed always that their only goal was the well-being of the clan, but he wondered what the secret desires of their hearts might be. What advancement to themselves did placating the Tohan bring? It did occur to him, then, that they might seek to usurp both his father and himself – such baseness seemed unbelievable, and he did not think the clan would ever allow it, but he also saw how ineffectual his father had become, and he feared pragmatic men like Endo and Miyoshi might, if not actively seek, at least accept a stronger head. Which will be no one but me, he swore to himself.

They sat in the great hall of the residence behind the castle itself. It had rained earlier, but now the sun had come out and it was very hot. Shigeru could hear the sea surging against the wall beyond the garden. All the doors stood open, and the deep verandas were cool pools of shade beyond which the summer light shimmered, making leaves a more brilliant green and the colours of the flowers – wisteria and lotus – more intense. The discussion continued all afternoon, while the heat intensified and the cicadas' shrilling grew more strident and men's tempers more frayed.

Finally, just before sunset, Lord Shigemori said he would like to delay the decision until he had been able to consult a shaman, who fortunately was visiting the shrine in the forest above the castle. A messenger was sent and the meeting broke up; it would be continued and a decision made the following day.

Shigeru spoke with the barest necessary politeness to his father and uncles, and went to walk in the garden to cool his temper. The sun was sinking below the hill on the western side of the bay, but the air was still stifling. His skin itched beneath the formal robes, and his head ached.

At the far end of the garden Takeshi was sitting on the stone wall overlooking the sea. Shigeru rarely saw his brother like this, sitting quietly, thinking himself unobserved, apparently wrapped in thought. He watched him for a few moments and found himself wondering what his brother's life would be like. He was so often the centre of attention, admired and praised, yet he was not the clan heir and, unless something happened to Shigeru, would never hold the power that he obviously longed for – and seemed created for. There were many instances in the chronicles of the clans where brother fought brother for power, where younger siblings turned against their elders, overthrew and killed them – or were defeated and put to death or forced to take their own lives. His father's brothers, right in front of his eyes, were proving themselves disloyal. They were half-brothers, it was true, from a different mother, but what if it were a sign of an inescapable part of Otori history that would be repeated in each generation? What if Takeshi were to prove disloyal to him?

How could he keep him occupied, and make use of all his talents? Really he should be given land of his own, a domain within the fief – maybe Tsuwano or even Yamagata.

Takeshi seemed to snap suddenly out of his reverie. He jumped from the wall and saw Shigeru. His face lit up in a smile so spontaneous and full of affection that it allayed some of Shigeru's fears.

'Have you come to a decision?' he demanded.

'Our father is consulting a shaman,' Shigeru replied, unable to keep the anger from his voice as he should have. 'We are to meet again tomorrow.'

Takeshi's smile vanished as quickly as it had appeared. 'It would be better to act immediately. That's what you think, isn't it?'

'Yes, I do, and everyone knows it by now. I have been saying it all afternoon. But I am not being listened to. Worse, I am constantly undermined by my uncles, who never cease reminding me of my youth, my inexperience and their great wisdom.'

'They have no wisdom,' Takeshi replied shortly.

Shigeru did not correct his brother for his disrespect. Takeshi glanced up at him and went on, emboldened. 'My older brother should act, for the sake of the clan.'

'I can do nothing against our father's wishes,' Shigeru replied. 'I must obey him in whatever decision he makes. The trouble is, he makes no decisions at all!'

Takeshi put on a voice like a mischievous child's and said brightly, 'My teachers can't forbid me to do things they don't know about. And if they don't forbid me, I'm not being disobedient.' The voice was a child's, but Takeshi's eyes were narrowed like an adult's. 'Mori Kiyoshige taught me that,' he added.

'Did he?' Shigeru said. 'Go and find Kiyoshige now and ask him to come to me. I'm thinking of trying the horses out – maybe early tomorrow morning.'

'Can I come?' Takeshi said at once.

'Probably not.'

Takeshi looked disappointed but did not argue. Instead he bowed formally to Shigeru, as a younger brother should to an older, and walked swiftly away.

He knows how to be obedient, Shigeru thought; he has had the best upbringing. I am sure I will always be able to trust him.

As they left the city he saw the girl again on the bridge: the miraculous bridge so perfect and beautiful. The river did not fight it now, but caressed its stone arches, whose footings had cost so many lives. Weeds were already attaching themselves to the lower stones, streaking the grey with dark, viscous green, and fish gathered in the shadow of the arches, finding shelter from the sunlight and from the sharp beaks of herons and gulls.

He noted the carved boulder he had erected – it had been a decisive act, like this dawn departure. But both were inspired by the same desire – for justice – and the same impatient intolerance of cruelty and disloyalty.

Even at this early hour there were people on the bridge, bringing offerings to the stonemason, and it made Shigeru think about death, and how this man's death, for all its cruelty, led to a sort of new life, inspiring people – the stonemason was as important and active in death as he had been in life: his memory would never die.

He could not see into the future, and therefore could not know how his own grave would become a centre of pilgrimage as long as the Middle Country endured, and how he would be worshipped as a god forever.

And although he meditated often on his own death, as Matsuda had taught him, and prayed that it would be honourable and significant, death did not weigh heavy on his mind this morning.

A sudden thunderstorm in the night had cleared the air and sluiced the streets clean. Huge grey-white clouds banked up on the horizon, tinged pink by the sunrise, as the sky began to deepen to blue. The horse beneath him was eager and excited, and he could feel its coiled energy through his legs and thighs. It was a young creature, like him. They were riding out together. He would not have to sit through another endless day of discussions, arguments, half-truths and evasions.

Ostensibly he was exercising the horses with Kiyoshige, Irie and about thirty men – but he did not intend to return to Hagi before the day's meeting started. In fact he did not intend to return for many days, for as long as it took to assess the border situation for himself, and deal with the Tohan if necessary.

The light below the clouds turned to yellow as the sun rose further, making their grey undersides gleam like newly polished steel. The riders followed the street that ran along the riverbank. Like most of the city streets it was unpaved, and the horses' hoofs sent showers of water splashing from the puddles.

Shigeru turned and looked back at the bridge. The low rays of the sun turned the water to silver. He had noticed the woman – Akane; he began at that moment to think of her as Akane – kneeling by the grave, head bowed as he rode past, and he had felt a sudden rush of recognition of a bond between them. He was not surprised now to see that she was gazing after him, with the look of someone peering out to sea, trying to make out some great ship nearing or leaving harbour.

He reined his horse back slightly, so he and Kiyoshige were riding side by side.

'When we come back, I would like to see her.'

'Who?' Kiyoshige replied teasingly.

'The stonemason's daughter. Akane.'

'Akane?' the younger boy repeated. 'I thought you were not interested.'

'I may be interested,' Shigeru replied. It was, it seemed, a day of decisions. He would choose his own war and his own concubine.

'It has already been arranged,' Kiyoshige said quietly, leaning sideways slightly in the saddle so only Shigeru could hear. 'She is waiting for you to send for her.'

Shigeru smiled; there was a host of things he might have expressed: pleasure, surprise, amusement at his friend's connivings. Kiyoshige laughed. There was no need to say any of them. They understood each other.

In the same way, he had not needed to explain his plan to Kiyoshige the day before. His friend had grasped Shigeru's intentions immediately. Irie had been invited to come and speak with the young men in the garden. Shigeru felt he needed at least one of his teachers to approve his scheme; and Irie, who had travelled with him to Yamagata and returned to the town to meet him in the spring, was the one he trusted most, suspecting from what he noticed about Irie during the meetings that the man's loyalties had been transferred to him. They had had no discussions; Shigeru had not sought advice. He had made up his mind, had told Irie of his intentions and asked – though ordered was closer to the truth – the older man to come with him.

The old warrior had obeyed impassively, but he had met them early, before the appointed time, and Shigeru felt his eagerness was as great as their own. Irie's outrage had been as deep as Shigeru's when they had uncovered the duplicity of Lord Kitano and his approaches to the Iida family, and he had been the most affronted by the Tohan version of Miura's death.

The men who came with them – ten from each one's personal retainers – were told nothing of the mission. Kiyoshige casually mentioned the need to try out the horses, and made sure his men rode the youngest, greenest colts to give some appearance of truth; but just like the man who had spoken to Akane on the bridge, what all the Otori men hoped for was the chance to confront the arrogant, insufferable Tohan, and teach them a lesson.

The last of the snows had melted and all the mountain passes were open. At first they followed the coast road towards Matsue; after three days they turned east, riding up and down steep mountain paths, sleeping wherever night overtook them, happy to be out of doors while the rain held off, away from towns and villages that might be infiltrated by spies, until they came to the edge of the wide plateau known as Yaegahara. It was circled by mountain ranges, that appeared ever more faintly one behind the other as far as the eye could see. The most distant were the High Cloud Ranges that formed a natural barrier to the Three Countries. Beyond the ranges, many weeks' travel to the east, lay Miyako, the capital of the Eight Islands – the seat of the Emperor, who, in name, ruled over them all. In reality, the Emperor's power was small, and outlying fiefs like the Three Countries virtually ruled themselves. If local clans and individual warlords rose to power and conquered and subdued their weaker neighbours, there was no one to object or intervene. Whatever rights might seem to be assured by inheritance or oaths of fealty were all subsumed by the final single legitimacy of power. Among the Tohan, the Iida family had risen to supremacy: they were an ancient house, high-ranking warriors, established at Inuyama for hundreds of years – but none of these things made them first among their equals as much as their lust for power and their ruthless and decisive pursuit of it. No one could be at ease with such neighbours.

Inuyama, the Tohan castle town, lay behind the mountains far to the south.

They camped on the edge of the plain, not knowing that most of their party would die there before they were three years older, and rode across it the following morning, urging their horses to gallop over the grassy slopes, surprising pheasants and hares that made the young horses startle and leap like hares themselves. It seemed the thunderstorms had brought an end to the spring rains; the sky was the deep blue of early summer, and it was very hot; both men and horses poured with sweat; the colts were excited and hard to control.

'It turned out a good exercise for them after all,' Kiyoshige said when they stopped to rest in the middle of the day in the shade of one of the few scattered woods on the grassy plain. There was a cold spring nearby where the steaming horses were watered and the men washed hands, faces and feet before they ate. 'If we were to fight an enemy on terrain like this, half our horses would be out of control!'

'We get too little practice,' Irie said. 'Our troops have forgotten what war is like.'

'This would make a perfect battleground,' Shigeru said. 'Plenty of room to move, and a good terrain. We from the west would have the sun behind us at the end of the day, and the slope in our favour.'

'Bear it in mind,' Irie said briefly.

They did not speak much, but dozed beneath the sonorous pine trees, half stupefied by the heat and the ride from the grasslands. Shigeru was almost asleep when one of the men posted as a guard called out to him, 'Lord Otori! Someone is coming from the east.'

He got to his feet, yawning and drowsy, and joined the guard on the edge of the wood, where a pile of large boulders gave them cover.

In the distance, a lone figure was stumbling across the plain. It fell repeatedly, struggled to its feet, sometimes crawled on hands and knees. As it came closer, they could hear its voice, a thin anguished howling that now and then quietened to sobbing only to rise again in a note that made horror touch the spines of the watching men.

'Keep out of sight,' Shigeru called, and swiftly the thirty men hid themselves and their horses behind boulders and among trees. Shigeru's second reaction after horror was one of pity, but he did not want to fall into a trap by showing themselves suddenly, or to frighten the man away.

As he came closer they could see that his face was a mass of blood, around which flies buzzed viciously. It was impossible to discern any features, but the eyes must have remained, and something of the mind, for it was clear that the man knew where he was going: he was heading for the water.

He fell at the pool's edge, and thrust his head into the water, moaning as its chill hit his open wounds. He seemed to be trying to drink, sucking at the water, heaving and retching as he choked on it.

Small pale fish surfaced at the smell of blood.

'Bring him to me,' Shigeru said. 'But be careful: don't frighten him.'

The men went to the water's edge. One of them put his hand on the fugitive's shoulder and pulled him up, speaking to him slowly and clearly. 'Don't be afraid! It's all right, we won't hurt you.' The other took a cloth from his pouch and began to wash the blood away.

Shigeru could tell from the man's posture that he was terrified anew, but as the blood was washed away and he could see the face more clearly, behind the pain and the fear there was intelligence in the expression of the eyes. The men lifted him and brought him to where Shigeru stood, and set him down on the sandy ground.

The man's ears had been sliced off, and blood oozed from the holes.

'Who did this to you?' Shigeru said, disgust creeping across his skin.

The man opened his mouth, moaned and spat out blood. His tongue had been ripped out. But with one hand he smoothed the sand, and with the other wrote the characters Tohan. He smoothed the sand again and traced, incorrectly, clumsily.

Come. Help.

Shigeru thought the man near death, and was reluctant to inflict further suffering by moving him. But he himself made a gesture at the horses, indicating that he would guide them. Tears poured from his eyes when he tried to talk, as though the realization that he had been silenced forever had only just sunk in – yet neither agony nor grief would deter him from his entreaties. All those gathered around were moved to something like awe at such courage and endurance, and could not refuse him.

It was hard to know how to transport him, since he was rapidly losing his remaining strength. In the end, one of the strongest of the retainers, Harada, a man with a broad solid build, took him on his back, like a child, and the others bound him tightly on. The two were helped on to one of the quieter horses, and, touching the man who carried him on the left or right side of his chest, the suffering creature guided them to the far side of the plain.

At first they went at a walk to spare him extra pain, but he moaned in frustration and beat his hands against the chest of the man carrying him, so they urged the horses into a canter. It was as if the colts sensed the new gravity of their riders, and they went forward sweetly and smoothly, as gently as mares with foals.

A stream flowed from the spring, and they followed the slight depression it made between the rounded slopes for a little while. The sun was lowering towards the west and their shadows rode before them, long and deep. The stream widened and flowed more slowly, and suddenly they were in cultivated land, small fields cut from the limestone, diked and filled with the river's silt, where the young seedlings glowed green. The horses splashed through the shallow water, but no one came out to grumble at the damage to the plants. The air smelled of smoke, and something else, charred flesh and hair and bone. The horses flung up their heads, eyes huge and nostrils flared.

Shigeru drew his sword and all of them followed, the steel blades sighing from the scabbards in unison. Harada turned his horse in response to his guide's bloodied hands and rode to the left along the dike.

The fields were the outermost of a small village. Hens were scratching on the banks, and a wandering dog barked at the horses, but otherwise there were none of the usual sounds of village life. The horses' splashing sounded astonishingly loud, and when Kiyoshige's grey whinnied and Shigeru's black replied, their neighs echoed like a child crying.

At the far end of the dike a small hill, hardly more than a mound, rose abruptly among the flooded fields. Its lower half was covered in trees, making it look like a shaggy animal, and craggy grey rocks crowned it. Their guide signalled to them to stop, and by his contortions indicated to Harada to dismount. He gesticulated towards the other side of the mound, holding his hands to his ruined mouth to tell them to be silent. They could hear nothing except the hens, the birds, and a sudden crackling sound like branches breaking. Shigeru held up one hand and beckoned to Kiyoshige. Together they rode round the side of the hill. Here they saw steps cut in its side, leading up into the dark shade of oaks and cedars. At the foot of the steps, several horses were tethered to a line between two trees; one of them was trying to tear leaves from a maple. A guard stood near them, armed with both sword and bow.

The horses saw each other and neighed. The guard immediately took aim with the bow and let the arrow fly. He shouted loudly, drew his sword. The arrow fell short, splashing into the water near the horses' feet. Shigeru urged the black into a gallop. He had no idea who this sudden enemy was, but thought he could only be from the Tohan. Their own Otori crests were clearly visible: only the Tohan would attack them so boldly. Kiyoshige had his bow in his hand, and as his horse broke into a gallop alongside Shigeru's he turned his body sideways in the saddle and let the arrow fly. It hit the other man in the side of the neck, finding the gap in his armour. He staggered and fell to his knees, clutching vainly at the shaft. Kiyoshige passed Shigeru and cut the horses' lines, shouting and flailing at them to scare them away. As they splashed off through the fields, kicking and squealing, their riders appeared, leaping down the steps, armed with swords, knives and poles.

There was no exchange of words, no challenge or declaration, just the immediate grappling in battle. They were equal in numbers. The Tohan had the advantage of the slope, but the Otori were mounted, could withdraw and attack with speed, and in the end the horsemen prevailed. Shigeru killed at least five men himself, wondering as he did so why he should end the lives of men whose names he did not know, and what fate had led them to his sword, late in the afternoon of the fifth month. None asked for mercy when the outcome became clear, though the last few remaining alive threw down their swords and tried to run through the shallow water, stumbling and slipping, until the pursuing horsemen brought them down, and their blood drifted across the sky's peaceful reflection in the fields' mirror.

Shigeru dismounted and tethered Karasu to the maple. Ordering some of the men to gather the bodies and take the heads, he called to Kiyoshige to come with him and began to climb the steps, sword still in his hand, alert to every sound.

After the clashing and screaming of the short battle, the hillside's usual sounds were returning. A thrush was calling from the bushes, and wood pigeons cooed in the huge oaks. Cicadas droned plaintively, but beneath all these everyday noises, beneath the rustle of leaves in the breeze, something else could be heard: a dull moaning, hardly human.

'Where's the man we brought?' Shigeru asked, stopping on the step and turning to look back.

Kiyoshige called to Harada and the soldier came running. The tortured man had been removed from his back, but his clothes and armour, even the skin of his neck, were soaked in his blood.

'Lord Shigeru, he died during the battle. We laid him down out of harm's way, and when we returned, his life had left him.'

'He was very brave,' Kiyoshige murmured. 'When we find out who he was we will bury him with honour.'

'He will surely be reborn as a warrior,' Harada said.

Shigeru did not reply, but went on up the steps to discover who it was the man had sought so desperately to help.

Just as the sound had been hardly human, so the bodies that hung from the trees were barely recognizable as men and women – and, he saw with a searing mixture of disgust and pity, children. They hung head down, slowly circling in the smoke of the fires lit below them, the skin swollen and roasted, eyes bulging from reddened sockets, pouring useless tears that the heat dried instantly. He was ashamed of their suffering, that they could be treated worse than beasts, that such humiliation and pain could be inflicted on them and they still remained human. He thought with a strange longing of the swift and merciful death brought by the sword, and prayed that such a death would be his.

'Cut them down,' he said. 'We will see if any can be saved.'

There were fifteen in all: seven men, four women and four children. Three of the children and all the women were already dead. The fourth child, a boy, died immediately when they lifted him down, as the blood flowed back into his body. Five men still lived, two because their skulls had been opened to stop the brain swelling. One of these had had his tongue torn out and died from loss of blood, but the other could speak and was still conscious. Once he had been strong and agile. His muscles stood out like cords. Shigeru could see in his eyes the same gleam of intelligence and strength of will as he had seen in their rescuer. He was determined this man should live, that the other man's fortitude should not have been in vain. The remaining three were so near death it seemed kindest to give them water and end their suffering, and Kiyoshige did so with his knife, while the conscious man knelt with joined hands and spoke a prayer that Shigeru had never heard before.

'These are Hidden,' Irie said behind him. 'That is the prayer they use at the moment of death.'

When the dead were buried, while it was still light, Shigeru went with Irie to the top of the hill where the Tohan heads were laid out before the entrance to the shrine. The place was deserted, but signs of their enemies' encampment were still evident: stores of food, rice and vegetables, cooking utensils, weapons, ropes and other more sinister instruments. He gazed impassively on the dead, while Irie named those he recognized from their features or from the crests taken from their clothes and armour.

Two were, surprisingly to Shigeru, warriors of high rank: one, Maeda, closely related to the Iida family through marriage, the other, Honda. He wondered why such men should defile their reputation and honour by participating in torture. Had they been acting on Iida Sadayoshi's orders? And what were the Hidden, that they aroused this vindictiveness and cruelty? His mood was sombre as he descended the steps again. He did not want to sleep near the shrine, tainted as it was with torture and death, and he sent Harada and some other men to look for alternative shelter. The one survivor of the atrocity was being looked after in the shade of a camphor laurel that grew on the bank. Shigeru went to him; fireflies were beginning to glitter in the blueness of twilight.

His face and head had been washed, and salve applied to the burns. The slashes in the skull oozed dark blood but looked clean. He was conscious, eyes open, staring upwards at the dark shade of the tree, where the leaves were rustling slightly in the evening breeze.

Shigeru knelt beside him and spoke quietly.

'I hope your pain has been eased.'

The man's head turned towards his voice. 'Lord Otori.'

'I am sorry we could not save the others.'

'They are all dead, then?'

'Their suffering is over.'

The man said nothing for a moment. His eyes were already glistening and reddened. It was impossible to tell if he wept or not. He whispered something Shigeru could not quite hear, something about Heaven. Then he said more clearly, 'We will all meet again.'

'What is your name?' Shigeru asked. 'Do you have any other family?'

'Nesutoro,' he replied. The name was unfamiliar: Shigeru could not recall ever hearing it before.

'And the man who came to us?'

'Tomasu. Is he already dead too?'

'He had great courage.' It was the only consolation Shigeru could give.

'They all had courage,' Nesutoro replied. 'Not one recanted, not one denied the Secret One. Now they sit at his feet in Paradise, in the land of the blessed.' He spoke in gasps, his voice rasping. 'Last night the Tohan lit a great fire in front of the shrine. They taunted us, saying, "See where the light bursts forth in the east. Your god is coming to save you!"' Tears began to well in his eyes then. 'We believed it. We thought he would see our suffering and our fortitude and come for us. And we were not wholly wrong, for he sent you.'

'Too late, I'm afraid.'

'God's ways are not for us to question. Lord Otori, you saved my life. I would offer it to you, but it already belongs to him.'

There was something in the way he said it, an attempt at humour that raised Shigeru's spirits, almost comforted him. He felt an instinctive regard for this man, a recognition of his intelligence and character. At the same time the words bothered him. He did not fully understand the man's meaning.

It was nearly dark by the time Harada returned, his men carrying torches that flamed and smoked, hastening nightfall. The village from which the Hidden had been taken lay a short distance away. Some of its buildings still offered shelter, though most had been destroyed during the Tohan attack. Many of its inhabitants had escaped, run away and hidden; they returned when they saw the Otori crest. A rough stretcher was made for the injured man, and two men carried him on foot while the rest rode, leading their horses and three others whose masters had died during the clash with the Tohan. A narrow stony track led from the hill along the side of the cultivated fields, following the course of the stream. The water babbled and sparkled in the torchlight; frogs were croaking among the reeds. The summer evening air was soft and caressing, but Shigeru's mood was dark as they approached the village, and the sight of the destruction there angered him still more deeply. The Tohan had crossed the border and come deep into Otori land. They had tortured people who, whatever their beliefs, were Otori, and who had been unprotected by their own clan. He regretted he had not acted earlier, that these attacks had not been punished before. If the Otori had not appeared so weak and indecisive, the Tohan would never have grown so bold. He knew he had been right to come, right to engage in the brief battle, but at the same time he was aware that the deaths of the Tohan warriors, especially those of Honda and Maeda, would enrage the Iida family and worsen relations between the two clans.

Grief and distress hung over the village. Women wept as they brought water and prepared food. Fifteen of their community had died – it must have been close to half: neighbours, friends, relatives.

Shigeru and his men were given makeshift accommodation within the small shrine, sitting under the carved figures and the votive pictures. The armour from the dead Tohan was presented to the shrine. The priest's wife brought water to wash their feet, then tea made from roasted barley. Its pungent smell made Shigeru realize how hungry he was. It did not look as if much food would be available; he tried to put all thoughts of eating away. The gratitude of the villagers, the warmth of the welcome in the midst of suffering, only increased his unease, though he gave no outward sign of it, sitting impassively as the headman knelt before him to give his account.

'Every village from here as far as Chigawa has been attacked,' he said bitterly. He was a man of about thirty, blind in one eye but otherwise healthy and strong-looking. 'The Tohan act as if this were already their land, exacting taxes, taking whatever they please, and trying to eradicate the Hidden as they do in Iida's own domain.'

'Already?' Shigeru questioned.

'Forgive me, Lord Otori: I should not speak so bluntly, but polite lies don't help anyone. Everyone fears the Iida plan to attack the Middle Country once they've unified the East. This must also be known in Hagi. For months we have been asking ourselves why no help comes, if we will be handed over to the Tohan by our own lords.'

'To what domain do you belong?'

'To Tsuwano; we send rice every year, but we are so far from them – only you and your father can save us.

Help must come directly from Hagi. We thought you had already forgotten us. And anyway, Lord Kitano's sons are in Inuyama.'

'I know it,' Shigeru replied, fighting to master his anger. Kitano's ill-considered decision to send his sons to the Tohan capital had proved a fatal weakness in the Otori position. The boys were hostages in all but name: no wonder their father took no action on the Eastern borders. Shigeru feared his former companions might pay for his attack with their lives, but the fault did not lie with him: it had been their father's decision to send them away, a decision that Shigeru already regarded as near treachery. If the outcome was the death of his sons, it would be no more than justice.

'If this sect fled from the East, they should be returned there,' Kiyoshige said, for no one was free just to walk away from their own land.

'It is true that some of the Hidden are from the East,' the headman replied. 'But most have always lived here in the Middle Country, and are of the Otori clan. The Tohan lie about them as they lie about everything.'

'They live among you, peacefully?'

'Yes, and have done for centuries. Outwardly they act the same as any of us. That is why they are called the Hidden. There are a few differences: we worship many gods and honour them all; we know we have salvation through the grace of the Enlightened One. They worship the one they call the Secret One, and they will not take life: they will not kill either themselves or others.'

'Yet they seem courageous,' Kiyoshige observed.

The villager nodded in agreement. Shigeru felt the man had more to say on this matter but something held him back, some other tie or loyalty.

'You know the man who survived, Nesutoro?'

'Of course. We grew up together.' After a pause he swallowed hard and said, 'My wife is his sister.'

'You are one of them?' Kiyoshige exclaimed.

'No, lord. I have never been a believer. How could I? My family have been heads in this village for generations. We have always followed the teachings of the Enlightened One and we honour the gods of the forest, the river and the harvest. My wife does the same, but secretly in her heart she worships the Secret One. I forbade her to declare the truth openly, like those who died: she had to trample on their sacred images...'

'What are they?' Shigeru asked.

The man shifted uncomfortably and stared at the floor. 'It is not for me to say,' he said finally. 'Speak to Nesutoro. He will know if he can tell you or not.'

'So you saved your wife's life?' Irie had been silent till now, watching and listening carefully.

'She is not dead, nor are our children; but she does not thank me for it. She obeyed me, as a wife should, but she feels she disobeyed the teachings of her god. Those who died have become martyrs, saints, and live in Paradise. She is afraid she will be cast into Hell.'

'This is the reason the Tohan hate this sect so much,' Irie said later, after the headman had been dismissed and they had eaten a sparse meal. 'Wives should obey their husbands, vassals their lords, but these people have another loyalty – to an unseen power.'

'Unseen and non-existent,' Kiyoshige said briefly.

'Yet we've seen tangible proof of the strength of their belief,' Shigeru observed.

'Proof of the belief, not of the god's existence.'

'What proof is there of the existence of any spirit?' Shigeru said, but then remembered how he himself had seen – had talked to – a fox spirit who could appear and disappear at will.

Kiyoshige grinned. 'It's better not to question too closely. The monks and priests could occupy you for years with their discussions.'

'I agree,' Irie said. 'Religious practices should keep the fabric of society in good shape – they should not unravel it.'

'Well.' Shigeru stretched his legs, then settled himself cross-legged and changed the subject. 'From tomorrow we will ride the length of the border, from sea to sea. We must know the full extent of Tohan incursion. We have nine weeks – maybe three months before the first typhoons.'

'We have few men for a long campaign,' Irie said. 'And the Tohan will be seeking revenge for this recent defeat.'

'I will write tonight to Yamagata and Kushimoto. They can each send a couple of hundred. You and Kiyoshige may go north with half of them. I will go south with the others.'

'I should accompany Lord Shigeru,' Irie protested. 'And, forgive me, Lord Kiyoshige is too young to undertake such a mission.'

'That's a matter of opinion,' Kiyoshige muttered.

Shigeru smiled. 'Kiyoshige – and all of us – need all the experience we can get. That is why you will go with him. We are not engaging in a major battle; we are simply demonstrating to the Iida that we will not tolerate encroachment of our borders. But I fully expect these skirmishes to lead to all-out war. You can wait for the extra men in Chigawa. We will ride there together tomorrow. I will send Harada tonight with the letters. And then I wish to speak to the man we rescued.'

He had carried writing materials and his seal with him, as always, in the saddle bags, and now he asked for more lamps to be brought, and water for the inkstone. He mixed the ink and wrote swiftly to Nagai at Yamagata and to Lord Yanagi of Kushimoto, ordering them to send men directly to Chigawa. Then he gave the letters to Harada, saying, 'There is no need to contact Hagi or anyone else. Above all, Kitano must not be told. You must impress upon them both: they must obey at once.'

'Lord Otori.' The man sprang into the saddle with no sign of fatigue, and accompanied by two soldiers carrying torches rode off into the night.

Shigeru watched the lights shrink until they were indistinguishable from the fireflies or the stars against the utter blackness of the Yaegahara plain.

'I hope you approve,' he said to Irie, who stood beside him. 'Am I doing the right thing?'

'You have acted decisively,' Irie replied. 'That is the right thing, whatever the consequences.'

Those I have to live with, Shigeru thought, but did not say it to Irie. He felt the sense of liberation that action brought. Irie was right: far better to act decisively than to sit in endless discussion and consultation, paralysed by superstition and fear.

'Now I will speak to Nesutoro,' he said. 'There is no need for you to come with me.'

Irie bowed and went back to the shrine. As Shigeru walked to the house where the village headman lived and where his brother-in-law was being tended, Kiyoshige joined him out of the shadows.

'The horses are tethered and fed. And guards have been set all around the village. There's not a lot to eat, but the men are not complaining. In fact they're happy – they can't wait to have another go at the Tohan.'

'I think they'll get that soon enough,' Shigeru replied. 'Word of this encounter will reach Inuyama within days, and the Tohan will respond. But by then we'll have re-inforcements. And from now on our borders will be patrolled and guarded properly.'

They came to the headman's small house. It had an earth floor with a tiny raised matted area for sleeping. Here Nesutoro lay, a woman kneeling beside him. When she saw the visitors she bowed to the floor, staying low until her husband spoke quietly to her. Then she rose and brought cushions for them, placing them on the step near the injured man. She helped her brother to sit, and leaned his head against her own body, acting as a support to him. In the dim lamplight her face was drawn, bruised with grief and tears, but Shigeru could perceive the likeness to her brother, in the planed cheekbones and almost triangular eyes.

Nesutoro's eyes glittered like coals with fever and pain, but the sharp features softened into a real smile at the sight of Shigeru.

'Are you able to talk a little?'

The man nodded.

'I am interested in your beliefs and want to know more about them.'

Nesutoro looked anguished. His sister wiped the sweat from his face.

'Answer Lord Otori,' the headman pleaded, then added apologetically, 'they are so used to keeping everything hidden.'

'There is no danger from me,' Shigeru said impatiently. 'But if I am to protect you from the Tohan I must know what I am defending. I leave here at dawn. You are not fit to travel with me. So, if you are able, we must talk now.'

'What does Lord Otori want to know?'

'For a start, what are the images that you have to defile?'

The woman made a slight sound as if she were about to sob.

Nesutoro moved his hand and traced a character on the matting, two lines crossing each other, as in the number ten.

'What does it signify?'

'We believe the Secret One sent his son to earth. The son was born to an ordinary woman and lived as a man. He was put to death in the cruellest way, nailed to a cross, but he came back from the dead, and now sits in Heaven. He will judge us all after death. Those who know him and believe in him will join him in Heaven.'

'Everyone else goes to Hell,' the headman added, sounding remarkably cheerful about it. His wife was weeping silently now.

'Where does this teaching come from?' Shigeru questioned.

'From far away in the West. Our founder, the saint whose name I bear, brought it from Tenjiku to Shin over a thousand years before, and from there teachers came to the Eight Islands hundreds of years ago.'

It sounded like any other legend to Shigeru, possibly founded in truth but overlaid by centuries of human imagination, wishful thinking and self-delusion.

'You may think we are mad,' Nesutoro said, sweat pouring from him. 'But we know our God's presence: he lives inside us...'

'They have a ritual meal,' the headman explained. 'When they share food and wine, they believe they eat their god.' He laughed as if to show that he did not share such outlandish beliefs.

The wife spoke suddenly. 'He gave himself for us. He suffered so we might live. Everyone, anyone – even me, a woman. In his eyes I am as good as a man, as my husband, even as –'

Her husband slammed his fist into the matting. 'Be quiet!' He bowed low to Shigeru. 'Forgive her, Lord Otori; her grief makes her forget herself.'

Shigeru was astonished by her words, and equally by the fact that she had dared to speak in his presence at all. He could not remember ever hearing a peasant woman speak directly to him. He was both affronted and intrigued. He felt Kiyoshige tense next to him, and held up his hand to restrain the younger man. He thought Kiyoshige might draw his sword and cut her down – anywhere else the woman would have been punished immediately for her insolence, but here in the bare, impoverished house, alongside the suffering man, it was as if they had moved into a different world, where the rigid codes of his society no longer applied. He felt compassion stir within him. He had, after all, enquired about the beliefs of these people called the Hidden: now he was learning about them, not only through words but directly through the person of the woman in front of him, who believed herself to be his equal.

'There is another image,' she said abruptly. 'Lord Otori should know...' Again she glanced directly at him, but after that one look she lowered her eyes again. Her voice became softer – he had to strain to hear it, leaning forward towards her. 'It is the mother and child,' she whispered. 'She is the mother of God, the child is God's son. Our way honours women and their children and seeks to protect them against the cruelty of men. God will punish those who persecute us: even the Iida lords.'

CHAPTER SEVENTEEN

When they left early the following morning, smoke still rose from the charred beams and thatch; it tasted raw in Shigeru's throat. The smell of burning made the young horses nervous, and they jibbed and pig-rooted as the riders followed a narrow track through the rice fields and then up the side of a low range of hills, where the dry fields of vegetables – pumpkins, beans, onions and carrots – gave way to bamboo groves and then to an upland forest of beech and cedar. They went in single file, giving no chance for conversation, but when they stopped at the head of the range to let the horses drink from a shallow pool filled by a spring, Kiyoshige remarked, 'So this strange sect is to come under your protection?'

'To tell you the truth,' Shigeru replied, 'the sect does not bother me one way or the other. They seem harmless enough. But as long as they are Otori I will protect them against the Tohan. If they are to be eradicated, it will be our decision. We will not allow the Tohan to decide such things for us.'

Irie said, 'This is an entirely reasonable position. No one can find fault with it.'

'I've been thinking about Kitano,' Shigeru went on. 'We are within his domain – my first instinct was to try to keep this from him. But he will be told as soon as we arrive in Chigawa. So I believe it is better to confront him head-on and send messengers ourselves, demanding his sons be recalled from Inuyama, and that he himself come to Chigawa to reaffirm his vows of loyalty to my father and myself.'

'And if the Iida do not allow the boys to return?'

'We must find some way of applying pressure so they comply.'

'Like what?' Kiyoshige asked. 'There's not much we can bargain with.'

'Lord Irie?'

'I'm afraid Kiyoshige is right: we can threaten further attacks, but that's more likely to enrage and harden the Iida than persuade them. And we must be careful not to be drawn into full-scale war, for we are not prepared for it yet.'

'How long would it take the Otori to be ready for war with the Tohan?'

'Next year, the year after.'

'We are a match for the Tohan right now!' Kiyoshige said hotly.

'Man for man I don't doubt it, but they outnumber us; they have more foot soldiers.'

'All the more reason to keep men like Kitano loyal,' Shigeru said. 'We must also start increasing our men and equipment as soon as I return to Hagi.'

The townspeople of Chigawa were astonished and elated at the unexpected appearance of the heir to the clan. Like the villagers, they had feared they had been forgotten and before much longer would find themselves Tohan. Shigeru and his men were given an excited welcome and invited to the largest inn. Messengers were sent to Tsuwano; Irie and Kiyoshige waited in the town for Kitano's response and Harada's return with reinforcements, making the arrangements necessary to house and feed so many men and horses, and two days later Shigeru left with his own men to ride south, to see with his own eyes what the Tohan were doing to his people there.

Several young men from the town came with him, eager to act as guides and, he thought, probably hoping for a skirmish with the hated Tohan. They were typical of the people of the east, small and wiry, energetic and quick-tempered. As well as weapons, they brought with them ropes and lamps and a pan of coals with which to light wicks. Shigeru wondered why, but as they rode south the reason became clearer. South of Chigawa, the limestone upland of Yaegahara extended towards the border like a pointing finger. The road itself curved away from the border. The valley seemed open all the way to Inuyama.

'Surely we should have this area well guarded,' he said. 'It is a gateway to the Middle Country.'

'The land is treacherous through there,' the oldest of his guides said, a man of about nineteen or twenty called Komori. 'If you don't know the way, it's easy to wander off the track and fall into the caverns: many people disappear and never find their way out. Yet, to see the border itself, we should go that way, if Lord Otori will trust us to guide him.'

'Komori knows this country above and below,' one of the others said. 'The Underground Emperor, that's what we call him.'

Komori grinned and pointed to the ropes on his saddle bow. 'These are the Emperor's jewels. You can buy them for a few coins in any shop in Chigawa, but underground they're worth more than all the treasure in the capital.'

They left the road and headed east through the long summer grass bright with yellow daisies, small purple orchids, bugle and white yarrow. The grass seed-heads were forming in delicate, foamy tassels. Butterflies, blue and yellow, fluttered around the horses' hoofs. Tracks made by foxes, deer and wild boar criss-crossed the plain. There were few trees – occasionally a clump of alders grew around depressions where water gathered, and shrubs clung to the sides of the deep caverns, often hiding the mouth completely. Shigeru could see how easy it would be to miss the path and plunge into one of these natural prisons. No one would know where you were, and there would be no hope of rescue.

They had ridden for about three hours, skirting numerous deep holes, while Komori named each of them for Shigeru – Hell's Mouth, Lair of the Wolf, the Cauldron – names created by humans and intended to describe them, yet to Shigeru's mind no human language could encompass the menace of the dark openings, gaping suddenly and unexpectedly in the peaceful summer landscape.

Kites mewed above them, and once in the distance they saw eagles circling on the warm air. Occasionally a hare started up at their approach, bounding away in huge desperate leaps, its eyes bulging. Pheasants and partridge were also abundant, glossy in their summer plumage.

'It would be a good place for hawking,' Shigeru observed.

'You need your eyes on the ground, not in the skies,' Komori replied. 'Few people come this way.'

They saw no one all morning; the plain indeed seemed deserted. So it was a surprise to come over the ridge of a slope and see in the valley beneath it a group of horsemen milling round the edge of one of the caverns. Several had dismounted and were peering over the rim, shouting and gesticulating.

'Tohan!' one of the men exclaimed, and Komori said, 'Ah! Someone has fallen into the Ogre's Storehouse!'

The men around him shouted in triumph and derision and drew their swords, waiting expectantly for Shigeru's orders.

'Go forward slowly,' he said. 'There is no need to attack unless they do. Have bows ready to cover our approach.'

The bowmen immediately drew off to one side. The Tohan below noticed the Otori coming, and their confusion increased. They saw they were outnumbered and at a hopeless disadvantage. Three of the men on foot leaped immediately over the edge into the cavern, plunging without a sound into the darkness. The rest turned their horses and urged them into a gallop. The riderless horses ran after them, leaving one man stumbling helplessly behind.

'Capture him, but don't kill him,' Shigeru ordered.

The man fell to his knees as the horsemen surrounded him. He was carrying a carved bird perch with two hawks tethered by their jesses, trying to hold them upright and reach his sword at the same time. The birds shrieked and flapped in frenzy, striking out with their sharp, curved beaks. Shigeru's men disarmed the man before he could kill himself and brought him to Shigeru.

He was thrown down somewhat roughly, and sprawled on his face in an attitude of despair in the dusty grass.

'Sit up,' Shigeru said. 'What happened?' When the man did not reply, he went on, 'There's no need to be afraid.'

At that, the man raised his head. 'Afraid? Do you think I am afraid of any Otori? All I ask of you is to allow me to take my own life, or kill me yourselves. My life is over. I let my lord fall into the pit.'

'Your lord? Who is it down there?'

The man's face was white with horror. He was shaking with emotion. 'I serve Iida Sadamu, son of Lord Iida Sadayoshi and heir to the Tohan.'

'Iida Sadamu fell into the Ogre's Storehouse?' Komori said in disbelief.

'What were you doing here?' Shigeru demanded. 'You have crossed the border, with armed men! You were seeking to provoke the Otori into war!'

'No, we were hawking: we rode two days ago from Inuyama. He was leading, galloping ahead of us, following the bird.'

He pointed upwards, and they saw the small dark shape still wheeling in the sky. 'He and his horse went in together.'

'Hawking!' Shigeru thought it would have made a good excuse for Sadamu to ride to the border country to see for himself what the Otori were up to. As good an excuse as trying out young horses... He marvelled at the strange workings of fate that had brought them together in this way. The heir to the Tohan lay beneath his feet, dead or dying... The men grinned nervously, as if they felt the same awe and shock.

The birds' screaming quietened suddenly, and in the silence they heard a voice echoing up from the depths below.

'Can you hear me? Get me out of here!'

'He lives! It is Lord Iida. Let me go; I must go to him.' The man struggled against the hands that held him. Shigeru made a sign to Komori and they moved away to one side so they could talk unheard.

'Could he have survived?'

'People do, sometimes. It's not the fall that kills them – it's starvation, usually.'

'Is it possible to rescue him?'

'We'd do better to leave him there. Throw this man down too, and pretend we know nothing about it. If Sadamu's gone, Sadayoshi will go soft.' Komori's eyes were gleaming with excitement.

'The men who rode off saw us. They will construct more lies about what really happened and blame the Otori for Sadamu's death. It would give the Tohan the excuse for war. But if we rescue Sadamu and return him to his clan, it will give us many advantages.'

Like the return of the Kitano boys, Shigeru thought.

'If it is Lord Otori's will,' Komori said, sounding disappointed.

'You can get to him?'

'I can get to him. Whether he can follow me out – that's a different matter.'

'Would you descend through this opening?'

'No, it's too deep, and anyway there's nothing here to lash a rope to. But, luckily for Sadamu, there's a passage linking this cavern with another; less deep, and with trees round it. It's very narrow, though.'

Komori called to the Tohan man. 'How fat is Lord Sadamu?'

'Not fat at all!'

'But he's a large man, right?'

When the other man agreed, Komori muttered, 'I may have to persuade him to strip!'

'Help!' the voice cried from the darkness. 'Can anyone hear me?'

'Tell him I'm coming,' Komori said. 'Tell him it'll take a while.'

The man crawled to the side of the slope, where the land fell away towards the cave's opening. The grass was slippery and sharp-edged. He called out, his voice still weak with shock.

'Lord Iida! Lord Iida! Can you hear me?'

'He won't hear that,' one of the Chigawa men said scornfully. 'We should throw you in; then you can tell Sadamu in person.'

The man who had been so eager to join his lord in death had now had time to recall all the joys of living, and for his natural reluctance to leave them to reassert itself. He begged the Otori to spare him, to save Lord Iida, making many promises on behalf of his clan, the Iida family and his own. Shigeru left him to try to communicate with his lord, guarded by half his men, while he himself rode with Komori and the rest over the grassy hills for more than an hour, he thought, until they came to another depression in the earth, where the fragile limestone, eaten away by water and weather, had collapsed into the honeycomb of caverns below.

The hills formed a gentle slope here, and water oozed from where it had collected between the rocks. Several pines grew in the moistened earth: two had sacred straw ropes around them, gleaming palely in the dark shadow of the trees, and a small wooden shrine stood between them and the cave's mouth, with offerings of fruit and flowers placed on it.

They dismounted, and Komori went to the shrine, clapping his hands to summon the cave god and bowing low three times. Shigeru did the same, and unexpectedly found himself praying for the life of his enemy.

They prepared the lamps and lashed the ropes to the pine closest to the edge. Komori stripped down to his loincloth and rubbed his body all over with oil, to slide more easily between the narrow rocks. He debated whether to take a weapon, but in the end decided against it.

'If Iida kills me he'll die there alongside me,' he said philosophically.

Two other Chigawa men were lowered down after Komori: they lit a small fire at the bottom to help guide him back. Shigeru sat on the edge of the slope by the rope, watching the flames below, waiting for the time to pass.

The sun crossed the sky above them; the sky was bright blue and cloudless. Slowly, the shadows swung from one side of the grove to the other. The sun was low over the rim of the hills when Shigeru heard the sound of hoof beats. One of his men came at a gallop, shouting, 'Komori has reached Lord Iida and they are on their way back!'

He tried to imagine the drama that was taking place below him: the darkness, the narrow passage. What beings dwelt in the caves? Bats, spiders, snakes probably, and maybe goblins or demons. Komori's courage was a rare kind – he would rather face a hundred warriors than go into that underground world.

The sun set and the flames below seemed brighter. The fire smoked blue in the twilight; the shapes of the men round it became dark and featureless, and seemed to float above the ground like ghosts.

Then suddenly there was movement, shouts of relief. Komori crawled from the narrow opening, turned and pulled another figure after him.

The heir to the Tohan clan was naked, soaked in oil and water, skin lacerated and bleeding from a hundred tiny cuts and grazes. With the help of the ropes he was raised to the surface, where Shigeru gave him Komori's clothes to dress himself in, averting his own eyes, not wanting to humiliate the man further or to seem to be glorying in the situation.

Sadamu went to the spring and crouched by it, washing his body carefully, wincing now and then but not uttering a sound. Then he dressed himself in the borrowed clothes. He was a bigger man than Komori, and they did not fit well.

Shigeru gave orders for food to be brought. Fires were lit and water boiled. Sadamu drank soup and tea, and ate ravenously, his eyes flickering round at the men and horses. Leaving him surrounded by guards, Shigeru drew Komori aside.

'What about the others? Was he the only one to survive?'

'His horse must have broken his fall. It was dead beneath him. Two of the men we saw jump died instantly. The other was alive, unhurt, but Lord Iida ordered him to kill himself. He had me hold the lamp so he could watch. It seemed to assuage some of his fury.' Komori was silent for a moment and then said, 'I thought he would kill me, too. He brought his sword and his knife, but had to leave them, for he could not make it through the tightest passage with them. He could not bear for anyone to see him helpless. He wanted no witnesses. We have saved his life, but he will hate us for it. We should have left him there.'

No, I must make use of him, Shigeru thought. He returned to Iida and made a slight bow to him.

'I hope you are not hurt?'

Iida stared at him for some moments. 'I seem to be indebted to you. My thanks. I'll ask you to give me a horse tomorrow and see me to the border.'

'I think it is best that we return to Chigawa in case Lord Iida is not completely recovered.'

'You know who I am, then?'

'One of your men saw you fall, and told us.'

'Fools and cowards, all of them,' Iida spat. Shigeru studied him in the firelight, and realized that no compassion, remorse or fear would ever divert him; it gave him a rare strength of will.

He wore a small, neat beard and moustache: he was slightly below average height, but heavily built; he was still in his twenties, and it was easy to see how he would broaden and thicken as he aged. His features were unremarkable but his eyes were extraordinary, intelligent and powerful, snapping now with rage, the eyes of a man afraid of nothing in Heaven or on Earth. Shigeru thought briefly that he understood the ferocity of Iida's persecution of the Hidden: this man considered himself above any judgement from gods or men.

'And who are you?' Iida said, gazing back, seemingly irritated more by Shigeru's inspection.

'I am Otori Shigeru.'

'Are you indeed?' Iida laughed bitterly. 'No wonder you want to take me to Chigawa! And then what?'

'There are various matters that need to be settled between our clans,' Shigeru replied. 'Our chance meeting seems to offer an excellent opportunity for negotiation. When the negotiation is completed to everyone's satisfaction, you will be escorted to the border.'

'The Tohan are far stronger than the Otori. It's only a matter of months before you submit to us. I command you to take me to the border immediately – as soon as it is light.'

'I believe we are equals by birth and blood,' Shigeru returned. 'I don't know for what reason you came over the border, but you are in the Middle Country now, where you have no authority. I see no alternative but for Lord Iida to comply with my wishes. You may do so freely or we will bind you with ropes and take you as a prisoner. It is Lord Iida's choice.'

'I swear by Heaven I will see you bound with ropes before I die,' Iida replied. 'How dare you speak to me like that?'

'I am in my own country: I am heir to my clan. I can speak any way I like!'

'How old are you?' Iida demanded.

'I am fully adult. I made my coming of age this year.'

'Well, I've heard of you. You fought Miura –'

'It was a fair fight!' Shigeru interrupted.

'Oh, I don't doubt that, though it suits us to present it otherwise. I am sure Otori Shigeru would never do anything ignoble.'

The sneer in his voice made the blood rise in Shigeru's face. He fought to control his temper, realizing intuitively that the only way to deal with Iida was through self-control, calmness and courtesy.

'I was told that you were handsome,' Sadamu went on. 'But good-looking boys grow up to be weak men. They are spoiled by too much attention when they are young. If you are the best the Otori can produce, I don't think we have anything to fear.'

Shigeru could not help being amazed by the man's effrontery – alone, unarmed, surrounded by enemies, Sadamu was self-confident enough to be deliberately insulting.

'The man who saw me fall – you hold him too?'

Shigeru nodded in assent.

'Bring him to me.'

'He is still at the place where Lord Iida fell. He will join us tomorrow.'

Shigeru heard a murmur from the men who surrounded them of anger at the insulting tone, anger in response to Iida's rage. He knew it would only take a word from him – less, a single gesture – and Iida's life would be over. Yet he would not kill an unarmed man, nor would he take any action that would bring on war before the Otori clan was fully prepared.

If Iida was aware of his own vulnerability, he gave no sign of it. He appeared to accept the situation, and wasted no more time or energy on struggling against it. He stretched out beside the fire, adjusted a rock under his head for a pillow, and seemed to fall instantly asleep.

Shigeru could not help admiring his equanimity: there was no doubt Iida Sadamu was a courageous man and a formidable enemy. He had already seen the evidence of his ruthlessness and his cruelty.

He sat up with the guards keeping watch. None of his men slept much, apart from Komori, who was exhausted by the rescue. They shared Shigeru's restlessness, as though they had captured a tiger or a bear that might suddenly attack them and rip them apart. It was a soft, mild night, the constellations blazing across the vault of heaven. Just before dawn there was a shower of falling stars that made the men gasp and caused the superstitious among them to clasp their amulets. Shigeru thought about Heaven, and the gods and spirits that ruled the lives of men. He had been taught that the test of government was the contentment of the people. If the ruler was just, the land received the blessings of Heaven. He wanted to ensure justice throughout the Middle Country, to realize his vision of his fief as a farm. Yet men like Iida seized power and dominated those around them by sheer force of will, their desire for power unhindered by compassion or the desire for justice. You either shared their view and submitted to them in return for their protection, or opposed them by meeting their will with your own and by being stronger. He was grateful for this strange meeting. He would never forget that he had seen Iida Sadamu naked and powerless.

They rose at first light, as larks called their morning song, and prepared the horses, ate a sparse meal of cold food and departed. Iida rode Komori's horse, ropes tied to its bit and held by warriors on either side lest he attempt to escape, while Komori himself ran at Shigeru's stirrup, guiding them back through the treacherous country.

After an hour they came to the Ogre's Storehouse. The men who had spent the night there were prepared for departure. The Tohan man stood beside the horses, holding the bird perch with the hawks still on it. Hungry, they raised their feathers and called piercingly.

When the man saw Iida, he tried to bow to the ground without letting go of the birds, his movements made clumsy by fear.

'Bring the birds,' Iida commanded from the horse. The man rose and went to him, holding the perch so that it was level with his lord's chest. Iida seized one bird in his bare hands. It struggled and screamed, trying to slash with beak and talons. He broke its neck and threw it to the ground, then killed the second in the same way. This he threw directly in the face of his retainer.

No one spoke. No one would plead for the man's life. He was Tohan: Iida could do with him what he wanted. The man laid the perch down in the grass, his movements no longer awkward but almost graceful in their delibera-tion. He undid his overgarments – he had already taken off his leather armour – and said quietly, 'I ask you to give me back my sword.'

The Otori warriors led him away from Iida to the edge of the pit. Afterwards they threw the body down.

'Ogre's breakfast,' one of them said. The birds lay in the dust, the brightness fading from their plumage. They already had ants in their eyes.

•

Irie and Kiyoshige were surprised to see them return so soon, and even more astonished when they learned the identity of their companion.

'Lord Iida Sadamu has had a terrible experience,' Shigeru said. 'He was lucky to escape death. He will be our guest while he recovers.'

He explained briefly what had happened and accompanied Iida to the best room in the inn, treating him with exaggerated courtesy and insisting that the highest quality clothes and food be supplied. He made sure Iida was well guarded, then he himself bathed and changed his own clothes, dressing with great care in formal robes, and having a barber come to shave his face and head and dress his hair.

Then he conferred with Irie and Kiyoshige. 'Since Lord Kitano is on his way here, I think it would be pleasant for him to see his sons. I intend to ask Sadamu to send letters to Inuyama requesting their presence. Once they are here and Kitano has formally reaffirmed his loyalty, we will escort Lord Iida to the border.'

'We should get assurances that the border violations will cease,' Kiyoshige said. 'I can't believe he fell into your hands like this! What a stroke of luck.'

'We will – but there is no guarantee that he will keep his word, and we cannot hold him for long. Irie, have a doctor come and tend to him. He can testify that Sadamu is too weak to travel.'

'Weak is hardly a word you would use to describe Sadamu!' Kiyoshige said, grinning.

After another explosion of rage, Sadamu gave in and wrote to his father. Within a week, Tadao and Masaji arrived in Chigawa; they were reunited with their father, Lord Kitano, the following day. All three of them made solemn declarations of allegiance in Sadamu's presence, and Sadamu himself undertook to maintain the borders and prevent any more incursions into Otori territory. The doctor pronounced Sadamu fit to travel and Shigeru accompanied him to the border, where he was met by a large force of Tohan warriors. Their faces were grim beneath their helmets, and they did not speak to or even acknowledge the Otori contingent. The leaders leaped from their horses to prostrate themselves before Sadamu, expressing their joy and relief at his return. He spoke to them sharply, ordering them to remount immediately and not to delay their departure any longer.

Once the horsemen had splashed across the river that marked the border, several of them turned to wave their swords and jeer at the Otori. Bows were armed and raised in reply, but Shigeru spoke swiftly to forbid retaliation.

'Not even a word of thanks!' he observed as Sadamu and his retainers galloped away.

'You have made an enemy,' Irie replied.

'He is Tohan: we were born enemies.'

'But now he hates you personally. You saved his life and he will never forgive you for it.'

•

The plum rains began and Shigeru spent the following weeks based in Chigawa; the reinforcements arrived and patrols were sent out to set up stations all along the border until the end of autumn. He also took the time to examine the agricultural conditions of the district, advised Kitano that taxes were too high and he must take no more than thirty per cent of the harvest, and spent two days listening to various grievances that the peasants held against officials and merchants.

He visited the silver and copper mines with Komori and discussed ways of increasing production, realizing anew how important it was to keep the mines out of Tohan hands. He would have been happy to stay all summer, but at the end of the month messengers arrived from Hagi with a letter from his father.

'I am summoned home,' he said to Kiyoshige. 'I wish I had not read the letter, but having done so, I suppose I must obey.'

He allowed Lord Kitano's younger son to return to Tsuwano with his father, but he had decided Tadao, the elder boy, would accompany him to Hagi and stay there, to encourage his father to remain loyal.

CHAPTER EIGHTEEN

Shigeru rode home in a cheerful mood, feeling he had every reason to be pleased with the results of his decisive action. His popularity and reputation were increased among the ordinary people, who came out to welcome him at every town and village, showering him and his men with gifts of food, fruit, rice wine. The weather continued hot and fine; the harvest would be good: everyone, it seemed, was happy.

But his reception at the castle was less enthusiastic. He had hardly dismounted in the outer bailey when Endo Chikara himself came to welcome him home, saying, 'Your father has asked you to go to him at once.'

'I will wash and change my clothes,' Shigeru replied. 'The effects of the journey...'

'Lord Shigemori did say "at once",' Endo demurred. Shigeru passed the reins to Kiyoshige. The two young men exchanged a glance. Kiyoshige raised his eyebrows slightly but said nothing.

Now I am to be chastised, Shigeru thought ruefully. But even though he expected it, it was no easier to bear. His uncles were very angry, his father bemused and sorrowful. His father's displeasure was caused more by the fact that Shigeru had acted alone without consultation or permission; his uncles, whose attendance annoyed Shigeru intensely, were more concerned about what they described as the unfortunate results: the deaths of Honda and Maeda, the unnecessary provocation of the Tohan...

'If I had not been there, Sadamu would have died!' Shigeru retorted. 'At least lies cannot be fabricated about his death. Furthermore, he swore in front of witnesses to control his men and prevent any more incursions into the Middle Country. We will have peace in the border region, and the mines around Chigawa are secured.'

'Lord Kitano is somewhat displeased at your meddling in his affairs,' his older uncle said.

'Kitano reaffirmed his allegiance to me personally, as did his sons,' Shigeru said, trying to control his anger. 'Tadao will stay close to me in the meantime . . .'

It was no longer a question of being right – although he was sure he was – but of whose will would prevail, who was the stronger. He reminded his uncles that he was the heir to the clan, that he was now an adult and that he expected their complete loyalty for the sake of the clan. He made no apologies either to them or to his father, and left the meeting close to rage. He felt his father should have supported him, and deplored Shigemori's indecision and vacillation. Filial duty bound him to defer to his father – but if the security of the Otori clan itself demanded contrary action, what should he do, what course should he take?

Kiyoshige had escorted Tadao to the retainers' quarters, and Irie had returned to his own house in the town beyond the castle wall. Shigeru went alone to his rooms in the residence. It was almost evening: the sun had already sunk below the steep hill on the west side of the gardens. He requested for a maid to come to the bathhouse at the hot spring between the rocks. The girl scrubbed the dirt from his skin and the stiffness from his limbs; then he sent her away and eased himself into the scalding water.

After a while he heard Takeshi's voice in the garden. He called out to him, and his brother came through the bathhouse, undressed and began to wash himself. Then he joined Shigeru in the water.

'Welcome home! Everyone's talking about what you achieved. It was wonderful – how I wish I had been with you!'

Shigeru smiled. His brother's admiration was a shadow of what he had hoped for from his father – but its genuine enthusiasm cheered him. He studied Takeshi: the boy had grown during the summer, his legs much longer, his chest filling out.

'And you met Iida Sadamu. I would have fought and killed him.'

'He was unarmed – and as naked as you are now! By the time he was clothed again, it seemed more sensible to negotiate with him.'

'The Tohan never keep their word,' Takeshi muttered. 'Don't trust him.'

Kiyoshige called from outside, 'Lord Shigeru?'

'Come and join us,' Shigeru exclaimed as Kiyoshige appeared at the threshold. 'We'll all eat together.'

'I have already made arrangements to eat with Kitano Tadao. I thought Lord Takeshi might accompany us.'

'I want to eat with my older brother,' Takeshi said, 'and hear about his exploits.'

'Shigeru won't tell you anything,' Kiyoshige said. 'He is far too modest. Come with me and I'll tell you what a hero he is and how much the people love him.'

'So am I to be left alone?' Shigeru said, stretching out in the water and thinking about sleep.

'Not exactly.' There was something in Kiyoshige's voice that alerted him.

Takeshi unconsciously imitated his brother, stretching in the same indolent way, linking his hands behind him and resting his head on them. 'I'll stay with you,' he said – and at almost the same moment, Shigeru was saying, 'Go with Kiyoshige, Takeshi. It will honour Tadao. It is the correct thing to do.'

Kiyoshige said, 'I'll tell you how Sadamu strangled his own hawks!'

'I don't think you actually witnessed that,' Shigeru observed.

'No, but Komori and the other Chigawa men related it to me.'

Takeshi sat up and looked towards Kiyoshige. 'He strangled his own hawks? Why?'

'Presumably because they led him into the Ogre's Storehouse!'

'I have to hear this.' Takeshi leaped from the water, splashing Shigeru as he went. 'You don't mind?'

'It's what you should do. Be polite to Tadao. We don't want him to pine for Inuyama.'

When Kiyoshige and Takeshi had gone, Shigeru dressed in a light cotton robe and returned to his apartments, half expecting to spend the night alone, half expecting... he was not sure what. But his pulse had quickened and his veins tingled, not only from the heat of the water.

It was almost dark. Lamps had been lit in the doorway and inside the main room, making the pale colours of the flowers on the painted screens gleam in the shadows against the golden background. The eyes of the finches among the blossom glinted as if they were alive. A spray of jasmine had been placed in the alcove, and its fragrance filled the room.

At the same time as he stepped out of his sandals, he could smell beneath the jasmine another scent – perfumed hair and garments. He paused for a moment, allowing himself to experience the moment, the anticipation of pleasure as acute as the pleasure itself would be.

She had had the lamps placed so they lit her face. He recognized her at once: the white skin, the eyes shaped like willow leaves, the strong cheekbones that stole true beauty from her face but gave it character that somehow added to her charm – Akane, the daughter of the stone-mason. He heard the soft rustle of her clothes as she bowed to the floor and said quietly, 'Lord Otori.'

He sat cross-legged in front of her.

She raised herself and said, 'I came to thank Lord Otori for his kindness to myself and my mother. You honoured my father in death. We are forever in your debt.'

'I am sorry for your father's death. The bridge is one of the marvels of the Middle Country: its construction adds to the glory of the clan. His death enhanced that. I thought it should be commemorated.'

'My family have sent gifts – nothing of any significance, food and wine. It's asking too great an honour, but may I serve you them now?'

His single instinct was to touch her, to hold her, but he also wanted to treat her with courtesy, to respect her grief; he wanted to know the woman who had cried out in the moment when her father was entombed, not merely the courtesan who would eventually give herself to him because he had expressed a desire for her.

'If you will share them with me,' he replied. His heart was pounding.

She bowed again and went on her knees to the door, where she called quietly to the maid. Her voice was soft, yet she spoke with complete authority. A few moments later he heard the soft pad of the maid's socked feet, and the women exchanged a few words. Then Akane returned with a tray of food and wine, bowls and shallow dishes.

She gave him one of the dishes and he held it with both hands as she poured wine into it. He drank it in one gulp; she refilled the dish, and then, when he had drunk a second time, held out her own so he could pour wine for her.

The food was chosen and prepared to increase the sensitivity of mouth and tongue: the orange melting flesh of sea urchin, slippery oysters and scallops, a delicate broth flavoured with ginger and perilla. Then fruits, cool and juice-filled: loquats and peaches. Both of them drank sparingly: just enough to set their senses on fire. By the time they had finished eating, Shigeru felt he had been transported to an enchanted palace where a princess was bewitching him completely.

Watching his face, Akane thought, He has never been in love. He will fall in love for the first time with me.

She was also beginning to ache with desire.

He had not known it would be like this: the driving compulsion to lose himself within the body of this woman, the complete surrender to her skin, her mouth, her fingers. He had expected there would be the physical release – as in dreams, or by his own hand – under his control, swift, pleasurable, but not overwhelming or annihilating. He knew she was a woman of pleasure, a courtesan, who had learned her craft with many men; he was unprepared for the fact that she seemed to adore his body and took the same delight in it as he did in hers. He had never known intimacy, had barely talked to a woman since his childish conversations with Chiyo: it was as if half his self, which had been asleep in darkness most of his life, had suddenly been caressed and startled into life.

'I have been waiting all summer for you,' she said.

'I have been thinking about you since I saw you at the bridge,' he replied. 'I am sorry you had to wait so long.'

'Sometimes it's good to wait. No one appreciates what is easily acquired. I saw you ride away. People said you were going to teach the Tohan a lesson! I knew you would send for me. But the days seemed endless.' She paused for a moment and then said very quietly, 'We met once before; you will not remember. It was so long ago. It was I who helped you when your brother nearly drowned.'

'You will not believe how many times I dreamed about you,' he said, marvelling at the workings of fate.

He wanted to tell her everything: the torture of the Hidden, the dying children, the courage of Tomasu and Nesutoro, the fierce satisfying skirmish with the Tohan; Iida Sadamu; his disappointment and anger at his father's reaction; his distrust of his uncles. He knew he should be guarded, that he should trust no one, but he could not help himself. He opened his heart to her as to no one else in his life, and found her mind as receptive and willing to accommodate him as her body.

He knew he was in danger of the very thing his father had warned him against – becoming infatuated with Akane. You will not fall in love with her, his father had told him. Yet how could he prevent that happening when she delighted him completely? At midnight it seemed impossible, but when he woke again at dawn he lay thinking about his father's words, making a huge effort to pull back from the edge of the pit, as dangerous and inescapable as the Ogre's Storehouse. He told himself that she was not beautiful, that she was a prostitute, that he could never trust her: she would never bear his children, she was there only to give him pleasure. It was unthinkable to fall in love with such women: he would not repeat his father's weakness.

She opened her eyes, saw he was awake and drew him to her again. His body responded and he cried out again at the moment of release, but afterwards he spoke to her coldly, told her to leave after the first meal was served without saying she was to come again or what future arrangements might be made.

He spent the rest of the day in some turmoil, wishing she was still with him, hoping he had not offended her, longing to see her again, yet fearing becoming entrapped by her. He wished he was back in Chigawa – dealing with the Tohan seemed simple and straightforward.

Akane sent for her palanquin and left with as much dignity as she could muster, but she was offended and mystified by his sudden coldness.

'He doesn't like me after all,' she said to Haruna. 'He seemed to at first, very much: he even talked to me, as if he had never talked to a woman in that way in his life, but he sent me away this morning.' She frowned. 'It was almost insulting,' she added. 'I won't forget it.'

'Of course he liked you,' Haruna said. 'There isn't a man alive who wouldn't like you. But he is the heir to the clan: he's not going to fall in love with you. Don't expect him to. He's not another Hayato.'

But Akane still missed Hayato. She liked having men in love with her. She had been flattered by Lord Shigeru's interest in her, and she found him very pleasing. She wanted to be with him again; she wanted him to love her.

'I don't expect we'll be hearing from him again,' she said. 'Everyone knows I spent the night at the castle – and why. It's so humiliating. Can't you put it about that I spurned him?'

'I give him three days,' Haruna replied.

Akane spent the next few days in a very bad temper, quarrelling with Haruna and being spiteful to the other girls. It was still very hot – she would have liked to walk to the volcano, but she could not go out in the sun. The business of the pleasure house went on all around her, day and night, sometimes arousing her desire, sometimes her scorn for the insatiable lust of men. On the evening of the third day, after the sun had set, she walked to the shrine to see the flowers and shrubs planted by the old priest. Some exotic yellow flower whose name she did not know gave out a heavy sweet fragrance, and huge lilies gleamed white in the dusk. The old man was watering them with a wooden bucket, his robe hitched up into his sash.

'What's up with you, Akane? You've been alone all summer! Don't tell me you've gone off men!'

'If I had a grain of sense, I would,' she replied.

'You need one of my amulets! It'll spark your interest again. Or better still, come and live with me. I'd make you a good husband.'

'I'll do that,' she said, looking at him fondly. 'I'll make you tea and scrub your back, clean the wax from your ears and pluck your beard.'

'And keep me warm at night, don't forget that!' He laughed so much that he began to cough and had to put the bucket down.

'Don't excite yourself, grandfather,' Akane said. 'It's bad for your health at your age!'

'Ah, no one ever gets too old for that, Akane! Here.' He took a knife from his sash and carefully cut a spray of the yellow flowers. 'Put this in your room: it will perfume the whole house.'

'Does it have a special power?' she said.

'Of course. Why else would I give it to you?'

'Do you have spells to make men fall in love?' she asked idly.

He looked curiously at her. 'Is that your problem? Who is he?'

'No one. I just wondered.'

He leaned towards her and whispered, 'Spells to make them fall in love, and charms to bind against love. The plants have many powers, and they share them with me.'

She walked back, carrying the spray, conscious of the fragrance enveloping her. She walked past Haruna's room and called mockingly, 'Three days, eh?'

Haruna stepped out onto the veranda. 'Akane! You're back! Come up for a moment.'

Still holding the yellow flowers, she stepped out of her sandals onto the veranda. Haruna whispered to her, 'Mori Kiyoshige is here.'

She went into the room and bowed to him. 'Lord Kiyoshige.'

'Lady Akane.' He returned her bow and studied her frankly, his eyes glimmering with amusement and complicity. His courtesy told her everything. She did not allow herself to smile but sat with impassive face and lowered eyes.

'Lord Otori was very satisfied with our last collaboration,' Kiyoshige said. 'He has another assignment for me. I am to arrange for a house to be built for you. Lord Otori thought you would prefer to have your own establishment rather than moving to the castle. I've spoken to Shiro, the carpenter. He will come tomorrow and discuss the design with you.'

'Where is it to be built?' Akane said.

'There is a suitable piece of land near the castle, by the beach, in a small grove of pines.'

Akane knew the place. 'Is it to be my own house?'

'You understand the arrangement, of course?'

'It's far too great an honour for me,' she murmured.

'Well, everything is written down – servants, money and so on. Haruna has read it and says she approves.'

'Lord Shigeru is extremely generous,' Haruna said.

Akane pouted. 'How long does a house take to build?' she demanded, irritable.

'Not long, if the weather holds.'

'And in the meantime?'

'You may return to the castle now with me, if you have no other plans.'

It irritated her further that he should think she had nothing else to do with her life. 'It's almost dark,' she said.

'No one will see me.' She did not want to appear to be smuggled into Shigeru's rooms.

'I will provide torches,' Kiyoshige said. 'We will make a procession, if that is Lady Akane's wish.'

He made me wait, Akane thought. I will make him wait for me. But only for one night.

'I should read the agreement,' she pleaded. 'And discuss it with my mother. I will do that tonight, and tomorrow, if you would be so kind, you may return – a little earlier, I think, before sunset.' She was already imagining how it would look, the palanquin, servants with huge sunshades, the Mori retainers on horseback.

Kiyoshige raised his eyebrows. 'Very well,' he agreed.

Haruna brought tea, and Akane served him. When he had left, the women hugged each other.

'A house!' Haruna exclaimed. 'And built specially for you by the best carpenter in Hagi!'

'I shall make it so beautiful,' Akane replied, now visualizing the house under the pines, surrounded by the constant sighing of the sea. 'I will see Shiro first thing in the morning. He must show me the site – or does that appear too eager?'

'There is no hurry,' Haruna said. 'You can take your time.'

The building of the house was delayed by the first typhoons at the end of the summer, but it was sheltered in the lee of the mountain range and was not damaged. It rained hard for a week and umbrellas replaced the sunshades when Akane made her thrice-weekly visits to the castle. As her relationship with the heir to the clan progressed she became more flamboyant, and people began to line the street to watch her palanquin go past as if it were part of a festival.

By the time the nights had begun to cool and the maples to put on their brocade, the house was finished. It was built facing south to catch the winter sun, thatched with grass-reed stalks, with wide eaves and deep verandas of polished cypress. The screens were decorated by an artist who had long been one of Haruna's clients. Akane herself had slept with him several times, though neither of them referred to the past. At her request he painted flowers and birds according to the seasons. Akane chose beautiful bowls and dishes in the local earthenware, made by the most famous craftsmen; mattresses and quilts filled with silk cocoons; carved wooden headrests.

When the house was complete she had a ceremony performed to purify and bless it. Priests came down from the shrine and performed the rituals, sprinkling water and burning incense. After they had departed, late that night when she lay next to Shigeru, listening to the sea, she marvelled at what fate had given her, and what her life had become.

CHAPTER NINETEEN

Shigeru now came from the castle every day around dusk. They ate and talked, or played go, which Shigeru had learned from childhood and was now reasonably skilled at; he taught Akane, and she grasped the game quickly and intuitively and came to love its intricate and implacable essence. Usually after they made love he returned to his own apartments; occasionally he stayed with her for the whole night. He did this rarely, for it was then that he felt most in danger of falling in love with her, in the surrender of self that came with falling asleep in her arms and waking in the night and in the early morning to make love again.

Usually after staying the night he would go away for several days; there were always matters to attend to: he wanted to keep an eye on the borders, visit Tsuwano with Kitano Tadao to reinforce that family's loyalty, oversee the harvest in his mother's estate across the river, as well as the everyday affairs of the clan, in which he now immersed himself. He tried not to think of her during that time, but he did not want to sleep with anyone else, and when he returned his heart thumped with as much excitement as on their first night.

He frequently visited his mother at her house by the river, to tell her what he was doing with the fields and forests that belonged to her. She came from a high-ranking family: her brothers had died within months of each other, leaving no children; the estate had passed to their sister to be held for her sons. The castle possessed many other lands, but this estate was especially dear to Shigeru: it seemed to belong to him personally, and it was here that he could put into practice all he had learned from Eijiro's writings, which he still kept with him. His mother said nothing about his arrangement with Akane, though she could hardly be ignorant of it – Akane had made sure the whole city knew of her new elevated status, with all the honour and prestige it entailed. However, some time after the house under the pine trees was finished, around the middle of the eleventh month when the first frosts were beginning to silver the rice stubble, Lady Otori announced to Shigeru that she intended to move to the castle.

'Why?' he said, astonished, for she had often expressed pleasure at the warmth and comfort of her house compared to the castle in winter.

'I feel it is my duty to take my place there and to look after Takeshi and yourself, especially if you are to be married.'

'I am to be married?' He had known, of course, that this would happen sooner or later, but had not been told of any firm arrangements.

'Well, not immediately, but you turn seventeen next year, and there is a very suitable young woman. I have been discussing it with Ichiro, and with Lord Irie. They have broached the subject with your father, and he is inclined to give the match his approval.'

'I hope she is from the Otori,' he said. 'I do not want my wife selected from the Tohan.'

He had spoken lightly, partly joking; his mother pursed her lips and looked sideways; when she spoke her voice was lowered.

'Of course she is from the Otori – from one of our oldest families. And she is a relative of mine: her father is a distant cousin. I agree with you, the Tohan have no right to decide who you will marry.'

'Surely everyone is agreed on that?'

'I'm afraid your uncles are of the opinion that a political marriage might prevent further difficulties with the Tohan. Apparently the Iida have a girl in mind.'

'Absolutely not!' Shigeru replied. 'I will not be married to anyone from the Tohan: above all not to anyone chosen by Iida.'

'Lord Irie said this would be your reaction. Of course, I have to follow my eldest son's wishes, and my husband's. But to avoid misunderstandings, the betrothal should take place before the Iida make a formal request. That way they will not appear to be insulted.'

'If that is your desire, I will obey you and my father,' Shigeru replied.

'Your mother is jealous of me,' Akane exclaimed when Shigeru told her about this conversation.

'Jealous of you? She did not even mention you!'

'She is afraid of my influence over you. She is moving to establish herself within the castle so she can influence the selection of your wife, and after your marriage the girl herself. Who is she, by the way?'

'She is some distant relative. I forgot to ask her name.'

'I suppose you will always act with such indifference,' Akane said. 'Truly, the women of your class have wretched lives.'

'I am sure I will respect her, and we will have children, of course.' It was a cold night, and Akane had ordered the rice wine to be warmed. Now she called for another flask and filled his cup; he filled hers in return and she drank it in one gulp.

'Something has upset you?' he said as he filled her cup again.

'What will become of me when you are married?'

'I imagine our arrangement will continue.' He smiled at her. 'If you want it to, of course. If you don't, this house is yours, as long as you are discreet.'

'Discreet? What does that mean?'

'I cannot bear the thought of another man here,' he admitted, surprised himself by the sudden pain the idea gave him.

'You see, no one is immune to jealousy, not even warriors!' Akane said with an air of triumph. 'You must have come to care for me!'

'I think you know that,' he replied. 'And do you care enough for me to be jealous of my wife?'

'Don't joke about jealousy,' she said, drinking again. 'I've seen women driven insane by it, by the casual behaviour of men they've fallen in love with. Love affairs are just a distraction for men: for women they are our whole life.'

'Have you ever been in love, Akane?'

'No, nor do I intend to be!' She saw a look of disappointment flash briefly across his face. We are all the same, she thought. We want to be loved, yet will not fall ourselves.

'What about the man called Hayato?'

'Hayato was very kind to me when my father died.'

'He is said to be driven out of his mind by his love for you.'

'Poor Hayato,' Akane said. 'If I had not come to your attention, then I would be living with him now.'

The wine had made her speak with honesty, yet she saw that she had displeased him and regretted saying so much.

'It is better that neither of us fall in love,' said Shigeru, the coldness that she feared returning.

'Lord Shigeru, you are young, forgive me for pointing it out. I am older than you – three years older; I propose we make a pact. We will not fall in love, but we will try not to give each other cause for jealousy. You have to marry, you have to have children. You must treat your wife with honour. But I also have certain claims on you now, and I expect you to honour them.'

He was surprised by her seriousness, and found himself admiring her. The lamplight accentuated her cheekbones: something about the strength of her face reminded him of the woman from the Hidden who had spoken to him as if she were his equal.

He had little knowledge of what made a marriage: his own parents lived separate lives, and he had barely spoken to his uncles' wives, who lived in the deep interior of the castle with their attendants and servants. He cast his mind around further, and suddenly remembered Otori Eijiro and his wife: there had been affection and respect between them, and the woman and her daughters had moved freely and on equal terms with the men. It is the influence of the Maruyama, Eijiro had said, and then had told him about Lady Naomi...

'What are you thinking?' Akane said, surprised by his long silence.

'Of marriage, of what happens between men and women; of Maruyama, where they say women have greater freedom.'

'Maruyama will go the way of all the other great domains,' Akane said. 'And Naomi will be the last female head of the clan.'

'You know of her?'

'I listen to men talking, and that's what they say. Her husband has close connections with the Tohan, and they hate the idea that a woman should inherit.'

'And do the Seishuu hate the Tohan in return? Enough to enter into an alliance with the Otori? What do you hear about that?'

It was the first time the idea had occurred to him: an alliance with the Seishuu – if a marriage would secure that, he would agree to it.

'Men gossip about all sorts of things at Haruna's,' Akane said. 'But they don't know what they're talking about half the time. Most of them have never been out of the Middle Country.'

'We should send a delegation to Maruyama or to the Arai at Kumamoto,' Shigeru said, thinking aloud. 'Find out what their true opinions are.'

Akane did not want to talk about politics. She called softly to the maids, and when they came to remove the dishes, asked them to spread out the bedding. Shigeru was as passionate and responsive as usual, but he did not stay with her, saying he had affairs to discuss with Lord Irie. After he had left, she returned to bed. It had grown even colder, the wind off the sea rattling the shutters and moaning through every chink in the walls. She wished she had a man alongside her to keep her warm, thought of Hayato with some regret, and then with uncharacteristic anxiety about her future. Men did fall in love with their wives; it was not uncommon, and the woman within the house held many advantages over the woman of pleasure. She had told Shigeru she had certain claims on him, but in reality she had none: his wife would have children, he would love them with all the warmth of his nature, and surely that would lead him to love their mother. She could not bear the thought of it. He will fall in love with me, she vowed.

It was not only that she feared being abandoned by him, unable to take any new lover: the idea of him with another woman clawed at her heart despite the rational words she had spoken earlier. Then the idea came to her to go to the old priest and seek a spell from him that would make the wife barren, that would make Shigeru hate her.

She had been careful not to conceive a child: Haruna had supplied her with pessaries that annulled the male seed and potions to drink should her bleeding be delayed, and she knew enough about her body's rhythms to avoid the days when she was fertile. But she often fantasized about having Shigeru's child: it would be a boy, of course, of great beauty and courage; his father would adore him, would acknowledge him or even better adopt him; he would become the heir to the Otori clan... If Shigeru loved her, he would want to give her a child. The thought warmed her; she drew the covers closer around her and drifted into sleep.

Shigeru discussed the subject of marriage with Irie, suggesting the idea of a closer alliance with one of the great families of the West. Following this, further deliberations were entered into by the elders, by Shigeru's father and his uncles. Meanwhile, his mother moved to the castle, appropriating the best rooms in the deep interior for herself and offending her sisters-in-law, who had to move out to make room for her. In subtle ways her presence changed the balance of power among the Otori lords, and though Shigeru resented her interference in his private affairs – she managed to make it clear that she disapproved of Akane without ever mentioning her, and often seemed to find it essential to speak to him at the end of the day when it was his custom to go to the house beneath the pines – he was grateful for her implacable opposition to any appeasement of the Tohan, and above all any marriage dictated by them. His father, who now spent more time with his wife than at any other period in his life, came gradually under her influence, and began to share her views and to rely on her advice rather than on the shamans.

His uncles opposed the idea of the Seishuu alliance on the grounds that it would insult and enrage the Tohan – and in any case, they argued, who was available? Maruyama Naomi was already married; the Arai had no daughters; the Shirakawa had girls, but they were mere infants. So a compromise was reached, and in the end it was agreed, as Shigeru's mother had first said to him, that the best strategy would be to arrange a betrothal as soon as possible to an Otori girl, and pretend that it had been a longstanding commitment.

Her name was Yanagi Moe: her family was closely related to the Otori lords and to Shigeru's mother. They lived in the mountain town of Kushimoto, and were a proud, austere family of the old style. Moe was their oldest child and only daughter, and had been brought up to think highly of herself, her family and her forebears. The Otori marriage was exactly what she had hoped for, believing it to be no more than her right. She had been born the year before Shigeru, and at seventeen was small and very slight; charming and graceful enough, reserved by nature, over-protected by her family, with little knowledge or interest in the world beyond the walls of her parents' house. She was fond of reading, wrote passable poetry and liked playing draughts, though she never mastered chess or go. She had been well taught how to supervise the running of a household, and knew how to reduce a maid to tears with a few words. She secretly had no very high opinion of men, having several younger brothers who had replaced her completely in her mother's affections.

The betrothal took place in Yamagata a little before the winter solstice, and the marriage in Hagi in the spring. There were huge celebrations: gifts of money, rice cakes and wine were distributed among the townspeople, singing and dancing went on late into the night. Akane listened to the sounds from her house with a bitter heart. She drove her nails into her palms when she thought of him with his bride. Her only consolation was the charm she had received from the old priest. He had laughed when she told him what she wanted, and had looked at her with sharp, serious eyes.

'Be careful what you wish for, Akane. It will come true, you know.'

She had let him fondle her breasts in payment, and the charm now lay buried in the garden, together with clippings from Shigeru's hair and fingernails, and drops of Akane's menstrual blood.

She did not see Shigeru for a week and had begun to despair, but when he finally came, after dark, alone except for two guards, he took her in his arms at once, without even waiting for the beds to be prepared, and made love with a ferocious desperation that she had never known in him before but which aroused her passion in response. Afterwards she held him while he wept – she had never seen him cry – and wondered what had happened to so bruise his sense of self.

It seemed indelicate to pry into the reasons for his distress. She said very little, called for wine to be brought and poured it for him. He drank several cups in swift succession, and then said abruptly, 'She cannot make love.'

'She was a virgin,' Akane replied. 'These things can take time. Be patient.'

'She is still a virgin.' He laughed bitterly. 'I was not able to get her to open. Everything I did caused her pain – and, it seemed, terror. She shrank from me: she had no desire at all for me. I think she has already come to hate me.'

'She is your wife,' Akane said. 'She cannot continue to refuse you: you must have children together.' She spoke quietly and calmly, but inwardly she was rejoicing. I'll let the old man suck my mouth! she vowed.

'I never expected it,' Shigeru said. 'I thought I could please her; I thought she would be like you!'

Akane took his hand and rubbed her fingers against the ball of the thumb. She liked the feel of the muscle below the skin, strong and flexible from years of practice with the sword.

'What will I do?' he said. 'It is clear that I have not deflowered her.'

'Be patient,' Akane said again. 'If you still have no success, it is your mother's duty to instruct her. Surely she can show her books, reassure her that it is all quite normal. If everything fails, you can repudiate her.'

'And be laughed at from here to Inuyama?'

'Cut yourself and spill blood on the bedding,' Akane said. 'It will be enough to silence gossip in the castle. It will give you time. She must come to love you.'

She gazed on him, thinking how any woman in her right mind would do so, inveighing against the fate that had made Yanagi Moe his wife and not Akane herself. If I were married to him, how I would love him, she told herself. I would make him happy.

Maybe the charm had greater powers than she thought; maybe the sight of his vulnerability had weakened her; she found herself suddenly trembling, fearful in an unfamiliar and exquisite way. I am on the brink, she thought. I must not fall. How I will suffer if I do. Yet her defences seemed so thin and poorly founded, especially against his need.

And his need for her became more apparent. He visited more often and seemed genuinely reluctant to leave. He spoke little about his wife, but she knew matters had not improved between them. Sometimes she felt guilty about what she had done, but then she rejoiced as the strength of their feelings for each other increased.

CHAPTER TWENTY

Yanagi Moe had anticipated her marriage with delight, but by the time the plum rains had ended it was clear to her that she could expect nothing but suffering from it. Her body had betrayed her by its rigidity and tension: she knew she was a failure as a wife. Shigeru's mother, Lady Otori, dominated and bullied her; the other women of the deep interior treated her with icy politeness that barely disguised their contempt.

And he, her husband, whom she had imagined she would respect and please, must also despise her. It was open knowledge among everyone that he kept a concubine – that did not shock her; it was common enough among men of his class, but the women of the deep interior often talked about Akane, about her charm and wit, and whispered among themselves that Shigeru was besotted by her.

If Shigeru had been as inexperienced as she was, they might have reassured each other; if he had been older, he might have treated her with more patience and restraint. But he was enmeshed in his first adult affair, which already gave him deep physical and emotional pleasure. Moe's reluctance and frigidity repelled him; he could not bring himself to demand what was so clearly repugnant to her. He was angered by her in the end, knowing that he must create heirs for the sake of the clan, not wanting to hurt her or insult her family, unable to decide what the solution to such a problem might be, reluctant to discuss it with anyone but Akane. And Akane always said the same thing: 'Be patient,' all the while smiling secretively.

Moe, in her turn, became angry with him. Once she knew about Akane, she placed all the blame for the failure of the marriage on her. Her pride was wounded deeply; she came to detest both her husband and the woman she thought he loved.

The end of the rainy season brought some relief from a situation that had become poisonous. Shigeru returned to the border country and spent the summer there with Kiyoshige and Takeshi. They took Miyoshi Kahei with them; like Takeshi he was only thirteen, but the situation did not seem threatening and his father wanted him to benefit from the experience. Kitano Tadao was allowed to return to Tsuwano. The threat from the Tohan seemed to have subsided a little. The borders were quiet, apart from the customary to-and-fro of merchants on the high road to Inuyama. They brought news from the Tohan capital – most significantly of the death of Iida Sadayoshi and the subsequent elevation of Sadamu to the leadership of the clan. Kiyoshige and Shigeru entertained the boys by repeating the story of Sadamu's unfortunate accident; they would not have laughed so uproariously had they known how many Tohan spies in Chigawa watched Shigeru's every move and reported back to Inuyama.

Akane found the long, hot days intolerably boring, but she was not altogether sorry that Shigeru was away. If he was not with her, nor was he with his wife, and his absence gave her a little space to regain control over her emotions. She behaved with discretion, visited her mother, the temples at Daishoin and Tokoji, where she always made generous donations, and various merchants from whom she ordered luxurious items: perfumes, teas, lacquerware, new robes for autumn and winter. She did not go to Haruna, but she often visited the garden near the volcano: she was more than a little impressed by what the old man's charms had achieved. The hot weather did not agree with him: she arranged for medicines to be delivered to him, cooling teas and herbs to purify the blood, and instructed her gardeners to help him water his plants while she kept him company. One day she was returning through the garden to where she had left the palanquin: it was almost a year to the day since her first night with Shigeru, and she was recalling it with mixed feelings as she passed the hedge that bordered the rear garden of Haruna's house. She quickened her step, not wanting to be seen by anyone there, but as she went by the entrance she heard running footsteps. Her former lover, Hayato, called out to her, 'Akane! Akane!'

He burst through the gate: she had to stop or run into him. They gazed at each other for a moment. She was shocked by the changes she saw in him: his face was gaunt, the skin yellow-tinged, the eyes sunken and glittering.

'You have not been well?' she said, moved to sudden pity by his appearance.

'You know why. Akane, why did this happen to us? We loved each other.'

'No,' she said, and went to walk on, but he seized her by the arm.

'I cannot live without you. I am dying with love.'

'Don't be a fool, Lord Hayato. No one dies for love!'

'Let's run away together. We can leave the Three Countries, go north. Please, Akane. I beg you, come with me.'

'It's impossible,' she said, trying to twist out of his grip. 'Leave me alone or I'll call for the guards.' She was alarmed, being with him when he was so distressed, fearing he might take her life and his own rather than live without her.

He looked down at his own hand in surprise, as if someone else had placed it round her wrist. When she had struggled, he had gripped her more tightly, hurting her. Now he let go suddenly. She rubbed the bruise.

'I don't want to hurt you,' he said. 'I'm sorry. That's the last thing I want to do. I want to touch you, like I did before. You must remember how good it was.'

She did not reply, but turned at once and walked rapidly away. She thought she heard him speak her name, but she did not look back. The porters leaped to their feet when she approached, and the guard who always accompanied the palanquin helped her into it and picked up her sandals once she was inside. She left the oiled silk curtains down, though it was stifling inside and one bold mosquito was whining annoyingly round her neck. She was afraid Hayato was in the grip of an all-devouring jealousy, as if afflicted by a wasting disease. She had said, 'No one dies for love,' but she could see how he might die, or kill himself, and then his angry ghost would haunt her... and she was afraid too of what charms he might use against her. Now she had entered the dark world of magic herself, she was all the more aware of its power.

She went to the household altar and burned incense, lit candles and prayed for a long time for protection against all the ills that might surround her. The night was heavy and dense: thunder rolled round the mountains, but it did not rain. She slept badly and rose late, had hardly finished dressing when Haruna arrived. Haruna was as elegantly dressed as always, but she could not disguise the fact that at some time that morning she had been weeping. Akane felt the clutch of fear that the premonition of bad news brings. She called for tea and exchanged pleasantries with Haruna, then sent the maids away, drawing close to the other woman so they sat knee to knee.

Haruna said quietly, 'Hayato is dead.'

She had half expected this news, yet it left her reeling with shock and grief. You must remember how good it was: his last words came back to her, and she did remember, she remembered everything good about him, and began to weep unrestrainedly for the pitifulness of his life and death, and for the life that they might have had together.

'I saw him yesterday. I feared he would take his own life.'

'He did not kill himself. It would have been better if he had. Lord Masahiro had him killed. His retainers cut him down outside my place.'

'Masahiro?'

'Lord Shigeru's uncle. The youngest brother. You know him, Akane.'

She knew of him, naturally, and had seen him on occasion – the last time was at her father's entombment. His reputation throughout Hagi was not good, though few dared express their opinions openly. In a city that was not easily offended, he was considered lecherous, and, more gravely, people said he was a coward.

'Why? What had Hayato ever done to offend Masahiro? How could they have even crossed paths?'

Haruna moved uncomfortably and did not meet Akane's gaze. 'Lord Masahiro has been visiting us from time to time – he gives another name, of course, and we all pretend we don't know him.'

'I had no idea,' Akane said. 'What happened?'

'Hayato was quite drunk – he had been drinking since he saw you, I gather. I tried to get him to leave quietly, but when he finally went outside he noticed Masahiro's men in the street. He began to rail at them, to curse the Otori lords, in particular Lord Shigeru – forgive me for telling you such a terrible thing. They were very forbearing, tried to get him to calm down: of course they were all in unmarked clothes; it was easy to pretend they were not personally insulted; everyone knows Hayato, he's always been well liked, and they would have ignored him, but Masahiro came out and heard his remarks, and then it was all over.'

'No one will blame Masahiro,' Akane said, weeping again at the sadness of it.

'No, of course not, but he has gone further: he has given orders for the family to be turned out of their home, their lands to be given to him, and for the sons to be killed as well.'

'They are only children!'

'Yes, six years old and eight. Masahiro says they must pay for their father's insults.'

Akane said nothing. The harshness of the punishment chilled her, yet it was Lord Masahiro's right to act as he pleased.

'Will you go to him, Akane? Will you plead with him to spare their lives?'

'If Lord Shigeru were here I might approach his uncle through him, but he is away in the East. Even if we sent the swiftest messenger it would be too late. I don't suppose Masahiro would even receive me.'

'Believe me, I am sorry I am asking you. But you are the only person I know who has any influence at the castle. I owe it to Hayato to try and save his children's lives and their inheritance.'

'Masahiro will be insulted by me even requesting an audience. He'll probably have me put to death too.'

'No, he is interested in you. He has often been heard to express his regret that you are no longer at my house. He compares all the girls to you.'

'That could be worse,' Akane said. 'I will be putting myself at his mercy. If he spares the children, what will he want in return?'

'You are under Shigeru's protection. Even Masahiro will not dare take advantage of you.'

'I am afraid it will displease Shigeru,' Akane said, wishing he were there and she could speak to him directly.

'Lord Shigeru has a compassionate nature,' Haruna replied. 'He would not exact such a punishment.'

'I cannot do it,' Akane said. 'Forgive me.'

'They will die tomorrow then.' Haruna wept as she spoke these words.

After the older woman had left, Akane went to the altar to pray for Hayato's spirit, to ask his forgiveness for the part she had played in his tragic fate and the disaster that his love for her had brought upon his family. He loved children, she thought. He wanted me to have his children. Now he is to lose his sons: he will have no one to carry on his line; his family will become extinct. There will be no one to pray for his soul.

People will blame me: they will come to hate me. What if they find out I used charms against Shigeru's wife? They already say I have bewitched him...

Her thoughts continued to writhe and twist like a nest of adders, and when the maids brought the midday meal she could not eat.

As the afternoon wore on, it grew hotter, and the cicadas' shrilling seemed more oppressive. Gradually her turmoil gave way to a numbness and lassitude: she felt so weary she could hardly move or think.

She asked for the bed to be prepared, changed into a light summer robe and lay down. She did not expect to sleep, but almost immediately she fell into a kind of waking dream. The dead man came into the room, undressed and lay down beside her. She felt the familiar smoothness of his skin; his smell surrounded her. His weight covered her as it had when they had first made love and he had treated her with such tenderness, and the day her father died, when her need for him had been so intense.

'Akane,' he whispered. 'I love you.'

'I know,' she said, feeling the tears spring into her eyes. 'But you are dead, and now there is nothing I can do.'

His weight changed against her, no longer the comforting solidness of the living man but the dead weight of the corpse. It pressed down on her, squeezing the air from her lungs, forcing her heart to pump frantically. She could hear her breath gasping and feel her limbs flailing uselessly.

Suddenly she was awake, alone in the room, dripping with sweat, panting; she knew she would never be free of his ghost – he had come to possess her – unless she made some kind of retribution.

Now she was seized by a feverish anxiety that it would be too late. Despite Haruna's words, she had no confidence that she would be allowed to speak to Lord Masahiro. She called for the maids, took a bath, and prepared herself while she tried to think of the best way to approach him. Her impatience, her sense of the rapid elapse of time, made her realize her only path was to write to him directly. It was the boldest thing she could think of: if it failed, there was nothing else she could do. She called for ink and paper, and wrote swiftly – her father, who could write as easily in stone as most scholars on paper, had taught her, and her handwriting was strong and fluid, reflecting her character. She used the phrases of courtesy, but nothing elaborate or flowery, simply asking if Lord Masahiro would permit her to come and speak to him.

He will never allow it, she thought, as she handed the message to one of the guards. I will hear nothing, and this time tomorrow Hayato's children will be dead.

Dressed in her finest clothes, she could do nothing but wait. Night had fallen, bringing a little relief from the heat. Akane ate a bowl of cold noodles with fresh vegetables and drank a cup of wine. She was afraid to sleep, afraid of Hayato's spirit. Again there was thunder in the distance, but no rain fell. The shutters were open and the scent of the garden flowers, mingled with the smell of the sea and with pine needles, drifted into the room. In the east, the moon was rising behind massed clouds, lighting their wild shapes as though they were shadow puppets in a play.

A huge flash of lightning had just lit up the southern sky when she heard the tread of feet and low voices outside beyond the wall. A few seconds later, one of the maids came in and whispered, 'Lady Akane, someone has come from the castle.' Her voice was tinged with alarm.

'A messenger?' Akane stood, trembling.

'Maybe... or maybe...' The girl laughed and her face twisted: she hardly dared to speak his name. 'You know, the uncle...'

'It cannot be!' Akane replied, wanting to slap her for her stupidity. 'What did he say?'

'He asked to see you.'

'Where is he now?'

'I asked him to wait in the entrance hall – but, Lady Akane, if it is him, how insulting of me! What should I do?'

'You had better show him in at once,' Akane said. 'And bring some more wine. Let him come in alone. If he brought anyone else with him, make them wait outside. You also must stay outside, but come at once if I call you.'

As soon as the visitor stepped into the room, despite the informality of his robes and the lack of crest, she knew at once that it was Masahiro. He was a short man, much shorter than Shigeru, and already showing signs of the corpulence of middle age. Her first thought was, He thinks he will sleep with me, and she felt a rush of terror, for she knew that if that happened, Shigeru would never forgive it.

She bowed deeply to him, then sat, trying to arm herself with steel and coldness.

'Lord Otori, this is far too great an honour.'

'Your letter said you wanted to speak with me. And I have long wanted to meet you. It seemed like a golden opportunity, especially as my nephew is away.'

She poured wine and made a comment about the heat of the night and the strange beauty of the moonlit clouds. He drank, staring at her in an appraising way, while she, less openly, was trying to assess him. She already knew of his constant pursuit of sexual novelty, which led him not only to Haruna's establishment but also, gossip said, to far seedier places and far more unusual pleasures. His skin was sallow in colour, and marked by several large moles.

She thought she should make her request directly, before any misunderstandings arose between them.

'I feel a certain responsibility for the sad event that took place last night,' she said softly.

'You mean, the intolerable insult to the Otori lords?'

I mean the death of a good man, she thought, but did not say it. 'I wanted to apologize to you in person.'

'I accept your apology, but I don't think you can be blamed if men fall in love with you,' he replied. 'I am told that is why Hayato acted as he did. Apparently he was infatuated with you. I've heard my nephew is too.'

There was a slight question in his voice. She said, 'Forgive me, Lord Otori, I cannot discuss Lord Shigeru with you.'

He raised his eyebrows slightly and drank again. 'And was that all you wanted? To apologize?'

He will never agree. I am merely humiliating myself, Akane thought, but then she felt the dead man's exhalation against her neck, as though he knelt behind her and would at any moment wrap his cold arms round her. She took a deep breath.

'Lord Hayato's sons are very young. His family have always served the Otori faithfully. I am asking you to be merciful and to spare their lives.'

'Their father insulted Shigeru: I am only protecting his name.'

'I am sure if Lord Shigeru were here, he would also plead for them,' she said quietly.

'Yes, he's a kind-hearted boy, so people say; I, on the other hand, do not have that reputation.' His voice was scornful, but she thought she also heard envy in it, and her suspicions were confirmed when he went on. 'My nephew is very popular, isn't he? I hear reports from every corner of the Middle Country praising him.'

'It's true,' she replied. 'People love him.'

She saw him flinch under the lash of his jealousy.

'More than his father?'

'Lord Shigemori is also very popular.'

Masahiro laughed. 'I would be surprised if that were true.' His upper teeth were slightly protruding, giving his lower jaw a look of weakness. 'Where is Shigeru now?'

'Lord Otori must know: he is in Chigawa.'

'Do you hear from him?'

'He occasionally writes a letter.'

'And when he is here – and I must tell you, the house is superb: elegant, comfortable; I congratulate you – does he tell you everything?'

She made a slight movement with her shoulders and looked away.

'Of course he does,' Masahiro said. 'You are an experienced woman, and my nephew, for all his admirable qualities, is still very young.'

He leaned forward. 'Let us deal frankly with each other, Akane. You want something from me, and I want something from you.'

She looked quickly at him then, and to hide her alarm she allowed an expression of scorn to form slowly on her face.

'I'm not going to suggest we sleep together. It's certainly what I want, but even I concede that it would be indelicate. And I'm sure it's asking you to pay too high a price for the lives of your old lover's children.'

She continued to stare at him, making no attempt to mask her dislike and contempt. He laughed again. 'But I would like to know what Shigeru's up to. You can surely assist me in that.'

'You are asking me to spy on Lord Shigeru?'

'Spy is rather a blunt word,' he returned. 'I am merely asking you to keep me informed.'

Akane was thinking rapidly. It was so much less than she had feared. She would never betray Shigeru's secrets, but she could easily make something up, enough to satisfy Masahiro.

'And in return you will spare the boys' lives and allow the family to remain in the house?'

'It would be very merciful of me, wouldn't it? Maybe I also will gain a reputation for compassion, and share in Shigeru's popularity.'

'Lord Masahiro is indeed compassionate,' she replied. 'I will make sure it is widely known.'

She felt Hayato's hand on the nape of her neck, a slight pressure, almost a caress. Then he was gone.

Farewell, she said in her heart. Be at peace now. She prayed he would find peace, and an auspicious rebirth, and would not come back to haunt her.

After Masahiro's departure, Akane tried to tell herself she was not displeased with the outcome of the encounter. Haruna would be overjoyed, and would almost certainly shower her with gifts; she had fulfilled her obligations to the dead, and she was sure that the agreement would not force her to betray Shigeru. She did not have any great opinion of Masahiro, and she felt quite confident of her ability to give him snippets of unimportant information. But as the days passed and she had time to reflect, she became less and less happy about what she had done, almost as if she knew unconsciously that she had taken the first step on a path that would deliver her into the power of a corrupt and cruel man.

Her greatest concern was that reports of Hayato's death and her intercession on the family's behalf would reach Shigeru, in some distorted form, and anger him. His absence and Masahiro's visit had combined to produce a sense of insecurity in her. Her role as the mistress to the heir to the clan gave her great pleasure: she could not bear the thought of losing it. And apart from that ignominy, she suffered from an unfamiliar anxiety – that Shigeru would think the less of her, that she would disappoint him, that he would turn away from her.

He will only love a woman who wins his respect, she realized clearly. He will not overlook or forgive any failing of character, any disloyalty. The idea that Masahiro might somehow inform him of their agreement unsettled her. Nothing could calm her unease. She wrote several letters and burned them, finding their tone falsely innocent, thinking her suggestions and suppressions, her embroidery of the truth, were blatant and would be easily discerned by him.

Her house, its exquisite objects, the garden, the pine trees, the sea, had all lost their power to charm her. Her appetite waned; she began to sleep badly and was short-tempered with the maids. The sight of the moon on the water, the dew on the first buds of the chrysanthemums and on the webs of the gold-orb spiders, moved her first to tears and then to despair. She longed for him to return from the East, yet dreaded his arrival; longed for winter, which would keep him in Hagi; dreaded what his uncle might tell him through spite or intrigue, and what she in turn would have to report to Masahiro.

CHAPTER TWENTY-ONE

The first typhoon of late summer swept up the coast from the southwest, but though it brought heavy rain its main force had abated by the time it reached Hagi; the eastern parts of the Middle Country were hardly touched, and Shigeru did not hasten his return home. It was true that he missed Akane from time to time, but he had no desire to go back to the intrigue in the castle or to the uncomfortable situation with his wife. The life of a warrior on the borders had a simplicity about it that was straight-forward and refreshing. He was treated by everyone with undivided respect and gratitude, which he found flattering, and which gave him ever-increasing confidence in himself and in his role as the leader of the clan. No one argued with him: everyone deferred to his opinions.

It was almost as if they were still boys, playing at stone fights, but with real soldiers and real lives at their command now. They kept a constant watch on the entire border from coast to coast, sleeping outside for nights on end beneath the soft summer sky with its huge blurred stars. Every couple of weeks or so they returned to Chigawa, where they took advantage of the hot springs and the plentiful food of late summer.

On one of these occasions, late in the eighth month, on an early evening just before sunset, Takeshi and Kahei came into the lodging house, hair still wet from the bath, laughing loudly. They also had become more relaxed during the last few weeks, released from the stern discipline of study and training that had filled their lives in Hagi. Both were on the cusp of manhood, their bodies filling out, limbs lengthening, voices breaking. In a year or two, Shigeru thought, listening to them now, they should be sent to Terayama, to learn as he had done the self-discipline that would bind together all they had been taught so far. He had watched his brother closely in the past weeks, trying to check Takeshi's recklessness and impetuosity, noting how the men adored and encouraged him, admiring his fearlessness. In Shigeru's opinion, Kahei had a more dependable character: his courage was not tinged with rashness; he was willing to seek advice and follow it. Yet Takeshi shone with something additional – the inborn Otori ability to inspire devotion. Shigeru wondered again how best to give his brother the responsibilities he needed. Takeshi showed no interest in crops and agriculture, the running of estates or the development of industry; his passion was all for the art of war. If his rashness could be tempered, he might make a great general;

at the moment, he was more interested in individual heroic exploits than in the careful planning of strategy and tactics. He was even less interested in the diplomatic negotiations that ensured peace. He and Kiyoshige frequently deplored the absence of war and longed for the opportunity to teach the Tohan a lesson like the battle at the shrine, which Kiyoshige described in bloodthirsty detail on more than one occasion.

Kiyoshige liked Takeshi, and their shared adventures while Shigeru had been at Terayama had formed a strong bond between them. Shigeru noticed how Kiyoshige encouraged the younger boy, tacitly approving his rashness because it matched his own. Shigeru deliberately kept them apart while they rode out on patrols, sending Kiyoshige with Irie and keeping Takeshi with him, but when they met in Chigawa it amused Kiyoshige to take Takeshi around with him.

'There was a man outside with a message for you,' Takeshi said. 'Just about the ugliest man I've ever set eyes on.'

'He's been roasted like a chestnut,' Kahei added.

'We sent him packing,' Takeshi laughed. 'What impudence, expecting you to speak to him.'

'Roasted?' Shigeru questioned.

'His face was puckered and red as if he'd been burned.'

'Hideous,' Takeshi muttered. 'We should have put him out of his misery. What does a man like that have to live for?'

Shigeru had thought more than once about the man he had rescued the previous year, but the Hidden seemed to have vanished underground again, true to their name. There had been no more reports of attacks over the border, and though occasionally what he had learned about their strange beliefs floated into his mind, he dismissed it as yet another superstition: he had enough of these from his father. Now he remembered Nesutoro, and the sister who had considered herself his equal because of the teachings of her god, and wondered what the man wanted and if it was too late to speak to him.

'Kiyoshige, go and see if this man is still there. You must remember him. Nesutoro, the one we rescued last year.'

Kiyoshige returned to say the man had disappeared. The innkeeper did not know how to find him, and there was no sign of him in the streets around.

'You should have treated him more gently,' Shigeru told his brother. 'He is a brave man who has suffered a great deal.'

'He's just some peasant who got drunk and fell in the fire!'

'No, he was tortured by the Tohan,' Shigeru replied. 'He is one of the reasons we fought them last year.'

'One of the strange sect? Why does everyone hate them so much?'

'Perhaps because they seem to be different.'

'They believe everyone is born equal – in the eyes of Heaven,' Kiyoshige said. 'And they claim their god will judge everyone after death. They don't know their place, and they make everyone else feel guilty.'

'They could be very destabilizing within society,' Irie added.

'And my elder brother protects them,' Takeshi said. 'Why?'

'The Tohan had come into Otori territory,' Shigeru replied. It was the reason he had always given; yet he knew, if he were truthful to himself, that it was not the only one. The scene at the shrine would never be erased from his mind: the cruelty, the courage, the suffering, all part of the terrible fabric of human life. The beliefs of the Hidden seemed outlandish and unlikely, but then so did his father's superstitions. Could anyone fathom the truth of life? Could anyone read the secret hearts of men? Just as cutting back a shrub made it grow more vigorously, so suppressing strange beliefs gave them more life. Better to allow people to believe what they wanted.

'I had never seen children tortured in that way,' he added. 'I find such cruelty offensive.'

There was a kind of pride there too: the Tohan might act in such an inhuman way, but the Otori would not. And a defiance: if the Tohan persecuted the Hidden, the Otori would protect them.

'Would you have spoken to him?' Takeshi looked a little discomfited. 'I'm sorry I turned him away.'

'If it is important, he will probably return,' Shigeru said.

'I don't think so. Not after the way we dealt with him. I should have been more gentle with him.'

'We can reach him through his brother-in-law,' Irie said. 'The headman from the village.'

Shigeru nodded. 'Next time we ride that way, we will make a point of speaking to him.'

Shigeru put the matter out of his mind, but the next morning Kiyoshige was called to the front of the inn and returned to say that the man's sister was waiting in the street.

'I'll send her away,' he suggested. 'You cannot be expected to receive every peasant who thinks they have some claim on you.'

'Did she say what she wants?'

'Just that she comes on behalf of her brother, Nesutoro.'

Shigeru sat silent for a few moments. Kiyoshige was right: he should not make himself freely available to anyone and everyone. If he showed favouritism or particularity to one group, it would only cause envy and discontent among others. But the woman had intrigued him, and there had been some connection between him and the man – some recognition on both sides of their shared humanity – and shared qualities, too, of courage and patience.

'Let her come in. I will talk to her.'

She came in on her knees, face to the ground. When Shigeru told her to sit, she did so reluctantly, her head kept low, eyes cast down. He studied her, noticing how she had made every effort to present herself: the faded robe was clean, her skin and hair clean too. He remembered the sharp planes of her face: they seemed more acute than ever, carved and hardened by grief. She had brought a companion with her, a girl of about fourteen or fifteen years, with the same high cheekbones and wide mouth.

The girl did not venture into the room, but remained kneeling in the doorway.

'Lord Otori,' the older woman began, haltingly. 'I do not merit your kindness. Your goodness is beyond words.'

'I trust your brother is recovered.'

'Thanks to your mercy. He is well, in himself, but...'

'Go on,' he prompted her. He listened impassively, neither flattered nor offended. Her words were formal, appropriate to her role as supplicant; he also felt his role descend on him, timeless and impersonal, nothing to do with his own seventeen-year-old self or his personality: the role of leadership he had been born into and trained for.

'He is losing his sight. His eyes became infected after the... after the fire, and he is nearly blind. My husband does not want him with us: it is too much of a burden, and there is no one left from his family to look after him.'

He was aware of her conflict – torn between her duty as a wife, her love for her brother, her role as headman's wife, her religious beliefs, shame that her husband would consider her older brother a burden. He was not surprised that her voice broke again, and tears began to flow silently.

'I am very sorry to hear it,' Shigeru replied. For a man of Nesutoro's age, too old to be taught the traditional skills of the blind, massage or lute-playing, blindness usually meant becoming a beggar.

'Forgive me,' she said. 'I could not think of anyone to turn to but Lord Otori.'

'What can I do for you?' He was amazed at her boldness, the same boldness with which she had spoken to him the previous year.

Irie, who was sitting next to Shigeru, leaned forward and whispered, 'I would not advise giving money or any other form of support. It would be misinterpreted by many, and would set a dangerous precedent.'

The woman waited until Irie had finished speaking, and then said quietly, 'I am not asking you for money. I would never do that. My brother expressly forbade it. But many of his people live peacefully in the West, among the Seishuu. My brother seeks your permission to leave the Middle Country and join them. All we are asking from Lord Otori is a letter stating this.'

'Will he be allowed across the border? And how will he travel if he is nearly blind?'

'There is a young woman who will go with him.' She turned and indicated the girl on the veranda. 'My second daughter.' The girl raised her head for a moment; he could see she had the same strong face as her mother.

'Your husband does not mind if she leaves?'

'We have four daughters and three sons. We can spare one child for a man who lost all his children. I come with my husband's permission. I would never act against his wishes, as Lord Otori already knows.'

'Lord Otori may not recall every detail of the lives of everyone he meets,' Kiyoshige said, not knowing that Shigeru did recall everything about the night – the injured, feverish man, the woman daring to address him directly, her husband's anger and incomprehension.

'Have the letter written for the two of them,' he said to Irie. 'They have my permission to travel to the West. I will stamp it with my seal.'

•

'You will not become like our father?' Takeshi said later, when the brothers were alone.

'What do you mean?' Shigeru replied.

'Consulting priests all the time, taking advice from all sorts of undesirable people.' Takeshi caught his older brother's look of disapproval and said rapidly, 'I don't mean any disrespect. But everyone talks about it, and deplores it. Now you receive this woman, and extend your protection to her brother... why? It seems so strange. I don't want to hear people deploring my older brother's behaviour.'

'What people say about it should not matter, as long as I hold the behaviour to be correct.'

'But your reputation is important,' Takeshi said. 'If people admire you and love you, they are more likely to do what you want. The more popular you are, the safer you are.'

'What are you talking about?' Shigeru smiled.

'Don't laugh at me: you should be on your guard. I hear things, you know: I keep my ears open, and moreover Kiyoshige and Kahei tell me a lot. You don't go to the places Kiyoshige takes me to.'

'You should not go to them either!' Shigeru interjected.

'People don't take any notice of me after a while, especially if they are drinking. I pretend to be still a child – '

'You still are a child!'

'Not really,' Takeshi replied. 'But I don't mind acting like one. Often I pretend I'm asleep and curl up on the floor while they loosen their tongues above my head.'

'And what do these loose tongues have to say?'

'I am not being disloyal myself: I am simply repeating what is said because I think you should know.'

'I understand.'

'They fear our father's indecisiveness in the face of Tohan aggression. They are concerned about the role our uncles play in the clan's decisions. They predict that the East will be handed over to the Tohan rather than defended.'

'Not while I live,' Shigeru said. 'We will spend the autumn and winter preparing for war; it is my intention to start gathering men and training them.'

Takeshi's eyes brightened with excitement. 'Just don't start a war until I'm old enough to fight!'

By now Shigeru had seen many men die. He would never forget the moment when life left the body of the first man he had killed – Miura. He did not fear his own death, though he still intended to make it significant, but the idea of Takeshi's death was unendurable. All the more reason not to delay the confrontation with the Tohan. But if it is next year, as it probably will be, Shigeru thought, at fourteen, he will not be too young to take part. How can I keep him out of the battle?

'Anything else you can tell me?' he asked.

'Maruyama Naomi's husband is in favour of an alliance with the Tohan. This is causing unease among the other Seishuu families – especially the Arai. People say we should join with the Seishuu before they support Iida Sadamu and we find ourselves caught between them and pincered.'

Shigeru sat in silence for a while, remembering his earlier thoughts on an alliance through marriage with the Seishuu. 'I have never been to the West,' he said finally. 'I would like to go there; I would like to see how they arrange affairs in Maruyama, for instance.'

'Take me with you,' Takeshi begged. 'There is still plenty of time before the snows begin – and autumn is a fine season for travelling. And let's go to Kumamoto too. I want to meet Arai Daiichi – they say he is a mighty warrior.'

'The eldest son?'

'Yes – he is only young but he is said to be the best swordsman in the Three Countries! But he is probably not as good as my elder brother,' Takeshi added loyally.

'I suspect you will be a better swordsman than I,' Shigeru said. 'Particularly if you go to Matsuda Shingen at Terayama.'

'I would like to be taught by Matsuda – but I don't know that I could stand all those months in the temple.'

'You would learn a lot. Maybe you should spend the winter there. We will call on Matsuda on the way.'

'On the way back,' Takeshi pleaded.

'You should stay at least a year,' Shigeru said, thinking, He will be far from the battlefield there.

Takeshi groaned. 'Too much studying.'

'Training the body is of no use unless you also train the mind. And besides, the study is fascinating in itself, as well as being a means to an end.'

'These things interest you – you are like our father! That's why I'm warning you not to get drawn in, as he has. Let's not take any notice of signs or omens or what the gods say or don't say. Let's just put our trust in ourselves and our swords!'

A few moments beforehand Shigeru had said his brother was still a child, and Takeshi's voice was full of a boy's enthusiasm and optimism; nevertheless Shigeru felt that this was their first conversation as adults. Takeshi was growing up, and a new element had entered their relationship. Twice now Takeshi had offered advice and Shigeru had taken it.

CHAPTER TWENTY-TWO

Shigeru decided that night to entrust the patrolling of the eastern borders for the rest of the year to Lord Kitano, and to his wife's family, the Yanagi of Kushimoto. Since the previous year, both families had supplied men and horses. He summoned the captains and told them he was returning to Hagi, leaving careful instructions on the frequency and size of the patrols and ordering them to send weekly messengers to the city to keep him informed on every detail.

The apparent lack of activity among the Tohan across the border made him uneasy. He wished he had a network of spies, as the Tohan had, to bring accurate news back from Inuyama. He was careful to tell no one else of his half-formed plan to travel West and see what alliances could be made with the Seishuu, fearing such a development would be seen as unnecessarily aggressive and would provoke Iida into open warfare.

Two days later they rode north to the sea, then turned west and followed the coast road to Hagi. The typhoon season had been a mild one, and seemed to be over early. Clear autumn weather made the journey enjoyable, and the men were cheerful at the prospect of returning home.

In the open country, Shigeru rode ahead with Irie to discuss his idea with the older man. Ever since they had journeyed together to Terayama, Irie had become his most trusted advisor. Ascetic and taciturn by nature, Irie was tireless and clear-sighted. His hair was grizzled with age, but he was still as strong as a twenty-year-old. He was a realist, but he was different from the fickle pragmatists, Kitano and Noguchi, for example. His loyalty to Shigeru and the Otori clan was absolute, undivided by self-serving or opportunism. And his grasp of the complex situation now facing the Three Countries was acute. He put no faith in signs and talismans, but he was cautious by nature, and would not lightly take the sort of action that would plunge the Three Countries into war, which Shigeru knew was what the young men – Kiyoshige, Miyoshi Kahei, his own brother – desired, and the outcome he himself favoured. He felt he needed Irie to check his own impulsiveness, to help him be decisive but not rash.

The horses slowed to a walk. Away to their left, the Yaegahara plain was turning tawny under the autumn sun. The tasselled heads of the grasses shimmered palely, and brown and orange butterflies flitted round the horses' hoofs. Bush clover and yarrow flowered purple and white.

To the east lay range after range of mountains. Already the breeze smelled of the sea.

'It will be good to be home,' Irie said. 'My first grandson was born a month ago. My son wrote to say he looks like his grandfather. I am looking forward to seeing him.'

'I am sorry, I am hoping you will come away with me again, and quite soon. I am thinking about travelling to the West, possibly entering into negotiations with the Seishuu.'

'Have you told anyone else about this plan?' Irie asked.

'No, only my brother, Takeshi. He was relating some gossip to me – of how people fear we will be squeezed by Iida using Maruyama Naomi's marriage as an alliance. I am sure that could be prevented if we act now.'

'Of course I will come with you, whenever you decide to go. In my opinion there's a great deal of merit in such an undertaking. I believe Iida has also been making approaches to the Arai, though they have a history of antagonism to the Tohan and have never entered into marriage alliances with them. It's a shame you have no sisters, for the Arai have four or five sons and none of them are married yet. No doubt Iida is lining up wives for them now!'

He glanced at Shigeru and said, 'Your wife has not yet conceived?'

Shigeru shook his head.

'I hope there are no problems. Your uncles have too many sons, your father and yourself not enough. Of course, you have not been married long; there is plenty of time. But you should stay at home with your wife more; that's my only reservation about travelling away so soon. See if you can't stay long enough to give her a child before you leave.' Irie chuckled.

Shigeru did not reply to this, beyond pretending to laugh too; for him the situation had nothing to laugh at in it. He missed Akane and looked forward to being with her with excited anticipation, but he dreaded seeing Moe and having to try again to overcome her fear and her coldness. He sometimes found himself wishing she would die and disappear from his life, and then he would be pierced by guilt and an uneasy pity for her.

'Or maybe you should take her with you,' Irie continued. 'She has not yet made the formal return to her parents' home, has she? This could be a good opportunity. And the freedom of travelling, the pleasures of the journey, may help bring on a child. I've seen it happen before.'

'I had been wondering whether to travel in state, or to go in unmarked clothes with you and only a few attendants. If the purpose of my journey is to escort my wife home and to take Takeshi to Terayama, I can travel openly without unduly arousing Tohan suspicions.'

'We could arrange some suitable celebration and invite the Seishuu families to attend,' Irie suggested.

'Will they come?'

'If the right language is used, I believe they will.'

'And if Iida Sadamu hears of it, will he suspect we are plotting against him?'

'He believes that already,' Irie replied shortly.

'All the same, I think we should send messengers secretly,' Shigeru said. 'Can it be done without it being generally known in Hagi? Do you have individuals you can trust?' He remembered an earlier conversation he had had with Irie. 'I almost wish we could employ the Tribe.'

'There is no need for that. Many Hagi merchants trade with the Seishuu; there are many family ties: there are several lines that we can explore.'

'Of course!' Shigeru exclaimed. 'My cousin, Otori Eijiro, is married to a woman from the Seishuu. He would make a good go-between. I'll send messages to him as soon as we get home.'

Shigeru's mother, Lady Otori, was as concerned as Lord Irie by her daughter-in-law's failure to conceive a child, especially as the girl had been her choice and she felt it her responsibility to turn her into a perfect wife and mother. Moe was losing her looks, growing thin and sallow, and Lady Otori feared that her obvious unhappiness would drive Shigeru further into the arms of Akane, who seemed to become more attractive and alluring every day. The tragedy of Hayato's death had not, it seemed, tainted her with any scandal: people decided it proved her desirability and her devotion to Shigeru. The mercy shown to Hayato's children was held to be the result of her compassionate intercession, and such fulfilment of obligations to a former lover was thoroughly approved. All this increased popularity infuriated Lady Otori. She feared above all that Akane would bear Shigeru's child, and that her son would acknowledge it – such a disaster had to be forestalled by Moe conceiving a legitimate heir.

She gave Moe advice on how to woo a husband, supplied her with illustrated books that depicted an interesting range and variety of techniques and positions, and had Chiyo come and take care of the young woman, remembering her own inability to bear live children, and Chiyo's solutions.

Moe looked at the pictures with repulsion, for they showed exactly what she was so afraid of: the uncomfortable and embarrassing positions, the taking, the intrusion – and she feared the outcome, too, though she knew it was what everyone expected of her, the only thing they expected. She had a deep dread of childbirth, and a premonition that she would die of it.

Chiyo had her own ideas of where the problem might lie. She saw in Moe a woman completely unawakened, unaware of the pleasure centres of her own body, too inhibited and too selfish to discover her husband's. It distressed her personally on behalf of the young man she had raised from infancy, and she was also aware of the political implications, which could be disastrous for the whole clan.

She brewed a tea that had a very strong narcotic effect, both soporific and hallucinatory. She persuaded Moe to drink it, and when it had taken effect and the girl was almost asleep, thrust her fingers up between her legs and realized the hymen was still unbroken. Even in her drugged state, the touch was enough to arouse panic in Moe. Her

muscles clenched and went rigid; she cried out in fear.
'Don't hurt me; oh please, don't hurt me.'

Chiyo tried to calm her by stroking and caressing her,
but there was no natural flow of wetness. She had thought
to break the hymen herself, but the membrane seemed
unusually resistant, and even the use of a smooth oiled
wooden phallus could not penetrate.

Moe had no clear memories afterwards, just an obscure
sense of violation and abuse. She began to believe that a
demon had come in the night and lain with her, and her
fears increased – that she had been unfaithful to her
husband and would bear a goblin child as a result: everyone
would see her shame. She trembled when Chiyo came
near her, and was reluctant to take food or drink prepared
by her. Lady Otori despised her all the more, and bullied
her more too.

It was with mixed feelings that Moe heard the news
of Shigeru's imminent return. She had enjoyed the respite
of his absence, especially knowing that he was also absent
from Akane, but she was deeply unhappy, and intelligent
enough to realize that her only hope of happiness lay in
a reconciliation with her husband.

Her mother-in-law swept into her room that evening
with the same idea in mind.

'You must look your best for him. He will come
straight to you. You must do whatever he wants, and
above all, please him.'

Chiyo took Moe to the bathhouse and scrubbed her
skin with bran; after the bath she rubbed lotions all over
her body; the scent of jasmine filled her nostrils, making

Moe's head swim. Her hair was combed carefully and left loose so it fell around her. She was dressed in night robes of silk. The attention flattered her, and as she sat waiting for him she felt for the first time a pleasant ache between her legs, and a flutter of excitement in her belly. She sipped a little wine and felt the blood pulse in her veins.

It is going to be all right, she thought. I will not be afraid of him. I won't hate him any more. I must love him. I must desire him.

Night fell; the hours passed, and Shigeru did not come. Finally she said to Chiyo, 'He must have been delayed on the road.'

At that moment, from the adjoining room they heard Takeshi's voice, greeting his mother.

Moe did not move for several moments. Then she picked up the wine flask and flung it across the room. It hit a painted screen and did not break, but spilled the wine in one ugly splash across the deep pink flowers.

'He has gone to Akane,' she said.

Akane, when she realized Shigeru had come straight to her before even going to the castle, was jubilant. The sight of him, dusty and travel-stained, his smile when he greeted her, swept away most of her anxiety. She made a great fuss over him, pretending to be horrified at how dirty he was, scolding and teasing him, then going herself to the bathhouse to help the maid scrub his back. She washed every part of his body, thinking with anticipation of how she would feel him against her soon – but not too soon.

She wanted to delay the moment, feeling her own skin tingle and her muscles soften with the languor of desire. It was a little over a year since the first time they had made love, when he had returned, like tonight, from the Eastern borders. She ordered the same food to be prepared: cool, glutinous, juice-filled. Night fell, and she called for the lamps to be lit, hardly taking her eyes off him as he ate and drank. He had changed from boy to man in that year. I changed him, she thought. I taught him how to be a man.

After they had retired and had satisfied their desire with passion, she lay against him. 'Now you will stay in Hagi till spring,' she said contentedly.

'I will spend the winter here. But before that, I have another journey to make.'

'You are cruel!' Akane said, only half pretending. 'Where are you going?'

'I will take Takeshi to Terayama. He can spend a year there: he wants to study the sword with Matsuda, and the discipline will be good for him.'

'He is very young – you were fifteen, were you not?'

'He turns fourteen in the new year. I have other reasons too. I think we will be at war next year. If my brother is at the temple, he will not be able to run away and fight.'

'He would do that,' Akane said. 'Lord Takeshi is bolder than men twice his age.'

'He should learn to fight properly – and grow to his full stature.' Shigeru paused and then went on. 'I am also escorting my wife to her parents' house in Kushimoto. She has not yet made her formal visit home.'

'Your wife is travelling with you?' Akane felt the stab of jealousy, thinking of the days and nights they would spend together on the road.

'You know I must have children – so I must sleep with my wife. Travel, getting away from a place she obviously dislikes, may make her care more for me. I'm sorry if it makes you jealous, Akane, but you have to accept the situation.'

'I would give you children,' Akane said, unable to stop the words, though she knew it was foolish even to think them.

'You give me cause for jealousy too. Kiyoshige told me about Hayato,' Shigeru said. 'They say you interceded with my uncle for his children's lives.'

'I would have appealed to you, if you had been here. I hope it does not offend you.'

'I was surprised my uncle was swayed by you. It made me wonder what he had demanded in return.'

'Nothing,' she said hastily. 'I believe he welcomed the chance to demonstrate his compassion. He was drunk when he had Hayato killed. In the morning he regretted his hastiness and wanted to make amends.'

'It does not sound like my uncle,' Shigeru said quietly. He moved away from her, rose and began to dress.

'Will you not stay?' she said.

'No. I can't tonight. I must see my parents in the morning, and my wife, and start making arrangements for the journey.'

'But I will see you before you go?' She heard the note of pleading in her own voice at the same time as disappointment and despair sprang into her heart. I am in such danger, she thought. I am falling in love with him. Immediately she feigned indifference. 'But of course, you will be very busy. Very well, I will await your return.'

'I will come again tomorrow night,' he said.

After he had gone and the sound of the horses had died away, she lay listening to the sea and the wind in the pines, berating herself for her stupidity. She feared loving him, the pain it would cause her: she feared losing him, to his wife, or in battle – why had he spoken of war? – or because of her pact with Masahiro.

He came as he had promised the following night, and talked a little more about his journey, planning to leave the next day while the weather was still fine. She tried to hide her feelings and devote herself purely to pleasing him, but the meeting left her unusually restless and dissatisfied.

She was even more disturbed when, after Shigeru had left the city, a message came suggesting she should make one of her customary visits to Daishoin that afternoon. It was not signed, but she had no doubt who it was from. She could not decide whether to go or not: the day was hot and she was tired and dispirited, but the prospect of spending the entire day moping indoors did not appeal to her either. In the end she ordered the palanquin and dressed with care.

The heat made the temple roofs shimmer; white doves sheltered under the deep eaves, and their cooing mingled with the insistent cheeping of sparrows and the drone of cicadas. Red autumn dragonflies danced above the cool water of the cistern in the front courtyard. Akane rinsed her hands and mouth, and bowed before the entrance to the main hall of the temple. The dim interior seemed to be deserted, and she walked, followed by the maid she had brought with her, into the shade of the sacred grove around the shrine. Here it felt a little cooler: water trickled from a fountain into a series of pools where gold and red fish swam lazily.

A man squatted beneath the trees, watching the fish. She recognized Masahiro. He stood when Akane approached. He did not greet her, or bother with any other courtesies.

'I was wondering if you had any news for me.'

'Only what Lord Otori must already know: your nephew has left to escort his wife home.'

'But was that the real purpose of his trip, or does he have other intentions?'

'Takeshi is to go to Terayama.'

'Yes, and Hagi will be a much pleasanter place without him.'

'I am sorry, he did not tell me anything else.'

'I expect he had other things on his mind.' Masahiro let his gaze linger on her form. 'And who can blame him?'

She felt a pang of fear at his lust; she had to invent something for him. She recalled a conversation from some time ago. 'He is interested in the Seishuu families. Maybe he plans to meet someone from the Arai or Maruyama.'

'He said that?'

'I am sure I have heard him mention it.' She knew Shigeru had not told her this explicitly, but the news had the desired effect on Masahiro, and distracted his attention from her.

'I suspected as much,' he muttered. 'I must inform my brother.'

It's not true, Akane thought as the palanquin carried her home, so it surely cannot do him harm.

CHAPTER TWENTY-THREE

The journey was leisurely, for they had several weeks of fine weather ahead of them, and since its purpose was ostensibly of a domestic and peaceful nature they took every opportunity to stop at famous places and sites of beauty along the way, as well as making formal visits to various Otori vassals and retainers. Shigeru's true purpose in travelling so slowly was to allow the messengers he had sent to reach Otori Eijiro and bring back his reply; he also had to allow time for Eijiro's two oldest sons to ride to Kumamoto and Maruyama to arrange a meeting with representatives from the Arai family and the Maruyama.

Kumamoto lay in the far southwest of the Three Countries, seven to ten days' hard ride away. Maruyama was about seven days' journey due west from Yamagata. As Shigeru and his retinue of mounted warriors, servants, foot soldiers and pack horses, palanquins for his wife and her women, banners and sunshades wound its way through the autumn landscape, the rice fields golden, the autumn lilies brilliant red, his thoughts were miles away with those distant messengers, urging them on their way, praying for a fruitful outcome to his swift planning. The messengers were from his own men, one of them Harada, who had ridden on a similar mission the year before to bring reinforcements to the border from Yamagata and Kushimoto. Harada had been deeply affected by the death of Tomasu, the man he had carried on his back across the Yaegahara plain. He was implacably opposed to the Tohan, and alert to any kind of weakness among the Otori that might lead to appeasement. Shigeru had entrusted the letter to Eijiro to Harada, also instructing him to travel on himself with the two sons. He recalled riding on the same road over two years before, when he had gone to Terayama to be taught by Matsuda. He looked back on his fifteen-year-old self with amazement. What a child he had been! He could see clearly how much he had grown up since then, and the changes that Matsuda's teaching, Irie's constant support and the circumstances of his life had wrought in him.

Once back in Hagi, he had moved rapidly to bring about the desired meeting with the clans of the West. But he had kept this true motive secret, sharing it only with Irie and Kiyoshige. He had sought his father's permission to take his wife to Kushimoto and Takeshi to Terayama, but it had been merely a formality. He had been making his own decisions for more than a year now, and the strength of his personality and character had increased to such an extent that his father now conceded to him on almost every issue. Shigeru no longer even kept up the pretence of consulting his uncles. Occasionally, when their protests and complaints annoyed him, he considered advising them to leave the castle, exiling them to distant country estates, but on the whole he preferred to keep them within Hagi, where he could keep an eye on their activities.

He discovered within himself an ability to dissemble. He took on an exterior that seemed affable, bland and relaxed. But beneath the mask lay a different personality, watchful and tireless. Now the austere training from Terayama began to show its results. He needed very little sleep, could endure endless meetings as well as the campaigns on the border. He became accustomed to making quick decisions and never regretting them, acting immediately to put them into practice. His decisions were invariably proved right, which won him the trust of warriors, merchants and farmers alike. Now he had a new idea that he would bring into being: an alliance that would bring peace to the Three Countries and protect the Otori against the Tohan. He was so sure of the justice and sense of this endeavour, he felt he could create it purely through the strength of his will.

This new ability to hide his true feelings helped him maintain a semblance of harmony with his wife during the journey. Moe was relieved to escape from the oppressions of life in the deep interior of the castle, but she was not a good traveller, did not care for horses and found the movement of the palanquin disagreeable. She was anxious about the dangers of the road – sickness, bandits, bad weather – and the minor discomforts of fleas, stuffy rooms and cold water irritated her. Shigeru spent as little time in her company as he could, though he treated her with unrelenting politeness. The rooms of lodging places with their flimsy screens did not encourage intimacy, and though he knew he should follow Irie's advice and keep trying to approach her, despite his own words to Akane and his best intentions he made no move towards her. He intended that she should spend the winter with her parents; when she returned to Hagi in the spring, they might be able to make a fresh start. He would be freed from anxiety about her and would be able to concentrate on the preparations for the war that he was increasingly convinced would break out within the next year.

It was with relief that he left Lord Yanagi's house at Kushimoto and set out for Terayama on the journey home. He would leave his brother at the temple. He had taken Takeshi everywhere with him, wanting the boy to see the country and meet the retainers and the vassal families for himself, hoping to share with him his ideas of the fief as a farm, the need to support warriors to defend it. Takeshi was astute when it came to assessing the reactions of the Kitano, for example, and he got on well with the Yanagi boys, but it was obvious that he was more interested in swords and horses: he himself said so. Shigeru responded that without rice they would have neither: the warrior's heroism was no use among the starving, and preparations for war included tilling the land as much as training men and arming them. However, he found little support for this view among the ruling families apart from Eijiro; they were more interested in how taxes could be increased: farming methods were old-fashioned, innovation if it happened, was piecemeal and inconsistent. After the war is won, I will rehaul the entire fief, Shigeru promised himself. But now the most important task was to ensure the loyalty and military readiness of the whole clan. And that could only be done by confirming allegiances and not antagonizing anyone.

On the journey out, he had made a point of staying two nights in Tsuwano, where Lord Kitano and his sons received him with chilly deference. The close friendship Shigeru had had with Tadao and Masaji seemed to have evaporated after Shigeru had demanded their return from Inuyama the year before. All three repeated their vows of allegiance, and gave detailed reports of the troops they had sent to the eastern borders.

'I am a little surprised your sons are in Tsuwano,' Shigeru said. 'I expected them to be in Chigawa until the beginning of winter.'

'Their mother has been unwell,' Kitano replied smoothly. 'At one stage we feared for her life.'

'I am glad to see her so perfectly recovered!' Shigeru replied.

'If I may offer a word of advice, Lord Shigeru, it is better not to provoke Iida Sadamu any more than you already have. We have heard many reports of his bitterness against you. You have given him cause to hate you.'

'He seizes on any pretext to justify his aggression and lust for power,' Shigeru replied. 'He knows that I am not afraid of him.'

'You must be aware that the Tsuwano domain would suffer the most from a Tohan attack.'

'All the more reason to ensure that it is properly defended.'

Kitano's words stayed with him after he left Tsuwano, causing him some anxiety. He would have liked to journey further south and meet Noguchi Masayoshi again. The memory of their first meeting also made him uneasy. Noguchi had accompanied Kitano's sons to Inuyama: since then, Shigeru had had no word of his movements, other than the formal interactions demanded by their relationship within the clan, the payment of rice levies and other taxes on the lucrative trade through Hofu. Matsuda had described Noguchi as a coward and an opportunist, and called both him and Kitano pragmatic. I should have insisted the boys come back to Hagi with me, he thought – and if only I had time to travel to Hofu.

One afternoon towards the end of the tenth month, when they were on their way back to Yamagata, Takeshi, who had been riding ahead with Kiyoshige, came cantering back to Shigeru.

'I thought you might like to know: the man we sent away in Chigawa, the burnt one, is on the road ahead. I can't imagine you want to talk to him, but... well, I was sorry I treated him so badly before, since he is in your favour, so I'm trying to make amends.'

Shigeru was going to tell Takeshi to send a servant to ask after the man's health and give him some food, but the beauty of the autumn day and the lightening of his spirits since leaving Moe at her parents' home suddenly prompted him to say, 'We will stop for a while and rest. Tell the young woman to bring her uncle to me.'

A makeshift camp was swiftly set up beneath a small grove of trees, mats spread on the ground and covered with silk cushions, fires lit and water boiled. A small chair was provided for Shigeru. Takeshi sat next to him, and they drank the tea Moe's parents had given them, picked on the southern slopes of Kushimoto, and ate fresh persimmons and a sweet paste made from chestnuts.

The air was crisp and clear, the sun still pleasantly warm. Ginkgo trees in the grove scattered their leaves in drifts of gold.

He can see none of this, Shigeru thought with pity as the girl led Nesutoro towards him.

'Uncle, Lord Otori is here,' he heard her whisper as she helped him kneel.

'Lord Otori?' He held his face up, as if trying to look with the last of his sight.

'Nesutoro.' He did not want to insult a man of such courage with pity. 'I am glad to see your journey is progressing well.'

'Thanks to your kindness, lord.'

'Give him some tea,' he said, and the servants came forward with a wooden bowl. The girl took it from them and placed her uncle's hands round it. He bowed in thanks and drank.

The girl's movements were deft and graceful. Shigeru was aware that Takeshi was watching her, and remembered how he had begun finding his eyes drawn to women. Surely Takeshi was too young! Was he going to be as precocious in this as in everything? He would have to talk to him, warn him against the dangers of infatuation. But the girl was attractive, reminding him of Akane, of how much he missed her.

'What will you do when you get to Maruyama?' he said.

'I believe the Secret One has some plan for my life,' the man replied. 'He has spared me; he has brought me this far.' He smiled, making the scars and the sightlessness suddenly less ugly.

'I am glad to have seen you,' Shigeru said, and told the servants to give the girl some rice cakes. 'Take care of him.'

She nodded and bowed in thanks, too awed, it seemed, to speak.

Nesutoro said, 'May he bless and keep you always.'

'The blessing of their god seems more like a curse,' Takeshi remarked when they resumed their journey.

Shigeru turned in the saddle to catch a last glimpse of the girl leading the blind man along the road. Lit by the afternoon sun, the dust around them made a golden haze.

'I hope he will have a safe and happy life from now on. But can you ever recover from such suffering?'

'Better to take your own life – and far more honourable,' Takeshi said.

'The Hidden are forbidden to kill themselves,' Kiyoshige told him. 'Just as they are forbidden to kill.'

It was the complete opposite to everything Takeshi had been brought up to believe. Shigeru could see the idea was incomprehensible to him. He was not sure he understood it himself. Yet it seemed wrong that those who would not kill should be tortured and murdered: it was like slaughtering children or women for no reason, or killing an unarmed man. He had seen for himself the results of bloodlust and unbridled cruelty, and now realized the wisdom he had absorbed from Matsuda Shingen. The warrior had been given the right to kill; his class loved the way of the sword. But the right brought responsibility, and love of the way of the sword must never be allowed to become a love of killing for its own sake. He hoped Takeshi would learn this too in the coming year.

They were met outside Yamagata by Nagai Tadayoshi, who had shown Shigeru so much of the town, the surrounding area and the records of both during his stay two years before. Nagai was an austere and undemonstrative man, but he could not hide his pleasure at the meeting. Shigeru was equally glad to see him again, feeling he could trust Nagai completely, and delighted to be in Yamagata, the town with whose people he had formed such close bonds.

The annual business of government took up many hours of each day. Shigeru devoted himself patiently to these affairs, determined not to leave Yamagata before he had word from Eijiro or his sons or Harada about the outcome of their negotiations. At first Takeshi attended the meetings too, but seeing his boredom and fearing he would exhaust too soon the concentration and discipline he would need for his time at Terayama, Shigeru allowed him to go with Kiyoshige and the other captains to assess the capabilities and readiness of the Yamagata warriors, a task Takeshi took to with alacrity.

They met in the evening to bathe and eat; Kiyoshige then usually took himself off to get the feeling of the town, as he put it. Shigeru did not allow Takeshi to go with him, knowing that getting the feeling of the town usually took place in pleasure houses among the beautiful women of Yamagata, but he found the information Kiyoshige gleaned from these excursions useful. Nagai had somewhat reluctantly suggested that Shigeru also might like to meet some beautiful women, but he had declined. It seemed unnecessarily insulting to his wife and, he realized, he did not want to hurt Akane by breaking his promise not to make her jealous. Besides, his refusal had so delighted Nagai it had been worth it for that alone.

So when Kiyoshige sent a message early one evening to say he had returned with a woman he wanted Shigeru to meet, Shigeru was at first inclined to refuse. The day's meetings had been long and demanding; his head ached and he was hungry. He did not intend to sleep with Kiyoshige's woman, however attractive she was, and so there seemed no point in meeting her. He sent a reply to that effect, but an hour later, while he was finishing the evening meal and talking to Nagai about the following day's arrangements, Kiyoshige himself came to the room and drank wine with them.

'When you are finished, Lord Shigeru, spare me a few minutes of your company. This girl will intrigue you, I promise. She is from Kumamoto; she plays the lute and sings. I think you will like her songs.'

Kumamoto: home of the Arai.

'Maybe I will join you for a little while,' he replied.

'We are at the Todoya,' Kiyoshige said. 'Come any time; we will wait all night!'

Nagai sat saying nothing, a look of disapproval on his face. Shigeru regretted the tarnishing of his bright reputation, but it was more important to keep his negotiations with the Seishuu secret. He did not leave immediately, not wanting to insult the older man; they talked for another hour or so, at first about administrative affairs, and then, after a third flask of wine, about Nagai's passion for gardening. Finally Shigeru stood and wished him good night. He went to the privy to relieve himself, and then, calling for two guards to come with him, walked from the residence through the inner courtyard to the castle gatehouse.

It could hardly be called a castle, though the foundations and the moat walls were of stone. Lying in the heart of the Middle Country, Yamagata had never come under attack and was not built to be defended. Shigeru thought about this as he crossed the bridge over the moat. The residence buildings were all wooden. They stood behind walls and strong gates, but he saw how easily they could be taken. Iida Sadamu was said to be building himself a mighty castle at Inuyama. Should the Otori be fortifying their towns in the same way? It was something else to discuss with Nagai.

It was about the second half of the Hour of the Boar. There was no moon, but the constellations of stars were brilliant in the cold clear night. There was a hint of frost in the air, the men's breath was visible, and a slight mist rose from the surface of the water. On the bank, bulrushes emerged like lances, and the willows' long branches, now almost bare, were wreathed in the pale vapour.

The town was quiet, most people already asleep. Only a few inns and pleasure houses still had lamps outside, their glow warm orange. From inside came sounds of music, women singing, men laughing, their voices made loud by wine.

The Todoya was built on the riverbank, its verandas extending out over the water; long boats were moored beneath them, and lanterns hung on the corners of the eaves and on the ends of the boats. Braziers had been carried onto the verandas, and several people sat outside, wrapped in animal pelts, enjoying the brilliance of the autumn night. There were two of Kiyoshige's men outside the main entrance; when they recognized Shigeru one of them called inside to a maid to fetch Kiyoshige, while the other knelt to unfasten Shigeru's sandals.

Kiyoshige appeared, gave him a knowing smile and led him to a room at the back of the house. It was a private room, reserved for special guests, spacious and comfortable, warmed by two charcoal braziers though the doors were open onto the garden. The night was windless. Water trickled from a fountain, echoing slightly like a bell. Occasionally there was a rustle as a leaf detached itself and fell.

A young woman, around seventeen years of age, knelt by one of the braziers. She was small, but not slight and fragile like his wife. Her limbs were strong, almost muscled, and beneath her robe her body was compact and firm. She bowed to the floor when he entered the room, and sat up when Kiyoshige told her to. She kept her eyes down, and her whole demeanour was modest and refined, but Shigeru suspected it was partly assumed, and his suspicions were confirmed when she glanced at him, met his gaze and held it. Her eyes were extraordinarily sharp and intelligent. She is more than she seems, he thought suddenly. I must be very careful what I say.

'Lord Otori,' she said. 'It is a great honour.' Her voice was soft, also refined, her language formal and courteous. Yet she was in a house of pleasure: he could not place her. 'My name is Shizuka.'

Again he sensed disguise: the name meant tranquillity, yet he felt this woman was far from tranquil. She poured wine for him and Kiyoshige.

'You are from Kumamoto, I believe,' he said, as though making idle conversation.

'My mother lives there, but I have many relatives in Yamagata. My family name is Muto. Lord Otori may have heard of them.'

He recalled, from Nagai's records, a merchant of that name, a manufacturer of soybean products, he thought, and could even place where the house was.

'You are visiting your relatives, then?'

'I often come to Yamagata for that purpose.' She glanced at Kiyoshige and dropped her voice. 'Forgive me, Lord Otori, if I come closer. We do not wish to be heard by the wrong people.' She shuffled towards him until they sat knee to knee. He could smell her fragrance and could not help thinking how attractive she was; her voice when she spoke had not lost its feminine note, but her speech was direct and matter-of-fact, like a man's.

'Your relative, Otori Danjo, came to Kumamoto two weeks ago. He is the same age as Lord Arai's eldest son, Daiichi. They met at Maruyama when they were boys; both were taught by Sugita Haruki. But I expect Lord Otori is already aware of this.'

'Of course I knew Danjo's mother is from the Sugita family. I did not know he was already acquainted with Arai Daiichi.'

'He and Danjo were happy to see each other again; and Lord Arai was very pleased to have such good news of Lord Otori's health. I am also closely acquainted with Lord Arai,' Shizuka went on. 'That is why I am here. I come at his request.'

Closely acquainted? What did she mean? Were they lovers? Was she Arai's acknowledged mistress, as Akane was his? Or was she a spy, sent by Iida to trap him into revealing his plans?

'I hope I will have the pleasure of meeting Lord Arai himself,' he said non-committally. For a moment he felt like the Otori symbol, the heron, peering into opaque water, waiting for something to move that he might stab at it.

She gazed at him frankly for a long moment, then reached into the folds of her robe and took out a small roll of paper. 'I have a letter from him. He accompanied Danjo back to Kibi, just across the border.'

He took the note and unrolled it, seeing the vermilion seal with the Arai characters.

'Lord Arai says he had heard that I am in Yamagata and invites me to visit him, since he is, by coincidence, in Kibi,' he said to Kiyoshige. 'He suggests we go hawking on Kibi plain.'

'Hawking is a very popular pursuit,' Kiyoshige remarked. 'As long as no one is swallowed up by the earth.'

'Why did he send the letter with you?' Shigeru asked the woman. 'Any messenger could have brought it to me.'

'Most messengers would simply have delivered it,' she replied. 'I was to see you first, and...'

'And what?' He did not know whether to be affronted or amused.

'And decide if we should take matters further.'

He was surprised by her boldness and confidence. She spoke as if she were one of Arai's senior advisors, rather than a concubine.

'You decided very quickly,' he said.

'I am able to sum up a character very quickly. I believe Lord Otori is to be trusted.'

But are you? he thought, but did not speak it.

'Ride towards Kibi tomorrow. Just over the wooden bridge there is a fox shrine. A horseman will meet you there. Follow him towards the southwest. Bring only a few men, and let everyone know that you ride out for pleasure.'

'We should have hawks,' Shigeru said to Kiyoshige.

He nodded. 'I will arrange it.'

'It will be a perfect day for hawking,' the woman called Muto Shizuka said.

CHAPTER TWENTY-FOUR

After the long days of discussion, reading, meetings and reports, Shigeru was glad to be out early on horseback, with his friend and his brother, on what was indeed a beautiful day, one of those days of late autumn when the last warmth of summer and the first chill of winter meet in perfect balance. The grasses were fawn and russet; the last leaves glowed golden and orange; the sky was a deep, unbroken blue, but the mountain peaks were already frosted with snow.

His black horse, Karasu, was eager and spirited after several days of inactivity. Three men rode with them, including the falconer carrying the hawks on their perch. The birds also were active and lively. A fourth man followed, leading a pack horse, for Kibi was half a day's ride away, and they would surely have to stay overnight somewhere or even sleep out of doors – the last time, Shigeru thought, before winter set in.

A broad river flanked by rice fields marked the border between the Middle Country and the West, but it was not manned in the way that the Tohan guarded their border. The Seishuu and the Otori had never been at war, the Seishuu being a group of several large clans who sometimes quarrelled among themselves but had never united to fight a common enemy, nor been dominated by one powerful family as the Iida dominated the Tohan.

The river was low and calm, though it was possible to see how high it rose in the spring floods; it was spanned by a wooden bridge, and on the far side Shigeru could see the grove of trees around the shrine, on this day a mass of leaves like flame against the dull green of the river and the pale brown stubble of the fields. Little white statues of the fox god shone like ice among the brilliant leaves.

A horseman waited as promised among the trees. He raised his hand in greeting, and without speaking turned his horse and set off at a canter away from the river and the road, towards the southwest.

'Who's that?' Takeshi called, his own horse pulling against the bit and bucking in its eagerness to follow. He had been told nothing of the true purpose of the outing.

'Someone we hope will show us where the best hawking is,' Shigeru replied, urging Karasu forward.

Their guide led them at some speed along a narrow track which eventually opened out onto a broad plain. Here the horses tossed their heads and snorted and began to gallop, and their riders let them run across the tawny plain like ships driven by the wind across the face of the sea.

Hardly a tree or a rock broke the smooth undulating surface of the plain, and the wind whipped tears into his eyes, blurring his vision, but as the horses began to slow Shigeru could see the figure a long way in the distance, the single horseman. They drew nearer; the man raised his hand again, and as the horses, trotting now, came up the slope towards him, Shigeru saw behind him a small group of men who had set up a kind of camp in a slight depression in the plain. Cloth screens had been erected on three sides, giving protection from the wind; matting had been laid on the ground and cushions placed on it. On either side of the open space fluttered long banners emblazoned with the bear's paw of the Arai and the setting sun of the Seishuu. Two folding stools had been prepared, and on one of these sat a young man who he assumed was Arai Daiichi. Beside him, on the ground, was Danjo, Eijiro's oldest son.

As Shigeru dismounted, Arai stood and declared his name, then dropped to his knees and bowed to the ground. Danjo did the same. When they rose, Arai said, 'Lord Otori. What a fortunate coincidence brings us to this meeting.'

His voice was warm, with a Western accent. It was hard to tell his age: he was already a big man, a little taller than Shigeru and a lot broader; his features were strong, his eyes sparkling. He radiated energy and strength.

Shigeru thought briefly of Muto Shizuka and wondered where she was now. He had half expected to see her here, since she and Arai had seemed so close.

'It's very fortunate that you were able to meet up with an old friend,' Shigeru replied, 'and a great pleasure for me that you happened to be here.'

'The hawking is excellent at this time of year. I often come to Kibi in the tenth month. You've met my companion, I think?'

Shigeru turned in surprise and saw Shizuka dismounting from the horse they had been following. He tried to hide his astonishment. He could not believe someone who now appeared, despite her riding clothes, so womanly – soft, gentle even – could have fooled him into thinking she was a man. In the brief moment of dismounting, everything about her had changed – almost, he would swear, her height and size.

Arai was laughing. 'You didn't suspect it was her? She's clever like that. Sometimes even I don't recognize her.' His eyes caressed her.

'Lord Otori.' She greeted Shigeru demurely, and bowed respectfully to Kiyoshige and Takeshi. Takeshi was trying in vain to hide his admiration.

'Lady Muto,' Shigeru said formally, honouring her, for it was obvious to him that Arai was deeply in love with her and that she held an unequalled position with him. He wondered if she loved him as much and, watching her, decided that she did, and felt a strange pang, envy perhaps, knowing that he would never allow himself to fall in love in that way and never expected to be so loved by a woman.

He suspected Arai was a man who seized what he wanted with no hesitation and no regrets. It was impossible to tell what effects his thoughtlessness would have on his character in later years, but now, in his youth, this appetite for life was an attractive quality, and Shigeru warmed to it.

'Sit down,' Arai said. 'We've brought food from Kumamoto. You may not have tasted such things before; we are close to the coast. These are just an appetizer; later we will cook and eat what our hawks catch for us.'

Dried roe from sea cucumber, flakes of preserved squid, unhulled rice wrapped in kelp, orange mushrooms shaped like fans, pickled in rice vinegar and salt. First they drank wine; afterwards water was boiled and tea served. The conversation was general: the autumn weather, the birds of the plain that they might expect to catch; then, in response to a question from Takeshi, various matters pertaining to the sword: the best swordsmiths, the greatest teachers, the most famous fighters.

'My brother was taught by Matsuda Shingen,' Takeshi said, 'and I am to go to Terayama to be instructed by him.'

'That will turn you into a man, like Lord Otori,' Arai replied. 'You were very fortunate to be accepted by Matsuda,' he said to Shigeru. 'It is rumoured that Iida Sadayoshi invited him to Inuyama and Matsuda refused.'

'Matsuda is one of the Otori,' Shigeru replied. 'There could be no reason for him to teach the Tohan.'

Arai smiled, but did not make any further comment. However, at the end of the day, after they had spent the afternoon galloping across the plain in pursuit of the swift hawks with a recklessness that impressed even Takeshi, and while the birds' prize catches of pheasant, partridge and a couple of young hare were braising over charcoal, Arai returned to the subject of the relationship between the Otori and the Tohan.

Dusk was falling, the smoke from the fires rising in grey plumes. The western sky was still pale yellow from the last of the sunset. Shizuka, who had ridden with them with all the skill and fearlessness of a man, poured wine for them. Arai drank in the same way as he rode, with no restraint and with reckless pleasure. From time to time the woman's hands brushed his and a look flashed between them. Her presence disturbed Shigeru, not only for the obvious and unsettling attraction between her and Arai, but also because he did not trust her.

Arai said, 'Sadamu has increased his invective against the Otori, so we hear, and has taken something of a dislike to you.'

'I made the mistake of saving his life,' Shigeru replied. 'He can turn any action into a studied insult.'

'And how do you intend to respond?' Arai spoke lightly, but a new seriousness had crept into the conversation, and Shigeru was aware of it. Only Kiyoshige and Takeshi sat close enough to hear. And the woman.

'Forgive me, Lord Arai, I would like to discuss my response with you, but it is a private matter for your ears only.' He glanced at Shizuka.

She sat without moving, a slight smile on her face. Arai said, 'You may speak freely in front of Muto Shizuka. You are not accustomed to the way we do things in the West. You must get used to women taking part in these discussions if you are also to talk to Maruyama Naomi.'

'Am I to have that pleasure?'

'It seems she is on her way to Terayama. She is a great admirer of the work of Sesshu, both the paintings and the gardens. You will meet her there – quite by chance, of course.' Arai laughed again, seeing his words had not quite dispelled Shigeru's misgivings, and turned to Shizuka. 'You will have to make a formal oath to Lord Otori to convince him.'

She came forward a little and said in a calm, clear voice, 'Lord Otori's secrets are safe with me. I will never reveal them to anyone. I swear it.'

'There,' Arai said. 'You can trust her. I promise it.'

She touched her head to the ground before him. Shigeru had to be satisfied, or risk offending Arai.

'It is true that Sadamu considers himself offended by me,' he said. 'But it is convenient for him; it gives him an excuse to do what the Iida have long intended: to expand into the Middle Country at the expense of the Otori. The silver mines around Chigawa, the rich sea port of Hofu and the fertile lands in the south all attract them. But Sadamu will not be satisfied with the Middle Country alone: he seeks to control the entire Three Countries; sooner or later he will move against the West. I believe an alliance between the Seishuu and the Otori would dissuade him in the first instance, and would defeat him if it came to war.'

'You must know that the Seishuu prefer to keep peace through diplomacy and alliances,' Arai said.

'I can hardly believe this is your own preference. Your family have never cared for the Tohan, so it is said.'

'Maybe not, but I am just one small part of the clan. My father is still alive and I have three brothers. Furthermore, Lady Maruyama's marriage, and several others – my own wife will probably be chosen for me from a family sympathetic to Iida, if not actually related to him – have brought the whole of the West much closer to the Tohan.' He leaned forward and said quietly, 'The Otori are a great clan, a historic family, possibly the greatest in the Three Countries – but what has happened to them? What were they doing while the Iida were negotiating these alliances? You know what people say: that while the Otori skulk in Hagi, the rest of the Middle Country will be stolen from them, and they won't even notice!'

'That's an insult –' Takeshi began, but Shigeru silenced him, putting his hand on his brother's shoulder.

'Many mistakes have been made,' he admitted, 'but surely it is not too late to remedy some of them.'

'I will speak to my father,' Arai said. 'But I can make no promises. We may not care much for the Tohan, but to be honest with you, we have little love for some of the Otori allies either, in particular our nearest neighbours, the Noguchi. It may be very imprudent for us to openly defy the Tohan at this time. We have nothing to gain from it. I came to meet you because I liked what I'd heard of

you, and I don't mind telling you I like what I see now.
But my preferences can have very little influence on the
policies of the West.'

'At least give us the assurance that you will not stab
us in the back while we fight the Tohan in the East.'

'So it will come to war?'

'I believe Sadamu will attack the Otori next summer.
We will defeat them, but not if we have to fight on two
fronts.'

'If Maruyama Naomi agrees to that, then there's every
possibility the Arai will too. And Lady Naomi will almost
certainly choose the more peaceful solution, for that is the
Maruyama way.'

The meat was ready, but despite its succulent, gamy
flavour, the day's vigorous exercise and the crisp night air,
Shigeru ate with little appetite, and his sleep was restless,
not only because of the many flasks of wine and the hard
ground. His earlier confidence of the wisdom and desirability of the alliance was replaced by a more realistic
appreciation of its difficulties, the many obstacles: the
need for months of careful diplomacy, months he could
not spare.

'It was a mistake to come,' he said to Kiyoshige as
they rode back to Yamagata.

'You never know. You have established a relationship
– one that could become a friendship. And you know that
you will meet Lady Maruyama before you return to Hagi.'

Shigeru made no reply, remaining unconvinced.

'Anyway,' Kiyoshige said, 'it was worth it for the
food alone!'

'And the hunting,' Takeshi agreed. 'My only regret is I did not watch Lord Arai use the sword. If he fights in the same way as he rides, it would be something to see.'

'It doesn't look as if you will ever have that opportunity,' Shigeru said. Their boyish cheerfulness irritated him. 'Arai will never fight alongside us. The most we can hope for is not to make an enemy of him.'

The heaviness of his spirits was not dispelled when they returned to Yamagata and told Irie of the outcome of the meeting.

'I cannot remedy the neglect of years in a few short months,' Shigeru concluded his account. 'We have wasted all of our opportunities while the Iida have been negotiating, making marriages and alliances. We are hemmed in on all sides. There is every sign that Sadamu is preparing an attack soon. I hoped to strengthen us against it, but I may simply be precipitating it. Will we ever be ready?'

'We must spend the winter preparing men and arms and planning strategy,' Irie replied. 'The southern and eastern provinces are the most vulnerable. Rather than return to Hagi with you, I suggest I go to Noguchi and impress on him the need to stand firm and not give in to Tohan intimidation.'

'And to start preparing men,' Shigeru said. 'They must be in readiness to advance along the Eastern border in spring.'

'Should I stay there for the winter to oversee it?'

'Send messages before the snow to let me know how the situation looks. I'll decide then.'

Shigeru fell silent. 'I am most concerned about spies,' he said finally. 'I feel Sadamu watches us all the time and will know my every move. What can I do to escape his net?'

'Be very careful who you talk to, and who else is there,' Irie replied. 'Surround yourself only with warriors you know and trust. Choose servants only from Otori families.'

'Easier said than done,' Shigeru replied, thinking of Muto Shizuka.

CHAPTER TWENTY-FIVE

The following day, they left early in the morning to ride to Terayama. The beauty of the autumn weather and the prospect of seeing Matsuda Shingen raised Shigeru's spirits a little, even though he had few hopes of the meeting with Maruyama Naomi. He knew her husband was from the Tohan; the husband's daughter was married to a cousin of Iida Sadamu, Nariaki. Naomi was only a year or so older than Shigeru himself. Despite what everyone kept telling him about the Maruyama way of doing things, he doubted if she had any real power, if she would ever act against the wishes of her husband and his family – which would be those of Iida Sadamu.

In fact, the more he thought about it, the more reluctant he was to meet her; mingled with his fears was a kind of anger at his own family, his father, his uncles, who had allowed this situation to develop. He couldn't help wondering why they had not approached the Seishuu themselves, years before, when he and Naomi had been children: they were almost the same age; they could have been betrothed then. And why had the Seishuu not considered the Otori heir, rather than a binding alliance with the Tohan? Did they, and most of the other clans in the Three Countries, consider the Otori an insignificant force, a declining clan destined now to be wiped out by the Tohan?

By the time they arrived at the foot of the mountain, he had decided he did not want to meet her, and hoped she would not be there. The journey had unsettled him further, though he should have been delighted by the rapturous welcome he received along the way. The progress was slowed by so many people wanting to greet him, talk to him, offer presents to himself and his men, and meet Takeshi.

'You will have to learn to be more standoffish,' Kiyoshige said, after the fourth or fifth halt to examine some innovative farming technique or be informed about a new taxation levy. 'They will eat you alive. You cannot be available to all these people. It's like being nibbled by a pool full of carp!'

'And we'll never get to the temple,' Takeshi added.

Shigeru saw what he had become, a sort of symbol for these people who put all their trust and hope in him. If he failed them, they would fall under Tohan rule: he could not bear to see that happen. Yet was he ready to take the measures that would bring war on the whole fief? And he was saddened in some way by the adulation. It had little foundation and was like a fantasy, unrealistic and unsustainable. He wanted their lives to have a sounder base: justice because it was Heaven's will, not on the whim of some idealized hero.

There were several retainers already at the inn at the foot of the mountain, wearing the Maruyama crest on their surcoats. They stared at Shigeru and Takeshi with undisguised curiosity as the brothers dismounted from the horses, leaving them in Kiyoshige's care.

'We'll go straight to the temple,' Shigeru said.

'Yes, I've eaten and drunk enough to last me for days,' Takeshi replied, for they had been fed at every stop.

As they made the climb Shigeru recalled the day when he had made it alone. He had been fifteen: more than a year older than Takeshi was now. He had found the early days almost unbearable, had longed to leave. Would Takeshi find it unendurable? There would be other boys as young as him, but they would be novice monks, not the son of the head of the clan. He thought he might speak to Matsuda, ask him to treat Takeshi leniently; and then corrected himself. Takeshi would be treated by Matsuda as he needed to be, and leniency was the last thing he needed if he was to learn to curb his recklessness and remedy the effects of his mother's indulgence.

At first Takeshi leaped ahead up the path, but as the climb steepened his pace slowed. The thought of the coming months was perhaps turning him serious.

They were greeted by the monks with a quiet, undemonstrative pleasure, and taken immediately to Matsuda Shingen, now the Abbot of the temple. He made them welcome, openly delighted to see Shigeru again.

Matsuda studied Takeshi carefully, but said little to him beyond commenting that in looks, at least, he was very like his brother. Then he called for two young boys who were in simple clothes and whose heads were shaven, and asked them to take Lord Takeshi and show him around while he spoke to Lord Otori.

The boys left in deferential silence, but before they were beyond the cloisters Shigeru could hear Takeshi's eager questions, and soon laughter from all three.

'It is very early for your brother to be here,' Matsuda said. 'I wonder if he has the maturity...'

'I'm hoping he will learn it here,' Shigeru replied. 'He does not receive the discipline he should in Hagi: my parents spoil him, Mori Kiyoshige leads him astray, and he has little respect for anyone. I want him to stay here for at least a year, possibly more. His education and training must be the same as mine –'

'I have other responsibilities now,' Matsuda interrupted gently. 'It is not possible for me to absent myself from the temple for long periods, as I did with you.'

'Of course, I understand that. But I hope you will be able to teach him, here, much of what you taught me.'

'If he is willing to learn it, I can promise you I will.'

'I have another reason for sending him here at this time,' Shigeru said. 'If we are to be at war next year, he will be out of harm's way, and if I meet my death on the battlefield, the heir to the clan will be in safe hands. I trust you where I do not trust my uncles.'

'You are right, in my opinion, both about the coming war and about your uncles,' Matsuda said quietly. 'But are the Otori prepared? You must delay as long as possible, while you build up your forces.'

'I suspect Sadamu will attack us early, through Chigawa. I intend to concentrate our defence around Yaegahara.'

'You must beware of a double attack, from the south as well as the East.'

'That is why I have sent Irie to Noguchi to claim his support. And my wife's father will guarantee the support of Kushimoto.'

'I'm afraid next year is too soon,' Matsuda said. 'Try not to provoke Sadamu into an early attack.'

'I must be prepared, yet I must not provoke him,' Shigeru said, smiling. 'It is not possible to do both.'

'Whatever you choose to do, you have my support always,' Matsuda said. 'And Lord Takeshi will be safe while he stays with us.'

As Shigeru rose to leave, the older man said, 'Let us walk in the gardens for a while; it is such a beautiful day.'

Shigeru followed him along the polished wooden floor that gleamed in the dim light: sunlight spilled through the open doors at the end of the corridor and he could smell wood smoke and pine leaves from outside, mingled with incense from the main hall of the temple.

At the end of the corridor they crossed a small courtyard and stepped into another wide room, whose doors were all open onto the garden beyond. The matting glowed gold. Two painted screens stood at either end; he had seen them often before but never failed to be moved by their beauty. When he had first come to the temple, the other boys had recounted the legends about their creator, the artist Sesshu, who had lived in the temple for many years. The bare panel was said to have once been painted with birds, so lifelike they all took flight, and the gardeners complained Sesshu's horses roamed at night, trampling and eating the crops, and demanded he should tether them.

A wide veranda gave onto the garden, facing south, warm with the autumn sunshine. They paused on the silvered cypress-wood boards while a monk brought sandals, but before Matsuda stepped into his, the other man whispered to him.

'Ah!' Matsuda said. 'It seems my presence is requested for a few moments. If you will excuse me, Lord Shigeru, I'll join you later.'

Shigeru could hear the waterfall in the distance and walked towards it, for it was one of his favourite parts of the garden. To his left lay the drop to the valley below: the slopes turning crimson and gold, the ranges beyond folding one after the other against the sky, already hazy in the afternoon light. To his right, the mountain itself formed the background to the garden, deep green with cedars, against which bamboo trunks stood out, slender and graceful, and the white splash of the waterfall fell like spun threads over the gleaming rocks. He climbed a little among the ferns, and looked back down on the garden. From here the rocks looked like mountains, the shrubs like entire forests. He could see the whole of the Middle Country in this small plot of land, its ranges and rivers. Then the illusion was broken by a figure appearing through the bushes – but not before, for a moment, she had seemed like a goddess walking through her creation.

He saw a young woman of great beauty, which surprised him, for no one had told him she was beautiful. Her hair, long and thick, framed her pale face with its small mouth and leaf-shaped eyes. She wore a robe of a yellow the same colour as the falling ginkgo leaves, embroidered with golden pheasants. She made no sign of having seen him, but went to the edge of the stream where a wooden stepped bridge had been built across the iris beds, and gazed away from him out over the valley, as though drinking in the perfection of the view.

Despite her beauty – or maybe even because of it: he had been imagining her as a ruler; now he saw her as a woman, a very young one – he thought he would leave without speaking to her; but she stood between him and his way out. He thought, If she speaks to me I will stop. If she says nothing I will simply pass by her.

He stepped down the path and across the stream. She turned at the sound of his feet on the small pebbles of the path, and their eyes met.

'Lord Otori?' she said.

In the years that followed, he would watch her grow into a woman of composure and self-control. At that moment he was aware of the girl she still was, not much older than him, despite her apparent calmness, unsure, not quite grown up, although she was a married woman and already a mother.

He bowed in response, but said nothing, and she went on, a little hurriedly, 'I am Maruyama Naomi. I've always wanted to see this garden. I am a great admirer of the work of Sesshu. He was a frequent visitor to my home town. We almost consider him one of ours.'

'Sesshu must belong to the entire world,' Shigeru replied. 'Not even the Otori can claim to own him. But I was thinking just now how this garden reflects the Middle Country, in miniature.'

'You must know it well?'

'I spent a year here. I have brought my brother for a similar stay.'

'I saw him earlier; he is like you.' She smiled. 'And then you will return to Hagi?'

'Yes, I'll spend the winter there.'

They were both silent after this brief exchange. The noise from the waterfall seemed even louder. A flock of sparrows rose from the ground and fluttered into the branches of a maple tree, scattering the crimson leaves.

There is no point in saying anything, Shigeru thought. She is only a girl: she can be no help to me.

'Lord Otori is fond of hawking, I believe,' she said suddenly.

'When I have the time; it is a fine pursuit.'

'Did the plains of Kibi give you satisfaction?'

'I enjoyed the outing, but had hoped for a greater catch.'

'Sometimes the catch is greater than you bargain for,' she said, with the hint of a smile. 'As it must have been at Chigawa!'

'Does everyone know this story?' Shigeru asked.

'Probably too many people for your good,' she said, gazing intently at his face. 'You are in great danger.' She gestured towards the garden. 'The Middle Country is open to the East.'

'But protected to the West?' he questioned.

'Let us walk a little,' she said, without replying directly. 'There is a pavilion, I believe. My woman will make sure no one disturbs us.

'You may know,' she said when they were seated in the pavilion, 'that my marriage allies the Maruyama closely with the Tohan. Everyone expects this to bring our domain into line with Iida. But I am reluctant to allow ourselves to be controlled by the Tohan. I am afraid above all that our ancient tradition of inheriting from mother to daughter will be abolished. I have a three-year-old daughter. I am determined she will inherit from me. Despite my marriage, despite the alliance, I will always resist any attempt to change this.

'My husband has told me repeatedly how much the Iida family dislike and resent this tradition. The Iida hate everything that they suspect questions or challenges their right to absolute power. I have been to Inuyama; I have seen the way they treat their women, how women have been reduced, over the years in which the warrior class has risen to power, to the level of objects, to be used in marriage alliances or to give their husbands children, but never to be allowed equal rank or even any real power. Only Maruyama is different.'

She looked away over the valley, and then her eyes returned to his face. 'Will Lord Otori help me to protect my domain and my people?'

'I was looking to the Seishuu for help,' he admitted.

'Then we must help each other. We will be allies.'

'Can you bring the whole of the West into alliance with the Otori?' he queried, and added, 'I need more than sympathy. I don't mean to be insulting, but I have seen how the Iida operate in the East, the way they have dominated the Tohan, destroying those families that will not submit to them; their use of children, especially daughters, as hostages. Forgive me, but you are particularly vulnerable. You say you have a three-year-old daughter: your husband has strong ties with the Iida family; your daughter will be sent to Inuyama as soon as she is old enough.'

'Maybe. I have to be prepared for that, but at the moment not even Iida Sadamu has the power to demand hostages from the Maruyama. And if the Otori can hold him in check, he never will.'

'The Middle Country is a useful defence,' he said, with some bitterness. 'But if we fall, you will follow.'

'The Seishuu know this,' she replied. 'That is why Iida will find no allies among us.'

'We cannot fight on two fronts,' he said. 'But I also should not leave Yamagata undefended, to the south and west.'

'You have my promise that we will not attack, nor permit any Tohan incursions.'

He could not help staring at her, filled with doubt. How could she make such assurances? Even Arai Daiichi, a man, an eldest son, had not been able to promise this. She could have come to him with Iida's knowledge, acting as a decoy to give him false security.

'You can trust me,' she said quietly. 'I swear it.'

So Muto Shizuka had also sworn to him – and in front of witnesses. Here they were overheard by no one other than the sparrows.

'Do you trust no one?' she questioned, when he had been silent for a long time.

'I trust Matsuda Shingen,' he said.

'Then I will swear it in front of him.'

'I believe your intention,' Shigeru said. 'It is your ability to achieve it that I have to doubt.'

'Because I am a woman?'

He saw anger flash briefly in her face, and felt obscurely disappointed in himself for persisting in insulting her. 'Forgive me,' he said. 'Not only that – because of the circumstances –'

She interrupted him. 'If we are to deal with each other we must be honest from the start. You think I am not used to the way you look at me. I have been accustomed to it since I was a child. I know all your thoughts: I have had them voiced to me with far less courtesy and forbearance than you show, all my life. I am used to dealing with men, older than you, with less hereditary power maybe, but certainly with more deviousness. I know how to achieve my own ends and how to enforce my will. My clan obey me; I am surrounded by retainers I can trust. Where is my husband now, do you suppose? He stayed in Maruyama, on my orders. I travel without him when I please.' She stared at him, holding his gaze. 'Our alliance will only work, Lord Otori, if you understand all of this.'

Something was exchanged between them, some deep recognition. She spoke from the same assurance of power that he had, so profound it was as if it formed the marrow of his bones. They had both been raised in the same way, to be the head of their clan. She was his equal; she was Iida Sadamu's equal.

'Lady Maruyama,' he said formally, 'I trust you and I accept your offer of alliance. Thank you: you have my deepest gratitude.'

She replied in similar vein. 'Lord Otori, from today the Maruyama and the Otori are allies. I am deeply grateful to you for championing my cause.'

He felt the smile break out on his face, and she also smiled frankly at him. The moment went on a little too long, and she spoke into a silence that had become almost awkward. 'Will you return to the women's rooms with me? I will prepare tea.'

'Gladly,' he replied.

She bowed deeply and rose to her feet. Shigeru followed her along the path, between the rocks and the dark-leafed shrubs. They walked around the side of the main halls and courtyards of the temple, and descended the slope to where a group of small buildings were set aside for the use of women visitors. The main guest rooms lay a little further up the hill, around the hot springs, and beyond them, beneath the huge cedars, were the graves of the Otori lords and their retainers, the moss-covered headstones and lanterns dating back for hundreds of years. Doves were croo-crooing from the roofs, and the sparrows chattered in the eaves. From the forest beyond came the poignant autumn cry of kites. In the inner depths of the temple, a bell pealed out clearly.

'It will be cold tonight,' Lady Maruyama remarked.

'Will you stay here?'

'No, I will stay at the inn at the foot of the mountain, and return to Maruyama tomorrow. You will remain here for a few days?'

'Two at most. I must make sure my brother is settled in, and there are several matters on which I need to seek Matsuda's advice. Then I have various affairs to deal with in Yamagata – the fief is administered from there at this time of year. But I will be back in Hagi before the solstice, before the snow.'

They came to the veranda of the women's guest house, and stepped out of their shoes onto the boards. A woman a few years older than Naomi came out to greet them.

'This is my companion, Sugita Sachie,' Lady Maruyama said.

'Please come in, Lord Otori. It is a very great honour.'

When they were seated, Sachie brought tea utensils and hot water, and Lady Maruyama prepared the tea. Her movements were precise and elegant; the tea was bitter and foaming. After they had drunk, Lady Maruyama said, 'You are acquainted with Sachie's older sister, I believe. She is married to Otori Eijiro.'

Shigeru smiled. 'I am hoping to break my journey with them on the way home. It will be a pleasure to report this meeting to your sister. I admire your brother-in-law greatly.'

'Sachie writes very often to her sister,' Lady Maru-yama said. 'You may receive messages from her, from time to time.'

'I look forward to it,' Shigeru said. The family connection reassured him. They conversed in general terms about Eijiro's family, and then about painting, and poetry. Her education seemed as broad as his, and she could obviously read men's language. Then the conversation became more personal – he found himself sharing with her his concerns for the well-being of the people, his desire for justice.

'Our recent confrontation with the Tohan in the East took place because they came across the borders, and were torturing and killing our people.'

He remembered the woman from Chigawa who had told him that many of her sect, the Hidden, sought refuge in Maruyama; indeed Nesutoro, the man he had rescued, was on his way there with Shigeru's letters of protection.

'We heard something of this.' Lady Maruyama exchanged a swift glance with Sachie. 'The Tohan persecution of the Hidden is another reason why I will never let them take over Maruyama. I do not speak of this openly, and I am trusting you not to divulge it, but these people are under my protection.'

'I know very little of them,' he replied, half wanting to ask her more, directly. 'But I find torture abhorrent: its use to force people to deny a deeply held belief is barbaric, not worthy of our class.'

'Then we have another reason to unite against Iida,' she said.

He rose to take his leave; she remained seated, but bowed deeply to the ground, her hair parting slightly to reveal the nape of her neck. He was surprised and rather ashamed of the strength of his desire to slide his hands under the silky mass and feel the shape of her head in the cup of his palms.

CHAPTER TWENTY-SIX

Two days later, Shigeru bade farewell to his brother and began the journey back to Hagi. The weather changed and became showery. The rain was cold; the easterly wind had a frosty bite, reminding him of the coming snows of winter. Kiyoshige was waiting with the horses at the foot of the mountain, together with Otori Danjo and Harada, the messenger he had sent to arrange the meetings with the Seishuu. They rode to Misumi, Danjo's home, and the two men told Shigeru their opinions of their undertaking.

'Arai Daiichi has not really changed since we were boys – he was always the leader, always fearless,' Danjo remarked.

'He is a man of huge abilities,' Shigeru replied. 'And, I would think, very ambitious.'

'He is irked, I suspect, by his position among the Seishuu – heir to a remote, not very wealthy domain, threatened by his nearest neighbours, the Noguchi, and kept from real power by his father's refusal to die or retire. He is attracted to the Otori alliance because it would give him equal power with Lady Maruyama, but he dare not support it openly – such negotiations would seem like treachery to his father or to Iida, and either one would not hesitate to demand he take his own life.'

'I had hoped for much more,' Shigeru admitted.

'Our efforts have not been a complete failure,' Danjo replied. 'I believe the Arai will follow Maruyama's lead, and not join in an attack from the East. At this stage, it may be the best you can hope for. And you may have started an alliance which can only be good for the Middle Country. You, Arai Daiichi, Maruyama Naomi are all young. Who knows what great things you might achieve in the future?'

'You are optimistic, like your father,' Shigeru said, smiling.

'I agree with Lord Danjo,' Harada said. 'Lady Maruyama seemed to grasp immediately the significance of your journey and your desire to meet her. She had been considering approaching your father, but early attempts had not met with much encouragement.'

'I knew nothing of them,' Shigeru exclaimed. 'So much time has been wasted!'

'You cannot blame yourself,' Kiyoshige said. 'We have been fully occupied in the East for the past two summers.'

'And will be next summer,' Shigeru replied. They rode in silence for a while, each wrapped in thoughts of the coming war.

Harada said, 'Lord Otori, I thought you would like to know, I saw the man we rescued, Nesutoro, in Maruyama. He is settled with some of his people, and is learning a trade – basketmaking or something of that sort. His niece, the girl, Mari, has found work in the kitchens of the castle.'

'I am glad they are safe,' Shigeru replied, a little surprised that Harada should know the girl's name, should have remembered it. He shot a look at his retainer, but the man's swarthy face revealed nothing. Yet Shigeru knew how moved Harada had been by the courage, suffering and death of Tomasu, and by Nesutoro's fortitude. He wondered if some deeper connection had been made: was it possible for a warrior like Harada to be attracted to the beliefs of the Hidden? He would have to question him further about it.

How little he really knew about any of these men, of their inner beliefs, hopes, ambitions and fears. He expected their loyalty and their obedience to his wishes: in their turn they demanded the same obedience from the men who served them, and so it went, through the whole interlocking hierarchy of the clan, everyone linked to everyone else through a net of loyalty and obligation. But someone like Nesutoro stood outside the net: he would only obey some unseen force, a supposed god who was above all human rulers and who would judge them after death. And he would not take life; neither his own nor anyone else's.

It was hardly the sort of thing he wanted to think about while he was preparing for a battle in which he would have to take the lives of many, and which he himself might not survive.

They did not linger at Misumi, spending only one night there. Shigeru talked till late with Eijiro, and received his assurances that the branch family would start preparing for war and mustering men, as far as the snow permitted: if Irie were successful with the Noguchi he now had the whole of the Middle Country preparing for war. The Western borders were safe from attack; he resolved he would send Kiyoshige and Harada back to Chigawa before the end of the year. He wished he knew what Sadamu was up to, how many men he was assembling, what alliances he was brokering... but at least Kiyoshige and Harada would keep an eye on what was happening beyond the border, and would give warning of any imminent attack. He was not displeased with the work of the past year. But the hardest task that lay ahead of him, he suspected, would be in Hagi itself, where his adversaries were his own family, his father and his uncles.

Shigeru's first resolve was to take control of the castle, and on the second day after his return he requested a private meeting with his father. When he arrived in the early afternoon, his mother was already in the room: she clearly intended to stay, and on the whole he was glad of it, for he knew he could count on her support against his uncles. He had given orders that they were not to attend;

if they came to the hall they were not to be admitted. It was the first time he had opposed them so openly, but he had even more unpleasant commands in store for them, and he felt confident enough in his increased popularity and authority to confront them now.

His father did not look well, and when Shigeru enquired after his health said he had been troubled by back pain, urinated frequently and consequently slept badly, and had little appetite. Wine only made his symptoms worse, and he dreaded the cold. Despite the charcoal braziers, the room was already freezing. His father's skin was tinged with yellow, and his hands trembled as they plucked at the amulets he carried in his sleeve. A special tea was brought, heavily laced with valerian; it seemed to alleviate the shivering, but made his father's mind sluggish and confused.

Shigeru conveyed formal greetings from the branch families and vassals, and then told his parents the essence of his activities: the preparation for war, the agreement with the Arai and the Maruyama. His father looked troubled, but his mother gave him her open approval.

'I should inform my brothers,' Shigemori said.

'No, Father, that is precisely what I do not want you to do. All these negotiations must be kept as secret as possible. I know you think my uncles have been of some support to you in the past, but I believe their influence has not been beneficial to the clan. Now I am of age there is no need for them to involve themselves so closely in our affairs.'

'They could be sent away,' his mother observed. 'They both have country estates that are pitifully neglected. There are too many people in the castle – all those children they keep producing. Lord Shigeru is right: we no longer need your brothers' advice. You must listen to your son.'

Shigeru was delighted with this advice from his mother, and, with his father's reluctant permission, immediately put it into practice. He summoned his uncles the following day and told them of his desires, was unmoved by their fury or their arguments, and insisted that they retire to Shimano and Mizutani at once.

Unfortunately, it proved harder to get rid of them than either he or his mother had expected. There were endless excuses: one of the wives was about to give birth, a child fell ill with a dangerous fever, the day was inauspicious, the river was in flood, horses could not be found; there was even a small earthquake. Then the year turned; the festival had to be celebrated in Hagi. As Shigeru returned home from the temple at Tokoji in the early hours of the morning on the first day of the year, snow was falling. It fell almost without let-up for six weeks, closing the city off from the rest of the country, and equally preventing his uncles from leaving.

CHAPTER TWENTY-SEVEN

Snow fell over the Three Countries, turning the land-scape white, covering the forests with the heavy blossom of winter, muffling sound and masking colour, putting an end to all outdoor activity from farming to war.

It fell on Inuyama, where Iida Sadamu planned his spring campaigns; on the temple at Terayama, where Otori Takeshi chafed against the bitter cold and the harsh discipline; on Maruyama, where Lady Naomi realized she was expecting another child; on the plain of Yaegahara, where only wolves and foxes left their tracks; on Kushimoto, where Shigeru's wife Moe refused to answer her mother's probing questions about marriage and grandchildren, listened to her father's fears about the coming war, and hoped war would come and that her husband would be killed in it, for she could see no other honourable escape from her marriage.

The snow filled Akane with delight, for it would keep Shigeru in Hagi and his wife in Kushimoto. She loved winter, despite the cold and the hardship: she loved the look of the snow-covered roofs, the icicles hanging from the eaves, the icy branches of trees etched delicately against the pale winter sky. The hot spring baths were even more pleasing when the air was freezing and snow melted on hair and skin. And what could be more pleasurable than the warmth of her lover's body on a cold night under piles of quilts when the snow fell too heavily for him to go home?

She was glad that Moe was away and that there was no sign of reconciliation or, more importantly, of a child. The longer the marriage went without producing a child, she reasoned, the greater were her chances of being permitted to bear one. For Shigeru had to have heirs for the continuity of his family and the stability of the clan. She had to time it right, to find herself pregnant at just the right moment, and then to give him a son.

When the weather permitted, she went to see the old man, taking him charcoal and padded clothes, hot stews and tea. And she brought back secretly the gifts he gave her in return: mummified roots like half-formed embryos, dried leaves and seeds with a bitter taste, tassels woven from human hair, all charms to help her capture Shigeru's love and protect the child that would be born from it.

She shared, for different reasons, Shigeru's eagerness to see Lord Shoichi and Lord Masahiro leave the city, and was angry and disappointed when their departure was prevented by the first snows. Masahiro had not contacted her again, but she was aware that he had her watched, and that sooner or later he would demand another payment for his leniency towards Hayato's family.

Her unease about this was increased by some indefinable change in Shigeru's attitude towards her. There was no indication that the charms were working – it would be more true to say the opposite. She told herself it was because of the preoccupations of politics and war, that she could not expect him to remain the passionate boy who had been on the brink of falling in love with her. He still took delight in her company, was indeed still passionate in bed, but she knew he was not in love with her despite all the charms she had tried to bind him with. He came to her frequently – Kiyoshige was away in Chigawa, Lord Irie still in the south, Takeshi at Terayama, and he had few companions – and they talked as they always had, yet she felt he was withholding something from her: he was growing away from her. She did not think she would ever see him weep again.

Their relationship settled into what it was supposed to be: she could not complain about it; she had accepted it, knowing what it was to be; no one had rushed her or forced her; yet she had hoped for much more, and now the new coolness in Shigeru's attitude inflamed her love for him. She had told herself she would never make the mistake of falling in love, but she found herself consumed by her need for him, her desire for his child, her craving for his love. She did not dare express it, or even speak to him about jealousy any more. When he was not with her, she longed for him with physical anguish; when they were together, the thought of him leaving was as painful as if her arm were being wrenched from her body. Yet she gave no sign of her feelings, telling herself she must enjoy what she had, how great her fortune was compared to many. There was no doubt it was a convenient arrangement for him; it gave him a great amount of pleasure with very little cost or pain. But he was the heir to the clan, she a nobody, not even a warrior's daughter. And wasn't the world arranged for the convenience and pleasure of men? She visited Haruna from time to time to remind herself of this. Haruna returned her visits and once brought Hayato's widow and her sons to thank Akane. The boys were intelligent and good-looking. She thought they would be kind, like their father. She became interested in their welfare and sent the family gifts. She had saved their lives – in a way, they became her children.

She went to the stone bridge at least once a week to take offerings to her father, and to listen to his voice in the icy water as the tide pulled it through the arches. One bleak afternoon, when the light was fading fast, she stepped from her palanquin and walked to the centre of the bridge, her maid following her with a red umbrella, for a few flakes of snow were falling.

The tide prevented ice forming on the surface of the river, but the ground on the banks was frozen hard, and the rushes stiff with frost and frozen snow. Someone had placed winter oranges in front of the stone, and they were also frozen solid, embedded in the crusted snow, tiny ice particles glinting against their bright colour in the last of the light.

She took a flask of wine from the maid and poured it into a cup, tipped a few drops out onto the ground and drank the rest herself. The wind off the water brought tears to her eyes, and she allowed herself to weep for a few moments, for her father, for herself, in their imprisonment.

She could not help being aware of the picture it must make: the red umbrella, the woman bent over in grief, and wished somehow Shigeru might be watching her while she was unaware of his gaze.

As she clapped her hands and bowed to her father's spirit, she realized that someone was watching her from the other side of the bridge. There were a few people in the streets, hurrying home before nightfall, heads bent against the snow, which was falling more heavily now. One or two of them glanced at Akane and called out a respectful greeting, but none of them lingered, except this one man.

As she returned to the palanquin, he crossed the street and walked beside her for the last few paces. She stopped and looked directly at him: she did not know his name but recognized him as one of Masahiro's retainers. She felt the sudden thud in the pulse of throat and temple as her heart seemed to plummet.

'Lady Akane,' the man said. 'Lord Masahiro sends you his greetings.'

'I have nothing to say to him,' she replied hastily.

'He has a request to make of you. He instructed me to give you this.' He drew a small package from his sleeve, wrapped in an ivory and purple coloured cloth.

She hesitated for a moment, then took it abruptly and handed it to the maid. The man bowed to her and walked away.

'Let us hurry home,' Akane said. 'It is so cold.' She was indeed chilled to the bone.

By the time they arrived at the house, night had already fallen. The wind soughed in the pine trees, and a dull moaning came from the waves on the beach. Suddenly Akane was sick of winter, sick of the endless snow and the cold. She gazed briefly around the colourless garden. Surely the plum, at least, would be in blossom? But the branches were still dark – the only whiteness snow and frost. She hurried into the house, calling for the maids to bring braziers and more lamps. She craved light and warmth, sunshine, colour and flowers.

When she was a little warmer, she told the girl to bring Masahiro's package. She untied the knot and slipped the silk wrapping away. Inside was a fan: she had seen similar ones at Haruna's establishment. It was exquisitely painted: on one side a woman in a spring robe gazed at wisteria flowers; on the other side the robe had fallen open; the scene was less delicate.

She was not shocked by the fan: the painting was beautifully executed and pleasingly erotic in mood. At any other time she would have been thrilled with this gift. The artist was well known and widely admired; the fans were collected avidly: they were extremely expensive. It was not something she wanted to receive from a man like Masahiro, but she could not bring herself to send it back or to throw it away. She wrapped it up again and told the maid to put it in the storeroom. She could not help thinking that she might have need of such treasures, one day, when Shigeru tired of her, or if he died...

Then she took up the letter that came with the present.

Masahiro wrote in couched sentences: an enquiry after her health, a desire to hear her news, comments about the harsh weather and how he worried for his children when there was so much sickness around, a warmly expressed hope that they might have the pleasure of meeting soon, and his most humble and heartfelt regards to his nephew. She told the maid to bring the charcoal brazier outside into the garden, and wrapping herself in a silky fur robe she tore the letter up and fed it piece by piece into the flames. The garden seemed full of sadness and ghosts; a sleety snow was falling against the smoke. Akane felt haunted, by her dead lover and by her own sorcery. The charms by which she had closed Moe's womb lay a few paces from her, buried in the frozen ground. Hayato too lay in the cold earth, along with the children they might have had together.

Even when the letter had been reduced to ash, indistinguishable from the sleet, she felt its veiled hypocritical phrases coil around her heart.

What did Lord Masahiro really want? Were he and his brother seriously seeking to usurp Shigeru? Or were his actions merely those of a malicious and inquisitive man who, deprived of real power, liked to play these spiteful games? She read his message without difficulty: the references to 'news' and 'children' were all too clear. She wished she had not met the boys: their faces with their smooth childish skin and clear eyes rose before her, as demanding as their father's ghost. They had found their way into her heart: she could not sacrifice them now.

She wondered if she should tell Shigeru of his uncle's demands, but feared too much losing his good opinion of her – or worse, losing him altogether: if he suspected her of spying on him or of compromising him in any way, she knew he would stop seeing her; and now his love and need for her were diminishing... She would be shamed in front of the whole city; she would never recover. I must continue to play them both, she thought. It should not be too hard: they are only men, after all.

When she returned inside she was shivering, and it took a long time to get warm.

Throughout the winter she delivered snippets to Masahiro that she thought might keep him interested. Some she made up; some were loosely based on what she gleaned from Shigeru. None, she thought, was of any great importance.

CHAPTER TWENTY-EIGHT

Muto Shizuka spent the winter in the southern town of Kumamoto, with Arai Daiichi, the eldest son of the clan lord. She could have seen herself openly acknowledged as Arai's mistress, for it was said he was so infatuated with her that he would deny her nothing, but beneath her lively, charming exterior she was secretive by nature as well as by upbringing and training, and she preferred to keep the relationship hidden.

Her father had died when she was twelve years old, and her mother lived with relatives in Kumamoto, a merchant family by the name of Kikuta whom the Arai knew mostly as money-lenders. Her father had been the eldest son of a Yamagata family called Muto, and Shizuka was very close to his relatives, writing to them almost every week and often sending gifts. She told Arai stories about this family, embroidering them with warmth and humour, entertaining him with their petty feuds and follies, until he felt he almost lived among them. What he did not know was that the Kikuta and the Muto were the two most important families of the Tribe.

Like most of the warrior class, Arai knew very little about the other castes that made up the society of the Three Countries. Farmers and peasants worked the land and provided warrior families with rice and other basic supplies; they were usually easy enough to handle, having no fighting skills and very little courage. Occasionally starvation made them desperate enough to riot, but it also weakened them, and unrest was usually quelled without difficulty. Merchants were even more despicable than peasants, since they lived and grew fat on other people's labour, but they seemed to become more essential every season, producing foodstuffs, wine, oil and soybean paste as well as many luxuries that added to the delights of life – fine clothing, lacquered boxes and dishes, fans and bowls – and importing expensive and exotic items from the mainland or from distant islands to the south: spices for cooking, herbs for medicine, gold leaf and golden thread, dyes, perfumes and incense.

Arai was a sensual man with a prodigious appetite for all life had to offer, and enough good taste to demand the best. He knew of the Tribe – had heard them spoken of – but thought they were some sort of guild, no more. Shizuka never told him that she had been born into the Tribe, was related to the Masters of both the Muto and the Kikuta families, had inherited many skills, and had been sent to Kumamoto as a spy.

Both families at that time were employed by Iida Sadamu as spies and assassins; and through them Iida, determined to deal with his traditional enemies the Otori, and in particular with the man he had come to hate more than anyone else in the Three Countries, Otori Shigeru, kept a close watch on the movements and intentions of the Seishuu in the West.

In the early spring, Shizuka sought her lord's permission to visit her relatives in Yamagata. She would have visited them without his permission, but it suited her to plead with Arai and then express her gratitude for his generosity. She had received a request to visit from her family there: she had much to report to her father's younger brother, Muto Kenji, who was about to take over the mastership of the family from her grandfather, and a personal matter to discuss with him, one that filled her with a mixture of joy and trepidation.

She went by the same route she had travelled with Arai when they had gone to Kibi to meet Shigeru, but she already knew that she would be returning by the more easterly road through Hofu and Noguchi. She did not know what the purpose of the mission was to be, but suspected it would be some secret communication between Iida and the Noguchi family, something so secret it called for the most skilled of messengers.

She went straight to the main Muto house in Yamagata, and was greeted with warmth and hardly given time to wash the dust from her feet before her uncle's wife, Seiko, said, 'Kenji wants to talk to you as soon as possible. I'll tell him you're here.'

Shizuka followed her aunt into the interior of the house, through the shop, where a cheerful older woman was packing soybean paste into wooden containers and a thin man was using an abacus and writing accounts on a scroll. The smell of fermenting beans pervaded the whole house: she could picture the vats in the sheds behind, weighted down with boulders to press the essence from the beans.

'Could I just have a mouthful of rice?' Shizuka said. 'The journey has made me feel a little nauseated; if I eat something it will pass.'

Seiko looked at her sharply and raised her eyebrows. 'Do you have news for us?'

Shizuka tried to smile. 'I should speak to my uncle first.'

'Yes, of course. Come and sit down. I'll bring food and tea, and Kenji will come to you in a little while.'

Her uncle was twenty-six years of age, only eight years older than she was. Like most of the Muto family, his appearance was unremarkable, his height average, his build deceptively slight. He managed to convey a mild, almost scholarly air, could discuss art and philosophy endlessly, enjoyed wine and women but never got drunk and never apparently fell in love, though there were rumours that he had been enthralled by a fox-woman in his youth, and for this reason was sometimes known by the nickname, the Fox. He had been married for several years to Seiko, who was from the Muto family too, and they had one child: a girl of about eight years, Yuki. It was commonly held to be a disaster that Kenji had no more children, legitimate or illegitimate – it was certainly not due to any lack of activity on his part, though the old women of the Tribe muttered that he scattered his seed too liberally; he should concentrate on one field and sow that – for in him all the ancient skills of the Tribe seemed to have been concentrated to an unusually high degree, along with the equally important character traits of ruthlessness and cynicism, and for those not to be passed on to future generations was considered unfortunate in the extreme. Everyone's hopes were pinned on Yuki, and she was spoiled, in particular by her father, though her mother was less indulgent. The girl was already showing signs of great talent, but she was headstrong and self-willed, and Shizuka knew it was feared she would not live long enough to have children of her own, but would meet an early death through her own recklessness or carelessness. Talents were of no use unless they were linked with character and controlled by training.

Yuki came running in now, a tray in her hands.

'Careful, careful,' Shizuka said, taking it from her.

'Cousin!' the girl cried. 'Welcome!'

Her face was vivid, dark-eyed and heavy-browed. Not beautiful, but full of life and energy. Her hair was thick, and she wore it plaited.

'Mother said you were hungry. We have been making rice balls. Here, eat. This one is salted plum, and this one dried octopus.'

Shizuka knelt and set the tray on the floor. Yuki knelt down beside her, waited with hardly concealed impatience for Shizuka to help herself, then took a rice ball and crammed it into her mouth. Almost immediately, she leaped to her feet again and announced that she would bring tea, and, running from the room, collided with her mother. Seiko just managed to rescue the tray, laden with tea and cups; she placed it on the floor and gave her daughter a slap.

'Go and tell your father his niece is here,' she screeched. 'And walk, like a girl should!'

'She drives me mad,' she said to Shizuka. 'Sometimes I think she is possessed. Of course, her father spoils her. He wishes she was a boy, and treats her like one. But she's not going to grow up to be a man, is she? She'll be a woman, and she has to know how to behave like one. Take my advice, Shizuka: if you have children, make sure you have sons.'

'If only one could choose,' Shizuka said, without smiling. She took the bowl of tea and drank.

'Seedlings can be thinned out,' Seiko commented, referring to the practice common among villagers of leaving newborn infants to die, especially if there were too many girls already.

'But all the children of the Tribe are valued,' Shizuka replied. 'Girls as much as boys.' She felt suddenly cold and feared she might vomit; a year ago she had been given a brew of herbs by Seiko in this very house. All the fibres of her body trembled in the memory.

'If they are talented. And obedient.' Seiko sighed. They heard Yuki's footsteps, pounding like a pony across the yard. The little girl stopped abruptly and stepped out of her sandals onto the boards of the veranda with exaggerated decorum. She came into the room, bowed gracefully to Shizuka, and said, using formal language, 'My father will attend on you presently.'

'There,' Seiko said approvingly. 'You can behave nicely when you want to. Be like your cousin. See how pretty Shizuka looks, how elegant her clothes are. Do you know, she has captured the heart of a mighty warrior with her charms. You would never know she has the ruthlessness and the fighting skills of a man!'

'I wish I were a boy!' Yuki said to Shizuka.

'To tell you the truth, I wished the same thing at your age,' Shizuka replied. 'But if it is our fate to be born into a woman's body, we must make the best of it. Be thankful you were born into the Tribe. If you study and train hard, you will have a better life than any woman of the warrior class. And if you are obedient and do exactly as you are told.'

'I am to go away this summer,' Yuki said, her eyes glowing. 'I am going to my grandparents, in the secret village.'

'You will have to behave there!' her mother told her. 'Your father will not be there to run to every time you don't get your own way.'

'It will be the making of her,' Shizuka said, remembering the years she herself had spent in the Tribe village, Kagemura, in the mountains behind Yamagata, developing her talents and learning all the skills of the Tribe. 'She has a great future ahead of her.'

Even as she spoke, she wished she could take back the words. She felt a premonition, as if she had tempted fate. She feared that Yuki's life would indeed be short.

'Be careful,' she said, as she heard her uncle step onto the veranda.

'She doesn't know the meaning of the word,' Seiko grumbled, but she took Yuki's hand gently and caressed her before leading her from the room. In that moment Shizuka saw that Seiko, for all her criticism, loved her daughter as deeply as her husband did.

'Welcome, Shizuka: it's been a long time,' her uncle said, using the customary greeting perfunctorily. 'You are well, I hope.' His gaze swept over her and she felt he saw everything about her. She gazed at him in the same way, her eyes trained to detect the slightest changes in expression and demeanour, to read the language of the body, particularly hard in Kenji's case as he was so adept in disguising his own self and assuming any number of other roles.

'We'd better go within,' he said. 'No one will overhear us or disturb us there.'

There was a concealed room in the centre of the house, behind a false wall released by turning one of the decorated bosses in the rafters. Kenji lifted the wall aside effortlessly, and replaced it from the inside. It fell into place with hardly a sound. The room was narrow, the light dim. Kenji sat cross-legged on the floor, and she knelt opposite him. He drew a small package from the breast of his robe, and placed it on the floor.

'This is an exceptionally important document,' he said. 'I've just brought it myself from Inuyama. It contains a letter from Sadamu to Noguchi Masayoshi. I'm not supposed to know its exact contents, but naturally I've opened it and read it. You are to give it to Kuroda Shintaro and to no one else. He will hand it on to Lord Noguchi.'

Shizuka bowed slightly. 'Am I allowed to know what the message is?'

He did not answer her directly. 'How are things between you and Arai?'

'I believe he loves me,' she said in a low voice. 'He trusts me completely.'

'It's very satisfactory,' Kenji said. 'Of course, no one knew this would happen when you were sent back to Kumamoto, but it couldn't have worked out better. Well done!'

'Thank you, Uncle.'

'And you? I trust you are not going to lose your head over him?'

'Maybe there is some danger,' she admitted. 'It's impossible not to respond when such a man loves you.'

Kenji snorted disparagingly. 'Be careful. He may turn against you as suddenly as he fell for you, especially if he feels deceived or affronted by you. He is as big a fool as any other warrior.'

'No, he is not a fool,' she replied. 'He is quick-tempered and rash, but his mind is astute and he is very brave.'

'Well, this flirtation with Otori Shigeru has irritated Sadamu enormously. You'd better warn Arai to dissociate himself from the Otori and make a clear declaration of support for the Tohan, or he'll find himself dispossessed this time next year, if he's still alive.'

'So Iida will fight the Otori this year?'

'Any time now. He will move into the east of the Middle Country as soon as the Chigawa river subsides – three or four weeks by my reckoning. Your report last autumn of Shigeru's meetings with Arai and Lady Maruyama gave Sadamu the excuse he needed to attack without warning. He'll declare that the Otori provoked him and were themselves preparing to attack the Tohan. Everyone knows Shigeru has been mustering armed forces for the last year.' He tapped the package. 'But your report made Sadamu think about the west and south. He first made advances to Shirakawa, hoping to have him host the Tohan for a rear attack, but Shirakawa's a vacillator and will wait and see which way the wind blows before he makes up his mind, and Iida needs a firm ally in the south. Hence this letter.' Kenji smiled almost with glee, but his voice held an uncharacteristic note of regret. 'How I love treachery,' he said softly. 'Especially among the warrior class, who talk so much about loyalty and honour!'

'Yet people talk of Lord Shigeru as an honourable man. Have you ever met him?'

She had never seen Kenji look uncomfortable before. He frowned and tapped his leg with his hand impatiently. 'As a matter of fact I have. There is something about him... Well, there's no point talking about it.'

'I swore to Lord Otori that I would not betray him, but I did,' Shizuka said. She wanted to say more, but did not know how to express her feelings, indeed was not even sure what those feelings were. She knew Otori Shigeru was doomed by the letter that lay on the floor beside her, and could not help but be saddened. She had liked what she saw of him; people spoke highly of him and she knew many in both Yamagata and Chigawa pinned their hopes for a safe and peaceful existence on him. Their lives would be far more wretched under the Tohan.

She had entered his world and had made an oath to him according to the codes of that world. He was not to know that she was from the Tribe, who held no oaths binding, who answered only to themselves. Her betrayal was not great, perhaps, but it made her uncomfortable nonetheless. She had been obedient to the Tribe, but if she had been able to follow her own leanings...

Kenji was watching her closely. 'Don't become seduced by warriors,' he said. 'I know that their beliefs and their lives have a certain appeal: all that talk of honour and character, physical and moral courage; the clans, the ancient houses with the crests and swords and heroes. Most warriors are thugs and bullies, usually cowards: the ones who aren't cowards are in love with death.'

'The Tribe sent me to live among them,' she said. 'To a certain extent, I have to take on their beliefs.'

'Pretend to take them on,' Kenji corrected her. 'We expect your obedience to us above everything.'

'Of course,' she replied. 'Uncle, that is always without question.'

'So I believe,' he said. 'But you are still young and in a dangerous situation. I know you have the skills to survive, but only if your emotions are not involved.' He paused, and then went on: 'Especially if you bear Arai a child.'

She was startled despite herself. 'Is it obvious? I have told no one yet, not even Arai. I thought I should tell you first, in case...'

She knew if it did not suit the Tribe, they would make her get rid of it, as they had before. Her aunt Seiko, like all Tribe women, had many ways to abort unwanted children. She would be given the brew immediately, the child would be gone by nightfall. She felt the muscles of her belly clench in fear.

'Normally, as you know, we are not in favour of mixing the blood,' Kenji said. 'But I can see many advantages in your having this child. It will certainly give you a lasting relationship with Arai, even after your passion for each other wanes – it will, it will, believe me – but more importantly it may inherit your talents, and the Tribe has need of them.' He sighed. 'We seem to be dying out slowly: fewer children born every year, and only a handful of them showing any real talent. Deaths of people we can't afford to lose – your father, Kikuta Isamu – Isamu had no children, your father and myself only one... We must not get rid of any more children; any Tribe blood must be maintained. So have this child, have others. Arai will be delighted, and so will the Tribe – as long as you remember where your loyalties lie, and who the child ultimately belongs to.'

'I am happy,' she said. 'I really want it.'

For a moment a look of affection flickered on his face, softening it. 'When will it be born?'

'At the beginning of the tenth month.'

'Well, look after yourself. After this mission I'll try not to ask anything too difficult of you. Just the usual pillow talk from your warrior, which is obviously not disagreeable to you!'

As Shizuka took the package from the floor and tucked it inside her robe, she said, 'What happened to Isamu? No one ever speaks of him.'

'He's dead,' Kenji replied shortly. 'That's all I know.'

She knew from his tone there was no point in asking any more. She put the matter aside, but she did not forget it.

'Where shall I deliver the letter?' she said.

'You can stay in Noguchi at the inn near the bridge, run by the Kuroda family. Kuroda Shintaro will contact you there. Give it to no one but him. Now there's another terrible waste. Shintaro, the most talented assassin in the Three Countries, is also without children.'

She wanted to ask him more, about the exact contents of the letter, but decided it was better that she did not know why Iida Sadamu was writing to Lord Noguchi or what he was offering him. She would obey her uncle and deliver the letter as instructed, but she could not help recalling the Otori brothers, and their young companion, Mori Kiyoshige; she remembered the undisguised admiration in their glances and pitied them.

'Where will this battle take place?' she asked.

'Almost certainly on the plain of Yaegahara.'

CHAPTER TWENTY-NINE

Spring came late that year to the Three Countries, and when the thaw finally came it brought widespread flooding, rivers breaking their banks and bridges being washed away, hampering the movement of armed forces and communication between allies.

The first news Shigeru had was when Irie Masahide returned at the end of the third month from the south. Irie brought Moe back from her parents' house, where she had spent the winter. He was in an unusually optimistic frame of mind, having received firm assurances of support from Noguchi as well as from the Yanagi, Moe's family. Thus the south and the west were secured.

As soon as the weather allowed, Shigeru renewed his efforts to remove his uncles from the castle, persuading his father to impose a kind of exile on them, sending them away to the country and ordering them to refrain from any public activity. To his surprise, Shoichi, Masahiro and their families left without demur, in extravagant processions that had the townspeople gaping at the expense and cheering their departure all the more enthusiastically.

Masahiro sent one final letter to Akane, telling her he hoped she would not miss him too much, but not to concern herself: he would be back before very long. This letter she also burned, and she kept its message to herself.

Harada came from Chigawa with messages from Kiyoshige. As soon as the snow had melted, he said, Tohan troops had been gathering along the northeastern border, and seemed prepared to attack at any moment. Shigeru had two weeks at most to gather the Otori army.

Shigeru took this news to his father and called an urgent meeting with the elders and senior retainers, at which he announced his decision to move troops immediately along the coast road towards the border, to meet the Tohan on the plain of Yaegahara.

His uncles, of course, were not present, and though the option of trying to placate Iida by pulling back from Chigawa was put forward by Endo Chikara and others, Shigeru dismissed it at once, saying he would not yield a single acre of Otori land to the Tohan. He revealed now what he had kept secret all winter: the Western alliance, the securing of the south, and the readiness of the Otori forces. His opinion was that the Otori could defeat the Tohan now, on the battleground of their own choosing and on their own terms. If they were to appease the Tohan they would lose both these advantages, and would never recover them.

His father gave his full support both in the meeting and afterwards.

'You should stay in Hagi,' Shigeru advised him, but the old man had made up his mind.

'We will fight side by side. We must let no one say afterwards that the clan was divided, or that you acted alone and without my consent.'

'Then surely my uncles should also join us,' Shigeru said.

His father agreed, and messengers were dispatched to their country retreats; but first Shoichi and then Masahiro sent regretful answers: Shoichi had sprained his shoulder falling from a horse, and Masahiro's household was in the grip of some ominous illness, possibly measles or even smallpox. Spreading contagion could not be risked.

Lord Shigemori was enraged by these replies, but despite the insult Shigeru was relieved. If his uncles were not in wholehearted support of this policy, it was better that they stayed away. He would deal with them after the battle; in the meantime he was free from the irritation of their presence and their influence over his father.

Yet he was uneasy about their true intentions, and it seemed his father shared his suspicions. For many nights before their departure they had discussed preparations of the army, strategy and tactics; often his mother was also present. One night Shigemori dismissed the servants, saying he wished to speak in private to his son. Lady Otori also rose to leave.

'You may stay,' he said. 'There must be a witness to what I have to say.'

She sank to her knees and bowed to her husband before sitting erect again, silent and composed.

Lord Shigemori took his sword from the rack at the end of the room and placed it on the ground in front of Shigeru. It was the legendary snake sword, Jato, a long sword cast by one of the great swordsmiths in the capital, its scabbard and hilt decorated with bronze and mother-of-pearl settings. It had been given to the Otori hero Otori Takeyoshi, who had also been given one of the Emperor's concubines in marriage at the same time.

'You know the reputation of this sword?'

'Yes, Father.'

'It is said to choose its master: maybe this is true; I have no way of knowing. It came to me directly when my father died – he did not have the good fortune to die in battle, fighting his enemies, as I may have soon. He died of old age, surrounded by his sons; the sword passed to me as the eldest son.'

Lady Otori said, 'Your stepmother desired otherwise.'

His father smiled bitterly. 'Neither Shoichi nor Masahiro will ever hold Jato. They will never lead the Otori: they must not. Since your return from Terayama and your exploits on the Eastern borders I have become aware of their ambitions and their jealousy, their constant attempts to undermine you in my eyes, their intrigue and backbiting. If I fall in battle, Jato will make its way to you. You must take it, and live. Whatever the outcome of the battle, you must not take your own life, but must live and seek revenge. This is my command to you as your father.'

'And if the sword does not come to me?' Shigeru questioned.

'Then you may as well kill yourself, for if Jato is lost, our family is lost too; our line will be extinguished.'

'I understand,' Shigeru said. 'I will obey your wishes in this as in everything.'

His father smiled again, this time with affection. 'Your birth was long awaited, but I hold it the most fortunate event of my life. Despite all my own weaknesses and shortcomings, I have been truly blessed in my son.'

Shigeru was heartened by these words, and by the unity of purpose shared with his parents. His father also seemed strengthened by their reconciliation, and though Lord Shigemori consulted his customary priests and shamans, he did not allow the day of departure to be unduly delayed. The first faintly auspicious day was decided on.

CHAPTER THIRTY

Early in the fifth month, Shigeru left the city of Hagi with close to five thousand men. His father came with him. Lord Shigemori had his armour prepared and his warhorse brought in from pasture. The decision seemed to strengthen him, and he rode erect in the saddle, Jato at his side.

Shigeru had gone to Akane the day before to say goodbye to her. She had been strongly moved, had clung to him and wept, her usual self-control abandoned. His leave-taking of his wife had been much colder. He felt Moe was glad to see him go and would be relieved if he did not return, though her father and brothers would be fighting alongside him, and if he fell they probably would too. He wished he was leaving children behind, but then recalled that if he was defeated they also would die, and was relieved that he was to be spared that sorrow. At least Takeshi was safe at Terayama.

He rode alongside his father across the stone bridge a little before midday. Akane stood by her father's grave, among the townspeople who had gathered to bid the army farewell. Shigeru's eyes met hers, and on the far bank he turned to look back at her, as he had once before.

He had received messages from Mori Kiyoshige at Chigawa, saying the Tohan were amassing just over the border, as he had expected. There was no element of surprise in the attack. Everyone knew the battle was inevitable. The villagers along the road from Hagi were digging earthworks and mounds to protect themselves. Along the way, the army was joined by more retainers with their own armed forces. Others, such as Otori Eijiro, had travelled south of the ranges and through the pass known as White Pine Pass, and they met up a week later on the western edge of the Yaegahara plain. A small range of hills extended into the plain, and on top of the most easterly one stood a wooden fort. The range curved round to the southwest road, and here Shigeru expected to find the Otori vassals from the south: the Yanagi and the Noguchi. He sent Irie with a troop of men to make contact with them, and set up camp along the western bank of the small river that flowed north from the plain.

Messengers were also sent to Chigawa, where Kiyoshige was under instructions not to attempt to defend the town but to retreat to the plain, bringing the Tohan army into the encirclement of the Otori forces. The messengers returned with Harada, who informed Shigeru that all the indications were that the Tohan would advance as soon as dawn broke the following day. Their forces were estimated at around twelve thousand – outnumbering Shigeru and his vassals by three or four thousand. But the advantages of the terrain lay with the Otori: from midday on the light would favour them, and they would be defending their own land against invaders.

The foot soldiers had all carried long wooden spikes with them, and these were now erected in lines of palisades to slow the attack and give cover to bowmen. As the sun set, the smoke from hundreds of small fires rose in the still air. The hum of the army, the noise of men and horses drowned out the evening song of birds, but when night fell and the soldiers snatched a few hours of sleep, owls could be heard hooting from the mountain. The stars were brilliant but there was no moon; towards dawn a mist rose from the river, and when day broke the sky had become overcast.

Irie returned as Shigeru was eating, to tell him that Kitano had taken up position on the far east of the plain, concealing his men on the slopes of a wooded hill, and Noguchi was a little to the west of him, covering the road to the south. Yanagi and his sons were between Noguchi and Otori Eijiro, who was within sight of Shigeru's main force. Shigeru remained in the centre and sent his father with Irie to the eastern flank, beneath the protection of the wooden fort.

The men readied themselves: rows of bowmen and foot soldiers behind the palisades and along the banks of the river; horsemen with drawn swords, the horses restless and sweating in the still, warm morning; bannermen holding aloft the crested banners, the Otori heron seen everywhere, white against the deep blue background, together with the family crests of the vassals: the twin carp of the Noguchi, the chestnut leaf of Kitano, the galloping horse of the Mori, the willow leaves of the Yanagi, the peach blossom of the Miyoshi; here and there the scarlet and gold of decorated armour, helmets topped with ancient moons, stag antlers or stars, and the flash of steel swords, knives and lance tips. The grass was shooting new bright green, and flowers dotted it, white, pink and pale blue.

Shigeru felt his heart swell with pride and confidence. He could not conceive that this magnificent army could be defeated. On the contrary, the day had come when the Otori would defeat the Tohan once and for all, and drive them back beyond Inuyama.

In the distance, across the plain, a cloud of dust signalled horsemen approaching, and before long Kiyoshige, Miyoshi Kahei, and most of their men rode up to the stockades. They had already had a taste of battle: the Tohan had taken Chigawa, and though Kiyoshige had retreated immediately as planned, the advance had been so swift and brutal they had had to fight their way through.

'The town is on fire,' Kiyoshige said. 'Many of the townspeople massacred. The Tohan are right behind us.'

His face was sombre beneath the dust and blood. 'We will win this battle,' he said to Shigeru, 'but it will not be easy, or short.'

They clasped hands briefly, then turned their horses towards the east, as the conch shells sounded and the Tohan warriors came pouring across the dusty plain.

It was around the Hour of the Horse and the sun had broken through the clouds and shone from the south-eastern corner of the sky, making it difficult to see the Kitano and Noguchi forces clearly. Since the Tohan were passing in front of their position, Shigeru expected the attack of arrows from moment to moment. From the northwest he could see Irie's men preparing to loose their arrows on the Tohan horsemen's right flank.

'Why are they delaying?' he said to Kiyoshige. 'They must move now. Ride to Noguchi and tell him to attack at once.'

Kiyoshige urged his grey, black-maned horse, Kamome, into a gallop across the plain towards the south. The Tohan horsemen were still beyond bow's range. The arrow that hit Kamome in the chest could not have come from one of them. It came instead from Noguchi's archers, and was followed by several more. The horse went down. Shigeru saw Kiyoshige leap from its back, landing on one knee and steadying himself before rising immediately, drawn sword in his hand. He did not have the chance to use it. A second burst of arrows came like a wave of the sea, dragging him under; as he struggled to get to his feet, one of Noguchi's warriors ran forward, severed his head with a single stroke, lifted it up by its topknot and displayed it to the soldiers behind him. An ugly shout rose from their throats, and the Noguchi surged forward, trampling over the headless body and the dying horse, racing not down the slope in the direction of the advancing Tohan force but up it, along the side of the plain, outflanking Shigeru's main force, pushing them up against the northern range, rendering the palisades useless.

Shigeru hardly had time to register anything – not the realization of betrayal, not grief at Kiyoshige's death – before he found himself fighting for his life against his own clansmen, rendered desperate and vicious by their treachery. Afterwards, scenes were engraved on his memory that would never be erased: Kiyoshige's head separated from his body yet still in some way living, eyes wide in shock; the gut-aching moment when he had to believe his own eyes and realize he had been betrayed; the first man he killed in a pure reflex of self-defence; the Noguchi crest; then the replacement of his own shock by a fury unlike anything he had ever experienced, a blood-lusting rage in which all emotions left him save the desire to kill the whole traitorous horde himself.

The foot soldiers were in disarray, mown down by the Tohan horsemen in front of them and the Noguchi bowmen to the side. Shigeru led his horsemen time and again against the Tohan, but as they were forced back towards the hills, each time there were fewer to follow him. He was aware of his father and Irie away to his left. The Kitano, whom he expected to reinforce him from the south, seemed to have vanished. Had they retreated already? Scanning the banners in vain for the chestnut leaf, he saw Irie lead an attack on the right flank of the Tohan; as he turned Karasu to urge him back into the fray, he spotted Eijiro with his oldest son, Danjo, alongside him.

They rode forward together, cutting a swathe into the foot soldiers, forcing them to retreat a little, but then Eijiro was struck from the side by a lance and went down. Danjo gave a howl of rage, killed the man who had killed his father; at almost the same moment a horseman rode at him and split his skull.

Shigeru fought on, possessed by the same blind fury. A fog seemed to have descended on the battlefield, dulling vision and hearing. He was vaguely aware of the screams of men and horses, the sigh and clack that preceded another deadly shower of arrows, the shouts and grunts that accompanied the heavy labour of slaughter, but he himself was dissociated from it, as though he saw himself in a dream. The fray was so intense it was almost impossible to distinguish his own men from the Tohan. Banners fell in the dust; crests on surcoats were obliterated by blood. Shigeru and a small handful of men were forced back up the course of a small stream. He saw his companions fall one by one around him, but each one had taken two Tohan warriors down with him. Shigeru was left facing two enemy soldiers, one on foot, one still mounted. All three of them were exhausted; he parried the hacking blows from the horseman, driving Karasu closer to the other steed and bringing his sword quickly back down as the horse stumbled. He saw his opponent's blood spurt and knew he had disabled him at least for a moment or two; he turned to counter the foot soldier on his right, killing him just as the Tohan man thrust up into Karasu's neck. The horse shuddered and plunged sideways, knocking the other horse in the shoulder; it fell, unseating its dying rider, and Karasu stumbled heavily, throwing Shigeru to the ground on top of his enemy, and collapsing over him, pinning him down.

He must have been stunned by the fall, for when he was able to extricate himself from the horse's body he was aware that the sun had moved to the west and was beginning to sink behind the mountains. The main thrust of the battle had passed over him like a typhoon and retreated: the small valley where Karasu's body dammed the stream was deserted, apart from the dead who lay in strange heaps, Otori and Tohan together, in ever-increasing numbers towards the plain.

We are defeated. The ache of misery, rage and grief for the fallen was too vast to contemplate for more than a moment. He set his mind now on death, welcoming the release it would bring him. In the distance he thought he could see Tohan warriors walking among the dead, severing heads to line them up for Sadamu's inspection. He will have mine too, Shigeru thought, a brash of rage and hatred washing through his belly, but I must not let myself be captured. He remembered his father's words: his father must be dead, and Jato was lost. He would cut himself open, the only way to assuage his pain, for no physical suffering could be greater than what he felt now.

He walked a little way up the stream and came to the spring itself, welling coolly from a gap in the black rocks. Ferns and bellflowers grew around it, the white flowers startling in the last of the light. In the rocks above the spring was a small shrine built from boulders and roofed with a single flat stone; another flat stone served as a sill for offerings. He took off his helmet and realized he was bleeding heavily from the scalp. He knelt by the spring and drank deeply, then washed his head, face and hands. He placed his sword on the sill of the shrine, prayed briefly to the god of the mountain, spoke the name of the Enlightened One, and took his knife from his belt. He loosened his armour and knelt on the grass, opened the pouch that hung at his waist and took out a small flask of perfume with which to scent his hair and beard, to honour his head when it was displayed to the gaze of Iida Sadamu.

'Lord Shigeru!' Someone was calling his name.

Shigeru had already embarked on his journey towards death, and did not take any notice. He knew the voice, but did not bother placing it: no one among the living had any hold on him now.

'Lord Shigeru!'

He looked up and saw Irie Masahide limping up the stream towards him. Irie's face was greenish-white; he clasped his side where the armour had been hacked away.

He has brought me Jato! Shigeru thought with profound sorrow, for he no longer wanted to live.

Irie spoke in gasps. 'Your father is dead. It is a complete defeat. Noguchi betrayed us.'

'And my father's sword?'

'It disappeared when he fell.'

'Then I can kill myself,' Shigeru said with relief.

'Let me assist you,' Irie said. 'Where is your sword? Mine is shattered.'

'I placed it on the shrine. Be quick; I fear capture above everything.'

But as Irie reached out to pick up the sword, his legs buckled and he pitched forwards. Shigeru caught the older man as he fell, and saw that he was dying. The blow that had cut his armour had gone deep into the stomach area. Only the lacing of the armour had held him together.

'Forgive me,' Irie gasped. 'Even I have failed you.' Blood gushed from his mouth. His face contorted and his body arched briefly. Then life fled from his eyes and his limbs relaxed into the long sleep of death.

Shigeru was moved deeply by the determination of his old teacher and friend to seek him out in the agony of his last moments, but the incident only reinforced the utterness of the defeat, and his aloneness now. Jato was gone: it was confirmed. He washed Irie's face and closed his eyes, but before he could kneel and take up his knife again, a shimmer at the corner of his eye made him turn, grasping for the knife, uncertain whether to plunge it immediately into his own belly or to deal first with this new threat. He was achingly tired: he did not want to fight, to dredge up from somewhere the energy to live; he wanted to die, but he would not let himself be captured.

'Lord Otori.' Another voice from the past that he could not place. The fading evening light seemed to fracture in a way that was vaguely familiar to his desperate mind. A fragment of memory from a different lifetime, a different light made greenish by the forest and the falling rain...

The fox spirit stood before him, holding Jato. The same pale, mobile face; the unremarkable, slight stature, the black opaque eyes that took in everything.

'Lord Otori!'

The man who had said he was called the Fox held out the sword in both hands, taking care to use the lightest touch, for any pressure on the blade would immediately slit the skin. Its scabbard was lost, but the bronze and pearl settings gleamed in the hilt. Shigeru took it with reluctant reverence, bowed to his benefactor, and felt the sword's power as it settled into his hand.

Life, full of unbearable pain and impossible demands, came rushing towards him.

Don't kill yourself. Was it the man's voice, or his dead father's, or the sword's? Live and get revenge!

He felt his face change as his lips parted. His eyes filled with tears, and he smiled.

He took Irie's empty scabbard from the warrior's belt and slid Jato's blade into it. Then he took his old sword from the shrine and held it out to the Fox.

'Will you take this in exchange?'

'I am not a warrior. I have no use for a sword.'

'You have the courage of a warrior,' Shigeru replied, 'and the Otori clan, if any survive, are forever indebted to you.'

'Let's get out of here,' the other replied, smiling slightly as if Shigeru's words had somehow pleased him. 'Take off your armour and leave it here.'

'You probably think I should take my own life,' Shigeru said, as he complied. 'I wish I had, still wish I could. But my father's last command to me was to live – if Jato, his sword, came to me.'

'I don't care one way or the other. I don't know why I'm helping you. Believe me, it's not my customary practice. Come on, follow me.'

The Fox had put Shigeru's sword back on the flat rock, but as they turned towards the mountain, shouts and the padding of feet came from below, and a small band of men burst upon the scene, the triple oak leaf clearly visible on their surcoats.

'I might need this after all,' the Fox muttered, seized the sword and drew it from the scabbard. At the same time, Jato came to life in Shigeru's hand. He had held the sword before, but this was the first time he had fought with it. He felt a flash of recognition.

They had the advantage of the slope, but neither of them had any protection and the Tohan men were in full armour, three carrying swords and two spears with curved blades. Shigeru felt his energy return as if Jato itself had infused new life into him. He parried the closest man's sword thrust, and with snake-like speed stepped sideways and let the man stumble past him; Jato hissed back through the air, and slid beneath the helmet into the back of the neck, severing the spinal cord. A spear thrust followed from below; but the Fox had gone invisible, and now reappeared behind the warrior, slashing with the long sword, cutting the man from shoulder to hip. The spear fell uselessly to the ground.

The Tohan men might have guessed who they were fighting, and their hopes of a huge reward spurred them on, but after the first two men died so quickly the second spearsman retreated backwards down the hill, clearly preferring not to be killed now the battle was over. However, he was shouting for help. At any moment, Shigeru knew, others would come pouring up the slope: if he was to avoid capture now, he must kill the remaining men and flee immediately, but he knew he was tiring and he was fighting them both at the same time, Jato moving through the air like a striking adder. He thought the Fox had abandoned him; then he realized the man was fighting at his side – and had been joined by a third, curiously similar in appearance. In the moment when their opponents were distracted, the Fox caught one man's sword arm with a return stroke, taking it off at the shoulder. Jato found the other's throat, and cut deep into the jugular.

'Ha!' the Fox said in some satisfaction, looking at the bodies and then at the sword blade before returning it to its scabbard. 'It's a good weapon. Maybe I'll keep it after all.'

'You have earned it twice...' Shigeru began, but the other man cut him off.

'You have a fine way of putting things, Lord Otori, but with all respect, there's no time for that now. You must know the entire Tohan army is looking for you. Sadamu has offered rewards for every Otori head, and the biggest one of all is for yours. I found you first and I'm not going to let anyone else get you.'

'You did not give me my father's sword in order to hand us both over to Sadamu?'

'No, if I wanted to kill you, I'd have done it by now, before you even realized it. I'm trying to help you.'

'Why?'

'I think we might discuss that later, when we get to wherever it is you want to go.'

'It seems I am to live,' Shigeru said, glancing briefly back towards the place he had thought would be his death scene. 'In which case, I must return to Hagi as soon as possible, and save what I can of the clan and the Middle Country.'

'Then we will go to Hagi,' the Fox said, and began walking swiftly up the slope into the darkness of the forest.

The last sounds of the battlefield faded as the forest deepened around them. It was almost completely dark, and the first stars had appeared: the Great Bear low in the northeast corner like an omen of evil to come. A vixen screamed, making the back of Shigeru's neck tingle. He remembered how he had followed this man before, when he had been just a boy, before he had killed even a single man, when his whole future had seemed full of hope… Then his world had been knocked out of kilter – by the collision with a supernatural reality. Now his world was again reeling – he did not know if it was within his power to steady it or if it would tilt and fall, hurtling him and everything that had any meaning for him into oblivion.

The vixen screamed again. She would be hunting to feed her young at this time of year – an undreamed-of feast awaited her on the plain below. He shuddered, thinking of the scenes dawn would bring, the crows feeding on the dead.

CHAPTER THIRTY-ONE

They walked most of that night, climbing all the time, through the wild mountain country that lay to the west of Yaegahara. For much of the time, Shigeru walked in a daze, his head wound aching, mind and body almost beyond exhaustion, one moment regretting bitterly the actions that had led to this disaster, the next inveighing against those who had turned against him, and bidding farewell to the dead who walked beside him. Scenes from the battle, devoid of any meaning, passed before his eyes. Who of his army was left alive? Would any return to the Middle Country?

They stopped to rest briefly at the top of the pass. It was so cold that swathes of snow still lay unmelted across the black rock of the mountain, gleaming ghostly white in the pre-dawn light; yet Shigeru did not feel it. He fell into a light feverish sleep and woke sweating, bands of dread tightening across his chest.

The Fox leaned over him. It was day, the first rays of the sun touching the peaks around them, turning the snow gold and pink.

'We must move on.' A flicker of concern crossed his face. 'You're burning. Can you walk?'

'Of course.' Shigeru got to his feet, swaying slightly as the blood rushed from his head. The cut was throbbing. He went to the snow and scooped up handfuls, rubbing them over his scalp and neck, wincing as he scraped the surface of the wound, then cramming clean snow into his parched mouth. He took several deep breaths in one of the exercises he had been taught at Terayama, gazing out across the unbroken green of the forest below.

'Let's go.'

The Fox led the way, and they clambered across boulders and began the descent. It was hardly a path that they followed, more a fox track. Often they went on all fours through dense undergrowth, as if tunnelling through the earth. From time to time the Fox turned back as though suggesting they should rest, but each time Shigeru indicated that they should press on.

He did not remember much about the journey, the alternations of fever and shivering, the throb in head and ache in lungs, compounded after the second day by bruised and cut feet and constant thirst. At the foot of the first range was a small valley, cultivated with rice fields and vegetable gardens. It took only half a day to cross it, and on the way a farmer gave them some early greens and carrot thinnings. He seemed to know the Fox, as did the other peasants working in the fields, but Shigeru had never been into this valley before, had not even known it existed, and in the hollow-eyed fugitive they certainly did not recognize the heir – now the head – of the clan. At its further side he could see another range of mountains, steeper and higher than the one they had just crossed, and behind it another. He forced himself not to think about the next ascent, and the one after, but to concentrate on walking, one foot after the other, keeping on only through the strength of his will.

They ate as they walked: the food brought the saliva back into his mouth and he began to feel a little better. Some time after midday they began to climb again: the fields around them were terraced steeply, tiny patches of earth cut out from the stony ground. The sun vanished early behind the mountains; they came quickly into the deep shade of the east-facing slope. Shigeru looked back briefly at the far side, which was still bathed in light and warmth. Between the bamboo groves and the cultivated fields there was no sign of any buildings; he wondered why the villagers had not built dwellings on that slope, to take advantage of the longer hours of sunlight – some ancient tradition or superstition, no doubt.

They climbed a little further and rounded a rocky outcrop; at that moment he realized the inhabitants of this valley had priorities other than afternoon warmth. Between the rocks and the cliff face, a massive log gate had been erected: it stood open now, but once closed it would seal off the hamlet inside. They passed through the entrance, the Fox greeting the guards who sat by it – powerful young men who looked more like warriors than farmers – and Shigeru found himself in what might have been a village, except that there were no wooden dwellings. The cliff here had been hollowed out, and these villagers lived in caves. There seemed to be ten or so, each with wooden doors and shutters, which all stood open on this mild afternoon of early summer; there was even a shrine, recognizable by its vermilion bird-perch-shaped gate. Women sat outside, preparing food, washing vegetables in the spring water that had been channelled into cisterns. The Fox went to one of these and brought water back in a bamboo dipper. Shigeru rinsed his mouth and hands, and then drank deeply. The water was cool and soft from the limestone.

'What is this place?'

'Somewhere you can hide and rest for a few days.'

'I have no intention of resting,' Shigeru said. 'I must get to Hagi as soon as possible.'

'Well, we'll talk about that later. Come inside, we'll have something to eat, and then sleep for a while.' The Fox saw Shigeru's impatient expression and laughed. 'You may not need to rest, but I do!'

In fact he showed no sign of fatigue, and Shigeru was sure the man could go for another week without sleep if he had to. He realized the fever was subsiding momentarily: he was thinking more clearly. He wondered if he were now a prisoner, if he would be allowed to walk out past the guards or if he would be held here until Sadamu's men came for him: presumably the Tribe would demand a huge payment in return. For he had fallen into the hands of the Tribe: he had no doubt about that. The Fox was no spirit, but a man with the astonishing abilities of the Tribe that his father had described to him.

He was both appalled and fascinated: ever since the conversation with his father, when he had learned of the existence of his older brother, he had kept in the back of his mind the idea that one day he would find out more about the Tribe and about his father's lost son. There seemed something preordained about this meeting: the man had even brought Jato to him. He glanced at the Fox – surely it could not be him?

A woman came from the dark interior of the cave and greeted them familiarly on the threshold.

'What brings you here, Kenji?'

'Just escorting my companion home.' He did not mention who his companion was.

'Sir,' she acknowledged Shigeru casually. 'What happened to his head?'

Her eyes ran over Shigeru and he felt she took in everything about him, including the sword.

'Just an accident,' the Fox, whose name was Kenji, replied.

'Cut yourself shaving, did you?' she said, glancing at Jato and then at Kenji's long sword. Her eyebrows went up.

Kenji shook his head slightly. 'Is there anything to eat?' he asked. 'It's been three days.'

'No wonder you both look half-dead. There's eggs and rice, fern shoots, mushrooms.'

'That'll do. And bring tea now.'

'Wine too?'

'Good idea,' Kenji grunted. 'And speaking of shaving, bring hot water and a sharp knife.' He addressed Shigeru. 'We'll take off your beard and find some other clothes. Anyone can see from your features that you are Otori, but it will make you a little less recognizable.'

They squatted down on their heels outside. A few hens were scratching in the dirt, and two children appeared and stared at them until Kenji addressed them teasingly and they giggled and ran away. The woman returned with a bowl of hot water, and Shigeru washed his face in it, then allowed the Fox to shave away the small beard with a knife blade of extreme sharpness. When they were finished, the woman brought rags – the remnants of old clothes – to wipe face and hands before they went inside.

It was dark and smoky within the cave, but there was a raised area for sleeping and sitting, and the straw matting was relatively clean. The woman brought bowls of tea: it was fresh and of surprisingly high quality for such a small, isolated village – but of course this was no ordinary village, Shigeru thought as he sipped the steaming liquid, grateful for the tea but apprehensive about the rest of the situation. He comforted himself with the fact that he still had his weapons. While he had them, he could defend himself or take his own life.

Kenji said suddenly, 'How old are you?'

He used a familiar form of speech that took Shigeru by surprise, for he had never been so addressed in his life, not even by Kiyoshige. Don't think of Kiyoshige now.

'I turned eighteen this year.' And Kiyoshige seventeen.

'Matsuda's training obviously worked.'

'You remember our previous meeting, then?'

'Luckily, as it turns out. I knew who to deliver the sword to.'

The warmth from the tea, and from the fire, made sweat prickle again on Shigeru's forehead and in his armpits.

'Did my father give it to you? Did you see him die?'

'Yes, I did. He fought bravely enough to the last, but he was outnumbered and surrounded.'

'Who killed him?'

'I don't know his name; one of Iida's warriors.'

How strange if this man were indeed Shigemori's son. 'How old are you?' Shigeru questioned.

'I am twenty-six.'

Shigeru made the calculation silently: too young to be Shigemori's son, too old to be his grandson – well, the coincidence would have been too great.

'Your name is Kenji?'

'Muto Kenji. My family are from Yamagata.'

Shigeru could feel the fever returning, bringing a strange lucidity to his thoughts. 'And one of them is Muto Shizuka?' he said without expression.

'She is my niece: my older brother's daughter. I believe you met her last year.'

'You know I did. I presume you know everything about those meetings, and that Iida Sadamu does too.' Shigeru moved his hand closer to the sword's hilt. 'What are you playing at?'

'What makes you think I am playing?'

The woman returned with food and wine, and Shigeru did not want to say more in front of her.

'You are safe with me, I swear it,' Kenji said with apparent sincerity. 'Eat. Drink.'

A starving man has no scruples: once Shigeru had smelled the food it was impossible to resist it. Whatever lay before him, he would face it better on a full stomach. He drank wine too, sparingly, watching Kenji closely, hoping it might loosen his tongue, but though the Fox drank two bowls to every one of Shigeru's, the wine seemed to have little effect on him other than flushing his pale face red. When they had finished, the woman took away the dishes and returned to ask, 'Will you rest now? I can spread out the beds?'

'Who is the god of the shrine?' Shigeru asked.

'Hachiman,' she replied. The god of war.

'I would like to have sutras said for the dead,' Shigeru continued. 'And cleanse myself from pollution before sleeping.'

'I will go and tell the priest,' she said quietly.

'You do not need to come with me,' Shigeru said to Kenji. 'You probably want to sleep.'

'Sleep can wait,' the other replied.

'It would be hypocritical to pray for the souls of the men you and the Tribe betrayed!'

'I did not betray anyone,' Kenji said calmly. 'I knew Noguchi would turn, but I did not induce him to. Iida Sadamu did that by making him an offer no sane man would refuse. Iida was driven to such generosity by his fear of an alliance between the Otori and the Seishuu.'

'Which your niece informed him of, after swearing she would not! It must have been her!'

'You cannot be outraged when people act according to their natures. And in this case everyone did. You should be angry with yourself for not recognizing those natures. This is what Sadamu is so good at, and why he prevailed against you and everyone else, and always will.'

Shigeru controlled his anger with almost visible effort as the returning fever set up a renewed throbbing in his veins. 'Unless I learn to do the same?'

'Well, you are not yet old. There is some hope that you can still learn.'

Shigeru said, 'In the meantime I must pray for the dead.'

He walked the few hundred paces to the shrine. Incense had been lit inside the gate and he let the smoke waft across him, breathing in the heavy fragrance.

The priest met him at the cave's entrance. He wore red and white robes and a small black hat, and he carried a stick crowned with tassels of pale white straw, but despite his religious garb he had the same warrior-look as the guards on the gate. Shigeru followed him into the dark interior. A few lamps burned smokily inside before the statue of the god. Shigeru knelt, took Jato from his belt and dedicated it silently to Hachiman. He began to pray. The Tribe maintain a shrine, he thought with fevered logic. They must also revere the gods and honour the dead.

'What is the name of the deceased?' the priest murmured.

'Not one, but many,' Shigeru replied. 'Let them just be known as warriors of the Otori clan.' How many? he wondered. Four thousand? Five thousand? He shuddered again, wishing he had been one of them. The chanting started; the smoke stung his eyes and he let them water, the moisture running unchecked down his cheeks and his newly shaven chin.

When the ceremony was over and he rose from his knees, he realized many people had come silently into the cave, and knelt or stood with bowed heads around him. He thought they did not know who he was, but it was clear they felt a certain sympathy for his sorrow, seeing him as a solitary warrior, masterless now, grieving for the deaths of companions and friends.

He did not think it was a pretence – if it was, it was both elaborate and cruel – and he was moved and puzzled, realizing that the character and customs of the Tribe had more depth and subtlety than their roles of spy and murderer would at first suggest.

He went back to the lodging place, Kenji a couple of paces behind him.

'It was good of so many to pray with me,' Shigeru said. 'Please thank them for it. But why did they do it?'

'They are Otori, after a fashion,' Kenji said. 'Their home is the Middle Country. They've heard of the battle by now: the losses are reported to be very heavy; maybe some of the dead were friends, even relatives. No one knows yet.'

'But to whom do they owe allegiance? Whose land is this? To whom do they pay tax?'

'These are interesting questions,' Kenji replied smoothly, and, yawning, changed the subject. 'You may have been taught by Matsuda to survive without sleep indefinitely; I need sleep now. How's your head, by the way? I can give you the same brew I gave you before, for Matsuda.'

Shigeru declined. They used the privy on the far side of the village, where the waste could be thrown directly down to the fields below. Back in the cave, he took off his outer garments and slipped beneath the hemp quilt, placing his weapons under the mattress. It smelled of smoke and some herb that he could not identify. He fell asleep almost immediately, but awoke burning and unbearably thirsty. It was light: he thought it must be the next morning, was seized by a terrible sense of urgency and began to get up, groping for his sword.

Kenji woke instantly, and groaned. 'Go back to sleep.'

'We must get going,' Shigeru replied. 'It must be long past daybreak.'

'No, it will be dark in an hour. You've hardly slept at all.' He called to the woman, who came after a little while with water and a cup of the willowbark tea the Fox had given Shigeru when they first met.

'Drink it, will you,' Kenji said with exasperation. 'Then we can both get some sleep.'

Shigeru gulped the water, its sweet coolness slaking his parched mouth and throat. Then he drank the tea, more slowly. The willowbark dulled the pain and suppressed the fever for a while. When he woke again, it was dark. He could hear the others breathing deeply as they slept. He needed to urinate, and got up to walk to the privy, but his legs would not obey him, buckling under him, pitching him forwards.

He heard Kenji wake and tried to apologize, was sure that the woman was his mother's old servant Chiyo, and began to explain something to her, but forgot almost immediately what it was. The woman brought a pot and told him to piss in it, just as Chiyo had done when he was a child. She brought rags soaked in cold water, and she and Kenji took it in turns to cool his body as sweat poured from him. Later the fever turned again to shivering; she lay next to him, giving her body's warmth to him. He dozed and woke, thought she was Akane and that he was in the house beneath the pines in Hagi, before the battle, before the defeat.

Between them they would not let him die. The fever was intense but short-lived: as the head wound healed, it burnt itself out. Two days later he began to recover, desperate with anxiety to return to Hagi, but more rational, and able to accept that he needed to regain his strength before travelling on.

The woman, whose name he never knew – Kenji addressed her familiarly as 'older sister', but that was how he would speak to any woman the same age or a little older than himself – spent the day in various household chores, her hands never idle. In the lethargy left by the fever, Shigeru watched her, fascinated by the skill and frugality of her daily life. She told him a little about the organization of the village: it was made up of three families, who unlike the lowest class of peasants all had surnames:

Kuroda, Imai and Muto. Most decisions were taken coop-
eratively, but the headman was always from the Muto
family – a relative of Kenji's. In the East they would be
Kikuta, she said, but in the Middle Country the Muto were
the leading family.

Kikuta: the name was familiar. Surely his father had said
the woman he had been infatuated with – or bewitched by
– had been called Kikuta. The conversation came back
clearly: all the griefs and disappointments of his father's life.

'And if the headman dies without adult sons, his wife
or his daughter takes over,' she added. 'I can talk to you
freely, even though you're not one of us, since you're an
old friend of Kenji's.'

'We are hardly old friends. Did he say so?'

'Not in so many words. I just assumed it. From the
way he's looked after you. He's not usually such a caring
person, believe me. He surprised me. He knows a lot
about plants and herbs, but he doesn't often use them to
heal, if you know what I mean.' Shigeru stared at her, and
she laughed. 'Must be some bond between you from a
former life.'

It was not a very satisfactory explanation, yet there
seemed no other. He did not want to talk too much in
front of the woman – or, indeed, within the village. He
did not want them to know his identity, and he suspected
some of them might have the supernatural skills that he
had heard about, and that he had already seen in Muto
Kenji. But when, a week later, they left together, they had
more opportunity to talk.

The night before they left, Shigeru gave the clothes he had been wearing during the battle to the woman, who promised to wash and mend them and present them to the shrine. She gave him in return an old, unmarked, indigo-dyed robe, and Kenji put on a similar one. Kenji bound the hilts of both swords with strips of dark sharkskin, hiding the decoration. The woman also provided them with new straw sandals and sedge hats that she had woven during the winter: Shigeru's concealed the half-healed slash across the side of his head.

'Now you look like brothers,' she said with satisfaction.

In the years to come, he would travel frequently in this way, crossing and recrossing the Three Countries through the vast tracts of forested mountains by little-known paths, his own strength and his sword's power disguised, but this was the first time he had made such a journey, no longer recognizable as the heir to the Otori clan, a humble traveller with few needs and few expectations. His mood was heavy with memories of the dead, but the day was beautiful, the air clear, the southern breeze soft and warm. Bell frogs and tree frogs called along the stream, and towards noon the forest was filled with the strident music of early cicadas. Vetch, daisies and wild orchids starred the grass, and insects hummed around the linden blossom.

They kept away from the high road, following instead a track that led over the mountain ranges; the climb was steep, the views from the top of the pass sublimely beautiful. To the north, beyond the white-fringed coastline, the sea stretched away into the distance, fishing boats tiny specks on its surface, and green islands rising up in it like mountains trapped by a vast blue flood.

They stayed the first night in an isolated farmhouse at the foot of the range. Here Kenji was known to the farmer, his sons and their families. They did not seem to have heard of the battle, and neither Kenji nor Shigeru spoke of it. They were in awe of Kenji, and treated both their visitors with such deference that no one spoke much at all.

The following morning, Shigeru took advantage of the wider path and gentler slopes to engage Kenji in conversation. His father was never far from his mind: his betrayal and death would have to be avenged, but Shigeru was also preoccupied with thoughts of the lost son from the Tribe, from the Kikuta family. He wanted to question Kenji about him, but some caution held him back. First he would try to fathom the man's true intentions, why he had helped him, what he expected in return.

'I suppose you will report my escape to Iida?' he said.

'I won't need to. Once you are back in Hagi it will be general knowledge. Iida will be disappointed. He'll make some other move against you. Do you trust your uncles?'

'Far from it,' Shigeru replied.

'Very wise.'

'That's why I am in a hurry to return. They will not wait for my death to be confirmed before they try to seize power.' After a few moments he said, 'Of course, that may have been why you detained me for so many days in the mountains.'

'I did not detain you! Did it escape your notice that you were delirious for two days, and then too weak to travel? I saved your life! Truly it's said that the man whose life you save will always hate you,' he added with a trace of bitterness.

'I am grateful to you,' Shigeru replied. 'I just don't understand why you did it. You have been working for Iida as an informant and a go-between: why return my sword to me and help me escape when your master wants my head?'

'No one is my master,' Kenji retorted. 'My loyalty is to my family, and to the Tribe.'

'Your family, like your double-faced niece. You speak of loyalty! You don't know the meaning of the word.'

Shigeru felt anger course through him, bringing renewed vigour. Kenji seemed equally enraged, but he said, trying to sound unmoved, 'Loyalty for the Tribe may not mean the same as to the warrior, but we know its meaning. If I were going to sell you to Iida, I would have done so already.' Kenji went on, 'I have been thinking about the future: Iida should not have everything his own way; we need to keep him a little unsettled; we need people to keep him awake at night while he worries about what they are up to.'

'So the Tribe controls us all?' Shigeru said.

'More than any of you suspect,' Kenji admitted.

'And it suits you now to support me, to maintain some kind of check on Iida?'

'That's my preliminary estimation.' Kenji glanced at him and then said, 'But of course, Shigeru, it is not the only reason.'

Shigeru did not correct him for the familiarity, but said sarcastically, 'Some bond between us from a former life?'

'Something like that. You know, I have never spoken to Iida. I have never even been admitted to his presence. I receive orders from his henchmen. But the first time we met, you spoke to me courteously, asked for my help, and thanked me.'

'I thought you were a fox spirit: I did not want to offend you.'

Kenji laughed and went on: 'And a few days ago you gave me your sword – a warrior does not do that lightly. Moreover, when I held your father's sword, I felt something of its power. I know you are its true owner – and a worthy one. You must know your reputation in the Middle Country, the respect and affection you command. The Tribe has different notions of honour: nevertheless, I don't want to be known as the man who sold Otori Shigeru to Iida Sadamu! So yes, there is a bond between us, for political and personal reasons.'

Shigeru said somewhat awkwardly, for Kenji's praise embarrassed him, 'I am more than grateful to you for saving my life, and for your help. I hope I can call on that help in the future. But what can I offer you in return?'

'Maybe no more than your friendship. It would be an interesting thing, to be friends with a warrior.'

And all my friends are dead, Shigeru thought. 'Would the Tribe work for me, as you have worked for Iida?'

'I am sure we can come to some mutually satisfactory arrangement.'

'Do you have any information now? Will Iida push on into the Middle Country? Do I need to reassemble my army immediately?'

'I don't know much – only what I saw with my own eyes at Yaegahara. The Tohan also suffered terrible losses. The Otori may have gone down, but they took their enemies with them. Iida will almost certainly demand that large parts of the Middle Country be ceded to him: Chigawa, the southern part, possibly even Yamagata – but he will not be strong enough to attack again, and not for some time.'

'They were brave,' Shigeru said.

'That was never in question. Nor is your own courage. But if you're going to survive, you need to acquire other qualities: discernment, deviousness and above all patience.'

'Above all deviousness,' Shigeru remarked. 'Maybe you can teach me that.'

'Maybe I can,' Kenji replied.

CHAPTER THIRTY-TWO

As reports began to come through from the battlefield, the city of Hagi went into mourning. People wept in the streets, rushed to the shrines to pray, beat gongs and bells to awaken the gods who had forgotten the Otori; the more courageous armed themselves with staves and knives, and villagers began to stream into the city from the surrounding districts.

After a few days, the remnants of the defeated army began to trickle back. Among the first was Miyoshi Satoru, with his oldest son, the fourteen-year-old Kahei. Miyoshi was one of Lord Shigemori's closest advisors, and one of Lord Shigeru's teachers. It was with the deepest sorrow that he reported her husband's death to Lady Otori.

'And Lord Shigeru?' she said, with no sign of grief.

'There is no clear knowledge of him: I cannot hide it from you. We fear the worst.'

Endo Chikara also returned, and the two retainers acted as swiftly as they could to protect what remained of the clan. Lady Otori, of course, was determined to secure Takeshi's position as heir, but Takeshi was only fourteen: a regent would have to be decided upon. As soon as Lord Shoichi and Lord Masahiro heard the news, they hurried back to the castle to make sure no negotiations took place without them. The extent of the disaster could not be minimized. Their clan and its young heir had attracted the anger and enmity of the most powerful warlord in the Three Countries. They would all suffer severe punishment – there was no doubt of that – but their main objective was to do all they could to ensure the survival of the clan.

Shigemori was dead, Shigeru missing, Takeshi still a minor and anyway a week's journey away in Terayama, which had every likelihood of becoming Tohan in the very near future. Shoichi and Masahiro, whatever their failings, were Otori lords: they were instated almost immediately as interim regents and given authority to begin negotiations with Iida Sadamu.

How to approach the conqueror was the next problem. Lord Shoichi himself suggested Tsuwano's Kitano, who had kept himself and his men out of the battle – which could be interpreted as neutrality. Shoichi already knew of Kitano's leanings towards Inuyama, the same leanings that had so offended Shigeru three years earlier.

Endo himself set out the next day for Tsuwano to make preliminary enquiries, while Shoichi and Masahiro made arrangements to move their wives and families back into the castle. However, while he was waiting for his wife's return, Masahiro went to visit Akane.

Haruna had gone straight to Akane as soon as she had heard the first news of the defeat. Akane spent that day and the next soaring and plummeting between hope and despair.

'He is only missing!' she kept repeating to Haruna, who sat by her, holding her hand, combing out her hair, massaging her neck and temples, encouraging her to eat and drink, anything to keep her from careering downwards into the deep pit of hopeless grief. 'No one saw him die!'

Haruna did not say what was uppermost in her mind: that all those who might have witnessed Shigeru's death were themselves dead. Mori Kiyoshige, for instance, murdered by his own clansmen – the name Noguchi had already become synonymous with traitor. She wept for the young man, so full of fierce vitality, and for all the others.

Akane bathed and changed her clothes over and again, repeating, 'He will need my love, when he returns. I must look beautiful for him: he will need my comfort as never before.' However, by the evening of the third day, she was sinking into desperation, though she still did not give way to tears. Just after sunset they heard the sound of horses in the street outside: hope returned with a stab of physical pain; brushing aside the maids, she ran to the front entrance. Harness jingled; the horses stamped and snorted. Men entered the garden, the Otori heron clearly visible on their robes. She thought she would faint with joy – but it was not Shigeru who followed the men into the garden.

'Lord Masahiro?' she said, her speech faltering.

'May I come in?' He stood for a moment while one of the men knelt to undo his sandals, then stepped up into the house.

'Who is here?' he questioned.

'No one – just Haruna.'

'Tell her to leave. I want to speak to you alone.'

His manner had changed, and it alarmed her: he was less ingratiating, more openly bullying.

She made an effort to stand up to him. 'I cannot receive you now. My deepest apologies; I must ask you to leave.'

'What are you going to do, Akane? Throw me out?'

He came close to her, swaggering a little. She stepped back, her flesh already feeling his hands and recoiling. Masahiro laughed and shouted towards the interior of the house. 'Haruna! I don't want to see your face here. Make yourself scarce before I come in.' He nodded towards the maids, who were waiting nervously in the shadows. 'Bring wine!' He strode into the main room.

The men stood at the front entrance. There was nothing Akane could do but follow him. He sat himself down and gazed out onto the garden. The summer air was moist and soft, smelling of the sea and the tides, but her mouth was dry and she felt parched, as if a fever were setting in.

One of the girls came in with wine and cups. She placed them on the floor and poured wine for them both. Masahiro waved her away: she cast an anxious look at Akane and retreated to the rear door, sliding it shut behind her. Masahiro drank deeply.

'I came to offer you my condolences,' he said; the words were appropriate but he could not hide the air of triumph behind them.

Akane whispered, 'Lord Shigeru is dead?'

He was the last person she wanted to hear this news from; it added another level to the unbearable pain.

'Either dead or captured. For his sake we must hope for the former.'

Never to see him again; never to feel his body against hers – the wave of grief started in her belly and swept through her. She thought she had felt grief at her father's death; now she knew that it had been nothing compared to this, a teardrop against the whole ocean. Sounds came from her mouth that she did not recognize: a deep moaning like the winter sea on a stony beach, followed by a sharp mewling like a seabird's cry.

She fell forward, hardly feeling the matting against her face, her hands tearing at it, then tearing at her own hair.

Masahiro leaned over and held her firmly, drawing her close to him as if to comfort her. She was hardly aware of his mouth against the nape of her neck, hardly felt his hands as they loosened her sash and lifted her robe. She knew what he would do: she could not stop him; she could not spare from her grief the energy or the will to resist him; she wanted him to get it over with as quickly as possible and then leave her alone. If he hurt her, it did not matter: no pain could come near what she already felt.

His lust made him clumsy and quick. Akane felt nothing but revulsion: men's desire, which she had once pitied and then adored, now seemed to her to be contemptible. She loathed everything to do with it: the invasion, the wetness, the smell.

The matting will be stained, she thought. I will have to replace it. But she knew that she would never do it: someone else would have to see to it, after her death.

Masahiro said, as he adjusted his clothes, 'In a way I have become the heir to the clan. So this house and its occupant are part of my inheritance.'

Akane said nothing.

'I am sure we will get used to each other, Akane. I know you are a very practical woman. I'll leave you now. But don't waste too much time grieving. Nothing will change in your life, if you are sensible.'

She heard him leave, heard the horses depart; then gave herself over to grief, keening and rocking herself, tugging at her hair and driving her nails into her skin. Her reason abandoned her, and she felt herself being pulled into the dark world of sorcery and spells. From where she lay, her eyes were drawn constantly to one spot – the place in the garden where she had buried the charm the old priest had given her. She had wanted to bind Shigeru to her: it seemed she had cursed him instead. She had wanted to control his desire for her, but she had used the desire of men to do it, and now she was trapped by her own sorcery. She ran barefoot into the garden, knelt in the dirt, scrabbling with her hands at the earth. The box smelled rank, like a coffin torn from a grave; when the maids came out, pleading with her to return inside, she raved at them and cursed them in a voice unlike her own, as if a demon had possessed her.

Haruna returned; the maids spoke to her in hushed voices, causing her to weep quietly. The women decided it would be better for Akane to be removed from the place where every room, every aspect and object spoke to her of her dead lover; and also from the scene of the unspeakable violation. She would not be separated from the box she had dug from the earth, but, cradling it in her arms, she allowed Haruna to help her into a palanquin and take her to the House of the Camellias. The house was quiet, the women all in mourning; indeed, many of them had returned to their families for the funeral ceremonies that were taking place all over the city. Haruna led Akane to the room she had slept in when she was a girl, washed her and dressed her in a clean robe and stayed with her till dawn. The change of surroundings seemed to calm her a little, and finally she gave in to exhaustion and slept. Haruna lay down beside her, and soon her eyes closed too.

Akane awoke with the dawn. Sparrows were chirping noisily from the camellias in the garden, and a bush warbler called piercingly. It was going to be another warm day. Soon the plum rains would begin. He will never feel sun or rain again, she thought, and grief tightened its vice round her heart.

She rose quietly, took the box from where she had left it beside the pillow block and slipped from the room. The garden sparkled with dew: there was no one around to see her, but she left clear footprints on gravel and grass.

She went to the old priest's dwelling, rousing him from sleep and demanding that he remove all the spells he had cast on her behalf. Half-fuddled, he tried to calm her, but his touch unhinged her further. Her madness gave her inhuman strength. As if a demon possessed her, she ransacked the hut, searching for something that would ease her pain. She threw his flasks and potions to the ground, scattering the dried roots and seeds. When he bent to collect them, she picked up his paring knife and cut his throat. It seemed to her that she killed Masahiro as he violated her, and that nothing but his blood would moisten her parched lips. May he die thus and thus again through all his lives, she cursed him; may he never find peace or salvation, may his children hate him and seek his death. Then she put her lips to the newly carved mouth and sucked from it.

Picking up the box with the charm that had bound Shigeru to her and turned his wife against him, she went to the shrine and prayed for forgiveness, for them all to be released. She wept for her dead love, and the tears brought clarity. I did not mean to love you, she told him, but I did, completely. Now you are gone, I will not live without you. Forgive me for the part I played in your death. The salt of tears mingled in her mouth with the taste of blood.

Clasping the box to her like a child, she climbed to the edge of the sulphur-smelling crater, and threw herself into the pit.

CHAPTER THIRTY-THREE

Kenji accompanied Shigeru to the south bank of the river. They arrived at the night ebb tide, when the air smelled of mud and salt. A new three-day moon hung low above the sea. Shigeru was a little reluctant to say goodbye, would have liked to keep his companion longer. He felt there was indeed some inexplicable bond between them, and suspected he would be in need of help in the coming months, the sort of help only the Tribe could provide – above all, information.

'Where will you go now? You are welcome to stay at my mother's house.'

'It's better for our friendship to remain hidden for now,' Kenji replied. 'There are places I can stay in Hagi.'

'Where can I reach you?' Shigeru asked.

'I'll send someone to you. I'll be in touch in some way through your household.'

Shigeru thought immediately of Muto Shizuka and was filled with misgivings – even if he had information from Kenji, how would he know if he could trust it? How could he control and use the Tribe when he knew nothing about them?

'Well, thank you again – for the sword, for all your help.'

'Lord Otori.' Kenji bowed formally. 'Look after yourself,' he added in more familiar speech, and turned to walk away.

Shigeru gazed after him for a moment, and saw the figure split in two. Two identical men walked side by side. Both raised a hand in farewell. They merged together, and Kenji, the Fox, vanished.

He is showing off, Shigeru thought: but what a marvellous skill to have.

Shigeru went first to his mother's house, crossing the river by the fish weir, remembering, as always, the day of the stone fight when Takeshi nearly drowned, and Mori Yuta did. Now the second Mori son was dead too...

He did not want to return to the castle like a fugitive. In the morning he would dress in formal robes and ride there as the head of the clan.

The dogs barked triumphantly; the guards opened the gate at the sound of his voice, their faces astonished, then contorted with emotion. Two of them, ancient grizzled men too old to fight on the battlefield, had tears coursing down their cheeks as they fell to their knees.

The household woke; lamps were lit, Chiyo wept as she prepared hot water and food. Ichiro forgot himself so far that he embraced his former pupil. Shigeru had returned from the dead, and no one could quite believe it.

Messengers were sent at once to the castle, and Shigeru's mother arrived at dawn. He had bathed and slept for a few hours, and was eating the first meal of the day with Ichiro when her presence was announced.

'You have come back just in time,' she said. 'Kitano is expected any day now with Iida's terms. Your uncles are installed as regents, but you can be sure they will not be as overjoyed as they should be at your return.'

'I will go to the castle at once,' Shigeru said. 'You must accompany me.' After a moment he went on: 'My father died fighting bravely, as did all his warriors. We were defeated by the treachery of the Noguchi. But Kitano is not blameless: his vacillation also contributed to the defeat.'

'This, however, makes him acceptable to Iida,' Ichiro observed. The older man's emotion had not affected his appetite, Shigeru noticed as Ichiro helped himself greedily to rice and salted plums. Yet he felt renewed respect for his teacher's learning and judgement, recalling his meticulous attention to detail and his scrupulous regard for truth. Moreover, Shigeru knew that he could trust him completely.

'You must refuse to negotiate through a traitor,' his mother said angrily. 'You must confront your uncles and take over the leadership of the clan immediately.'

'Forgive me for disagreeing, Lady Otori,' Ichiro said, 'but Lord Shigeru should be prepared to be flexible: it's not the willow's branches that break under the snow. The Otori have been defeated in battle: no matter whose the fault, the outcome is the same. Iida is going to make heavy demands, heavier than the worst blizzards of winter. If we are not to be broken completely, we must be prepared to bend.'

Lady Otori, affronted, opened her mouth to argue, but Shigeru held up a hand to silence her.

'What are these demands likely to be?'

'We must find out from Kitano. I am afraid he will ask for Chigawa, the silver mines, all of the eastern districts, and maybe even Yamagata.'

'We will never give up Yamagata,' Lady Otori exclaimed.

'And, though I dislike having to voice such things, your abdication, even your life, may be required.' Ichiro spoke in a dry, impersonal manner, as though discussing a point of legality, but a sudden fit of coughing seemed to overcome him, and he wiped his eyes with the sleeve of his robe, hiding his face briefly.

Lady Otori did not argue with this interpretation, but sat in silence, her eyes cast down, her face stern.

Shigeru said, 'My father's command to me was that I should take my own life only if Jato were lost. Jato came to me, as if by a miracle: therefore I must obey my father's wishes and live, in order to seek revenge.'

'The sword came to you?' His mother was shocked into speech. 'Where is it?'

He indicated where it lay beside him: the hilt disguised, the scabbard borrowed.

'That is not Jato,' she said.

'I will not draw it to prove it to you. But it is Jato.'

His mother smiled. 'Then we have nothing to fear. They cannot make you abdicate if you hold the Otori sword.'

Ichiro said, 'Iida Sadamu, it is reported, hates you personally. Your uncles may be tempted to deliver you to him for their own gain. The Otori army has been almost annihilated. We are in no position to defend ourselves. You will be in great danger. You must go very carefully.'

'Do I hold any advantages?' Shigeru asked.

'You are the legal heir to the clan; the people love you and will not give up their support of you quickly.'

'And the Tohan also suffered huge losses,' Shigeru said. 'Sadamu himself may not be able to attack the heart of the Middle Country or lay siege to Hagi. And maybe the Seishuu will stand by their pledges of alliance and come to our support.' And maybe the Tribe will be another check on Sadamu's ambition, he reflected, but did not speak of this.

'Well, that's better than I thought,' Ichiro said.

Shigeru gave orders for the most stately procession possible in the circumstances to escort him to the castle. Old men and boys were rapidly assembled from the remnants of the household guards. Somewhat to his surprise, Miyoshi Kahei and his younger brother Gemba appeared among them: Gemba was only six years old.

'I am happy to see you alive,' Shigeru said to Kahei.

'Not as happy as we are to see Lord Shigeru,' the lad replied, his former boyishness and cheerfulness extinguished by what he had seen of war. 'Kiyoshige's death was terrible,' he added quietly, his eyes bright with unshed tears. 'It must be avenged.'

'It will be,' Shigeru replied, as quietly. 'What news of your father?'

'He also lived. He is at the castle now. He sent my brother and me to be part of your escort, a pledge of his support in the coming months: many of our men died, but they have sons, the same age as me, or Gemba; we will be your future army.'

'I am grateful to him, and to you.'

'It is how the whole city, the whole country feels,' Kahei exclaimed. 'As long as Lord Shigeru is alive, the whole clan lives!'

Shigeru had a new scabbard brought for Jato, removed the black sharkskin from the hilt and carefully cleaned and polished the sword. He dressed in formal robes, subdued in colour, embroidered with the Otori crest, and placed a small black hat on his head. Chiyo plucked the regrowth in his beard and redressed his hair. A little before noon, he set out for the castle. He rode one of the Mori horses, a grey with a black mane and tail who reminded him of Kiyoshige's dead stallion. His mother accompanied him in a palanquin.

His mother's house lay some way from the centre of the town, surrounded by other small estates, with tiled white walls and tree-filled gardens. Canals ran alongside the roads, swimming with lazy fish, and the air was full of the trickle and splash of water. In the gardens, azalea bushes bloomed like red flames, and the canal banks were lined with irises.

In the distance other sounds could be heard, unrecognizable at first, then gradually distinguishing themselves into the beating of drums and gongs, people shouting, singing and clapping their hands. The streets became crowded: the townsfolk were dressed in bright colours and wore strangely shaped hats and yellow or red scarves. They danced as if afflicted by madness or possessed by spirits. At the sight of Shigeru's procession, their singing and their movements became more frenzied. The throngs of people parted as he rode between them, but their emotion rolled over him, consuming him until he felt no longer a human being, a man, but the embodiment of something ancient and indestructible.

This must never be allowed to pass away, he thought. I must live. I must have a son. If my wife will not give me one, I will have children with Akane. I will acknowledge her children and adopt them. No one can prevent me from making my own decisions now. He had hardly thought of either woman for days: now longing for Akane swept over him. He gazed towards the house beneath the pines, half expecting to catch a glimpse of her, but the gates were closed; the house seemed deserted. As soon as matters were under way in the castle, he would send a message to her. He would go to her that night. And he must speak to Moe as soon as possible to find out what had happened to her father and brothers. He feared they were dead, since the Yanagi had borne the brunt of the Tohan's first onslaught while being attacked on the right-hand flank by their supposed allies, the Noguchi.

Endo Chikara and Miyoshi Satoru greeted him in front of the castle, welcoming him home and expressing their condolences for his father's death. In contrast to the frenzy in the town, their mood was sombre. No one could pretend that the Otori did not face complete disaster. They rode over the wooden bridge together; in the first bailey Shigeru dismounted and strode towards the entrance to the residence.

When they stepped inside, Endo said, 'Lord Kitano will arrive tomorrow. He brings the Tohan demands.'

'Summon the elders and my uncles,' Shigeru replied. 'We must discuss our position before we meet Kitano. My mother will also attend our meeting. Tell me when they are all assembled. In the meantime I must talk to my wife.'

Endo spoke to one of the maids and she disappeared along the veranda, returning a few moments later and whispering, 'Lady Otori is waiting for you, Lord Otori.'

The room was dim after the brilliant sunshine, and he could not see Moe's expression clearly as she bowed to the ground, then welcomed him – but the stiffness of her body, and her stilted speech, disclosed to him her grief for the dead and, he suspected, her disappointment that he was not among them. He knelt in front of her, able now to see her reddened eyes and blotched skin.

'I am very sorry,' he said. 'I'm afraid you have suffered a great loss.'

'If you call the death of my father, all his sons, all our warriors, a great loss – yes, I have,' she replied with profound bitterness. 'My marriage bound my family to you, to your rashness and foolhardiness. They would have done better to copy Kitano and Noguchi. Our house is wiped out. Our land is to be taken from us and given to Iida's warriors.'

'This is still to be negotiated,' Shigeru said.

'What negotiation will bring my family back? My mother will kill herself rather than leave Kushimoto. They are all gone save me. You have destroyed the Yanagi.'

'Your father was loyal to my father and to me. Your family were not traitors. You should be proud of them.'

She raised her eyes to his face. 'You have also suffered a great loss,' she said with a mock concern. 'Your mistress is dead.'

He had thought she would express some formal condolences for his father's death, and briefly did not understand what he heard. Then he realized the depths of her hatred for him, the intensity of her desire to hurt him.

'Akane,' she went on. 'The courtesan. She killed an old man and then killed herself. Apparently, so the gossip goes, Masahiro visited her with the news of your death: it must have driven her out of her mind.'

She continued to stare at him, almost triumphantly. 'Of course, Masahiro had been in contact with her all winter. He must have slept with her often while you were away.'

His rage was so intense he wanted to do nothing but kill her. He fought against the wash of red that set the muscles in his arms and hands afire. He felt his fists clench and his face contort with new intolerable pain. Akane was dead? She had been deceiving him with his own uncle?

Both seemed equally unbelievable and unbearable. Then he remembered the stories about her former lover, Hayato; the gossip in the town when the man was killed on Masahiro's orders, his children condemned and then spared, thanks, everyone said, to Akane's intercession.

'You must be very tired,' Moe said in the same artificial voice. 'And I see you were wounded. Let me prepare you some tea.'

He knew if he stayed in the room a moment longer he would lose control. He stood abruptly, saying nothing more to his wife, thrust his hand towards the door, tearing the paper screen as he forced it open, and rushed towards the garden. The wall brought him up short. He crashed his fist down on it as though he could split the stone, and tears spurted from his eyes like fountains.

He stood gazing out to sea across the bay. Scarlet azaleas splashed the green of the opposite shore. The waves murmured against the huge sea wall and a slight breeze came off the sea, drying the tears on his cheeks. After the one first surge he did not weep again, but felt the heat of his fury subside and transform itself into something else, no less intense but controllable: an implacable resolve to hold onto what was left to him.

There was no one to whom he could talk, no one with whom to share his grief. Only Kiyoshige would have understood, and Kiyoshige was dead: he would never talk to him, never hear him laugh again. He himself was surrounded by people who hated him – his uncles, his own wife. He had lost his father, his closest friend, his most trusted advisor, Irie Masahide – and Akane, who would have consoled him, whom he would never hold again.

Endo Chikara came to him to tell him that the meeting was assembled. Shigeru had to put aside his grief and rage and face his uncles with composure. Now more than ever he was grateful to Matsuda and the monks at Terayama for the rigorous training that had taught him self-control. He greeted his uncles with no indication of his true feelings, received their condolences and enquiries calmly, scrutinizing their faces carefully but discreetly, assessing their stance and demeanour. He studied Masahiro covertly, repelled by the thought of Akane in the embrace of such ugliness. He did not believe it – she would never sleep with Masahiro, unless he had forced her. This idea caused him such revulsion he had to seal it away in order to be able to continue the discussions.

The meeting was stormy, marked with unease and fear, filled with recriminations: the first against the treacherous Noguchi, then, more subtly, against Shigeru himself, for inciting Iida's hostility, for confronting the Tohan directly. It ended in something of a stalemate, with Lord Shoichi declining to stand down as regent since it might be that the Tohan would refuse to negotiate with Shigeru, and someone had to be in authority to speak for the clan.

Endo, pragmatic as usual, was noticeably silent, but Miyoshi spoke warmly in support of Shigeru, making it clear that in his opinion the people in Hagi, indeed throughout the Middle Country, had been in favour of the war against the Tohan, and would vehemently resist any decision to submit to them. He believed, with Shigeru, that the West would not tolerate the complete domination of the Middle Country by the Tohan, and that they should put their confidence in the alliance with Maruyama, and use it as leverage.

'We must meet the Tohan demands with demands of our own,' Miyoshi counselled. 'After all, Sadamu attacked Chigawa unprovoked.'

'Unfortunately, he was all too provoked,' Shoichi retorted. 'By Lord Shigeru's conduct ever since the death of Miura.'

There seemed little point in arguing repeatedly over the same ground, and Shigeru called an end to the meeting, returning to his mother's house that night, since he wanted to talk in private with Ichiro, and he could not bear to be under the same roof as his uncles or his wife. Miyoshi wanted to accompany him, but Shigeru persuaded him to remain in the castle: he needed at least one loyal retainer there. Miyoshi sent reinforcements to guard the house, and Shigeru thought he knew why. At this point his sudden death would be a convenience for many. Assassination had become a strong possibility. He had never thought about it before; he had been protected by his undisputed position. Now as he returned through the streets, which were still frantic with milling crowds of people, he realized how easily an assassin could be hidden among them. His mother's house seemed pitifully unprotected, but at least he trusted her servants, unlike within the castle, where he could no longer trust anyone.

He told Ichiro all that had been discussed in the meeting, and his teacher offered to attend the following day's negotiations, agreeing with Miyoshi that the Otori had many grievances that needed to be addressed.

'I will remember everything that is said, and make a record of it,' he promised.

By the time they had bathed and eaten the evening meal, Shigeru was numb with fatigue. He wanted to question Ichiro about Akane – but what would Ichiro know? He wanted to grieve for her, as she deserved – but what if she had indeed betrayed him? It was too lacerating to think about. He shut his emotions away, as if in a box buried in the earth, and let himself fall into the deep river of sleep.

Just before sleep came to him, he thought, If anyone knows the truth about Akane, it will be Chiyo. He resolved to question the old woman later, and found some comfort in knowing that she would not lie to him.

Lord Kitano arrived in Hagi the following day, and was escorted with great ceremony to the castle. The dignity of his passage was somewhat marred by the frenzied behaviour of the townsfolk, still exorcising their grief and sense of betrayal in dancing and chanting, dressed, it seemed, in ever more garish and bizarre apparel. Kitano's procession found itself the target of abuse, stones and rubbish were hurled, and blood was very nearly spilled as a result.

Only Shigeru's appearance stopped the unrest from developing into something more ugly. He met Kitano, welcomed him formally and rode alongside him, his composure and courage reassuring and calming the people to some extent, as did the presence of Ichiro, who was widely known and respected as a man of great learning and integrity. It was a sultry, humid day: clouds were massing over the mountains and on the horizon. The plum rains would start at any time, and put a temporary halt to hostilities.

Men shouted angrily that they would burn their houses to the ground and destroy their fields rather than hand them over to the Tohan; women sang that they would throw themselves and their children into the sea if Sadamu ever rode into Hagi. Shigeru was glad that Kitano heard this: if the people were not placated, the harvest would not be brought in, food production would come to a halt, and everyone would starve before the next spring.

The meeting was to be small: just the Otori lords – Shigeru and his uncles – and Kitano. Ichiro was also present with two scribes, one from Hagi, one from Tsuwano. When they were all seated in the main hall and the formal courtesies had been exchanged, Kitano said, 'I am glad I am able to be of some service to the clan at this very sad time.'

He had a self-satisfied air, like a cat that had just scoffed stolen fish.

Shoichi said, 'We deeply regret recent events – we ourselves counselled against them. My brother and I will take responsibility for the future good behaviour of our clan. We hope we can make reparations that Lord Iida will find acceptable.'

'In return, he will recognize us as nominated regents until the succession is clarified,' Masahiro added.

'There is no need for such clarification,' Shigeru said, trying to speak calmly. 'I am Lord Shigemori's eldest son. I have an heir, in my brother, Takeshi.'

Kitano smiled urbanely and said, 'It is one of Lord Iida's basic conditions. No further negotiations will be carried out while Lord Shigeru is the head of the clan.'

When no one spoke, he added, 'I warned you not to incite his enmity. Unless you agree to step aside, there is little point in continuing this meeting. Lord Iida and his army have advanced as far as Kushimoto. We cannot prevent them from taking Yamagata. Then only Tsuwano lies between them and Hagi.'

'Hagi cannot be taken by siege,' Shigeru exclaimed.

His uncles exchanged glances. 'But we could be starved out, especially since it is early summer, and the rice harvest is still weeks away,' Shoichi said.

'Shigeru should take his own life,' Masahiro remarked dispassionately. 'Surely that would answer Iida's requirements, and be honourable.'

'My father's command was that I should live,' Shigeru replied. 'Especially since Jato came to me.'

Ichiro said from behind them, 'If I am permitted to speak, Lord Shigeru's death would plunge the whole of the Middle Country into turmoil. If the Tohan had defeated the Otori in a fair battle, it would be an acceptable outcome. But when treachery is involved, the rights of the defeated are stronger. The battle was fought in the Middle Country:

Lord Iida was the aggressor. All these considerations must be carefully weighed before we reach settlement.'

'The threat to lay siege to Hagi is an empty one,' Shigeru added. 'For the Seishuu will come to our aid. Tell Sadamu that. Anyway, our reports suggest he suffered too many losses to embark on a new campaign, especially during the rainy season.'

'All these contentions may have weight,' Kitano replied, 'but there is no point in discussing them, unless you accept that from this day on you are neither the head nor the heir of the Otori clan.'

'It is not something I can divest myself of, like a robe, or a hat,' Shigeru replied. 'It is what I am.'

'In that case, my presence here is futile,' Kitano remarked.

There was a short silence. Then Shoichi and Masahiro both began to speak at once.

'It's ridiculous...'

'Lord Shigeru must step aside...'

'Your brother is at Terayama?' Kitano said. 'I must tell you that the temple is surrounded by my men, under orders from Lord Iida and myself to attack it, kill everyone in it and burn it to the ground unless matters are settled satisfactorily within the week. The town of Yamagata will also be razed.'

'That would be an act of unsurpassed evil, even for you,' Shigeru replied angrily.

'I can think of a few apt descriptions of you, too, Shigeru,' Kitano retorted. 'However, I don't think insulting each other is constructive. We have to come to an agreement.'

There was a sudden rush of rain on the roof, and the smell of wet earth drifted into the room.

'We must put the good of the clan first,' Shoichi said piously. 'Lord Iida allows you to live, Shigeru. It's a huge concession. And your brother's life will be spared too.'

'You were defeated in battle: you must expect to pay some price for that,' Kitano added. 'Of course, if you insist on taking your own life, we cannot prevent it. But I agree with Master Ichiro – it would cause turmoil among the people, and for that reason, with considerable mercy, and because you once saved his life, Lord Iida will not insist on it.'

Their voices reached him as if from a great distance, and the room seemed full of mist. All he could think of was, *Yet Jato came to me. I must not die before I have sought revenge. It is impossible for me to cease to be the head of the clan. Jato came to me.*

Then he remembered how the sword had come to him, and the words of the man who had brought it to him. *Discernment, deviousness, and above all patience.* These were the qualities he needed to exploit to survive. He would start practising them now.

'Very well,' he said. 'I will step aside, for all the reasons you have mentioned, and above all for the good of the clan.'

'Lord Iida expects written assurances that you will retire from political life, and never take up arms against him again.'

Deviousness. Shigeru inclined his head. 'In return, my brother must receive a safe conduct to Hagi, and both Terayama and Yamagata spared.'

Kitano said, 'They will be spared from attack, but must be ceded to the Tohan, as well as Chigawa and the Yaegahara plain. I am also making sacrifices,' he added. 'I am to forfeit nearly half of my domain. I refrained from attacking you as Iida had requested I should. Noguchi, on the other hand, is being rewarded with the whole of the south.'

The negotiations went on for the rest of the day. The borders of the Three Countries were redrawn. The Otori territory was reduced to the mountainous area between Hagi and Tsuwano and a narrow strip along the northern coast. They lost Chigawa and its silver mines, Kushimoto, Yamagata and the rich southern city of Hofu. Two-thirds of the Middle Country passed into the hands of Iida's warriors. But Hagi was not attacked, and a sort of peace resulted that lasted for over ten years.

Too weakened by Yaegahara to attack them outright over the next few years, Iida also made demands of the Seishuu, for their alliance with the Otori. Arai Daiichi was ordered to serve Noguchi Masayoshi; Lord Shirakawa's eldest daughter Kaede was sent to Noguchi castle as a hostage as soon as she was old enough, and Maruyama Naomi's daughter Mariko was subjected to the same fate in Inuyama itself. Huge castles were built at Yamagata and Noguchi, and carefully guarded border posts set up on the high roads.

But all that lay in the future.

CHAPTER THIRTY-FOUR

For the next few days, Shigeru was fully occupied with the details of the surrender agreement, the exact placement of the boundaries, a revised system through which tax would be directed to the new rulers. Most of the time he found it easy to act calmly, as if it were all a dream from which he would sooner or later awake, and everything would be as it used to be. He moved with indifference through the unreality, doing what had to be done, meticulously and with as much justice as possible. He met endless groups of people: warriors, merchants, village headmen; explained the surrender terms as best he could to them, remaining as unmoved by their anger and lack of comprehension as by their frequent tears.

Gradually his seeming imperturbability had an effect on the frantic behaviour in the town. The dancing crowds dispersed, and people began wearing their ordinary clothes again as life returned to normal. He would not allow them to descend into self-pity and victimhood. That led only to impotence and a festering resentment which would do the Tohan's work for them and destroy the clan from within.

But from time to time Shigeru would find himself in the grip of uncontrollable rage. It came from nowhere, as if it were some demon assailing him. He usually rushed from whatever room he was in, for he feared above all killing someone without intending to; his right hand was often bruised from punching it against a wooden pillar or a stone wall once he was alone. Sometimes he slapped his own face, thinking he was surely going mad; then he would suddenly become conscious of the world around him again, a bush warbler calling from the garden, the scent of irises, the soft patter of rainfall, and the rage abated.

Occasionally when alone he was visited in a similar way by demons of overwhelming grief, for all the dead and for Akane, whom he missed with physical pain. The place of her death, the volcano's crater, had become a centre of worship for the women from the pleasure houses and for young girls in love. Shigeru occasionally visited it himself, and he often went to her father's grave on the stone bridge, made offerings and read the inscription he had had engraved there:

Let the unjust and disloyal beware.

Rage and grief were equally unbearable, and he struggled to keep them both at bay, but painful as they were, they made him feel real. Yet he could not allow himself to succumb to either.

Chiyo had told him what she had gleaned of the circumstances of Akane's death. He suspected his uncle Masahiro of more than lechery – the man had been actively conspiring against him. But Akane herself had been indiscreet, had not been completely faithful to him, had been swayed by Hayato's plight. Thoughts of revenge often came to him, but revenge would keep. He would be patient, like the heron that came every evening to fish in the streams and pools of the garden of the house by the river.

Chiyo, with her practical attitude towards matters of the body, recommended he should console himself with other girls, but he declined her offers, obscurely resenting all women for their attractiveness, their duplicity, and not wanting to become involved with anyone.

He took up residence in the house with his mother and his wife. Ichiro was delighted with the arrangement, assuring Shigeru that the life of a man retired from the world had many delights: the study of literature, religion and philosophy, the practice of aesthetic pleasures, and, naturally, the enjoyment of culinary ones.

Lady Otori and Lady Moe were less content. Both of them felt, at some level, that it would have been more honourable for Shigeru to take his own life. They would of course have joined him in this act, but while he insisted on living, they also were obliged to.

The house, while beautiful and comfortable, was not large, and Shigeru found a certain pleasure in a simple and frugal way of life. Moe missed the luxury and splendour of the castle; while she thought she had not liked the intrigue of the deep interior, now she found she missed that too. She was not fond of her mother-in-law; Chiyo's presence made her uneasy, arousing unpleasant memories; most of the time she had too little to occupy herself with, and she was bored. She was a wife, yet not a wife; she had no children; her family were dead, her house wiped out due to the rashness of her own husband. It was an insult to them that he still lived, and she reminded him of this daily with barbed comments in company and accusations when they were alone together.

With little to do herself, Lady Otori bullied Moe more than ever, often ordering her daughter-in-law to carry out tasks that the maids should do, and usually for no reason other than spitefulness. One evening, a few weeks after the battle, before the end of the rainy season, she told Moe, who was preparing for bed, to fetch her some tea from the kitchen.

It was raining heavily, and the house was dim. Moe filled the teapot from the iron kettle that hung over the embers of the fire, and took a cup to her mother-in-law.

'The water was too hot,' Lady Otori complained. 'You should remove it from the flame and let it cool a little before you make tea.'

'Why don't you ask Chiyo to make it?' Moe retorted.

'Go and make a fresh brew,' Lady Otori ordered. 'Take some to your husband, too. He is with Ichiro, looking at some records. See if you can't behave like a wife to him for once.'

Moe did as she was told, and, full of resentment, carried a tray with the cups of tea on it to the room that was Ichiro's favourite.

Shigeru was there alone, reading a scroll. Several paulownia-wood boxes stood around him, and the room smelled of old paper and rue. He was immersed in study and did not look up when she came in. She knelt and placed the tray on the floor. She was seized by the urge to attack him, wound him, make him suffer as she suffered.

'You sit there like some merchant,' she said. 'Why do you spend so much time in here? You are no longer a warrior at all.'

'Would you be happier if we lived apart?' he replied after a moment. 'I am sure some other arrangements can be made. We have both suffered. There is no point in us hating each other.'

His calm reasonableness infuriated her even more. 'Where would I go? I have nothing and no one left to me! The best way to separate would be through death. Yours first, and mine afterwards.'

He still would not look at her, but said quietly, 'I have already decided I am not going to kill myself. My father commanded me to live.' His eyes ran down and up the columns of writing on the scroll. He unrolled a little more.

'You are afraid,' she said scornfully. 'You are a coward. This is what the great Lord Otori Shigeru is reduced to – a coward, reading about rice and soybeans like a merchant, while your wife brings you tea.'

The day's incessant rain, the smell of damp and mould had already plunged him into depression, and he had been fighting rage and despair all day.

'Leave me alone,' he said, the anger erupting in his voice. 'Go away.'

'Why? Am I reminding you of what you would rather forget? The deaths of thousands on your account? The loss of two-thirds of the Middle Country, the destruction of my family, your own complete humiliation?'

The rage came swooping down on him. He was on his feet, prepared to rush out into the rain. She stood between him and the door. His hands came out to push her away, but she fell against him and he caught her smell, fresh from the bath, her hair fragrant and silky. He both hated her and wanted her. She was his wife: she was supposed to satisfy him and supposed to give him children. He recalled in a flash their wedding night, with its anticipation and disappointment. He was gripping her by the arm, his other hand against her neck, feeling the vulnerable bones at the top of the spine. He was aware of how fragile she was, and of his own power and strength, and was overwhelmed by desire for her.

He thrust her down onto the matting, feeling for her sash, pulling up her robe, loosening his own, wanting to hurt her, obscurely wanting to punish her. She made a small sound of fear. As abruptly as it had descended, the rage vanished. He remembered her fear and frigidity.

I was about to force her, he thought with revulsion.

'I'm sorry,' he said awkwardly, moving away from her, letting her go.

She made no effort to get up, or to cover herself, but gazed at him with an extraordinary look that he had never seen before. She said, 'I am your wife. This is the one thing you don't have to apologize for. If you are still capable, that is.'

The finest line separated the intensity of hatred from the intensity of love. Moe was more aroused by his rage than by his tenderness. She wanted his anger, when she had despised his gentleness. The act between them was as much one of violence as one of love. Yet at the moment of his surrender he felt a rush of tenderness for her, a desire to own and protect her.

Their married life assumed its own distorted pattern, woven from the fractured and twisted threads of their lives. Throughout the day Moe acted as an exemplary wife, quiet, deferential to her mother-in-law, hard-working. But when she and Shigeru were alone, she sought to incite his rage and then submit to it. She drew the anger to her as a tall pine draws lightning, and was herself both ignited and damaged by his response. He still moved and lived in a state of unreality, keeping himself busy during the day, studying, often with Ichiro, at night; the steady beat of the rainfall, the damp moist air, the smell of mould all came between him and the real world. Sometimes he thought he had become a living ghost and would drift away into the mist. The rage that Moe aroused in him, coupled with desire and its release, served a strange purpose in anchoring him to reality. He was grateful to her for it, but any expression of tenderness evoked scorn in her, so he never spoke of it.

By the time the plum rains ended, she had conceived a child. Shigeru was torn between delight and foreboding. When he saw himself, as he was occasionally able to, as a simple warrior-farmer, he imagined the joy children would bring into his life; when he considered his role as the dispossessed heir to the clan, he knew that a child, especially a son, could only add to the danger of his position. How long would he be allowed to live? If his uncles' rule was just, soon the Otori clan would forget him; they would settle down peacefully under it: his life would be irrelevant to them; his death would go unmourned. If, as he feared, Shoichi and Masahiro continued to exploit the resources of the clan for their own benefit and unrest increased, his survival would be even more precarious. He would become a focus for the hopes for the renewal of the world and the return to just government that turned into sparks and ignited revolts among peasants and farmers. His uncles would see him as a constant incitement to rebellion. If he was to live long enough to achieve revenge, he needed to walk a careful path between being too visible and being forgotten altogether. He feared a son would present too great a challenge to his uncles to ignore, yet he longed for a child: the heir to his father's blood, the true heir to the clan.

He feared also for Moe's health. The pregnancy was difficult: she could hardly eat and vomited often. From time to time the thought crossed his mind that their brutal coupling could only result in a monstrous child.

Moe no longer came to him at night: in fact, they hardly spoke any more. She retreated into the women's part of the house, where Chiyo looked after her, persuading her to eat, massaging her legs and back, brewing soporific teas to allay the sickness.

CHAPTER THIRTY-FIVE

Shigeru's next concern was the coming Festival of the Dead. It had been his custom, at this time, whenever possible, to visit Terayama, where many of his ancestors were buried. He had heard that his father's ashes had been taken there after the battle, but he had not attended the funeral, nor had any ceremony been conducted in Hagi – only his brief prayers in the Tribe village. It was his duty, he felt, to go there now, to pay his respects to his father and have prayers said for him, their ancestors and the Otori dead, and escort his brother home, for Takeshi was still at the temple. And he longed to see Matsuda Shingen, to hear from the Abbot some words of wisdom that would teach him the way to live the rest of his life.

He spoke to Ichiro of his desire to travel to Terayama, and the older man said he would approach the Otori lords and see if such a journey would be permitted. Rage swept through Shigeru at the implications of this reply: he was no longer free to travel through the Middle Country; he had to seek his uncles' permission in everything. But he was more able now to control his anger, and he gave no indication of it to Ichiro, merely asking him to seek permission as soon as possible, as arrangements needed to be made and he wanted to send messages ahead to Matsuda.

He did not receive a direct refusal, but constant evasive replies made him realize that permission either would not be granted or would be given too late to arrive at the temple before the first day of the festival. He decided to take matters into his own hands, and put on the disguise that he had worn with Muto Kenji: the old, unmarked travelling robe, the sedge hat; he wrapped Jato's hilt in sharkskin, took a small pouch of food and a string of coins, crossed the river at night by the fish weir, and began to walk through the mountains.

If anyone challenged him, he had decided he would say he was on a pilgrimage to one of the remote shrines in the mountains to the south of Hagi, but no one seemed to suspect his identity. The months after the battle had seen many masterless or dispossessed warriors crossing the Three Countries, making their way home or seeking refuge in the forest, often resorting to petty banditry to survive. He realized his face and person were not known: people did not recognize him. When they had looked at him before, they had seen not him, the individual, but the heir to their clan. Now that he no longer travelled with all of the trappings of Lord Otori, he was invisible. It was both a shock and a relief.

Many people travelled with their faces hidden, wrapped in scarves or concealed beneath conical hats like his. He walked, seemingly deep in his thoughts, as impenetrable as any black covering, but studying the land as he passed through it, taking note of the state of the rice fields, the management of the forests, the fields cut from the mountainside where villagers grew vegetables, fenced with stakes against wild boars. It was high summer, the rice fields brilliant green, the forests deep and shaded, sonorous with the strident cicadas, the air heavy and humid. As well as insects, the forest echoed with birdsong; and every night the cries of frogs rang from the dikes and pools.

He kept away from the high roads, following steep narrow tracks, getting lost from time to time but always continuing south, until he came to the hut where he had spent the summer with Matsuda. He arrived at dusk, startling the tanuki which dived under the veranda, and spent the night in the hut. It seemed to have been closed for some time: the air was musty, the embers in the fine grey ash long cold. It was filled with memories for him, of Matsuda's teaching, of Miura's death, of the fox spirit who had become a friend called Muto Kenji; he ate the last of the food he had brought with him and then sat in meditation on the veranda, while the starry vault of the sky wheeled above him and the tanuki went out on its night-time prowling; when it returned just before dawn, Shigeru also retired inside the hut, and slept for a few hours. He awoke refreshed, feeling somehow more whole than he had for months, breakfasted on spring water and resumed the last stage of his journey.

In the middle of the day, he rested for a while beneath the massive oak where he had seen the houou. He could still recall, clearly imprinted in his mind, its white feather, tipped with red. Matsuda had spoken to him then of death, of choosing the right path towards making his death significant – but now he was still alive when so many had died: had he made the right choice? Or would the result of his actions simply be to drive the houou away from the Middle Country never to return?

There was no sign of the warriors who Kitano had said were surrounding the temple – maybe when the surrender treaty was signed they had all returned to Yamagata, its many inns and beautiful women, or had gone home to Tsuwano to prepare for the harvest. Nevertheless, despite the apparent peace and tranquillity of the temple, the serene curve of the roofs against the deep green of the forest, the white doves fluttering around the eaves, endlessly croo-crooing, Matsuda Shingen could not hide his concern at Shigeru's arrival. Shigeru had just walked into the main courtyard and spoken to one of the monks raking the gravel and sweeping the paths – the temple was not fortified at that time, and the main gate was kept open from dawn to midnight. The monk, mistaking him for an ordinary traveller, had directed him to the guest rooms. It was only when Shigeru removed the hat he wore and asked to speak to the Abbot that he was recognized and taken at once to Matsuda's office. He knelt before the old man, but Matsuda rose, stepped swiftly towards him and embraced him.

'You have come alone, in these clothes? It is hardly safe for you. You must know what danger you are in.'

'I felt I had to celebrate the Festival of the Dead in this place,' Shigeru said. 'This year above all I must honour my father's spirit, and those of the fallen.'

'I will show you where Lord Shigemori's ashes were buried. But first, let me call your brother. You must long to see him.' Matsuda clapped his hands, and when the monk who had escorted Shigeru reappeared, asked him to fetch Takeshi.

'Is he well?' Shigeru asked.

'Physically he's in good health – excellent. But since the news of the defeat and your father's death, he has been very disturbed – angry and defiant. He has threatened to run away several times. For his own safety, I try to keep a close watch on him, but the constant supervision irks him.'

'In other words, he has become very difficult,' Shigeru said. 'I will take him off your hands. He must return to Hagi.'

'Lord Kitano has offered to send an escort,' Matsuda said. 'But Takeshi refuses to go with him, saying he does not keep company with traitors.'

'I have been concerned that Kitano might attempt to delay him in Tsuwano, thus turning him into a hostage,' Shigeru said. 'I would prefer to take him back with me.'

'But then your journey would be revealed to everyone,' Matsuda warned him.

'My journey was not sanctioned by my uncles, but it was completely justifiable,' Shigeru replied. 'I must perform the necessary ceremony for my father, here, where his ashes are buried, and at this time, the Festival of the Dead.'

'Iida will seize on the slightest pretext as proof that you broke the terms of the surrender. I don't see how he will allow you to live. He will have you either assassinated in secret or executed publicly. You are only safe if you stay in what's left of the Middle Country, in Hagi.'

'I don't intend to spend the rest of my life in what amounts to prison!'

'Then how will you spend it?' Matsuda gave no sign of sympathy, regret for the defeat, or recrimination. Shigeru had acted from the best of his knowledge and ability: he had been defeated, but the action had been the right one. This attitude strengthened and comforted Shigeru far more than any pity would have done.

'I will become a farmer, among other things; I will retire from the world. And I will wait.' These answers came to him now, in the quietness of the temple. 'But I need to know the land. I intend to walk it, and discover it. Even Iida cannot see that as a provocation. My self, my person, will be my weapons against him. Everything that Iida is not, I will become. I must live – to counter him; to defeat him, even if I only outlive him. If I can provoke him to murder me, my death will achieve what my life cannot. And I will come here every year I can; I hope you will continue to advise and teach me.'

'Naturally I will be glad to, as long as I am not endangering your life further.'

'I would have killed myself on the battlefield,' Shigeru felt bound to explain. 'But my father's sword, Jato, was delivered into my hands, and I believe it was a command to me to live.'

'If the sword came to you, it must be for a purpose,' Matsuda said. 'Your life is not yet fulfilled. But the path from here on will be much harder than the one you have already travelled.'

'I no longer know who I am,' Shigeru confessed. 'What am I, if I am not the head of the clan?'

'This is what you will learn,' Matsuda said. 'What it is that makes you a man. It will be a harder battle than Yaegahara.'

Shigeru was silent for a few moments. 'My wife is expecting a child,' he said abruptly.

'I hope it is a girl,' Matsuda said. 'Your uncles will be very disturbed if you have a son.'

They were interrupted by a sound outside, and the door slid open. Takeshi rushed in and threw himself at his brother as Shigeru rose to embrace him. Shigeru felt his eyes grow hot; he held Takeshi by the shoulders and looked at him. Takeshi had grown and filled out; his face was thinner and more mature, showing the high cheekbones and strong nose that gave the Otori their hawkish look. Takeshi's eyes were bright, and he sniffed a couple of times but fought back tears.

'Have you come here to kill yourself?' he demanded. 'You must let me join you. Lord Matsuda will assist us.'

'No, we are going to live,' Shigeru replied. 'It was our father's express wish. We will live.'

'Then we must take to the mountains and fight the Tohan there!' Takeshi exclaimed. 'We can rally what was left of the Otori army!'

Shigeru interrupted him. 'We can only do what is possible. I have signed the surrender treaty and have agreed to retire from political life. You must do the same, unless you want to serve our uncles, swear allegiance to the Tohan, and fight for them.'

He remembered his concern about Takeshi's future: he had hoped to give him a domain of his own. Now that would never happen. What would Takeshi do with the rest of his life?

'Swear allegiance to the Tohan?' Takeshi repeated incredulously. 'If you were not my brother, I would think you were insulting me! We must act with honour – it is all that is left to us. I would rather take my own life than serve my uncles!'

'That is something I forbid you to do. You are not yet an adult; you must obey me.'

'You are no longer the heir to the clan.' Takeshi's voice was bitter; it was clear he sought to wound him.

'But I am still your older brother.' Shigeru could understand that Takeshi was disappointed in him; nevertheless he found it painful.

'Lord Shigeru is right,' Matsuda said mildly. 'You must obey him. He wants you to return to Hagi with him.'

'I suppose anything's preferable to staying here,' Takeshi muttered. 'But what am I to do in Hagi?'

'There will be much to do: continue your studies, assist me.' And learn what I have to learn, Shigeru thought: how to be a man.

'Tomorrow we will bid our father farewell,' he said. 'As soon as the festival is over, we will return home.'

Takeshi did not weep during the short service but he obeyed Shigeru without argument and said goodbye to Matsuda with gratitude for all his teaching and what seemed like sincere affection. They returned the same way Shigeru had come, on foot, in unmarked clothes, through the mountains.

Takeshi asked once, 'Is this how we must always be, from now on?'

'It is very hard,' Shigeru admitted. 'And will get harder still. But it will not be forever.'

Takeshi's face which had been sullen and closed brightened a little. 'We will take our revenge?'

They were alone in a way that they might not be again for months or years. Shigeru said quietly, 'We will. I promise you that. Our father's death and our defeat will be avenged. But it means secrecy and deception, something neither of us has ever practised. We have to learn how to do nothing.'

'But not forever?' Takeshi said and smiled.

The weeks passed. Life resumed its rhythms: in order to keep Takeshi occupied, Shigeru found his own days filled.

Takeshi no longer trained in the castle areas with his cousins and the other boys and young men of the clan. Instead Shigeru taught him, on the riverbank or in the forest. Miyoshi Kahei and his younger brother Gemba often accompanied them, with their father's permission, and many other young men sneaked away to observe, for Shigeru, taught by Matsuda, had become a swordsman of great skill, and Takeshi seemed set to equal or even surpass him.

One day, Mori Hiroki, Kiyoshige's brother and the last surviving son of the horsebreaker's family, was among the small crowd at the edge of the river. He had been dedicated to the shrine of the river god six years ago, after the stone battle in which his oldest brother Yuta had drowned and Takeshi had nearly died. He was now fourteen years old. He approached Shigeru after the training session, and asked if he might speak to him.

Shigeru had always had a certain interest in the young man, who had been the subject of his first adult decision. He had suggested that Hiroki be sent to the shrine to serve the river god: he had advised the boys' father, Yusuke, not to take his own life but to continue to serve the Otori clan with his great skills as a horseman. He had watched Hiroki grow into a well-educated and perceptive young man, who had retained his love of dancing and become highly skilled at it.

'My father has certain things he wants to say to you,' Hiroki said. 'Would it be possible for you to come to visit him?'

'I would like to,' Shigeru replied, feeling there was much he should tell Kiyoshige's father about his son's life and death. He made arrangements for the following day, and left early in the morning, taking Takeshi with him. Ichiro had suggested Takeshi might be better employed in studying handwriting, history and philosophy. Takeshi might excel at the martial arts, but his energetic nature disliked inactivity, and he lacked the self-mastery required for diligent learning. Both Ichiro and Shigeru tried to impress on him how intellectual understanding enhanced physical skills, and how self-control was acquired through devoting oneself with as much enthusiasm to what one disliked as to one's favourite pursuits, if not more. Takeshi received all this advice with ill-concealed impatience, and often disappeared from the house, fighting in stone battles with boys from the town and even in forbidden sword-fights with warriors' sons. Shigeru was torn between anger at his brother's conduct and fear that Takeshi would be killed or would run away altogether and join the bands of lawless men who were living rough in the forest, preying on farmers and travellers, pretending to be unvanquished warriors but in reality little better than bandits. He made every effort to involve Takeshi in his own life and interests.

They did not cross the river by the fish weir, but walked across the stone bridge. Shigeru paused to make an offering and pray at the stonemason's grave, hoping Akane's restless spirit would find peace. He thought of her often, raged against her, missed her and grieved for her in equal measures, as Moe's body swelled with his child. Moe's sickness abated as the weeks passed, but she remained sallow-looking and thin apart from her belly, as though the growing child drained all nourishment from her, and her physical discomfort was replaced by a mental anguish as her time drew nearer, for she had always had a deep-rooted fear of childbirth.

They went on foot as Shigeru had no horse – Karasu had died in the battle, and he had not yet replaced him. Almost as many horses had been killed as men; the living ones had been appropriated gleefully by the Tohan: among all the Otori losses, the shortage of horses was one of the deepest felt and most resented.

They were accompanied by one of the few old men that remained of his mother's retainers. The man walked a few paces behind him, his demeanour subdued, yet he and Takeshi must have been aware, as Shigeru himself was, of the buzz that went ahead of them – the murmur, a mixture of sorrow and excitement that brought merchants from their warehouses and craftsmen from their workshops to stare in his direction, drop to their knees as he passed by, then rise to follow him with their eyes.

The Mori residence lay a short way upstream from the lands that belonged to Shigeru's mother, on the southern bank of the Higashigawa. It had become almost a second home to Shigeru during his boyhood: it had always been a place of quiet cheerfulness, despite the frugality and discipline of the Mori's way of life. It saddened him now to enter the untended garden, to see the deserted stables and meadows. There were a few mares with foals at foot, and the old black stallion who had fathered Karasu, but no full-grown horses, and only four two-year-old colts: two blacks, two black-maned greys.

Hiroki met them at the gate to the house, thanked them for coming and led them across the wide wooden veranda to the main room, where his father was already sitting. Fresh flowers had been placed in the alcove, and silken cushions spread on the floor for the visitors; an old man was trying to restore order to the garden, the rasp of his bamboo rake the only sound apart from the cicadas' constant background song.

Yusuke looked calm, but he had grown very thin, and the powerful horseman's muscles in neck and shoulder had wasted. He was dressed in a plain white robe, and Shigeru felt a pang of sorrow and regret, for the white robe signalled that Yusuke intended to kill himself and was already dressed for burial.

They exchanged deep bows, and Shigeru sat in the place of honour, his back to the alcove, looking out over the neglected garden. Yet even its wildness had a certain beauty: he could see how nature struggled to take possession of it again, the seeds sprouting where they fell, the shrubs bursting into their natural shape, escaping from the hand of man. This place of honour was no longer his, yet neither he nor Yusuke could conceive of any other way of relating to each other.

'I am very sorry for your son's death,' he said.

'They tell me he died through the treachery of Noguchi.'

'I am ashamed to have to report it,' Shigeru said. 'It is true.'

'It was terrible news,' Takeshi added. 'I cannot believe my friend died in such a way.'

'And Kamome?' the old man said, for his horses were nearly as dear to him as his sons.

'Kamome was brought down by the Noguchi arrows. Kiyoshige died with his drawn sword in his hand, as if he would fight the entire Noguchi clan himself. He was the best friend anyone could have.' They sat in silence for a few moments; then Shigeru said, 'You have lost both your sons to my family. I deeply regret it.'

He wanted to tell Yusuke that he intended to seek revenge, that he would wait patiently: that Iida and Noguchi would pay for Kiyoshige's death, and his father's... but he did not know who might be listening, and he knew he must not speak rashly. He prayed Takeshi would also keep silent.

'The lives of our entire family already belong to Lord Shigeru,' Yusuke replied. 'It's only through your wisdom and compassion that we have lived till now.' He smiled, and tears shone suddenly in his eyes. 'You were only twelve years old! But this is the reason I've asked you to come today. As I say, my life is yours. I'm asking you to release me from this obligation. I cannot serve your uncles. My only surviving son is a priest: I do not expect the river god to give him back to me. My only wish is to end my life. I seek your permission to do so, and ask that you will assist me.'

'Father!' Hiroki said, but Yusuke held up a hand to silence him. 'I see you have your father's sword,' he said to Shigeru. 'Use Jato on me.'

Again Shigeru felt the pull towards death. How could he take the life of this skilled and loyal man, and live himself? He feared Yusuke would be the first of many: fathers who had lost their sons, warriors who had survived the battle, who would not live with the shame and dishonour of defeat. The best of the Otori would follow those already lost; the clan would destroy itself. But if he were already dead, none of this would concern him... Better perhaps to accept it, order his wife, mother, brother to kill themselves, and die himself. He could almost feel Takeshi next to him willing him to do it.

He heard the stallion neigh from the field, a sound so like Karasu's it was as if he were hearing a ghost.

'We need more horses,' he said. 'I will release you from your obligations to me – indeed your son, Kiyoshige, has paid all debts many times over – but I have one more request to make of you: that you will build up the horse herds before you leave us.'

He could think of nothing that would better restore the clan's pride and spirit than to restore their horses.

The stallion neighed again, and one of the colts answered, echoing, challenging its father.

'I'd have to travel to look for some,' Yusuke said. 'We won't find any in the Three Countries for a while; the horses of the West are too small and too slow, and the Tohan certainly won't help us.'

'Father used to talk, in the past, of the horses of the steppes,' Hiroki said. 'Didn't Father always wish to travel to the mainland and see them for himself?'

'The horses from the edge of the world,' Yusuke murmured. 'Fiercer than lions, faster than the wind.'

'Bring back some of them as your last service to the Otori,' Shigeru said.

Yusuke sat in silence for many long moments. When he spoke, his voice, which had been so firm before, was broken. 'It seems I put on my funeral robe prematurely. I will obey you, Lord Shigeru. I will live. I will go to the edge of the world and bring back horses.'

The tears that he had not shed before were now coursing down his cheeks.

'Forgive me,' he said, wiping them away with the white sleeve. 'This is the grief I had hoped to escape. It is far harder and more painful to live than to die.'

Takeshi said very little but when they left he murmured to his brother, 'Lord Mori is right. It is harder to live.'

'For my sake you must live,' Shigeru replied.

'I would take my own life if you ordered me to; if you tell me not to, I suppose I must obey you. But it seems so shameful.'

'We are obeying our father, there is no shame in that. And never forget, it will not be forever.'

CHAPTER THIRTY-SIX

Moe's fears increased as the child grew. Everything conspired to alarm her. It was common knowledge in the city that Shigeru's uncles were not pleased by the prospect of the birth: people whispered of plots to poison mother and child, to assassinate Shigeru and Takeshi, to bring about Moe's death by spells and sorcery. The winter was unusually bitter, the snows coming early and lasting into the third month, the wind howling from the northwest, bringing freezing temperatures and fresh blizzards. Food and firewood became scarce, charcoal hardly obtainable; the ground was frozen hard as stone, and the weight of icicles broke roofs and trees.

Despite Shigeru's efforts the previous summer, the harvest had suffered from the setbacks of the defeat and its aftermath. Food was running short; beggars flocked to the city, where they died in the streets from starvation or cold. Moe did not dare step outside: it seemed death was everywhere, stalking her and her child. She rarely felt safe, except in the deep recesses of the house where Chiyo sat with her, massaged her shoulders and legs to relax her, and told her gentle tales about tiny magical children born from peach stones or bamboo trunks to allay her fears.

But neither the safety of the house nor all Chiyo's skill could protect her in the end. Her time was overdue: the baby was awkwardly placed, her labour prolonged and yet ineffective. Her screams went on for a day and a night, but before the end of the next chill day they were stilled. The child, a girl, never cried at all, but died at the same time as her mother, and was buried with her.

The passing of the young woman whom no one had particularly liked plunged the whole household into deepest sorrow. The deaths were trivial – a woman, a girl child – compared to the losses already sustained; yet they inspired almost inconsolable grief. Maybe it was felt that the child had promised a new life, a new start; and now even this small comfort had been denied. Maybe his own family began to believe that the house of Otori Shigeru was cursed.

Shigeru's grief, compounded as it was by remorse and regret, was the heaviest and most intractable. For several weeks he did not leave the house, except to attend the necessary ceremonies. He drank no wine and ate very little, and spent long hours in silent meditation, recalling everything about his wife and the distorted love they had crafted from their marriage. He remembered with shame how he had wished for her death; he had wanted to remove her from his life as one would slap a mosquito: she had been an irritation to him; more, they had hated each other but they had lain together to make the child that had killed her. They had both been forced down this path: they were husband and wife; their marriage had been designed to produce legitimate children. No one could blame him for giving his wife a child: it was the function of women to bear children.

However, it was his first experience of the danger and pain of childbirth. He knew how much Moe had feared it. Though he had been kept from the room, he could not remain unaware of her terror and agony. It amazed and saddened him that women should endure such things: they carried the full result of men's desire for their bodies; they went to the edge of the world and brought back sons and daughters. And often they did not come back, but were pulled, struggling vainly to live, into the darkness, their young, fragile bodies torn apart.

He dreamed of his daughter often, once most vividly of her body in the earth: as spring warmed the cold limbs, pale green plants sprouted from them like young ferns.

Both Akane and Moe had been given to him. Akane he had asked for and got; Moe had been supplied. And now both of them were dead, at just over twenty years old. He thought often about all that Akane had taught him; he wished he had told her that he loved her, that he had let his love for her flower instead of denying it; he wished he had loved his wife, that she had given herself to him willingly and ardently because she loved him. Maybe if they had lived ... but they were both gone. He would never see either of them again.

Then his grief would be intensified by longing. After a few weeks, Chiyo, with her usual practicality, arranged for one or other of the maids to linger after they had spread out the bedding, but Shigeru could not bring himself to touch them, telling himself he would never sleep with a woman again.

Spring came late, but with all the more intensity. The southerly breezes had never been so welcomed for their soft warmth; the sky had never seemed so deeply blue, nor had the new leaves ever been such a brilliant green against it. As the days lengthened, Shigeru mastered his grief, realizing that even though he no longer had any definable role in the clan, he still had a part to play in its recovery. If he could reshape his life, then so could the Otori clan.

In his time of meditation, he had thought much about his future. He would never give up the intention to confront and kill Sadamu, avenge his father's death and his clan's defeat; but in order to achieve this, he knew he must keep it completely hidden. He would make the world think he had genuinely retired, that he was no more than a farmer; he would be innocuous and blameless, and he would wait patiently for as long as he had to, hoping and praying that some opportunity would present itself.

He began practising this role at home. He dispensed with all formality in the house, somewhat to his mother's displeasure, took to wearing old, simple clothes, and concerned himself with the development of the garden and of his mother's estate. He talked to anyone who would listen about experimental farming, when the rains would come, how best to deter caterpillars, moths and locusts; such work was patently necessary, for the whole country had suffered the previous winter and food stores were almost completely depleted. It did not escape notice that while Shigeru was concerning himself with restoring the land in order that the people might be fed, Shoichi and Masahiro were living in luxury in the castle, expanding and redecorating the residence and making no concessions in their demands for taxation. Craftsmen and painters worked with gold leaf, ebony and mother of pearl while five hundred people died in a week on the streets of Hagi.

CHAPTER THIRTY-SEVEN

'Of course, it was a great relief to Sadamu,' Kikuta Kotaro remarked to Muto Kenji. It was over a year since the Battle of Yaegahara and the Tribe Masters had met by prior arrangement in the port town of Hofu, now ceded to the former Otori vassal, the traitor Noguchi. 'If Shigeru had had a son, followed by other healthy children, it would have added considerably to Sadamu's anxieties. Or so it was reported to me in Inuyama.'

Shizuka poured more wine into the bowls and the two men drank deeply. They were both her uncles, Kotaro on her mother's side, Kenji on her father's. She listened carefully to the conversation, hiding her feelings, which were complex towards Lord Shigeru. She had never been able to completely forgive herself for her betrayal of him. She felt a stab of pity for him now, wondering if he grieved for his wife's death; he must surely regret that of his child even if it were not a son. She thought with a sense of pride of her own son, now six months old, a robust and precocious child, the image of his father, Arai Daiichi. He was sleeping in another room, but she could hardly bear to let him out of her sight, and her pride was mixed with an anxiousness for him that made her breasts tingle and the milk start to flow.

She was half ashamed of her sentiments, she who had always been praised for her ruthlessness and lack of emotion, so valued by the Tribe. She pressed her arms across her chest, hoping the milk would not stain or smell, knowing that both the men in the room would catch the change in her scent.

Indeed, Kenji glanced at her in his amused, sardonic way as Kotaro continued, 'But the possibility of future sons has persuaded Sadamu that he made a mistake last year not insisting on Shigeru's death. He has become even more obsessed by him. Only Shigeru's death will free him and give him peace.'

'Why did he spare him before?' Shizuka asked. None of them were confidants of Lord Iida, but Kotaro lived in Inuyama, had his own spies there, and dealt with Iida's retainers, Ando and Abe. He knew the warlord's thoughts and intentions better than any of them.

'He had some curious idea that he was acting with honour. His vanity was undermined by the fact that he won the battle only through treachery, and that Shigeru had saved his life two years earlier in the underground caverns. He thought he was cancelling a debt.'

431

'It is as impossible for Sadamu to act with honour as it is for Shigeru to act with dishonour,' Kenji said and laughed as though he were joking.

'That's what many are saying,' Kotaro agreed, 'though not within earshot of the Tohan if they value their tongues and ears.' He laughed too and went on, watching Kenji's face closely: 'But I've received a request, though in fact it was not put quite that delicately, from Ando, for Shigeru to be removed, before the end of the year.'

Kenji gestured to Shizuka to fill his bowl and drank before replying. The three of them were sitting in the back room of a merchant's house; at the end of the room was a small veranda and beyond that an unpaved yard. Someone had placed a few pots of sacred bamboo and silver leaf around the edge of the veranda but the yard was filled with pallets, boxes and baskets; by the gate two pack horses and some porters were waiting patiently to be loaded up. From beyond the walls came the sounds of the port city. The rhythm of life in Hofu followed the winds and the tides; it was midday; the high tide and the sudden change of the direction of the wind had brought a flurry of activity that masked Kenji's long silence.

Finally he said mildly, 'I thought we agreed last year that Iida was better kept off balance, that Shigeru should remain alive.'

Shizuka reflected that she had never seen either of them lose their temper. When they became angry they spoke more and more gently, never relinquishing their iron self-control. She had seen both of them kill with the same cool precision and lack of emotion. She had a sudden vision of Shigeru under their knives and was astonished at the pain it caused her and a completely uncharacteristic feeling of guilt.

The wind rattled the flimsy screens. 'It is an easterly,' Kotaro said with some irritation.

'It will keep you in Hofu for a while,' Kenji remarked, for Kotaro was on his way home to Inuyama from the West. 'We will have time for a few more games.' The two men had been playing go and the tray holding the board and its pieces sat on the matting between them. 'What took you to Maruyama anyway?'

'Another extremely well-paid mission for Lord Iida,' Kotaro replied. 'It must not be repeated beyond these walls but I don't mind telling you. Sadamu's furious that the Western clans did not join him in the attack on the Otori. He lost too many men at Yaegahara to undertake any more military campaigns, yet he wants to punish the Seishuu, Lady Maruyama in particular. He hopes to persuade her to obey her husband's family as a good wife should.'

He glanced at Shizuka. 'Your warrior has had his wings clipped, has he not? Is he suitably shamed and repentant?'

'He tries to pretend to be,' Shizuka replied. 'His life depends on it. Underneath he is very angry. He resents being forced to serve a traitor and he fears his brothers will usurp him if his father should die while he is away from the domain with the Noguchi.'

'Serves him right!' Kotaro returned, laughing again. 'Make sure you keep a close eye on him as you did last year, especially if he is contemplating any more rash meetings, and let us know at once. You're in a perfect position to carry out any judgement and I won't have to make another long and tedious journey.' He leaned forward and said more quietly to Kenji, 'I had no idea there were so few Tribe families in Maruyama, and no Kikuta at all. That's why I had to go myself. Are we dying out? Why do we have so few children?'

He turned to Shizuka and demanded, 'What's your son like? Does he have Kikuta hands?'

It had been the first thing she had checked as soon as the baby was born, looking for the straight line across the palm that marked the Kikuta family, that she had inherited from her mother. She shook her head. 'He takes after his father.'

'Mixing the blood seems to mostly decrease the skills,' Kotaro grumbled. 'That's why the Tribe has always been against it. But it's disappointing; there have been exceptions where it increases them. I hoped he might be one of them.'

'His talents may develop as he grows older,' Kenji said. 'As the Muto's do. He has, after all, Muto blood in him.'

'How old is he?' Kotaro asked.

'He is six months,' Shizuka replied.

'Well, don't get too attached to him. Infants can pass away suddenly for a variety of reasons.' He grinned as he finished speaking. 'Like Maruyama Naomi's son, who died a few days ago. He was about the same age.'

'He died while you were in Maruyama?' Kenji said more coolly than ever.

'Sadamu wanted her warned. There's no better way to strike at a woman.'

'You killed her child?' Shizuka could not help exclaiming.

'Kill is a strong word. I hardly had to do anything. I just looked in his eyes. He slept: never to wake again.'

She tried to conceal the shudder that ran through her. She had heard about this skill that only the Kikuta possessed, to induce instant unconsciousness through their gaze. An adult, she knew, would wake from it, though they were more usually killed while they were disabled; a baby would be completely vulnerable...

Kotaro was proud of himself; she detected a trace of boastfulness in his voice. Suddenly she hated him, for the murder and for the pleasure he took in it. She hated these men who controlled so many lives, including her own, with their ruthlessness and cruelty. They had made her get rid of the first child she had conceived. Now she thought she discerned a threat against her living son, a reminder to obey them. She was filled with bitter resentment even towards Kenji, though she had always believed him to be genuinely fond of her.

She looked at him now. His face was expressionless with no sign of shock or disapproval.

'So Shigeru is next,' Kotaro declared. 'I admit, he will be harder.'

'We have not quite reached an agreement on Shigeru,' Kenji replied. 'Indeed the Muto family are under orders to take no part in any attempt on his life.'

When Kotaro made no immediate response to this Kenji went on, 'Shigeru is mine; I saved his life at Yaegahara; but apart from that he is more useful to all of us alive.'

'I don't want to fall out with you over this,' Kotaro said. 'The unity between the families of the Tribe is far more important than either Sadamu or Shigeru. Let's draw lots for him. We'll see if Heaven is on his side.' He scooped up a handful of go pieces from where they lay on the board after the last game and placed them in their bag. He held it out to Shizuka. 'Take one,' he said.

She drew it from the bag and laid it down on the matting between them. It was white. They all stared at it for a few seconds.

'Match it and he's yours,' Kotaro said. 'Shizuka, close your eyes. I will put one stone of each colour into each of your hands. Then Kenji will choose.'

She held her closed fists out to her uncle, praying that Heaven would guide him. Kenji tapped her left hand. She opened it; the black piece lay on her Kikuta-marked palm. Involuntarily, not trusting Kotaro, she opened her other hand. The stone was white.

Kenji said with infinite gentleness, 'This covers one attempt. I'll go along with that. But if you fail, Shigeru's life reverts to me.'

'We will not fail,' Kotaro said.

CHAPTER THIRTY-EIGHT

Shigeru took up travelling again, in unmarked clothes with his face hidden, taking care to change his appearance on every new journey, hoping to avoid recognition. In the course of the year, the new boundaries were established more firmly, and barriers set up at bridges and crossroads. The Otori had lost the whole of the south, and had been pushed back from the east into a narrow strip along the coast. Shigeru walked through all the remaining territory, knowing it intimately, talking to the farmers, feeling that they often suspected who he was but knew how to keep his secret. He learned about how they organized village life, who the headmen were, their indomitable readiness to confront their lords with their grievances.

When the plum rains put an end to his travels early in the sixth month, he spent the days making careful records of everything he had seen and heard, working until deep into the night with Ichiro.

Late one afternoon, as the rain fell steadily on the roof, dripping from the eaves, trickling down the chains, filling the new ponds in the garden, Chiyo appeared and told him a visitor had arrived.

'On a day like this?' Ichiro muttered. 'He must be a madman.'

Chiyo, who had become ever more familiar with her increasing age and the new informality of the household, said, 'Certainly, rather an unusual caller, if not a madman. He looks like some kind of merchant, but he asked for Lord Shigeru as if he were an old friend.'

'What is his name?' Shigeru said, only half paying attention.

'Muto,' Chiyo replied.

'Ah.' Shigeru finished the sentence he was writing and laid down his brush. He flexed his fingers for a moment. 'You had better show him in.'

Chiyo looked reluctant. 'He's very wet,' she said.

'Then prepare a bath and find dry clothes for him. We will eat together in the upper room. And bring wine,' he added.

'Who is it?' Ichiro inquired.

'Someone I met last year. I'll tell you about him later. But I want to talk to him alone first.'

'It's been a long time,' Kenji said as he came into the upstairs room. 'Thank you for your hospitality.'

'It's the least I can do, in return for yours,' Shigeru replied. 'I'm glad to see you. You said you would send someone to me, but I'm assuming you changed your mind?'

'Unh.' Kenji nodded. 'It seemed best not to draw attention to you. It's been a hard year for everyone. You were obviously reducing your household anyway. It might have been difficult to place someone new.'

'So I'm not currently employing one of your members?' Shigeru said, smiling.

'No, but Iida would be happier if you were!'

'Iida may as well forget about me: he has rendered me impotent against him.'

'Hmm.' Kenji made another of his expressive grunts. 'That may be how you present yourself to the world, but don't forget you are now talking to the man who delivered your father's sword to you, and who heard it speak.' He gestured towards the sword in its stand at the end of the room. 'You have not given it up, I see.'

'I will only hand it over to my heir when my death is inevitable,' Shigeru replied. 'But I am not seeking revenge. All that is behind me: I have become a farmer.' He smiled blandly at Kenji.

'Nevertheless, Iida is still very concerned with you. Almost obsessed, you might say. It's as if some invisible thread binds you to him. He seeks information about you constantly. He is tormented by the fact that he only defeated the Otori through treachery. He won the battle but lost his honour.'

Shigeru said lightly, 'Is there any real honour among warriors any more? These days, all men seize opportunities to advance themselves, and justify their actions afterwards. The Tohan chroniclers can write Iida Sadamu's version of events and make him the undisputed hero of Yaegahara.'

'I agree with you completely,' Kenji said. 'My work, after all, involves me intimately with the dark side of the warrior class. But men with the immense vanity of Iida want to appear honourable while acting dishonourably. It's beginning to dawn on him that he will never win that battle with you. And there are already many balladeers in the Three Countries making up songs about it!'

'I'm flattered,' Shigeru replied. 'But it in no way changes my situation. I have lost everything, except for this house and a small estate.'

'And the high regard and undiminished devotion of your countrymen,' Kenji said, studying Shigeru intently. 'You haven't heard of "Loyalty to the Heron"?'

'What is it?' It was not uncommon for groups to spring up under such names: Narrow Paths of the Snake, Rage of the White Tiger, usually made up of young men who decided to use their intelligence and ability to challenge the accepted order and renew the world. Peasants and farmers banded together with low-ranking warriors to form leagues to defend their fields and farms, and put pressure on their landlords.

'It's a supposedly secret group that's spreading through the Middle Country: they swear to support you when you challenge your uncles, as they all hope you will.'

'I'm gratified for their support, but I can only disappoint them,' Shigeru said. 'To challenge my uncles would bring civil war and destroy the Otori.'

'At the moment, perhaps. But you are not yet twenty years old, and you have patience.'

'You know a great deal about me,' Shigeru said, laughing as if the idea amused him.

'I hear about you,' Kenji said. 'I was sorry to learn of your wife's death. Do you plan to marry again?'

'No, never,' Shigeru replied abruptly. 'I had hoped to have children, but I've realized their existence would only threaten my uncles further, and they would become hostages, if not in reality then to fate. I cannot bear any more losses. Besides, I have my brother: I must act like a father to him now.'

'Well, keep an eye on him. He is in even greater danger than you, as are all your family and anyone you care for. Iida will do anything he can to humiliate you, demonstrate his power over you and cause you pain.' Kenji fell silent for a moment, then said quietly but deliberately, 'Be very careful. Change your routines, go nowhere alone, always be armed.'

'Iida can ignore me,' Shigeru said, pretending indifference, but noting the warning nonetheless. 'I have given up the way of the sword.'

'Yet you still teach your brother, and continue your own practice.'

'My brother needs to be kept occupied. I may be a farmer now, but Takeshi is a warrior's son. He must have the education of a warrior before he comes of age. Then he can choose his own way.' Shigeru went on: 'You seem to know all my activities. Do you have spies watching me all the time?'

'No, not at the moment,' Kenji replied. 'I only hear what's already spread on the wind. I keep my ears open, that's all.' He sounded sincere and Shigeru wanted to trust him, wanted to have this unusual and attractive man as his friend.

'What brings you to Hagi?' he said.

'I have relatives here. You probably know the brewery run by Muto Yuzuru.'

It was a little morsel of information, offered almost like a gift. Shigeru nodded. 'Your family are involved in winemaking, then?'

'Runs in our veins instead of blood,' Kenji said; Shigeru poured him another cup, which he downed in one gulp. 'I myself make soybean products – paste and sauce, in Yamagata. Most of our families are involved in one or the other.'

'And did you come to see me with any special purpose?'

'Not really. Just dropped in. I believe it is what friends do.' Kenji was grinning.

'It has not been within my experience so far,' Shigeru admitted. 'I have been isolated from such everyday pleasures. Sometimes I feel like Shakyamuni, before his enlightenment. He knew nothing of suffering or death; he had been shielded from them. But it was not until he lived in the world that his compassion was awakened.' He broke off, and apologized. 'Forgive me. I did not mean to

compare myself in any way to the Enlightened One, or
to become so serious. One of the consolations of my new
standing in life may be ordinary friendships like this.
Though, of course, I am not suggesting that there is
anything ordinary about you!'

'Just a humble merchant, as you are a farmer!' Kenji
replied.

'Let's drink to the friendship between them. The farmer
and the merchant!'

They both emptied their cups and refilled them.

'What other news do you have?' Shigeru asked.

'You may be interested to hear that Arai Daiichi was
forced to submit to Iida. He's been dispatched to serve
Noguchi in the new castle Iida's building for him.'

'Did your niece go with him?'

'Shizuka? Yes, she's living in the town. They had a
child, you know?'

Shigeru shook his head.

'A boy. They called him Zenko.'

Shigeru emptied his cup, poured more wine and drank
to hide his emotion. She had betrayed him; she was rewarded
with a son! 'Will Arai acknowledge him as his heir?'

'I doubt it. Anyway, Shizuka's children belong to the
Tribe. Arai's younger than you. He'll marry and have legitimate children. He would have been married by now, but
the Three Countries have been in chaos since Yaegahara.
The Western allegiances are all up in the air. They won't
fight Iida, but they'll make life difficult for him. He's
demanding concessions: the Shirakawa will probably have
to give up their daughters as hostages; the Maruyama

offended the Tohan by their refusal to attack the Otori from the West. Lady Maruyama's husband died in the autumn, just after the birth of his son, and the son died recently. She'll probably have to give up her daughter too.'

'Poor woman,' Shigeru said, after a moment's silence. He was amazed and grateful to her for her staunchness.

'If she were a man, she would have paid for her defiance with her life, but since she's a woman Sadamu doesn't really take her seriously. My prediction is he will marry either her or her daughter in order to claim the domain.'

'But he must already be married, at his age?'

'Yes, he is married, but there are many ways to get rid of a wife.'

Shigeru did not reply, reminded again sharply of the fragility of women, and the weeks of mourning Moe.

'Forgive me,' Kenji said, his tone of voice changing. 'I should not have spoken so, given your circumstances.'

'It is the reality of the world,' Shigeru said. 'Iida is an expert in such marriage politics. I wish my father had been as skilled!' Surely Lady Maruyama will never marry Iida, he thought.

After Kenji had departed the following morning, Shigeru went to Ichiro's room and took out a fresh scroll. It continued to rain, though not as heavily; the air smelled of mould, moist and humid.

Muto Yuzuru, he wrote. Brewer in Hagi.

Muto Kenji, the Fox, soybean-product manufacturer in Yamagata.

Muto Shizuka, his niece, concubine and spy.

Her son by Arai Daiichi, Zenko.

He looked at these sparse pieces of information for some time. Then he added:

Kikuta woman (name unknown).

Her son by Otori Shigemori (name unknown).

He rolled the scroll inside one on crop rotation and hid it in the bottom of a chest.

CHAPTER THIRTY-NINE

The rains came to an end, and the heat of summer followed. Shigeru rose early and spent the days in the rice fields, watching the farmers protecting the crops from insects and birds. No one ever spoke of the society Kenji had mentioned – Loyalty to the Heron – yet he was aware of some deep understanding of his desire for anonymity. Beyond his own estate, he was never addressed by name. Outside Hagi, few knew him by sight, and if he was recognized no one gave any indication of it.

Then the rice was harvested with sickles, the grain separated out with flails and sticks and dried on mats in the sun. Small children kept constant watch over it, setting up a cacophony with bells and gongs. In the vegetable fields, the water-powered deer-scarers beat out their erratic rhythm. The Festival of the Weaver Star was celebrated, and then the Festival of the Dead. Shigeru did not go to

Terayama, as in the previous year, but instead attended the memorial at Daishoin, where so many of the Otori of his generation had their final resting place, and where Moe and his daughter were buried. Custom dictated that his uncles should also be present at this ceremony, and Shigeru greeted them with deference and humility, knowing that he must convince them of his new identity if he was to live. He did not speak much to them directly, but talked enthusiastically about the harvest in their hearing. A few days later his mother, who still had some contact with the deep interior – the women's part of the residence – spoke to him, trying to conceal her displeasure.

'They are referring to you as "the Farmer". Can you not at least maintain some dignity, some consciousness of who you are?'

He gave the frank smile that was becoming second nature to him.

'"The Farmer." It is a good name. It is what I am: hardly something to be ashamed of.'

Lady Otori wept in private and goaded him when she spoke to him. He said nothing to her of his true intentions; nor did he tell anyone else, though from time to time he would catch Ichiro regarding him curiously, and wondered how much his astute old teacher suspected.

Takeshi did not hide the fact that Shigeru's behaviour puzzled and shamed him. The nickname of the Farmer spread, and Takeshi hated it, frequently getting into fights over it – and over other perceived insults to Shigeru or himself. He was at the age when the turbulence of becoming a man increased his innate recklessness tenfold.

He loved women, and while it was considered perfectly natural for young men of his age to visit the pleasure houses, Takeshi showed none of Shigeru's reticence or self-control. On the contrary, people began to whisper that he would become as lecherous as his uncle Masahiro.

Chiyo brought these rumours to Shigeru's notice, and he spoke to Takeshi severely about it, leading to angry scenes which surprised and distressed him: he had thought his brother would always be obedient to him and heedful of his advice. He tried to remind Takeshi obliquely of his resolve for revenge but he had no plans to spell out and Takeshi was impatient and dismissive. Shigeru realized the extent to which grief, humiliation and loss of status had undermined Takeshi's loyalty and loosened the bond between them. Not that the bond was any weaker on Shigeru's side. His love and concern for his brother were stronger than ever. Yet he could not allow understanding Takeshi's situation to lead to indulging him. Shigeru was strong-willed, Takeshi stubborn; the confrontations between them increased.

In the ninth month, violent rain and winds lashed the country as the first typhoons swept up the coast from the south, but when the storms abated, autumn had come, with clear blue skies and cool crisp air. The weather was an invitation to travel; Shigeru realized he was longing to escape the difficult atmosphere of the house, the confinement of the city, the stress of continually pretending to be what he was not. He felt he and Takeshi needed to be apart for a while, but feared to leave the younger boy with only Ichiro to supervise him.

Takeshi would make his coming of age in the New Year, yet in Shigeru's eyes he was immature and still had much to learn. Shigeru increased the time they spent together, dedicating long hours in the study to classical learning and war strategy, and on the riverbank to sword training.

One warm evening, when he had arranged to meet his brother, Takeshi kept him waiting. Several young men had turned up to watch the training sessions, among them Miyoshi Kahei. Shigeru practised for a while with Kahei, noting the young man's skill and strength, his unease at Takeshi's lateness increasing. When at last Takeshi arrived, he did not apologize; he watched the final bout with Kahei without expression, and when it was finished made no move to take the pole from him.

'Takeshi,' Shigeru said, 'do the warm-up exercises and then we will spar for a while.'

'I think you have taught me all you can,' Takeshi said without moving. 'I have promised to meet someone shortly.'

'You can still learn something from me, I expect,' Shigeru replied mildly. 'And your first promise was to me, your first obligation to your training.'

'What am I training for, since we do not fight?' Takeshi exclaimed. 'Why don't you teach farmers' sons how to use the hoe?'

Shigeru was aware of Kahei trying to control his reaction, and of the other young men: their shock, followed by their alert interest in how Shigeru would respond. His own immediate reaction was fury that Takeshi should challenge him in public: all the anxieties and irritations that his brother had caused him for months came boiling to the surface. He seized the pole from Kahei and thrust it towards Takeshi. 'Take it and fight, or I'll knock you out.'

Takeshi was barely ready before Shigeru's pole caught him on the right shoulder. Shigeru hit him harder than he had ever done before, unable to suppress the thought: That'll teach him a lesson. His brother responded with equal rage, and came back at him ferociously, surprising Shigeru with the intensity of the attack. He sidestepped and parried the thrusts, but each blow came more swiftly and powerfully than the last, and every response he made only increased Takeshi's fury.

He did not believe his brother was seriously trying to harm him until one blow got past his guard; he ducked in time but knew that Takeshi had been aiming with all his power at his temple, which the pole would have cracked like a piece of pottery. His own rage ignited in response: his next thrust caught Takeshi hard in the breastbone, winding him; as he bent forward, choking for air, Shigeru's pole returned to catch him in the side of the neck. Takeshi fell to his knees; the pole dropped from his hands.

'I concede,' he said, his voice muffled by rage.

'When you can get the better of me, then you may choose whether to continue your training or not,' Shigeru replied. 'Until that time, you obey me.' But he was thinking, We cannot go on like this; we will end up killing each other.

Kahei offered to help Takeshi home. The brothers did not speak for several days; their mother was distraught at

Takeshi's bruises and displeased with Shigeru for causing them. Takeshi had improved in character while he had lived apart from his mother, but now they were both in the same house her indulgence of the younger son and her disapproval of the older undermined Shigeru's authority and encouraged Takeshi's resentment.

Shigeru could see no solution other than to continue to insist on imposing his will, but he knew his disguise as the Farmer had lost him the respect of his mother and his brother.

A few days after the fight that nearly got out of hand, Kahei's father Miyoshi Satoru came to visit, ostensibly to ask if Ichiro might condescend to take Kahei and Gemba as pupils. This led indirectly and with great delicacy to the suggestion that Takeshi might like to spend more time with Satoru's sons, might even like to reside with them for a few weeks.

Shigeru was torn between gratitude and a fear that Satoru thought he was failing in his efforts to raise his brother, that Takeshi was out of control and everyone in Hagi knew it. Satoru deftly managed to give the impression that his older son, Kahei, would benefit greatly both from Ichiro's teaching and from the association with Takeshi, making it possible for Shigeru to agree without any loss of face. Nevertheless, he was reluctant to pass on his personal problems to another family: he thanked Lord Miyoshi for the offer and promised to consider it and discuss it with his mother and Ichiro.

He was sitting in Ichiro's room that night, talking with the old man, when his glance fell on what seemed to be a new addition to the boxes of scrolls that lined the walls. Somewhat to his surprise, Ichiro was all in favour of Lord Miyoshi's suggestion; his mother had argued against it, but more out of habit than through any serious objection.

'What is in this box?' Shigeru inquired.

'It was delivered a few days ago. I forgot to tell you. There's a letter inside, on the top. It's from Otori Eijiro's widow. The estate has been ceded to Tsuwano. She and her daughters are returning to the West. These are the last writings of her husband before he died: she wanted you to have them.'

'Well, I'll look through them.' It seemed a good distraction from the decision he had to make about Takeshi, though it brought its own griefs as he remembered Eijiro's family and the happiness of their lives. He found himself recalling the week he had spent there, and the deep impression it had made on him. It is the influence of the Maruyama, Eijiro had said.

Eijiro's wife was from the Sugita family. Lady Maruyama's companion, Sachie, was her sister. He was thinking about Maruyama Naomi as he took out the letter and unrolled the scroll. The widow's handwriting was strong and bold, the language restrained; he felt he could see her courage and her grief in both. Laying the letter to one side, he took out the next scroll. When he opened it, a smaller piece of paper was enclosed within it. The handwriting was different, neither Eijiro's nor his wife's – more fluid and graceful – and the piece was not a letter, nor was it records of farming.

It was the night of the full moon of the ninth month, and the screens were all wide open, revealing the garden bathed in light. The air was still, all the leaves motionless, the shadows dark and long. In the closest shrub, an orb spider was weaving a web: gold and silver glinted in the moonlight together. He read:

Like young fern shoots
my child's fingers curled.
I did not expect,
in the fifth month, frost.

Was it a message to him, or had it been included in the papers by mistake? Lady Maruyama had said she would write to him by this very means. She did not write of alliances or intrigues; she did not even address him by name. There was nothing that might link them under any suspicious scrutiny; she wrote of grief for a lost child, yet the image she used pierced him as if he had received a sudden cut to the flesh of his heart. She must have had news of his loss; she had suffered in the same way: he had lost his wife and daughter; she, her husband and son. She might have written differently, with words of commiseration, pledges of support, but these brief lines made him believe more than anything that he could trust her, and that she would be part of the pattern of his future. He thought of the game of go: a player might seem to be completely surrounded, powerless and defeated, but an unexpected move could break the tightening ring and reverse the situation. Such a move had suddenly come to him: for the first time since the battle, his patient persistence, dogged and grey, was coloured by the faintest tinge of hope.

He folded the poem and tucked it inside the breast of his robe, then turned his attention to Eijiro's last writings, marvelling at how the energetic, intelligent voice still spoke out to him. Eijiro had been experimenting with different strains of sesame seed, used for oil for cooking and lighting. Shigeru soon became absorbed in the subject, and thought he might try some of these in his own fields: he would write to Eijiro's widow to ensure seeds were retained and sent to him before she left for the West, and he would set aside some land to sow a crop in the spring, making sure the aspect, irrigation and fertilizing followed Eijiro's advice. Every time I light a lamp with the oil, I'll think of him – he could have no more fitting memorial.

The following day, Takeshi came to him and apologized.

'Kahei told me I should,' he said awkwardly. 'He explained to me how much I was in the wrong.'

'He is a good friend to you,' Shigeru replied, and told his brother about Kahei's father's suggestion. 'Let's walk outside for a while.' Once they were in the garden, beyond earshot of anyone, Shigeru explained a little of his continued pretence, repeated his intentions and the need to keep them secret; Takeshi promised to be patient. They agreed Takeshi should live with the Miyoshi family for a while and the young man seemed to welcome it as a new challenge.

'I know you think I am running wild,' he said quietly to Shigeru. 'Some of it is real, but like you I also play a role that is not my true self. I can't pretend I don't enjoy a lot of it, though! It must be more fun than being a farmer!'

Later that afternoon Shigeru was walking through the fields, thinking partly of the sesame crop and partly with some relief of Takeshi, when a man stepped out from the shade of a small group of peach trees and spoke his name.

He recognized the voice at once – his retainer, the warrior Harada – and turned towards him with joy, for he had not seen him since before the battle and had believed him to be dead. Yet the man who dropped to his knees before him was almost unrecognizable. His head and face were covered in a scarf of some deep yellow-brown material and he wore the short jerkin of a labourer; his legs and feet were bare. Shigeru momentarily thought he had been mistaken, but the man raised his head and spoke without getting up: 'Lord Otori. It is I, Harada.'

'I had heard nothing of you, and assumed you were dead,' Shigeru exclaimed. 'It's a great joy to see you, but you are so changed I hardly knew you.'

'Indeed my whole life has changed.' Harada spoke quietly and humbly, like a supplicant or a beggar. 'I am glad to find you alive. I was afraid you would have had to give in to the pressure to take your own life.'

'Many people think I should have joined the dead,' Shigeru said. 'But I have my reasons for remaining with the living. You must come to my house. We'll eat together, and I'll tell you them. Where have you been all this time, and why, may I ask, the change in your appearance and dress?'

He could see now that Harada carried no sword, nor, apparently, any other weapon.

'It is better that I don't come to your house. I don't want it to be known that I am in Hagi. Indeed, I can be of greater service to you if I remain unrecognized. Is there somewhere we can talk?' He dropped his voice further. 'I have a message for you.'

'There is a small shrine at the top of the valley. It's deserted except during days of festival. I am walking that way.'

'I will meet you there.' Harada lowered his head to the ground, remaining there while Shigeru walked on.

Shigeru was both pleased and disturbed by the meeting, delighted that Harada was still alive, puzzled by his strange appearance and his lack of weapons. He did not go directly to the shrine, but continued his careful inspection of the land, taking the time to speak to the farmers, who at that time of year were chopping the stubble and bean straw for fodder and collecting fallen leaves from the oak coppices to use as compost. Sesame needed a warm southerly aspect: in the rugged country south of the city such fields were scarce, and already used for beans and vegetables. The farmers grew enough of these for their own needs, but sesame would be a product they could supply to merchants in the city or directly to warriors' households. It would give them income, access to coins, and increased power over their lives.

Eijiro had written, as if in a direct message, Whenever sesame has been introduced, I have seen an improvement in the living conditions of the villagers and an increase in their well-being, including a greater interest in education. Several villages have even been inspired to have their young men taught to read at schools established in the temples.

A place like this might become a school, Shigeru thought as he approached the shrine. It was almost empty, apart from one young man of about fourteen years, the son of the priest from the nearest village, who kept guard. The villagers stored various farming implements there, hoes, staves and axes, as well as firewood, stacked neatly against the southern wall to dry out before winter. The boy was sitting on the faded wooden veranda, eating from a bowl. Behind him a young girl, obviously his sister, was preparing tea on the hearth. Shigeru could imagine her walking through the forest from her home to bring her older brother his supper.

He had spoken to the boy before, and now said, after greeting him, 'Someone is coming here to meet me. I will wait inside.'

'My sister will bring tea,' the boy replied, ducking his head but not making any other obeisance, as if he knew of Shigeru's desire for informality and anonymity. Ever since Kenji's visits during the plum rains, Shigeru had noticed among the people he met in field and forest similar tiny indications of 'Loyalty to the Heron'.

He removed his sandals and stepped into the darkened interior. The floor had been recently swept, but the air smelled musty. The shrine felt empty, as though the god slept elsewhere and only returned when awakened by the music of the festival.

He found himself wondering about the existence of the gods. Could they really be awakened or swayed by the chanting and prayers of men? This part of the forest, with its small grove, had a feeling of peace and tranquillity that was almost numinous. Did that mean it was truly a place where a god dwelled?

His musings were interrupted by the boy's voice, followed by Harada's. After a few moments the girl came into the shrine, carrying a tray with two wooden cups.

'Your visitor is here, sir.' She set the tray on the floor, and when Harada came in and knelt, placed a cup before him and one in front of Shigeru. Harada unwound the head covering, revealing a terrible scar that covered one side of his face. He had lost the eye, and the whole cheek seemed to have been cut away. The girl flinched at the sight of him, and turned her eyes away.

'Please call me if you need more tea,' she whispered, and left them.

Harada drained the cup at a gulp, causing Shigeru to wonder if he had eaten or drunk anything that day, and then reached inside his jerkin and brought out a small flat package.

'I am to give Lord Otori this to prove my message is genuine.'

Shigeru took it. The wrapping was of a silk as fine as gossamer, faded grey, very old. A faint smell of incense clung to it. He untied it and took from inside a small folded piece of paper. Inside this was a dried fern shoot, perfect in every detail yet, like the silk, faded in colour.

'You have been in Maruyama?' he said quietly.

Harada said, 'The message is that there is much the two parties need to discuss in person and in secret. The Eastern part of the other domain needs inspection. The other person involved will be just across the border.'

He named a mountain shrine, Seisenji, and spoke of the pilgrimage that the 'other person' intended to make while in the district.

'At the next full moon,' he added. 'What reply should I take back?'

'I will be there,' Shigeru said. He was about to ask more: why Harada had gone to Maruyama after the battle, how he had survived the injury, when there was a disturbance outside. The girl screamed loudly and angrily, the boy was shouting; there was a rush and tramp of feet on the boards and three armed men burst into the temple.

But for the dimness of the light, Shigeru would have had no chance, but in the second it took for them to adjust their eyes and recognize him, he was on his feet and Jato was in his hand.

He did not wait to enquire what their purpose was – he had no doubt they had come expressly to kill him; they each had long swords, drawn and ready. Their faces were hidden apart from their eyes, and their garments unmarked. He was outnumbered – Harada, he knew, was unarmed – and speed was his only advantage. To kill the first two was almost like a reflex: the blade moved of its own volition, in its snake-like way, in two jabbing strokes, the downward to the left that cut the first man deep in side and belly, the upward to the right that whipped back across the second's throat. The third assailant was a step behind them and could see better. His blade came whistling down at Shigeru's neck, but he had raised Jato in front of his face and was able to parry the blow and force the blade away.

His adversary was fast, strong and cunning – a fighter of great ability, possibly the most skilful Shigeru had ever encountered apart from Matsuda Shingen. In brief moments between the complete concentration of the fight, he wondered why Harada remained apart from it. This was no ordinary challenge but an unprovoked surprise attack. There was no honour involved. As he felt himself begin to tire, he wondered if Harada had in fact betrayed him, had lured him to this place precisely for such an attack. But the fern – no one knew of that – had she betrayed him? The thought filled him with such rage and despair that it gave him supernatural power. He drove at his opponent with fury, forcing the man to retreat a few steps onto the veranda. Here the boy, with great resourcefulness, thrust a pole between his legs and tripped him up, while the girl threw the tea kettle full in his face.

Shigeru finished him off, Jato taking his head. He was astonished by the intervention of the pair – normally villagers took no part in warriors' battles, large or small: he would have expected these two to run away and hide. The boy was trembling, perhaps partly at his own temerity, but he said to his sister, 'Go and tell Father,' and then, 'Are you hurt, Lord Ot – ' He broke off. 'Sir, I mean!'

'No, I thank you.' He was breathing hard, still in the grip of the shock and intensity of the sudden attack. 'Help me carry the bodies outside. And bring water. We will wash the blood before it stains the floor.'

'How did they dare!' the boy exclaimed. 'To attack you within the shrine! Truly the god punished them!'

'With your help,' Shigeru added.

'It was wrong of me! I should not have interfered. But I was so angry.'

With Harada's help, they dragged the bodies beyond the shrine precinct, and the boy brought water from the spring and sluiced the floor. The dead men stared with sightless eyes while their blood turned the clear water pink.

'Who were they?' Shigeru said to Harada.

'Lord Otori; I have no idea. This had nothing to do with me, I swear it.'

'Then why did you bring me to this place? And leave me to fight them alone?'

'You suggested the meeting place,' Harada said hurriedly. 'I could not have known – '

'You had time to inform your accomplices.'

'I did not! I would never betray you. You know who sent me. Sh – they are your ally, they have already proved that.'

'Yet you stood aside and did nothing.'

'This is what I wished to explain to Lord Otori. There is this matter I have to speak to you about.' Harada glanced around – the sound of scrubbing came from the shrine hall where the boy was fully occupied. The girl had not yet returned with her father. Harada said swiftly, 'I have to ask you to release me from your service.'

'You seem to have released yourself already!' Shigeru accused him. 'No arms, no fighting spirit. What has happened to you?'

'I have taken a vow never to kill again,' Harada replied quietly. 'That is why I ask you to release me. I can no longer serve you as a warrior should.'

'So you have become one of the Hidden,' Shigeru said. He recalled how this thought had occurred to him months ago, before the battle: he had wondered then what effect it would have on the allegiance of a warrior like Harada.

'I was wounded at Yaegahara,' Harada said, touching his empty eye-socket. 'When I lay near death, I had a vision. A being called to me out of a white light, and told me I was to live and to serve only him. I felt God had spoken to me. It seemed a miracle that I was not discovered and killed by the Tohan, a miracle that I recovered – proof of the truth of the vision. I made my way to Maruyama, and found Nesutoro and Mari. They taught me about the Secret God, and gave me rebirth in their custom, through water. I took the name Tomasu, after the man I carried on my back. Forgive me, Lord Otori: I cannot serve both the Secret One and you; I will never kill again, nor is it permitted to kill myself. I will understand if you feel it is necessary to take my life, and I pray that the Secret One will forgive you.'

Shigeru listened to this speech with mounting consternation. Harada was obviously completely sincere: in the past he had believed the man to be dogged in his devotion. Out of all the men he had known, Harada had a single-mindedness and simplicity about him: he was not given to fanciful imaginings; only the deepest conviction could lead him to take this extraordinary step and ask to be released from his allegiance. Only such a conviction, verging on madness, could make him stand by passively while his liege lord, the head of his clan, was attacked and nearly murdered.

His feelings also included embarrassment and an obscure sense of shame. His own warrior had failed him, while two peasant children had come to his aid. Truly his world had been turned upside-down! And Harada's world as well. But how could the man bear to live under such humiliation? It would surely be doing him a favour to release him into death, where he could commune with white lights and secret gods as much as he liked.

Harada seemed to read his thoughts, and extended his neck. His eyes were closed; he said a few words quietly and Shigeru recalled hearing them before, spoken by Nesutoro at the time of death of his wife and children and friends: the prayers the Hidden speak at the moment of their passing. He remembered his insight that the pruned bush grows more vigorously. Despite Iida's fiercest attempts to eradicate them, the Hidden still spread; their numbers increased. He had thought it an obscure belief of the downtrodden, the lowest levels of society: but it had emerged in one of his own warriors.

His hand had been on Jato's hilt and he had been about to wield it, but now he let his hand drop to his side.

'I ask one final service of you,' he said. 'Take my reply back. Once that is done, I release you from all obligations to me. You are no longer part of the Otori clan.'

The words struck him as appalling. He had never said them to anyone in his life. Harada had made himself masterless, a man of the waves, as it was said, by his own choice.

'There will be other ways I can serve you,' Harada murmured.

'Go now,' Shigeru ordered him. 'Before anyone else knows you came. Farewell.'

Harada got to his feet, muttering words of thanks, and walked swiftly away. For a while, silence returned to the shrine, apart from the splash of water and the hollow echo of the bucket, the wind in the oaks and the rustle as leaves fell. A thrush sang loudly. The air was growing cold, almost as if there would be a frost.

In the distance, Shigeru could hear people approaching. The young girl came running up the hill, followed by her father and most of the men of the village. They carried sticks, staves and mattocks, and their faces were set in anger.

'These men came to the village earlier,' the priest said. 'They asked for Lord Otori. We told them nothing, except to look for him in Hagi. But they must have hidden in the forest and followed you here.'

'Who would dare to do such a thing!' one of the younger men exclaimed.

'We know who would dare!' another replied, raising his sickle. 'We should go to Hagi ourselves and protest.'

Shigeru did not recognize the dead men. They wore no crests on their clothes, and when the bodies were stripped they had no tattoos or other marks, save the scars of old wounds. Kenji's warning came back vividly to him.

'Could they have been bandits?' he asked the priest; if bands of masterless men were operating openly so close to Hagi, they would have to be dealt with.

'I suppose it's possible,' the man replied. 'Many warriors were left without lords or land after Yaegahara. But we have not been attacked, nor have we heard of any such bands in these mountains. I am afraid you were their chosen target,' he added. 'We will show those in Hagi that such actions will not be tolerated in the Middle Country.'

The men around him shouted their agreement, and seemed set to march to Hagi at once, giving Shigeru even more cause for astonishment. It was surely a result of the upheaval of Yaegahara, and one that no one had foreseen: instead of being cowed by the defeat, the remaining Otori farmers were defiant; they would take up arms themselves rather than be handed over passively to the Tohan.

He dissuaded them from taking any action, instructing them to arrange for the burial of the dead, and returned home. By the time he reached the house, night had fallen; the moon was one night past full. The air was drier and much colder than the previous night, and the moonlight was no longer golden but pale and ghostly, the shadows suggesting the darkness that lay behind the world of appearances. Out of the day's events, the assassination attempt seemed the least astonishing. He had not even paid attention to the bloodstains on his clothes until Chiyo exclaimed in horror when she came to the door to welcome him, a lamp in her hand.

The news spread at once through the household, and the next day, despite Shigeru's orders for secrecy, had become widely known throughout Hagi. Rumours proliferated, adding to the unrest of the city. Shigeru's uncles were forced to deny publicly any involvement in the assassination plan and to receive Shigeru openly and with respect in order to allay the unrest. Nevertheless, disturbances continued throughout the autumn. As a result, his own position became a little less dangerous, and less restricted: permission to travel freely was granted. He still maintained his disguise, however, relishing the freedom and anonymity it gave him.

He had no way of knowing who had been behind the attempt: but given Kenji's warnings he had to assume it was Iida. Kenji, he thought, might have confirmed this, but the Fox did not reappear as he had in the sixth month, and though Shigeru thought of writing to him at Yamagata, in the end he did not. It concerned him that he was possibly spied on most of the time, and he became more watchful and secretive himself, but he was reassured also by the fact that the men had waylaid him on his own estate – an obvious place for him to be. They might have ambushed him far more successfully on the lonely mountain paths to Terayama, had they known his every movement. And he was heartened by the support of the farmers, by the realization of the hidden loyalty to himself that lay just below the surface like a vein of coal, ready to burn and forge steel.

He announced his intentions of visiting Eijiro's estate to bid farewell to his widow, and made arrangements for

Takeshi to move to Lord Miyoshi's residence while he was away. If all went well, Takeshi might stay there for the winter.

When the moon returned, he set out for Misumi. Mori Yusuke had not returned from his journey, but before he left he had entrusted his remaining horses to Shigeru, and Shigeru took the oldest colt, which had recently been broken in; he named it Kyu. The horse was lively, full of youth and energy: it was impossible to ride it and feel depressed. Truly, I am not made for despair, Shigeru realized, grateful for the upbringing that had made him so resilient. Even the week he spent at Eijiro's, though there was grief enough in the deaths of father and sons, and the loss of the estate, did not plunge him back into the black mood of the days after Moe's death. In the well-ordered fields, still maintained despite Eijiro's passing, he saw a lasting tribute to the man's foresight; and, in the courage of his wife and daughters, testimony to the value of their upbringing.

It will not all be lost forever, he promised silently. I will restore it.

He thought about it constantly, and pieces of strategy began to assemble themselves in the corners of his mind. One of the most important pieces, he knew, would be alliance with the West, with the Arai and the Maruyama. The attempt on his own life had also given him ideas. Iida had attempted to strike at him in the heart of his own country. Could he not strike back in a similar way? Could he bring himself to resort to assassination? Would the

Tribe ever work for him as Kenji had once suggested they would? Could he ever afford them?

A few days before the full moon, he left the horse at Misumi and went on foot into the mountains, letting it be known that he was going to look at the high country forests and would spend some time in retreat, praying for the souls of the dead. No one seemed to question this: his reputation was already established; he was interested in farming, he was more than usually devout, and he set great store by the proper respect paid to the dead.

The Western border of the Middle Country ran along a narrow valley between two steep mountain ranges. Further south, the border was guarded: local lords demanded taxes and tariff fees on goods and merchandise, and spies kept a close watch on travellers. Shigeru had written authority from his clan to travel where he pleased, but he did not want his movements known, and planned to get across the border in the wild mountainous country at the head of the river that flowed all the way north to Hagi.

He had some knowledge of the district on the lower eastern slopes from his previous visits to Eijiro, when they had ridden into the mountains and Eijiro had shown him the different trees grown for timber: cedar and pine, zelkova, paulownia and cypress. But once he was above the level of the forest, following narrow tracks over stony crags, he was in unknown country, finding his way by the sun during the day and the stars at night. The weather remained fine, day after day of clear autumn skies as the leaves changed colour, dyeing the forests red, the stain spreading perceptibly every day from the summit of the ranges downwards.

He had brought food with him, and also ate what the land provided: chestnuts, cobs and mulberries; some nights, early on, he found shelter in an isolated farmhouse, but in the high mountain there were no dwellings and it was too cold to sleep outside, so he walked all night as the moon waxed fuller.

He descended the first range and crossed the river. The area seemed deserted: no sign of any habitation, no smell of smoke. The river here was fast and shallow, hardly more than a stream, babbling to itself as it leaped over boulders. He slept a little in the middle of the day, warmed by the sun, but by nightfall the weather showed signs of changing. The wind swung round to the northwest; clouds banked up on the horizon. He came through a pass and stood on the highest rock to look towards the north, all the way to the coast. The sea was a dull violet smudge on the horizon beneath the solid grey sky. He knew he would be looking at Oshima, the island volcano, but he could not make out its shape. To his left, the range fell more gently, becoming the fertile land of the West, warmed by the coastal 'black current', protected by its mountains. Far away to the southwest lay the city and castle of Maruyama. Harada had told him the shrine she was visiting was less than a day's walk from the pass. He scanned the forest below; in the far distance smoke hung in the valley, but otherwise there was no sign of habitation, no curve of roof emerging from the deep green. On this side of the range, the autumn was slower to place its mark on the trees: only a few maples on the highest slopes had started to turn.

Just before dusk he smelled smoke, and another scent that brought a rush of water into his mouth and made his stomach growl; he followed both smells warily and came upon a small hut made from roughly hewn branches and bark.

Two men were roasting game birds on a fire, the flames bright in the fading light. Shigeru greeted them, startling them: their hands went to their knives and for a moment it seemed he would have to fight them. Guilt made them touchy and suspicious, but when they saw Jato they were more inclined to placate the solitary warrior.

He asked them if they knew the temple, Seisenji, and they gave him directions.

'But surely you won't walk through the night?' the older man said.

'I'm afraid the weather is changing,' Shigeru said.

'You're right! It'll rain tomorrow. Probably after midday.' He glanced at the younger man: they could be father and son, Shigeru thought. 'Stay here tonight. You can share our catch. We've been lucky this week.'

They had many birds, quail, pigeons and pheasants, hanging by the neck on cords from the rafters of the hut. The quail they supplied to a traveller, who transported them to a merchant in Kibi. The rest they dried and salted to feed their families. They were reluctant to reveal too much about their hunting, and he gathered that it was not exactly allowed, but the local lord overlooked it when it suited him.

The pigeon's flesh was dark and strong-flavoured. While sucking the bones, he asked the men if they had heard of the battle of Yaegahara. They shook their heads: they lived in their isolated village or on the mountain, where little news penetrated from the outside world.

He slept lightly, not quite trusting them. It was a cold night, and the younger man got up several times to put more wood on the fire. Shigeru woke each time, and lay for a while thinking about this chance meeting and how his life must be from now on: needing help and support as all men do, yet never able to trust anyone; relying on his own skill and watchfulness to discern threat and defend himself against it, but avoiding living in constant fear and suspicion, which would destroy him more slowly than the sword but as effectively.

They rose in the grey dawn, the men keen to return home before the rain began. They hung the strings of birds round their necks and waists, wrapped their loin-cloths and leggings over them, and covered their upper bodies with loose cloaks.

'Keeps you warm!' the younger man laughed, and pretended to shiver. 'Feels like my wife's fingers on my balls!'

Shigeru could imagine the caress of the soft down against the skin.

They walked together for several hours until the track forked at the head of two narrow valleys. Here they parted, the hunters going north, Shigeru south.

He thanked them and wished them well; they responded cheerfully and briefly, hardly breaking their stride, not bowing or using deferential language. They did

not seem in the least curious about him. He was glad they had no interest in the world beyond, and that they did not care who he was.

He had not gone far down the track before the rain started, at first a light drizzle, just enough to make the path slippery, then, as the wind picked up, heavier and drenching. The wide, conical hat protected his head and shoulders, but his legs were soaked, his sandals muddied and falling apart. He tried to quicken his pace, anxious to reach Seisenji before nightfall, but the track became more treacherous – in places water ran down it like a river – and he began to fear the deluge would force him to spend the night in the forest. He started to question what he was doing as the rain dripped from his hat and his feet lost all feeling. What did he expect from the meeting – if indeed they ever met? Why was he making this journey, unpleasant and dangerous as it was? Would she come at all? Would she come only to betray him?

He remembered vividly the moment when he had longed to slide his hands under her hair and feel the shape of her head, but he sternly tried to put this from him. She had rebuked him for seeing her only as a woman, for not taking her seriously as a ruler: he would not make that mistake again. If she were there at all... Anyway, he wanted no more involvement with women, dreading the pain and disappointment that passion dealt out – but her hair!

It was almost dark when the mountain path, now resembling a waterfall more than anything else, dropped steeply down to join a wider, more level road that led up

a slight slope. At the top of the slope, almost hidden by the driving rain and the dark cedars, was a small building with curved roof and deep eaves. Four horses, one a pretty mare, backs to the wind, were tethered beneath a barely adequate shelter roofed with straw which shook in the gusts of wind, shedding stalks and chaff like huge raindrops.

He stopped at the steps and removed his sandals and hat, sodden as they were. Despite the rain, the doors were all open. He stepped up onto the veranda and looked in.

The rain streamed from the eaves and splashed up from the ground, enclosing the building like a living curtain. Lamps were lit inside, but the main room of the temple was empty, the floor bare boards. It seemed hardly used: a wooden statue of the Enlightened One sat on a small platform; in front of him vases held fresh flowers, the yellow-flowered silver leaf and branches of red-berried sacred bamboo. There were few other decorations or artefacts; only, below the rafters, votive pictures of oxen and horses.

He called softly and heard her voice speak to her companion Sachie, heard the woman get to her feet and approach the doorway. She turned and whispered back into the interior room.

'It is he.'

He made a sign to Sachie, fearing she would speak his name, but she said simply, 'Come in. We are expecting you,' and bobbed her head. He remembered her as an elegant and refined woman of high rank, but now she looked younger and less polished, and the clothes she wore were plain, cut like a man's. The interior room was matted, and he hesitated on the threshold, not wanting to sit down in his wet, muddied clothes.

Lady Maruyama sat by a small lamp, but it was too dark inside to see her face. She stood and approached him. She also was in men's clothes, made from dark cloth, her hair tied back with cords. In contrast with Sachie, her garments made her look older, taller, in every way stronger, but they could not dispel the mystery of her long hair nor the new spareness that grief had brought to her face, revealing the beauty of the bones beneath the white skin. Her look was frank, her gaze direct and open.

'I am so glad to see you. Thank you for coming all this way. You must be tired. And you are wet through. Sachie, can we provide dry clothes?'

'I will ask the groom,' the woman replied, and went quietly from the room, through the worship hall to the veranda. After a few moments she returned with a dry robe that smelled faintly of horses, as if it had recently been unpacked from a saddle pannier.

Shigeru went with Sachie to the other side of the hall, where there was a similar space divided into storerooms and an office with matted floor. The temple's records were stacked in mouldering piles, and a cracked inkstone lay abandoned on a low writing table.

'Does no one live here?' he asked.

'The local people believe this temple to be haunted,' she replied. 'They won't come near it. Priests are driven mad here. They kill themselves or run away. No one will disturb us; and if anyone sees us they will think we are ghosts.'

She brought a bowl of cold water to the veranda and he washed his face, hands and feet.

'I will prepare something to eat,' she murmured. After she had gone he stripped off his clothes, dried himself and put on the borrowed robe. It had been made for a smaller man. He tied it as best he could, put Jato into the sash and his knife inside the breast. It was becoming colder, and despite the dry clothes his skin was beginning to tremble.

He returned to the matted room, and Lady Maruyama indicated that he should sit. She must have brought some furnishings with her on the pack horse, for there were crimson silk cushions on the floor that surely did not belong to the temple; a sword lay next to her.

'Thank you for your message,' he said. 'I was very sorry to hear of your son's death, and so soon after your husband.'

'I will tell you about it later,' she replied. 'You have also suffered terrible loss.'

'I felt you understood, better than anyone,' he said.

She smiled. 'I hope you did not lose everyone you loved.'

'No,' he replied, after thinking about it for a moment. 'My brother still lives, my mother, my teacher. I have at least one friend. I have a lot to thank you for,' he added. 'If you had joined Iida last year, the Otori would have been completely destroyed.'

'We had made an agreement. I gave you my word. I will never enter into an alliance with the Tohan.'

'Yet our acquaintance Arai Daiichi is now serving the Noguchi, whose name has come to mean traitor throughout the Middle Country.'

'Arai had no alternative; he was lucky not to be forced to take his own life. I believe he is biding his time, as you are. We keep in touch as much as we can, through Muto Shizuka.'

'It was she who betrayed us to Iida,' Shigeru said. 'Presumably Arai does not know, since they are still together, and she has borne him a son.'

'You are angry about that!'

'I am angry about many things,' Shigeru said. 'I am learning patience. But I would not trust the Muto woman not to betray us again. Do not tell Arai about this meeting.'

Sachie came quietly into the room with a tray on which stood two bowls filled with a kind of stew, mostly vegetables, with egg stirred through it. She returned in a few moments with a tea kettle and cups.

'It is very plain,' she apologized. 'We had to bring everything with us on the horses. But Bunta will go and find more food if the rain stops tomorrow.'

'I should return to Misumi tomorrow,' Shigeru said.

'Then let us eat quickly, for we have much to talk about,' Naomi said.

He found he was ravenous, hard put to eat slowly, but she ate sparingly as if she had little appetite, watching him all the time.

When they had finished Sachie took the bowls away; the young man, Bunta, brought in a small brazier with glowing charcoal, and then also retired. The rain continued to fall heavily; the wind soughed in the cedars. Night pressed in on them. The old building was full of strange sounds, as if its many ghosts talked in scratchy voices, their mouths full of dust.

Lady Maruyama said, 'I believe my son was murdered.'

'How old was he?'

'Eight months.'

'Infants die from many causes,' Shigeru replied. Indeed, many children were not named until the second year of their life, when their chances of survival into adulthood seemed more assured.

'He was an unusually robust child: he was never ill. But apart from that, I was given warnings that if I did not follow my late husband's family's wishes I would be punished in some way.' Her eyes had become more luminous in the lamplight, but she spoke calmly and dispassionately.

'I would ask you how anyone dared dictate to you,' he said. 'But the truth is I am in the same situation. My life is now subject to my uncles' wishes.'

'We are both betrayed by our closest relatives. Because your uncles, like my husband's family, are willing – eager even – to appease and accommodate Iida Sadamu and the Tohan. It is only to be expected: in the short term they profit from it. But eventually such self-serving behaviour can only lead to the downfall of the Western clans as well as the Otori. The Three Countries will be ruled from sea to sea by the Tohan with their cruelty. The female succession of Maruyama will come to an end.'

Shigeru leaned forward a little and spoke even more softly. 'I will confide in you, though I have never spoken openly of this. I will have my revenge on Iida and destroy him, no matter how long it takes. Even he must have some weakness. I said I was learning patience: I am waiting for some strategy to be revealed to me, waiting for him to let down his guard or make some mistake. That is the only reason I am still alive. I will see him dead first.'

She smiled. 'I am glad. It's what I hoped to hear from you. It is my secret desire also. We will work together and share information and such resources as we have.'

'Yet it must be kept secret – perhaps for years.'

'What is kept hidden from the world increases in strength and worth,' she replied.

'I heard a rumour that Iida seeks to secure the Maruyama domain by marrying you himself,' Shigeru said, hoping he did not sound too abrupt.

'This is what my husband's family hope to force me into. Neither the death of my son nor threats to my daughter's life will make me do that. I would rather be dead.'

After a pause she said, 'I should tell you something of my life so that you understand me. My husband, Ueki Tadashi, was from a small clan on the borders of the East and the Middle Country. He had been married before, to a woman from the East, and had three children: the eldest, a daughter, was older than I – already sixteen and married herself a cousin of Sadamu's, Iida Nariaki, whom my husband adopted, though Nariaki retained the Iida surname.'

'It is none of my business,' Shigeru said, 'but who arranged this marriage; did you choose your own husband?'

'I was somewhat against it, I confess. I did not like the idea of having stepchildren; I was uneasy about such a close alliance with the Iida family. But I allowed myself to be persuaded, and did not regret it at first: my husband was a delightful man, intelligent, kind and a complete support to me.'

Shigeru tried to dismiss a sudden pang of something akin to jealousy.

Naomi went on, 'But his children were another matter, and the very kindness of his nature meant he did not control them as he should. The daughter acted as though she were the heir to Maruyama. When my own daughter was born, she did not hide her rage and disappointment, but began to insist that she be recognized legally. My husband never refused her as such, but merely prevaricated. His health began to fail – when our son was born he seemed to recover a little, he was very happy – but this lasted only for a matter of weeks: his health had been poor all summer, and he died before our son was a month old, from a tumour, it was believed.'

'You have my deepest sympathy,' Shigeru said.

'I had not realized to what extent he protected me until he was gone,' she said. 'Since then, I have been assailed on all sides. I did not take the threats seriously until my son passed away. I had no proof that he had been poisoned, but he died so suddenly after having always been so strong. My accusations and suspicions were dismissed – I was held to be crazed with grief; opinions were voiced that a clan could not be led by a woman: a man would never be so weakened.'

He studied her face in the flickering lamplight. Her expression showed her sorrow, but he thought her character so steady that no grief would ever tip her into madness. He admired her enormously and wanted to tell her so, but he was afraid to reveal the depth of an emotion that he had not yet admitted to himself. He became awkward, speaking in short, abrupt sentences that rang falsely in his own ears. He wanted to tell her about his dream of his fern-child, and how much her message had meant to him, but he was reluctant to express his own grief, in case he were softened by it, and then...

The outcome of their conversation seemed thin and disappointing: he could offer her nothing in the way of political or military support, merely that they were united in their desire for Iida's death.

However, the gap between desire and reality seemed insurmountable. All he could promise her was silent support: years of waiting and secrecy. It was hardly worth putting into words. Finally even their desultory conversation failed completely and they sat in silence for many moments. The wind howled outside, shaking the roof, driving the rain against the walls, sending cold draughts through all the chinks.

'I suppose we may write to each other,' Shigeru said eventually and she made a movement of acquiescence with her head but did not speak except to wish him goodnight. He bade her goodnight in reply and went to the office, where he lay and shivered most of the night in the thin, ill-fitting robe, fighting down the thought that she slept not twenty paces from him and that she had summoned him with other reasons in mind, now that they were both unmarried.

It was impossible not to admire her: she was beautiful, intelligent, brave and possessed of deep feelings: everything a woman should be. But she had spoken of her husband so warmly: she had obviously loved him, and still mourned him; for his part, he did not want to be involved with any woman, least of all one of such high rank who was already desired by his greatest enemy – and whom, he already knew, he would never be allowed to marry.

When he woke, the rain had stopped, though the early morning sky remained overcast. His own clothes were still damp, but he put them on again, leaving the borrowed robe folded on the floor. Sachie and Bunta had gone to the neighbouring village to buy food for the return journey, for they were all eager to take advantage of the break in the weather.

Naomi invited Shigeru to stay until the others returned, so he could then take food with him, but he was anxious to cross the first pass before nightfall.

'Should I leave you alone?' he questioned.

She became almost angry with him. 'If you want to leave, go now! I am in no danger, and even if I were, I am perfectly capable of defending myself.' She indicated the sword next to her. 'There are also spears outside,' she said. 'I assure you I can fight with both.'

They parted formally, with a certain sense of disappointment on both sides.

A wasted journey, he thought. We are both hopelessly weakened. He could not see how they could help each other, yet he could not imagine achieving anything without her. She was his only ally.

The further he went, the worse he felt about leaving her. He wanted to tell her more; he felt he had not expressed his gratitude to her for supporting him against Iida, for understanding his grief, for making the journey to see him. It might be months before they met again: the thought was suddenly unbearable. He had walked for scarcely two hours when the rain began again, heavier than ever. Faced with the prospect of spending the night without shelter, he told himself it would be wiser to turn back; as soon as he turned his spirits lifted. He walked swiftly, often breaking into a run, hardly noticing the rain lashing at him, soaking him, his heart pounding from exertion, from anticipation.

He saw immediately that the woman, Sachie, and the groom had not returned. Only the one horse, the pretty mare, stood in the shelter. She turned her head at his approach and whickered gently. He splashed through the puddles, undid his sandals and leaped up onto the boards of the veranda.

He heard the sound of a sword sliding from the scabbard, and put his hand to Jato, calling out, yet not wanting to name either himself or her. As he stepped into the temple area, the door to his left slid open and she stepped out, the drawn sword in her hand. For a moment they stared at each other without speaking. A flush lay beneath her normally white skin, and her eyes were brilliant with emotion.

'I... came back,' he said.

'I did not expect it to be you.' She looked at the sword, and lowered it. 'You are soaked.'

'Yes. The rain.' He gestured towards the outdoors, where the rain fell in a solid curtain.

'Sachie and Bunta will have stayed in the village,' she murmured. 'Let me take your wet clothes.'

Pools of water were already collecting around him where his garments dripped on the floor. He took the sword from his sash and placed it inside the doorway of the matted room. She laid her sword next to it, then stepped towards him, her face still, her movements deliberate. He smelled her perfume, her hair, and then her breath. She stood close to him and her hands went to the knot in his sash. She undid it carefully and then looked up into his face as she pushed the outer garment back from his shoulders. Her hands brushed against the cold skin at his neck and he remembered the birds' plumage; she led him into the room, loosened her girdle and drew him down onto the crimson cushions. He thought, I must not do this, but he was beyond choice, and then he thought, Everything else is denied to me; this one desired thing I will have. He remembered all he had feared for women, their frailty, their weakness, but she did not receive him with passiveness or weakness, but gave herself to him, and took him, all his strength and his need, with her own strength and power. Beneath the silk undergarments her body was both slender and muscular, desiring his as much as his desired hers, astonishing and delighting him.

They clung to each other like fugitives in the deserted temple. While the rain fell, they were safe: no one would come as long as the rain kept falling. They were emperors in a palace above the clouds, in a world beyond time where anything was possible.

This is what it is to fall in love, he thought with a kind of wonder, never having expected to experience it, having always guarded himself against it on his father's advice; now realizing the impossibility of resisting it, he laughed aloud.

She was seized by the same merriment and became playful, like a child: she brought tea and poured it not like a great lady, but like a serving girl.

'I should serve you,' he said. 'You are the head of your clan, and I am dispossessed. I am nothing.'

She shook her head. 'You will always be Lord of the Otori clan. But we will serve each other. Here.' She spoke in familiar language. 'Take. Drink.' And the abrupt words coming from her mouth made him laugh again.

'I love you,' he said.

'I know. And I you. There is a bond between us from a former life – from many lives, maybe. We have been everything to each other – parent and child, brother and sister, closest friends.'

'We will be husband and wife,' he said.

'Nothing can prevent it,' she replied, adding frankly, caressing him, 'It is what we already are. I knew I loved you as soon as I saw you at Terayama. I recognized you in some way, as though I had known you deeply but had forgotten about you. My husband was still alive and I knew I could never admit my love for you. But I did not stop thinking about you or praying for your safety. When my husband and my son died, it was only the thought of you that sustained me. I decided that so much had been taken from me, I would grasp the one thing I truly wanted.'

'I felt the same,' he said. 'But what future is there for us? Before, you were a faint dream, a distant possibility. Now you have become my reality. What meaning will our lives have if we are only to be separated?'

'Why should we not marry? Come to Maruyama. We will marry there.' Her voice was warm and untroubled, and her optimism led him into a reverie where it was all possible: he would marry and live with this woman; they would establish a peaceful land in the West . . . they would have children.

'Would it ever be permitted?' he asked. 'My uncles are now the heads of the Otori clan. My marriage would be of some importance to them. They would never approve of a union that so increased my standing and power. And there is Iida Sadamu.'

'The Tohan decided my first marriage. Why should they have any further say in my life? I am a ruler in my own right. I will not be dictated to!'

Her imperiousness made him smile, despite his forebodings. He saw her confidence – the assurance of a woman who knows she is loved by the man she loves. Despite the losses of the previous year, she still had a look of youth. Grief had marked her, but had not corroded her spirit.

'Let us work towards it,' he said. 'But can we keep such a thing secret? We might be able to meet once or twice without being discovered but...'

'Let us not talk of danger now,' she interrupted him gently. 'Both of us know the danger; we have to live with it daily. If we cannot meet we may at least write to each other, as you said last night. I will send letters, as before, through Sachie's sister.'

It reminded him of her previous message, brought by his former retainer.

'You met one of my warriors, Harada? I was astonished by his conversion to the Hidden.' He spoke more quietly, though there was no chance of being overheard through the downpour, and tentatively, unsure of how much she would reveal.

'Yes, Harada had some sort of vision. It is not uncommon among these people: their god speaks to them directly when they pray to him. It seems, once heard, it is a voice that is hard to ignore.'

He felt she was speaking of some direct experience. 'Have you heard it?'

She smiled slightly. 'There is much that appeals to me in these teachings,' she replied. 'My children taught me how precious life is, how terrible it is to take it. As the leader of my clan, though, to give up the sword would condemn my people to immediate defeat by all those armed warriors who surround us. We must have some power to stand up to the cruel and the ambitious in their pursuit of conquest. But if everyone believed they faced a divine judge after death, maybe their fear of punishment would rein them in.'

He doubted it, feeling that men like Iida, who feared nothing in Heaven or on Earth, would be controlled only through strength of arms.

'Sometimes I think the voice is calling to me, but because of my position I believe I am unable to answer. It seems offensive to me that people who will not defend themselves should be persecuted and tortured,' she went on. 'They should be allowed to live in peace.'

'They give allegiance to a heavenly power, not their earthly rulers,' Shigeru said. 'Therefore they cannot be trusted. I deeply regret Harada leaving my service.'

'You can trust Harada,' she said.

'Would you stand by and watch me take on three men?'

'No, I would fight alongside you. I do not claim to be one of the Hidden, only to admire and respect some of their teachings.'

There was so much to talk about, so many things to tell each other, and everything they learned about each other only increased their desire. When desire was slaked they talked again, for the rest of the day, as the grey light slowly faded and night came, increasing their sense of isolation from the world, as if they had been transported to some bewitched mansion beyond time. The rain continued to pelt down; they hardly slept, totally absorbed in each other, body and mind, until exhaustion and passion blurred all barriers between them and it seemed they had truly become one person.

When the rain finally eased in the afternoon of the second day, the silence woke them as if from an intoxicated dream, calling them back to their separate lives, to a parting filled with anguish and joy. Sachie and Bunta returned before nightfall, full of apologies for the delay, but they fell silent when they saw Shigeru was there still; the young man went immediately outside to care for the horses. Sachie came inside and prepared food for them. They had hardly thought to eat and now were famished. She had bought eggs and winter greens, and made a broth with soybean paste and curd. Later she cooked rice, saying she would prepare rice cakes for the journey back. She retired to sleep in the room Shigeru had previously occupied, giving no hint of her feelings in either expression or demeanour, yet clearly she was aware of what had happened between them – the very air seemed silky and heavy with their passion.

'She will never say anything to anyone,' Lady Maruyama assured Shigeru.

'And the groom?' He did not really care: he was just grateful to spend another night with her, not to lie shivering fervently paces away as he had before. He reached out and slipped his hands under the smooth mass of hair and cupped her head in his palms.

'He is a discreet and silent young man. Sachie will swear him to secrecy. I am in my own domain; I may do as I please! No one will question me or betray me.'

'Yet Iida may have spies everywhere – even Arai's lover works for the Tribe, and therefore possibly for Iida. How can we ever know whom to trust?'

'I am aware of all this yet right now I feel no one can harm us,' she whispered.

When he poured himself into her he felt the same; yet he knew that this newborn passion could only mean greater danger for them both.

CHAPTER FORTY

Shigeru made the return journey in a state of exhaustion, yet buoyed up by emotions of hope and happiness that a week before would have seemed forever beyond his grasp. He knew in the uncertainty and violence of their world that they might never set eyes on each other again, yet what existed between them was eternal: it could never be taken from him. He felt again her head in his hands, the silky touch of her hair, and heard her voice – Take. Drink – and saw her face light up with laughter.

The weather continued to be changeable, with sudden drenching showers and gusts of wind tearing the leaves from the branches and massing them in drifts at the foot of the trees. As the leaves fell the forest opened up, the bare branches glistening in the soft autumn light. Several times he saw deer on the track ahead, their black scuts quivering as they plunged away from him, and at night the lonely cry of geese flying overhead echoed through the damp air. But for him the autumn wind did not sing of love grown cold, but of a love new and robust, one that would never be extinguished while he lived. He did not know when they would meet again, but now they were allies, more than allies: they were bound together. He waited for her to send another message to him.

She wrote once before winter, the letter arriving in the same way, concealed in more of Eijiro's writings. The letter was unsigned: one might have thought it a copy of a tale, for it read like a fragment of a ghost story, set in an isolated temple in the rain: a warrior bewitched by love, a spirit woman who seduced him. It was written with lightness and humour: he could almost hear his spirit woman laugh.

Then the year turned; the snows came and the city of Hagi was shut off from the rest of the Three Countries.

During the long winter months, when snow was piled high in the garden and icicles hung from the eaves like rows of white radishes, the unyielding harvest of winter, Shigeru often took out the letter and read it, recalling the isolated temple, the rain, her voice, her hair.

Sometimes he could not believe what had happened, that they had dared to take what they both so deeply desired, and he was amazed by her courage and grateful to her beyond words. Her risk was greater than his, for he had nothing that tied him to this world beyond her and his intentions of revenge, whereas she had a daughter and a domain to lose.

At other times their love for each other seemed so natural and preordained that he could see no danger in it. He felt they were invulnerable, protected by fate itself.

So when Naomi wrote in the spring, her letter concealed inside a package from Eijiro's widow containing samples of sesame seed for the first experimental plantings, telling him that she would be at a place called Katte Jinja on the northern coast of Maruyama at the full moon of the fourth month, Shigeru did not hesitate to make arrangements to go travelling again.

Over the last year he had become almost as interested in fishing as in farming, for it was from the sea that Hagi gained most of its food and its wealth. The families of fishermen had their own hierarchies, loyalties and codes, and, Shigeru knew, these often brought them into conflict with his uncles in the castle, who saw their rich, bountiful catches as a source of no less bountiful tax. Shigeru was particularly well acquainted with Terada Fumimasa, a thickset, immensely strong and endlessly shrewd man who ran his own fleet, and the port in general, with affable but unchallenged tyranny. He had, it was rumoured, fathered half the young fishermen in Hagi, but had one legitimate son, Fumio, a boy the same age as Miyoshi Gemba, who at eight years old already accompanied his father on all his voyages.

Terada had from time to time invited Shigeru to join them. Shigeru had never taken him up on it, but now a plan began to form in his mind. Terada lived near the port on the slopes of Fire Mountain. In the last year, Shigeru had often walked here, visiting the place where Akane had died, taking pleasure in the exotic gardens the old priest had created. He had made sure the gardens were not neglected after the old man's death: it had been a way to deal with his grief and anger at Akane, as well, he thought, as preserving a memorial to her beauty and vivacity. Many young men and women came here to pray to Akane's spirit to help them in all matters of the heart, and Shigeru half-consciously joined his prayers to theirs.

On this day in late spring, when the cherry blossom was at its peak, and the lusher scents of orange blossom also filled the air along with many perfumes of strange flowers that he could not identify, the shrine on Fire Mountain was thronged with people, all no doubt feeling like him the tug of spring in their blood, the longing for love, the desire for the beloved's body, the craving to lie down together and make new life.

He thought Terada would be home, for he had seen his ship in the port, getting ready to set sail on the next day's tide. Shigeru knew he had been recognized by many in the crowd: he had been aware of their respect and delight, and someone must have informed Terada, for the man himself came out to his gate and warmly invited him to step inside.

'Lord Shigeru! What an unexpected pleasure; and a great honour, if I may be so indiscreet.' He made no attempt to lower his voice, clearly believing he could do and say as he liked in his own home. No one would dare report any of his words to the Otori lords; their families would have felt Terada's punishment before such words left the mouth.

Terada issued several barking commands; maids brought tea, wine and morsels of raw fish just sliced from the living creature, still quivering, melting in the mouth with the salty essence of the sea itself. They talked about the moon and tides, the weather and the season, and then Shigeru said idly, looking out over the bay towards the other volcano, 'I suppose Oshima is very different from Fire Mountain.'

'Has Lord Shigeru never been there?'

Shigeru shook his head. 'I have always wanted to.'

'Fire Mountain is said to be more stable. Oshima is very unpredictable. No one would dare build a house like this next to the volcano there – though I have been tempted from time to time, especially when the castle tries to extract more and more money from us.'

He filled Shigeru's bowl again and drained his own. Shigeru made no reply and did not allow his bland expression to change. They spoke of other matters, but as Shigeru was leaving Terada said, 'There is nothing to prevent us from dropping by Oshima this week. Why don't you come with us?'

'I would be delighted,' Shigeru said, giving his customary frank smile.

'Meet us at the harbour tomorrow night: we will be away about a week.'

Shigeru went home and made the necessary preparations for the journey, informed his mother and Ichiro, and wrote a brief letter to his uncles, which he instructed Ichiro to deliver after his departure. He said nothing about extending his journey as far as the Maruyama shoreline, but the following evening, as Terada's ship sped across the waves, helped by the tide and the southeast wind, he asked the older man, 'Do you ever put in on the coast of Maruyama?'

'Occasionally we stop at Ohama, when the wind swings to the north and we can't get back to Hagi. Why? Did you want to go there?'

Shigeru did not reply immediately. Terada gestured to him to come a little closer.

'I have no secrets from any of my men,' he said quietly. 'But you may have things you prefer the whole ship does not hear, and I respect that. If you want to go to Maruyama I'll make sure you get there, and I'll ask no questions about your reasons, nor allow anyone else to.'

'You say the northerly keeps you from returning to Hagi,' Shigeru said. 'If you took me to Katte Jinja, might it keep me there for a few days?'

'It will if I tell it to,' Terada replied, grinning. 'It suits us as well; we'll put into Oshima and fish the sea between the island and the coast. We can come back for you whenever you desire.'

The light was fading and the full moon was rising. Shigeru gazed at the path it made across the waves towards the West and imagined walking its length to where she waited for him.

The fishing boats came to Oshima just before dawn, and hove to in the lee of the cliffs, waiting for daybreak. The breeze dropped; the sea was calm, lapping gently against the basalt rocks, so quiet that they could clearly hear the awakening birds on land.

The sun rose, a bright red sphere emerging from the unruffled ocean.

'It will be fair weather for a week,' Terada said, looking up at the cloudless skies, shading his eyes with his arm.

'Good for travelling,' Shigeru agreed, trying to mask his impatience with indifferent calm.

The men put out oars and rowed the boats into the rock-rimmed harbour. From a distance it seemed to be a natural basin, but when they had anchored and leapt ashore Shigeru realized that nature had been improved by carefully hewn stones placed to form a landing quay. The opposite side had been similarly built up into a protective wall.

Above their heads, the sides of the volcano rose steeply; the black rocks and old lava stood out between the forest that sought to cover them. Smoke and steam rose from the crater, and from the numerous hot springs at the volcano's foot, even from the surface of the sea itself where the boiling water burst through cracks in the ocean floor.

'Come, I'll show you around,' Terada said, and, leaving the men to prepare the nets and baskets, they scrambled over the rocks and followed a rough track up the side of the mountain.

'Does no one live here?' Shigeru asked, looking around, when they paused for breath about halfway up. He raised his eyes and looked towards the coast. Hagi lay to the east, lost in the haze.

'It's known as the entrance to Hell,' Terada replied. 'I like to encourage that reputation. The fewer people who come here, the better. Do you want to bathe? Take care, the water is scalding.'

They both stripped off, and Shigeru slid carefully into the pool, his skin turning red instantly. Terada could not help grunting as the water hit his powerful frame.

They sat half-submerged for a few moments without speaking; then Terada said, 'You weren't wounded in the battle?'

'Just a cut in the scalp. It's healed now; my hair covers it.'

'Unnh,' Terada grunted again. 'Forgive me – and shut me up if I'm speaking out of turn – but you will not always be so retiring and so patient?'

'Indeed I will,' Shigeru replied. 'I have withdrawn from power and politics; I am interested only in my house and lands.'

Terada was gazing at him searchingly. 'I know this is what people say; but there are still many who hope secretly –'

Shigeru interrupted him. 'Their hope is futile, and so is our discussing it.'

'But this journey?' Terada persisted.

'It is of a religious nature,' Shigeru replied, allowing an earnest note to creep into his voice. 'I have been told of strange visions and apparitions at this shrine. I will spend a few nights alone there and see if anything is revealed to me. Apart from that, I am interested in your work, your knowledge of the sea and its creatures, as well as the opinions and welfare of your men. And I like travelling.'

'You don't have to worry about my men,' Terada replied. 'They do what I tell them, and I look after them!' He chuckled, and gestured to the land around the pool.

'This is where I would build my house if I lived on Oshima. You can see all the way to Hagi, and no one would ever winkle you out.'

'Is this your island, then?'

'If I am the only one who dares to come to Oshima, then it belongs to me,' Terada said. 'It's my bolt hole: if your uncles get too greedy I'll not stay in Hagi and pay for their luxuries.' He glanced at Shigeru and muttered, 'You can tell them that, I don't care, but I'll not tell them your secrets.'

'I will speak to them about the fairness of the taxation system,' Shigeru said. 'To be frank, it has already concerned me. But your other secrets are safe with me.'

When they had dressed again and descended to the quay, the men had lit fires and prepared food. By midday they were again aboard; Terada had cushions placed on the high deck in the stern, and Shigeru reclined on these, half dozing, as the flowing tide carried the vessel towards the coast, the sail flapping in the breeze, the charms and amulets tinkling on the mast, the messenger pigeons cooing gently in their bamboo baskets.

Terada's son came and sat beside him with one of the tortoiseshell-coloured cats that sailors believe bring good luck, showed him how to tie knots for nets with a piece of resined cord and related stories about kindly dragons and magic fish, every now and then leaping to his feet when he spied a flock of seabirds or a school of fish. He was an attractive boy, plumpish, robust, very like his father.

The sun was low in the sky by the time they came to shore. Its light turned rocks and sand golden. They had seen no boats out at sea, but here, close to the coast, several tiny craft were bobbing in the water. The fishermen seemed both hostile and afraid at the sight of Terada's ship, and Shigeru suspected some earlier encounter might have turned violent.

'This is where Katte Jinja is,' Terada said, pointing towards the shore, where the shrine's roof could be seen between twisted pine trunks. 'You don't have to worry about these people; they won't hurt you.'

There was something more than the usual scorn in his voice, and Shigeru raised his eyebrows.

'They are Hidden,' Terada explained. 'So they will not kill, not even to defend themselves. You will find them interesting, no doubt.'

'Indeed,' Shigeru said. 'I might even question them about their beliefs.'

'They will tell you nothing,' Terada said. 'They will die rather than disclose or forswear them. How long will you stay?' he questioned as his men prepared to lower Shigeru over the side into the thigh-deep water.

For the rest of my life, he wanted to reply, but instead said vaguely, 'I suppose three nights of apparitions will be enough.'

'Three nights too many, if you ask me.' Terada laughed. 'Expect us at this time four days hence.'

The sailors gave him a basket of rice cakes and salted fish, and Shigeru took his own bundle of clothes, holding these over his head, along with Jato, as he waded ashore.

At the top of the beach were a few hovels; women and children sat outside them, tending fires around which small fish were drying on bamboo racks. They stopped what they were doing and bowed their heads without speaking as Shigeru walked past. He glanced at them, noting that the children, though thin, looked healthy enough, and that several of the women were young and not ill-looking. They all looked tense, ready to bolt, and he thought he could guess the reason: the presence of Terada's predatory, unprincipled men. No doubt, missing their own women, the sailors took these, knowing their husbands would not fight to defend them. He resolved to speak to Terada about it. These were her people. It was wrong that men from his clan should prey on them.

Like Seisenji, the shrine seemed abandoned, neglected. He could hear a bullfrog in the shrine garden. It was evening now, the last rays of the sun spilling onto the verandas of the old wooden buildings, casting shadows from every knot and irregularity of roof and floor. There were the horses, tethered in one of the outbuildings: the same mare, the same pack horse. His heart leaped suddenly with the realization, only half believed till this moment, that she was here, that he would hold her, hear her voice, smell her hair. All the pent-up desire and longing of the past six months rose like a flame within him.

His senses seemed unnaturally acute, as though one layer of skin had been stripped from him. He could already smell her perfume and the female scent that lay beneath it.

He called softly, 'Is anyone there?' his voice sounding like a stranger's to his own ears.

The young man, Bunta, came round the side of the building, saw Shigeru and stopped, looking momentarily startled, before dropping to one knee and bowing.

'Lord –!' he said, cutting his speech off before he uttered Shigeru's name.

Shigeru nodded to him, saying nothing.

'The ladies are in the garden,' Bunta said. 'I will tell my lady that a visitor is here.'

'I will go to her,' Shigeru replied. Despite Bunta's discretion, the man made him uneasy. He could so easily be a spy from the Tribe, could so easily betray them. Yet at that moment Shigeru knew that nothing, no threat of death or torture to himself or to anyone he loved, would stop him going to her.

I am bewitched, he thought as he walked swiftly round to the back of the shrine, remembering the tale she had written for him. The garden was overgrown and untended, the spring grass tall and green, studded with wild flowers; the cherry blossom was just past its peak, the ground covered in drifts of white and pink petals, like a reflection of the flowers that still clung to the branches.

Lady Maruyama and Sachie sat on cushions placed on stones around the pool. It was clogged with lily pads and lotus leaves, and one or two deep purple early irises bloomed at its edge.

She looked up at the sound of his footfall and their eyes met. He saw all colour drain from her face and her eyes go lustrous, as though the sight of him were a physical blow. He felt the same; he could barely breathe.

Sachie whispered something and Naomi nodded, her eyes never leaving Shigeru's face. Sachie stood, bobbed her head to Shigeru and disappeared into the shrine.

They were alone. He went and sat beside her, in Sachie's place. She leaned into him, resting her head on his shoulder, her hair spilling across his chest. He ran his fingers through it and over the nape of her neck. They stayed like that for a long time, neither of them speaking, listening to each other's breath and heartbeat.

The sun set and the air began to cool. Naomi drew back and gazed into his eyes.

'Just before you came, a heron alighted at the edge of the pool. Sachie and I agreed it was a sign that you would soon be here. If you had not come tonight I would have left tomorrow. How long can you stay?'

'Some fishermen from Hagi brought me. They will return in four days.'

'Four days!' Her face lit up even more. 'It is an eternity!'

Much later he woke, hearing the surge of the sea on the shingle and the noises of the night from the grove around them. He heard the horses stamp as they shifted their weight. Naomi was also awake; he saw the moonlight that drenched the garden glint on the surface of her eyes. They watched each other for a few moments; then Shigeru said quietly, 'Where were your thoughts?'

'You will laugh at me,' she replied. 'I was thinking of Lady Tora of Oiso, drowning in love.'

She referred to the well-known tale of the Soga brothers, their revenge and the women who loved them.

'Juro Sukenari waited eighteen years for his revenge, did he not? I will wait as long, if that is what it takes,' Shigeru whispered.

'Yet Juro died – his life fading with the dew of the fields,' Naomi replied, quoting from the ballad that was popular with blind singers. 'I cannot bear the thought of your death.'

He took her in her arms then; death had never seemed so distant, nor life so desirable. Yet she was trembling, and afterwards she wept.

The following day was sultry, unseasonably hot. Shigeru rose early and went to swim in the sea. When he returned he did not dress fully, but went half-clothed to the back of the shrine and began the exercises he had been taught by Matsuda. Both body and mind were tired, slightly dulled, drained by the slaking of passion. He thought of the night's brief conversation. It was only two years since his father's death and the betrayals of Yaegahara; was he really capable of maintaining the pretences of his present life for so many more years? And for what purpose? He could not raise an army against Iida. He would never meet him in battle, or indeed in any situation where he might come close enough to him to strike him down. He might allay Iida's suspicions against him, but how would he make use of this? He might be a better swordsman than Iida, though even this seemed doubtful this morning when he was so tired and so slow, but he did not have the skills to surprise him, to ambush him . . .

To assassinate him.

The idea kept returning to him. Now he did no more than note it, bringing his mind back to concentrating on the work. After a few moments he became aware that someone was watching him. He let the movement turn him, and saw Naomi beneath the trees.

'Where did you learn that?' she said, and then, 'Will you teach me?'

They spent the morning going through the exercises; she showed him the way that girls were taught to fight in the West, and then they found old bamboo poles in the outbuildings and sparred with them. Her strength and speed surprised him.

'One day we will fight side by side,' she promised him when the heat forced them to stop and retreat into the shade. She was breathing hard, sweat glistening on her skin. 'I have never let a man see me like this,' she said, laughing. 'Other than Sugita Haruki, who taught me to fight with the sword.'

'It suits you,' he said. 'You should appear like it more often.'

The heat continued, and after the evening meal Naomi begged Sachie to tell a ghost story.

'It will chill our spines and cool us,' she said. Her spirits were high, her look brilliant, her happiness over-flowing.

'This shrine is said to be haunted,' Sachie replied.

'Is there any that is not?' Shigeru asked, remembering Seisenji.

'Your lordship is right,' she replied, smiling slightly. 'Many dark things happen in these isolated places: uneducated people are afraid of their own violent thoughts. They turn their own fears and hatreds into ghosts.'

Her insight impressed him. He saw there was more to her than he had first thought. She was so quiet and self-effacing: he had been so obsessed with Naomi that he had overlooked her intelligence, her lively imagination.

'Tell us what happened here,' Naomi said. 'Ah! I am shivering already!'

Sachie began her tale in a deep, sonorous voice. 'Many years ago, these shores were inhabited by evil men who made a living by luring ships onto the rocks. They killed the survivors of the shipwrecks and burned everything except what they took for themselves, so that there would be no witnesses and no evidence. Mostly their victims were fishermen, occasionally merchants, but one night they wrecked a ship carrying a lord's daughter to her betrothal in a city in the south. She was thirteen years old; she was washed up on the beach when the ship sank and all her retinue were drowned. The cargo was of her betrothal presents: silk, gold and silver, boxes of lacquer and zelkova wood, flasks of wine. She begged them to spare her life, saying her father would reward them if they returned her to him, but they did not believe her. They cut her throat, filled her clothes with stones and threw her body into the sea. That night, while they were celebrating their catch, they heard sounds from this shrine, and saw lights. Flute music was playing, and people were singing and laughing.

'When they crept close to investigate, they saw the girl they had murdered, sitting in the centre of the room, surrounded by her waiting women and her retainers. At her side was a tall lord, dressed in black, his face hidden. They thought they were concealed, but she saw them and called out, "Our guests are here! They must come in and join the feast!"

'The evil men turned to run away, but their legs would not obey them. The girl's gaze pulled them in, and when they stood trembling before her, she said, "You betrothed me to death, and this is my marriage feast. Now my husband desires to meet you." And the man at her side stood; Death stared in their faces. They could not move. Drawing his sword, he killed them all, and sat down again at his wife's side.

'The feast went on even more wildly, and the dead men's wives said to each other, "Where are our husbands? They are enjoying the stolen goods without us." They ran to the shrine and burst in, and the girl said to them, "I am glad you have come. My husband desires to meet you." And the lord stood up and drew his sword again and killed every last woman too.'

'Did they have any children?' Naomi said. 'What happened to them?'

'Their fate is not recorded,' Sachie said. 'But after that this place was uninhabited.'

'Until a gentler people came,' Naomi murmured.

'The men who brought me told me the villagers here are Hidden,' Shigeru said, equally quietly. 'I believe they have suffered from these same men. I will take steps to put an end to it.'

'They are so isolated and so defenceless,' Naomi said. 'We can protect them from the land – each year we conduct campaigns against bandits and outlaws in these and other remote areas of the domain – but we do not have the ships or the resources to deal with pirates.'

'They are not pirates,' Shigeru replied. 'Not yet. But they are full of grievances of their own, so they prey on those weaker than themselves. I will speak to their leader and command him to keep them under control. His son told me a story,' he added. 'He is a boy of about eight years old, Fumio. His father adores him and takes him everywhere with him.'

'Tell us!' Naomi said.

It was around the first half of the Hour of the Dog; night had fallen completely. There was no wind, and the waves were muted. A pair of owls were calling to each other from the old cedars, and a few frogs croaked from the pool. Now and again some small creature scampered through the rafters. The flickering lights threw their shadows above them, as though the dead kept them company.

Shigeru began his story: 'Once a boy went fishing with his father. A storm came up unexpectedly and they were blown far out to sea. The father gave his son all the food and water he had, so after many days the man died but the child lived. Finally the boat washed up on the shores of an island, where a dragon dwelled. The child called to his father, "Father, wake up, we are saved!"

'But his father did not wake. The boy cried louder and louder, so loud that he woke the dragon, who came to the beach and said, "Your father is dead. You must bury him and I will take you home."

'The dragon helped the boy bury his father, and afterwards the boy said, "I cannot leave my father's grave. Let me stay here and I will be your servant."

'"I am not sure what you can do for me," the dragon replied. "Since I am a powerful dragon and you only a human being, and a small one at that."

'"Maybe I can keep you company," the boy suggested. "It must be lonely on this island all by yourself. And when you die I will bury you and say prayers for you at your grave."

'The dragon laughed, for it knew that the lifespan of a dragon far exceeds that of a human, but the boy's words moved it. "Very well," it said. "You may stay here and be to me what you were to your father."

'So the dragon brought the boy up as his son, and he became a great magician and warrior, and one day he will appear, Fumio says, and put an end to cruelty and injustice.'

'Even in stories told by children, we hear the people's longing for justice,' Naomi said.

When they had lain together the previous night, their desire had been overwhelming and uncontrollable. This night they were both more thoughtful, more aware of the risks they were taking, the madness of their actions.

'I am afraid we will make a child,' Shigeru confessed. 'Not that I do not long for it...'

'I do not believe I will conceive this week,' Naomi replied. 'But if I do...' She broke off, unable to voice her intention, but he knew what she meant, and was filled with sorrow and anger.

After a few moments she said, 'I long to give you children; I thought of that when you spoke of Fumio: you must want so much to have a son. It may never be possible for us to marry. I feel all we can do is steal these moments, but they will be very few, with long stretches of time between them, and always so dangerous. It claws at my heart to say it, but you should marry again, so that you can have children.'

'I will marry no one but you,' he said, and then, realizing the depth of his love for her, 'I will lie with no one but you, for the rest of my life.'

'One day you will be my husband,' she whispered. 'And I will bring your children into life.'

They held each other for a long time, and when they made love it was with a hesitant tenderness, as though they were made of some fragile material that one rough move might shatter.

Shigeru swam again the following day, Naomi watching him from the shore.

'I have never learned to swim,' she said. 'I do not care for boats. I suffer from seasickness and prefer to travel by land. It must be terrible to drown – it is a death I fear.'

He could see that her mood was made sombre by their imminent parting, though she tried hard to conceal it. It was a little cooler, the breeze stronger, shifting to the southwest.

'It is the wind you need to blow you home,' Naomi said. 'But I hate it. I wish the northerly would blow and keep you here forever.' She sighed. 'Yet I must return to the city.'

'You miss your daughter?'

'Yes, I do. She is delightful at this age. She is four years old; she talks all the time and is learning to read. I wish you could see her!'

'She will be brought up in the Maruyama way,' Shigeru said, recalling Eijiro's daughters.

'I pray she will never have to be sent away,' Naomi said. 'It is my greatest fear, that Iida will feel himself strong enough to demand hostages, and Mariko will go to Inuyama.'

It was one more constraint on them. By the end of the day they were both silent. Naomi was pale, and seemed almost unwell. He intended to refrain from touching her, but she threw herself against him as soon as they were alone, as though she would annihilate her fears with passion, and he could do nothing but respond. They hardly slept, and when dawn came Naomi rose and dressed.

'We must leave early,' she said. 'It is a long journey back, and anyway I cannot bear to say goodbye to you, so I must go at once.'

'When will we be able to meet again?' he asked.

'Who knows?' She turned away as the tears began to spill from her eyes. 'I will arrange something, when I can, when it is safe... I will write, or send a message.'

Shigeru called for Sachie, who brought tea and a little food, and Naomi regained her self-control. There was nothing they could say to each other; nothing would make the parting easier to bear. The horses were prepared, Bunta as silent as ever, the pack horse loaded with bundles and baskets. Naomi mounted the mare, Sachie and Bunta their horses, and the three rode off. Only the young man looked back at Shigeru.

CHAPTER FORTY-ONE

When he was alone, Shigeru went to the seashore and washed himself all over, plunging into the chilly water, welcoming the numbness it induced, wishing it would numb his emotions as well. Then he set himself to training vigorously, striving to regain his self-mastery, but he kept seeing her image before him, her brilliant eyes, the sheen of sweat on her skin, her slender body shaking, in passion, with tears.

At midday, one of the women from the village brought him some fresh grilled fish from the previous night's catch. He thanked her, and after he had eaten, took the wooden bowl back to her and helped the men prepare the nets for the evening's work. They spoke little: he told them he would warn Terada against attacking them when the ship's captain returned that afternoon. They expressed their gratitude, but he could tell they were not convinced – and indeed on the high seas and in these remote places Terada could act as it suited him, according to his own laws.

The ship appeared out of the afternoon haze, tacking against the southwesterly; Shigeru waded out to it and was pulled over the side. The decks were slippery with the blood of fish that had already been gutted and packed in barrels of salt. Huge vats of seawater held the living catch. The smell was strong, stomach-turning, the fishermen tired, dirty and keen to get home.

'Did you see any apparitions?' Fumio asked eagerly, and Shigeru told him the story of the girl betrothed to death, and the phantoms at the wedding feast.

'And you saw them in Katte Jinja?' the boy said.

'I certainly did,' Shigeru said in the same earnest tone, aware of Terada's eyes on him. 'I shall go home and write it down. One day perhaps you will read my collection!'

Fumio groaned. 'I hate reading!'

His father cuffed him. 'You will read Lord Otori's book and enjoy it!' he said.

They sailed into Hagi harbour early the next morning. Shigeru was awake most of the night, watching the stars and the waning moon, seeing the first hint of dawn and then the vigorous sunrise as the orange sphere pushed itself above the eastern mountains and spilled its extravagant light across the surface of the sea. He thanked Terada at the dock, and thought he saw again both scorn and disappointment in the older man's expression.

He ambled back to his house, stopping to talk to several shopkeepers and merchants along the way, discussing the spring planting, examining various goods introduced from the mainland, drinking tea with one, rice wine with another.

When he came to his own gate and walked through it, greeting the guards cheerfully, into the garden, he saw his mother seated inside the room that gave onto the eastern veranda. He walked round and wished her good morning.

'Lord Shigeru!' she exclaimed. 'Welcome back.' She glanced rapidly at his attire and said, 'You have not been out in the city like that?'

'I have been at sea for a few days,' he said. 'It was very interesting, Mother. Do you know they catch bream, squid, mackerel and sardines between Hagi and Oshima?'

'I have no interest in bream or squid,' she replied. 'You stink of fish – and your clothes! Have you completely forgotten who you are?'

'I'd better go and bathe, then, if I stink,' he said, refusing to be ruffled by her annoyance.

'Indeed, and take some care when you dress. You are to go to the castle. Your uncles wish to speak to you.'

'I shall tell them about the ghosts I saw,' Shigeru replied, smiling blandly. 'I'm thinking of compiling a collection of ancient tales of apparitions. What a fine title that would make! Ancient Tales of Apparitions.'

The expression on his mother's face was not unlike Terada's: disappointment, scorn. He was perversely annoyed that she should be so easily fooled, that she should think so little of him...

He considered making his uncles wait, sending a message to say he was tired after his journey, but he did not want to antagonize them or give them reasons to curtail his activities. After bathing and having his forehead and beard plucked and shaved by Chiyo, Shigeru dressed carefully in his formal robes, but chose the oldest and least ostentatious; before he left he placed Jato, its hilt still wrapped in its sharkskin cover, in his sash, and tucked the piece of cord that Fumio had given him inside his outer garment, all the while pondering on the best way to make the short journey to the castle. He decided to leave his black stallion Kyu behind: horses were still scarce and he did not want to be tricked into having to present his own to either of his uncles. He had settled on walking – it seemed suitably eccentric – but his mother's shock was so great he relented and allowed her to send for the palanquin.

The hot water after the sleepless night had brought fatigue closer. His eyeballs itched, and his head felt almost unbearably heavy. The time at Katte Jinja already seemed like a mirage, and his current state like the results of possession. When he arrived at the castle and emerged from the palanquin, he could not help recalling his father's words five years ago, warning him against infatuation – and Matsuda Shingen's observation that it was one of the faults of the Otori nature. Now he had succumbed in the same way; he did not know where it would lead him. He only knew it was too late to turn back.

He was greeted by Miyoshi Satoru, Kahei's father. They spoke for a while about Takeshi, who had been living in the Miyoshi household since the previous summer. Lord Miyoshi spoke favourably of the young man, who served under him in the castle guard. Takeshi had celebrated his coming of age; it seemed he was settling down.

They walked together to the residence, Shigeru noting the new decorations that had cost so much and been so resented in the town. It reminded him of the ever-increasing taxation that affected everyone, even Terada and his fishing fleet: he must speak to his uncles about it; he must stand up for his people, maintain his pretence... see her again.

His uncles made him wait: he had expected this and was not angered by it; rather, he was grateful, for it gave him time to sit quietly and control his breathing, re-gathering his thoughts and strengthening his resolve. Miyoshi sat in silence too, occasionally looking up as footsteps echoed within or on the outside veranda, and glancing at Shigeru as if he would apologize for the lords' lack of courtesy.

Eventually the steward of the household appeared, and with many apologies ushered Shigeru into the main reception room. The man was an elderly retainer who had served Lord Shigemori and whom Shigeru knew well. He thought he saw embarrassment in his demeanour, and regretted once more the disappointment and shame he had brought on so many in the clan. He wished he could express to this man and to so many others his perverse gratitude that they served his uncles loyally and would preserve the Otori until Iida was dead and Shigeru head of the clan.

His older uncle, Shoichi, was seated in Shigeru's father's former position, and the younger brother, Masahiro, where Shigeru used to sit on Lord Otori's left-hand side. Shigeru neither liked nor admired Shoichi, but these feelings were coldly indifferent compared to the hatred Masahiro aroused in him for his seduction of Akane. He gave no indication of any of these emotions now, merely greeted his uncles in formal language, bowing deeply to the ground, raising himself only when Shoichi returned his greeting and instructed him to sit up.

They exchanged enquiries about each other's health and families, and comments about the fine weather, the onset of summer and other innocuous matters. Shigeru spoke at some length about his farming experiments, allowing himself to ramble on enthusiastically about the possibilities of the sesame crop and the necessity of good fertilization. He was explaining his theories on the ideal way to treat horse manure when Lord Shoichi interrupted him.

'I am sure all the clan's farmers will benefit from Lord Shigeru's wisdom in such things, but we have more important matters to raise with you today.'

'Please tell me, Uncle. Forgive me for having been so tedious. I am becoming a bore about my hobbies, I know.'

'I suppose this recent trip with Terada was in pursuit of some other hobby?' Masahiro said, smiling unpleasantly.

His expression made Shigeru uneasy; Masahiro's lecherous character gave him a nose for sniffing out illicit love affairs. If he mentions her I will kill him here, and then myself. He forced his own smile.

'Indeed it was,' he replied. 'I am interested in fishing techniques. Terada showed me their best fields, their nets, the way they preserve the catch, both salt and fresh. And his son taught me some useful knots.' He took the cord from his breast and showed them Fumio's tricks. 'Delightful, aren't they? You should let me teach you, Uncle, and you can entertain your children.' He deftly twisted the cord into the pattern Fumio called the Helmet and displayed it. 'Of course, this was not the only hobby. I spent some time in a haunted shrine, and collected a fine account for my compilation.'

'Your compilation?' Lord Shoichi repeated in some puzzlement.

'Ancient Tales of Apparitions. That's what I have decided to call it. It will be a collection of ghost stories from the Three Countries. These stories are passed on by word of mouth: some are extremely old. I don't believe anyone has ever written them down.'

'You take after your father,' Masahiro said, grinning. 'He was also a believer in the supernatural, in signs and apparitions.'

'I am my father's son,' Shigeru replied quietly.

'Terada seems to grow more influential every day.' Shoichi leaned forward, looking intently at Shigeru. 'Did you sense any disloyalty towards us?'

'Certainly not,' Shigeru replied. 'He is as loyal to the clan as anyone in Hagi. But the increasing taxation irks him. He likes to make a profit – if the castle takes too much money from him he will be driven to resist.' He spoke calmly and rationally, hoping his uncles would see the sense in his argument. 'There is no need to take more than thirty parts in a hundred from anyone: merchants, farmers or fishermen. If we devote our energies to improving our crops, our small industries and our catch from the sea, everyone benefits and taxes can be reduced.'

He meant what he said sincerely, but also took advantage of the moment to discourse a little more on composting and irrigation. He saw scorn and boredom come into their expressions. Finally Masahiro interrupted him. 'Lord Shigeru, you are becoming too solitary.'

'Almost a recluse,' Shoichi agreed.

Shigeru bowed and said nothing.

'There would be no objection to you marrying again,' Shoichi said. 'Let us find you a wife.'

Shigeru felt it represented a turning point and rejoiced inwardly. If his uncles were willing to give him permission to marry and have children, it meant they now saw him as harmless, were taken in by the mask he had assumed.

'You are very kind,' he said. 'But I have not yet recovered from my wife's death, and do not wish to undertake the responsibilities of marriage.'

'Well, keep our offer in mind,' Masahiro said. 'A man cannot live without women.' He ran his tongue over his lips and gave Shigeru a glance of complicity, igniting the hatred again.

I will kill him, Shigeru vowed inwardly. I will wait for him outside one of his haunts and cut him down.

'The next matter we have to discuss is your brother,' Shoichi said.

'I believe Lord Miyoshi is pleased with his conduct,' Shigeru replied.

'He does seem to be settling down at last,' Shoichi said. 'I have no complaints about him at the moment, though Lord Masahiro may feel differently.'

'Takeshi's always been a problem, in my opinion,' Masahiro muttered. 'No more so than usual recently. All the same, it will be a pleasure to be rid of him for a while.'

'He is to go away?' Shigeru questioned.

'Lord Iida has suggested he should go to Inuyama for a few years.'

'Iida wants Takeshi as a hostage?'

'There is no need to put it in such blunt terms, Lord Shigeru. It is a great honour for Lord Takeshi.'

'Have you already replied? Is it all decided?'

'No, we thought we would discuss it with you first.'

'You must not do it,' he said urgently. 'It puts the Otori clan at an insupportable disadvantage with the Tohan. Iida has no right to demand this now: it was not part of the terms of the surrender. He is trying to bully you: you must not give in to him.'

'This was also Lord Miyoshi's opinion,' Shoichi said.

'Sooner or later we will have to enter into a closer alliance with the Tohan,' Masahiro objected.

'I would not advise it,' Shigeru said, trying to hide his anger.

'But you know more about farming than statecraft, Lord Shigeru. And you are certainly more successful with your crops than you were on the battlefield.' Shoichi smiled lightly. 'Let us make an agreement. Continue to confine yourself to your spirits and your sesame, and Takeshi stays in Hagi. If your behaviour causes us any disquiet, your brother will go to Inuyama.'

Shigeru forced himself to smile in return. 'These are my only interests, so I will not be deprived of my brother's company. Thank you, Uncle, for your wisdom and kindness.'

His mother questioned him closely about the meeting when he returned to the house; he told her about Terada and the suggestion of marriage but kept his uncles' discussion of Takeshi from her. However, later that night, exhausted as he was, he confided in Ichiro all that had been said, and the old man made a record of it, placing the scroll inside one of the many chests that filled the room.

'You seem like a different man when you enter this room,' he remarked, glancing at Shigeru.

'What do you mean?'

'Lord Shigeru, I've known you since you were a child, have watched you grow up. I know which is your real self and which is a role you assume.'

'My brother is now hostage to my role-playing,' Shigeru said with a deep sigh.

'I'm glad to see you have profited so from my instruction,' Ichiro said obliquely. 'Especially in the art of patience.'

•

Ichiro said nothing more on the subject, but it was a comfort to Shigeru in the coming months to know that his teacher, at least, understood his secret motives and sympathized with them.

In the sixth month, news came from Inuyama of the birth of a son to Iida Sadamu. Official celebrations were held in Hagi and lavish gifts sent to Inuyama, and Shigeru rejoiced privately, for if Iida's wife had given him an heir he had no reason to divorce her and look elsewhere.

The plum rains came, followed by the days of high summer. He was fully occupied with overseeing the harvest, rose early and retired late. When he had time, he gathered more ghost stories – and people, learning of this interest, went out of their way to bring him new material or to suggest haunted places for him to visit. In the autumn, after the typhoons had abated, he took a few days to travel north from Hagi along the coast, stopping at each village and temple, and hearing the local legends and folk tales. The journey was partly to maintain his new character, partly to test how much he might travel freely without being recognized or followed, but mostly to alleviate his restlessness as the months since his last meeting with Naomi stretched away with no word from her, nor any way of contacting her. He returned the night before the full moon of the ninth month with several fine new tales, reasonably sure that he had not been trailed, and was writing them down when Chiyo came to the door and said, 'That friend of Lord Shigeru's, the strange one, is at the gate. Do you want to see him tonight, or will we tell him to come back tomorrow?'

'Muto Kenji?' Shigeru said, delighted, for it was over a year since Kenji's last visit. 'Bring him in at once, and bring wine, and prepare something to eat with it.'

'Will you move to the upper room?' Chiyo inquired.

'No, let him come in here. I will show him my compilation.'

Chiyo looked pleased, for she had already supplied him with many grim and weird stories.

'He can probably tell you a few stories of his own,' she said as she left the room. 'If he's not an apparition himself.'

After they had exchanged greetings, Kenji cast an eye over the collections of scrolls and asked, 'What are you so engrossed in?'

'It is my compilation of supernatural tales, haunted places and so on,' Shigeru replied. 'Chiyo thinks you might be able to add to it.'

'I can tell you some chilling things, but they are not tales – though they involve ghosts and their masters.' Kenji laughed. 'They are all too true.'

'Histories of the Tribe?' Shigeru enquired. 'They would make an interesting addition.'

'They certainly would!' Kenji was studying him closely. 'Have you been away?'

'Just along the coast. I enjoy travelling – and now I have this new hobby...'

'Yes, a perfect excuse!'

'You are too suspicious, my dear friend,' Shigeru said, smiling.

'I like travelling, too. We should go together some time.'

'Gladly,' Shigeru said, and dared to add, 'There's a great deal I would like to learn from you.'

'I'll pass on to you all I can that helps you,' Kenji replied, and went on more seriously, 'I can tell you something of the Tribe too. I know we interest you. But to reveal all our secrets is impossible: I'm one of the two most important figures in the Tribe, but it would still cost me my life!'

Shigeru longed to question Kenji about his father's lover, the Kikuta woman, and her child – what had become of him, had he had children, was he still alive? – but he remembered she had warned his father never to speak of it; the Tribe had not known of the affair. Perhaps it was better that they never did. He put the matter aside for the time being.

'Do you have any news for me?'

'You've heard about Iida's son, no doubt?'

Shigeru nodded. 'Has it changed Iida?'

'It's calmed him down, temporarily. But now he has an heir it will spur him on to consolidate the Tohan lands and his new territories. My niece often asks after you, by the way.'

Chiyo returned with flasks of wine and cups, and trays of food. Shigeru poured wine. Kenji drained his cup in one gulp. 'Arai, it seems, still harbours some hopes of alliance against Iida.'

'I have given up all such ideas,' Shigeru said blandly, drinking more slowly. 'Shizuka betrayed both Arai and me,' he went on. 'I am surprised he lets her live!'

'Arai is less astute than you; I do not believe he ever suspected her. If he did he must have forgiven her, for they have another son,' Kenji remarked.

'They are lucky.'

'Well, children are always welcome,' Kenji said. 'Zenko was born the year of the battle: he is now two years old. The younger one is called Taku. But Arai is to be married next year, and that may make Shizuka's position more precarious.'

'Presumably you will look after her,' Shigeru said.

'Naturally. And more than any woman I know Shizuka can take care of herself.'

'But her sons must make her vulnerable,' Shigeru said. 'Who will Arai's bride be?'

'Someone selected by the Tohan; no one of any importance. Arai is still in disgrace.'

'Am I?' Shigeru said.

'Iida thinks you have been made harmless. He is not afraid of you, at the moment.' Kenji paused as though wondering if he should say what he said next. 'Your life was in some danger last year, but that danger is not so great now. If Iida feels anything for you, it is contempt. He often expresses it. He even refers to you as the Farmer!'

Shigeru smiled inwardly.

'Of course, the clever hawk hides its talons,' Kenji remarked.

'No, my talons are drawn, my wings clipped,' Shigeru laughed. 'And I believe Sadamu has given up hawking.' He reminded himself of the day he saw the now all-powerful lord of the Tohan naked. He was relieved and encouraged that his new role was accepted even as far away as the East. Moreover, he felt if any rumours of his meetings with Naomi had reached Kenji, the Tribe Master would have let him know. Kenji seemed to take pleasure in telling him things he knew about him: if he said nothing, it meant he probably knew nothing. The young man, Bunta, had not given them away: he was not from the Tribe. He smiled again at his own suspicions, and refilled the wine cups.

Kenji stayed for a few days, and the two men grew closer, the events from their past, a common delight in the good things of life, and a certain mutual attraction deepening their friendship. In fact Kenji was becoming the closest friend Shigeru had ever had, apart from Kiyoshige. Like Kiyoshige, the Fox was excessively fond of women, and often urged Shigeru to accompany him to the pleasure houses of Hagi, particularly the famous House of the Camellias, where Haruna still held sway. Shigeru always refused.

At the end of the week, they made a short journey into the mountains to the east of Hagi. Kenji was an excellent companion, endlessly knowledgeable about wild plants and animals, acquainted with many hidden paths that led deep into the forest, tireless, and prepared to endure all the discomforts and surprises of travel with sardonic good humour.

He also told Shigeru a certain amount about the Tribe: but when, once home, Shigeru started to write this information down, he realized it was largely superficial – an address, a family relationship, some old story of punishment or revenge. Kenji deftly avoided giving any real details. Shigeru began to believe he would never penetrate the wall of secrecy the Tribe had constructed around themselves and their activities, never discover his half-brother...

Kenji came once more before winter put an end to such journeys, and then again in the fourth month of the following year. He always brought news of events beyond the Middle Country, the continued good health of Iida's son, the warlord's various conquests, the sporadic persecution of the Hidden, Arai Daiichi fretting with impatience in Noguchi castle, the Shirakawa's oldest daughter, Kaede, who had been sent to the same castle that year as a hostage. Occasionally he had news from Maruyama, and Shigeru listened to it impassively, hoping Kenji would not discern his quickened heartbeat, silently giving thanks that she was well, that her daughter was not yet a hostage.

The summer was hot, with early, violent typhoons, bringing the usual anxieties about the harvest. Shigeru's mother was unwell on and off throughout the summer – the heat did not agree with her, and her temper became very unpredictable.

After the full moon of the tenth month, the weather finally began to cool. The meeting with Naomi the previous year seemed like something imagined. Shigeru had almost given up hope of ever hearing from her again when a messenger brought a letter from Eijiro's widow, saying that she had been given permission to make one last journey to her old home to dedicate a memorial to her husband and sons in their former local temple. Was it possible for Lord Shigeru to attend? It would mean so much to her and to the spirits of the dead. She would be travelling with her sister, Sachie. They did not expect an answer, but would be there at the next full moon.

Shigeru was puzzled by this message: did it mean she would be there too? Yet the occasion sounded a formal one: if he went, he would have to go as Otori Shigeru, not as some unrecognized traveller. Eijiro's lands had been ceded to the domain of Tsuwano, which was still part of the Middle Country but whose lord, Kitano, was in favour of alliance with the Tohan and no friend to Shigeru. Was Kitano setting up a trap for him on behalf of Iida Sadamu?

Yet for all his suspicions, the remote possibility of seeing her meant he had to go. He approached his uncles for permission to travel, and was surprised, delighted and alarmed in equal measures when this was readily granted. He put his affairs in order as far as he could, in case he should not return, and set out on Kyu with a few of his own retainers, reflecting that it was a very different way of travelling compared to his recent journeys with Kenji, on foot and in unmarked clothes. Now he wore the formal clothes of a lord of the Otori clan, and Jato rested undisguised at his hip.

The excessive heat and the typhoons had resulted in a poor harvest, and he saw signs of hardship in villages and farms, fields destroyed and buildings not yet restored. Yet the weather was fine and mild, the colours of autumn just beginning to stain the forest, as they had two years ago when he had travelled in secret to meet Lady Maruyama at Seisenji. It was the first time he had ridden this way since then, and he could not help being aware of the effect his appearance had on the people. They thronged out to watch him pass, and followed him with eyes in which he imagined he saw a desperate appeal, not to forget them, not to abandon them.

Eijiro's old house was still standing, and to Shigeru's surprise Lord Kitano's younger son, Masaji, greeted him when he rode through the gate.

'Father wanted me to take over the estate,' he explained, looking a little embarrassed, as though, like Shigeru, he was remembering the day when they had been made welcome here by Eijiro himself, had competed with his sons and daughters – the men of the family now all dead, the women in exile. 'Lord Otori Eijiro was a fine man,' he added. 'We are happy to accommodate his wife in this matter of the memorial and delighted Lord Shigeru could also attend.'

Shigeru inclined his head slightly but said nothing in reply.

'The ceremony will be held tomorrow,' Masaji said. 'In the meantime, you must enjoy our hospitality.'

The younger man was both uncomfortable and nervous, Shigeru realized.

'You would like to bathe, no doubt, and change your clothes. Then we will eat, with my wife and the ladies ... Lady Maruyama is also here; her companion is Lady Eriko's sister, and their brother Lord Sugita accompanied them.'

Relief, joy, desire all came flooding through him. She was here: he would see her. He nodded but still did not speak, partly because he did not trust his voice, partly because he could see Masaji was intimidated and unnerved by his silence. Despite all that had happened since they last met, Masaji still held him in awe and treated him with deference. It both amused him and consoled him.

The old house had been redecorated, new mats laid, new paper screens installed. Its intrinsic beauty was enhanced, but the warmth that had made it so charming was gone forever.

When he was shown into the room where the ladies were already seated, he did not dare look at Naomi. He was aware of her presence, could smell her fragrance. Again, it was like a blow. He concentrated his attention on Lady Eriko, thinking how unbearably sad for her it must be; indeed, her face was pale and strained, though her manner was composed. They greeted each other warmly, and then Eriko said, 'I believe you have met Lady Maruyama and my sister.'

Naomi said, raising her eyes to his, 'Lord Otori and I met by chance at Terayama several years ago.'

'Yes, I remember,' he said, amazed that his voice matched hers in calmness. 'I trust Lady Maruyama is well.'

'Thank you, I am recovered. I am well now.'

'You have been sick?' he said too rapidly, unable to mask his concern.

Her eyes smiled at him, as if trying to reassure him.

'Lady Maruyama was very ill for a long time,' Sachie said quietly. 'There has been a lot of plague in the West this summer.'

'My mother has also been unwell,' he said, striving for a conversational tone. 'But the cooler autumn weather has restored her health.'

'Yes, the weather has been beautiful,' Naomi said. 'I have heard so much about this place but have never visited it before.'

'My husband will show Lady Maruyama around,' Masaji's very young wife began nervously.

'Lord Shigeru is the farming expert,' Masaji interrupted her. 'He was always more interested in such things than the rest of us. And now he is called the Farmer.'

'Then perhaps Lord Otori will show me around tomorrow,' Naomi said. 'After the memorial service.'

'If it is Lady Maruyama's wish,' he replied.

The service was held in the small shrine in the garden, and tablets with the names of the dead man and his sons placed before the altar. Their bones lay in the earth of Yaegahara, along with ten thousand others'. Smoke from incense rose straight upwards in the still air, mingling with the sharp scents of autumn. A stag barked in the forest, and wild geese cried distantly as they crossed the sky.

Shigeru had spent the previous evening and the night swinging between sheer happiness at being in her presence and despair at being unable to touch her, take her in his arms, even to talk to her openly without watching every word. They had hardly addressed each other, and when they did it was in formal language, on unimportant matters. When they had the opportunity to walk alone together through the fields, still in sight though out of earshot, they were constrained and reserved.

'It has been such a long time,' Shigeru said. 'I did not know you had been ill.'

'I was very ill; I could not eat or sleep for weeks. I should have written to you, but my illness robbed me of confidence, and I did not know what to say to you, or even how to send it.'

She paused, and then went on in a low voice, 'I would like to hold you now, lie down with you here on the grass, but it is impossible this time. But I am feeling more hopeful – I don't know why: perhaps I am deluding myself – but I feel with Iida's son growing up a healthy boy, and with everything so settled now – I can see no reason why we should not marry.'

She glanced back at the house. 'I must talk quickly; I don't know how long we will have alone. I must leave tomorrow and we may not have another opportunity. I am resolved to discuss the question with my senior retainers and the elders of the clan. They will approach your uncles with offers and promises they cannot refuse: trade, gifts, ships, maybe even part of the border country. The Arai will be in favour, and so will the rest of the Seishuu.'

'It is my sole desire,' he replied. 'But we will only have one chance: if we make such a request, we risk exposing what we are to each other; if it is refused, we will lose what little we have.'

She was staring straight ahead, seemingly calm, but when she spoke he realized her self-control was near breaking. 'Come back to Maruyama with me now,' she begged. 'We will marry there.'

'I cannot leave my brother in Hagi,' Shigeru said, after a moment. 'I would be condemning him to certain death. And such an act would unleash war – not only on a battlefield like Yaegahara but throughout the Three Countries, in this peaceful valley, in Maruyama itself.' He added, with pain, 'I already lost one terrible battle. I do not wish to begin another war, unless I am sure of winning it.'

'You must start telling me about these crops,' she said swiftly, for Lady Kitano was approaching them. 'But first I will say that I am so happy for this chance of seeing you, no matter how painful it is too. Just to be in your presence fills me with joy.'

'I feel the same,' he replied. 'And always will.'

'Next year I will write to your uncles,' she whispered, before speaking more loudly about locusts and the harvest.

The following day, after farewells had been made and Lady Maruyama and her party had left to ride towards Kibi, Kitano Masaji accompanied Shigeru on his way north, saying he had a young horse that needed the exercise. Shigeru had been allowing himself to indulge in dreaming: that Naomi's plan would work, that they would marry, he would leave Hagi with all its painful associations of defeat and death and live with her in Maruyama. He replied to Masaji's comments and questions with only half his attention.

They had almost reached the pass at the head of the valley when a horseman appeared suddenly out of the forest on the eastern side. Shigeru's hand went immediately to his sword, and Masaji's did the same, as they reined the horses in and turned to face the stranger.

The man leaped from his horse, removed his helmet and fell on one knee, bowing deeply.

'Lord Otori,' he said, not waiting for the others to speak nor giving any formal greeting. 'You have returned. You have come to call us to arms again. We have been waiting for you!'

Shigeru stared at him. There was something familiar about the man's face, but he could not place him. He was young, less than twenty, his face gaunt and bony, his eyes glittering in deep sockets.

He is a madman, Shigeru thought, unhinged by some great loss.

He tried to speak gently but firmly. 'I have not come to call you or anyone to arms. The war is over: we live at peace now.'

Masaji drew his sword. 'This man deserves to die!'

'He is just a lunatic,' Shigeru said. 'Find out where he comes from and return him to his family.'

Masaji hesitated for a moment, long enough for the stranger, with the single-minded swiftness of the insane, to mount his horse again, and rein it backwards towards the forest. He cried out in a hoarse voice, 'So it is true what they all say. Otori failed us at Yaegahara and fails us now.'

He turned the horse and galloped back, weaving between the trees and quickly disappearing.

'I'll go after him and capture him,' Masaji exclaimed, and called to his men. 'Did you know him, Lord Shigeru?'

'I don't think so,' Shigeru replied.

'There are many masterless men between here and Inuyama,' Masaji said. 'They turn to banditry. My father is trying to eradicate them. Goodbye, Shigeru. I am glad we had this chance to meet again. I've long wanted to tell you I don't blame you for not taking your own life, as many do. I'm sure you had good reasons and it does not mean any lack of courage.'

There was no time to reply to this. Masaji and his men had already put their horses into a canter in pursuit of the madman. Shigeru urged Kyu into a gallop up the steep track to the pass, wanting to leave them both behind, the lunatic and the man who had once been a friend, and to forget their words which revived all too strongly his sense of failure and dishonour. It was only that night, just before sleep, that he remembered where he had seen the man before. It had been at his wife's parents' house in Kushimoto. The man was from the Yanagi, who had been all but wiped out in the battle by the traitorous Noguchi, whose very name had been eradicated. It was distressing and disturbing, awakening all his feelings of guilt and grief about Moe, his doubts about the path he had chosen, his feeling that death by his own hand would have been the braver choice.

Soga Juro Sukenari waited eighteen years to avenge his father. It was only three years since Yaegahara and his own father's death. Was he deluding himself that he would have the patience to wait as long as another fifteen years, suffering constant humiliations like those of today?

The turn of the moon had brought a change in the weather. It was much colder, and he could hear rain making its first tentative patter on the roof. He thought of the power of water: it allowed itself to be channelled by stone and soil, yet it wore away the first and washed away the second. He fell asleep to the sound of the rain, his last thought that he would be as patient as water.

CHAPTER FORTY-TWO

A couple of weeks later, just before the onset of winter, Shigeru was returning home on a bitterly cold day when he became aware that someone was following him. He turned once and saw a figure hidden by a hat and cape: it was impossible to tell if it was male or female, though it was of no great height. He walked faster, his hand prepared to go to his sword. The road was frozen solid and icy underfoot. He looked almost unconsciously for a piece of firmer ground on which to make a stand if he had to, but when he turned again his follower had vanished – though he had the feeling he was still there, unseen: he fancied he could hear the slightest footfall, the merest breath.

'Is that you, Kenji?' he demanded, for sometimes the Fox played similar tricks on him, but there was no response. The wind blew more coldly; night was falling.

As he turned to hurry home he felt someone pass by him, and caught the slight scent of a woman.

'Muto Shizuka!' he said. 'I know it is you. Show yourself to me.'

There was no reply. He said more angrily, 'Show yourself!'

Two men came round the corner, pushing a barrow laden with chestnuts. They stared at Shigeru in amazement.

'Lord Otori! What's wrong?'

'Nothing,' he replied. 'Nothing's wrong. I am on my way home.'

They will think I've gone mad. 'Not only the farmer but the crazy farmer,' he muttered as he came to the gate of his mother's house, certain that the two would go straight to the nearest inn and start gossiping about him.

The dogs got up, wagging their tails at the sight of him. 'Has anyone come in?' he called to the guards.

'No one, lord,' one replied.

Chiyo said the same when she came out to welcome him. He walked into every room: there was no one there. Yet he was sure he could still smell the faint unfamiliar scent. He bathed and ate distractedly, uncomfortably aware of his vulnerability to the Tribe. There might be poison in his food; a knife might suddenly come out of the air; a mouthful of needles might be spat out with supernatural force and speed, directed at the eye; he would die almost without knowing it.

He had removed his sword when entering the house. Now he called to Chiyo to bring it to him; he laid it on the floor next to him and placed it in his sash when, after the meal, he went to the room where he usually spent the evening reading and writing. Ichiro had retired early, suffering from a heavy cold. Chiyo had already placed two braziers in the room, but the air was still chill enough for him to see his own breath.

And someone else's. A tiny, hardly perceptible cloud hung at knee level.

'Muto,' he said, and drew his sword.

She came out of nowhere: one moment the room was empty; the air shimmered; the next moment she knelt on the floor in front of him. Though he had seen Kenji do this, it still made him dizzy, as though reality itself were dislodged. He took a deep breath.

'Lord Otori.' She lowered her brow to the ground and remained there, her hair spilling over her face, revealing her slender neck.

If he had met her in the street, or in the forest, if she had been standing, walking – in any position but this – he would have fought with her and killed her to punish her for her duplicity and treachery. But he had never killed a woman, nor an unarmed man – though she was hardly an ordinary woman she seemed to be unarmed; further-more, the idea of shedding blood within his own house repelled him. And she had kindled his curiosity: now he had seen with his own eyes what his father had seen, the Tribe woman who could disappear and reappear at will. Why had she come to him like this, putting herself, it seemed, in his power? And what might he learn from her?

He sat cross-legged, placing the sword next to him. 'Sit up,' he said. 'Why are you here?'

'There are many things I want to talk to you about,' she replied as she raised herself, looking directly at him. 'I came here because your house is safe: there are no spies here, no members of the Tribe. Your household are very loyal to you – as is most of Hagi.'

'Did your uncle send you?' he asked.

She nodded. 'Part of my commission is from him. I will tell you his news first. There's been an unfortunate development that he thought you should know about. There was an attempt to assassinate Iida Sadamu two weeks ago.'

'What happened?' Shigeru said. 'It failed, presumably. Who was behind it?'

'You had nothing to do with it?'

'Am I under suspicion?'

'The would-be assassin was from your wife's family, the Yanagi.'

Shigeru remembered the madman who had ridden out of the forest: he knew at once it must be the same man.

'He was apparently seeking to avenge the annihilation of the clan,' Shizuka continued. 'My uncle and I believe he was acting individually, out of rage and despair. It was a clumsy attempt: he tried to ambush Iida on the road when he was returning to Inuyama for the winter. He never got near him. He was taken alive and tortured for five days, but he said little except that he was the last of the Yanagi. He was a warrior, but Iida declared him stripped of all privileges: he died finally on the castle wall. Iida immediately assumed he was in your service. It has reawakened all his suspicions: he will demand some sort of retribution from the Otori.'

'I am in no way involved,' Shigeru exclaimed, appalled at the implications of this rash act of which he had had no knowledge. 'How can I be held responsible?'

'Many people would like to assassinate Iida; he will always see your hand behind it. And besides, something more implicates you: Kitano Masaji reported that the same man had spoken to you as you left Misumi. He said you must have given him some secret message or sign.'

'I thought he was a lunatic, and tried to prevent Kitano from killing him!'

'A grave mistake. He eluded Kitano's men and went straight to the high road between Kushimoto and Inuyama to attack Iida. My uncle's advice is to lie very low; don't leave the Middle Country, stay in Hagi if possible.'

'I only travel for agricultural research and religious duties,' Shigeru said. 'And both must be laid aside during the winter.' He gestured at the writing materials and the boxes of scrolls that filled the room. 'I have plenty with which to occupy myself until spring comes.' He gave her his open-hearted smile, but when he spoke again his voice was bitter. 'You may tell your uncle that – and Iida, of course.'

She said, 'You are still angry with me. I must also talk about this. I was acting on the orders of my family when I betrayed you and the man I love, the father of my sons. From the Tribe's point of view, I was doing my duty. It is not the worst thing I have done at their command. Yet I am deeply ashamed of it, and I ask you to forgive me.'

'How can I forgive you?' he replied, trying to control his anger. 'The betrayal and death of my father, my best friend, thousands of my men; the loss of my position – and after you swore to Arai Daiichi and to me that we could trust you.'

Her face was white, her eyes opaque. 'Believe me, the dead haunt me. That is why I want to make amends.'

'You must take me for a fool. Am I supposed to trust you again and express my forgiveness to ease your pangs of conscience? For what purpose? I have retired from politics; I have no interest in anything other than farming my estate and pursuing my spiritual duties. What is past is past. Your remorse cannot undo the battle or bring back the dead.'

'I will not defend myself against your contempt and distrust, for I deserve both. I just ask you to see things from the point of view of a woman from the Tribe who now wants to help you.'

'I know you are a consummate actor,' he said. 'You outdo yourself in this performance.' He was on the point of ordering her to leave, of calling the guards and having her thrown out, having them put her to death.

She held out her hands to him, palms upward. He saw the unusual lines that ran straight across the hand as though cutting it in half. He stared at them, trying to remember... something his father had said, about the Kikuta woman.

'Lord Otori, how can I convince you to trust me?'

He raised his eyes from her hands to her face. It was impossible to tell if she was sincere or not. He said nothing for a few moments, making an effort to curb his anger, trying to assess the dangers and the advantages to him in this sudden new development, thinking with brief sorrow of the young Yanagi man, his pain, his humiliation. He turned away from her and said abruptly, 'What do the lines on your hands signify?'

She glanced down at them. 'Some of us who have Kikuta blood carry this mark. It is supposed to indicate high skills. My uncle has told you something of these things?'

'If I wanted to know more about the Kikuta family, would you be able to help me?' he said, turning back to her.

She raised her eyes again to his. 'I will tell you anything you want to know.'

His distrust returned. 'Are you sure you are allowed to?'

'In this I am acting for myself. I am transferring my allegiance from the Tribe to Lord Otori.'

'Why?' He did not believe her.

'I want to make amends for the past. I've seen the cruelty of the Tohan at work. In the Tribe we are brought up not to care about the differences of right and wrong, nobility and baseness. We have other concerns: our own survival, our own accumulation of power and wealth. I have never been allowed to choose for myself; I have always done what I was told. Obedience is the character trait most highly valued by the Tribe. But since the birth of my sons I have felt differently. Something happened... I can't tell you exactly what it was but it shocked me deeply. It made me realize I would rather my sons lived in Lord Otori's world: not Iida Sadamu's.'

'Very touching! And quite unrealistic, since my world has vanished forever.'

'If you truly believed that, you would be dead,' she said quietly. 'The fact that you continue living tells me that your world can be restored, and that it is your hope. Arai too still hopes for it. Let us work together for this purpose.'

He glanced at her, saw her eyes were still fixed on his face, and then looked away. The night was growing colder; he could feel the icy air on his cheeks. He moved a little closer to the brazier.

'I swear on the lives of my sons,' she said. 'I've come to you not on the orders of the Tribe, or of Iida or your uncles or anyone else. Well, Kenji told me to come but he does not know why I was glad to obey him.' When he still said nothing, she went on. 'Arai is not alone among the Seishuu in hoping to see Iida overthrown. Lady Maruyama must also desire it. Especially since Iida has demanded her daughter be sent to Inuyama as a hostage next year.'

'Is Lady Maruyama also under suspicion?'

'Less than you. But she was also at Misumi. You spoke to her, perhaps in some secret language, Kitano thinks. And Iida hopes to control her domain either by marriage or by force. He is regrouping his armies, but he will seize on any pretext of disloyalty to act.'

Shigeru sighed deeply. 'Are you trying to tell me something about Lady Maruyama?'

'Lord Otori, the groom, Bunta, reports to me. Only to me. This is proof, if you like, of my loyalty to you. Bunta told me of your first meeting, and the next one.'

It was what he had feared all along. They had been watched: the Tribe knew, Iida knew. He could not speak, his muscles and blood frozen.

'I have never spoken of it until now,' Shizuka went on. 'No one else knows.' She added after a moment, 'You should not meet again. It has become extremely dangerous. Because Bunta reports only to me I have been able to keep it secret, but I cannot do that much longer. You should not even write to each other, once Lady Maruyama's daughter is a hostage in Inuyama.'

He believed now that she was telling the truth, and saw suddenly how much he needed someone like her, with all her Tribe skills, her longstanding connection with Arai, her relationship to Muto Kenji. Her appearance was the unexpected move that, as in go, opened up the whole game.

'There are things I would like to find out about the Kikuta.' He drew the writing table towards him and took up the inkstone, then said, 'It needs water. Wait here. I'll fetch us some wine. And do you want something to eat?'

She shook her head. He stood and went to the door, slid it open and walked through the next room towards the kitchen. Chiyo was nodding off beside the hearth. He told her to heat some wine and then go to bed.

She was full of apologies. 'Lord Otori has a visitor? I did not know.'

'Don't worry,' he said. 'I will take the wine myself.'

Understanding leaped into her eyes. 'Your visitor is a woman? Excellent, excellent. You won't be disturbed, I'll make sure of it!'

He did not correct her, but smiled to himself as he returned, carrying the small ceramic flask and cups.

'I'm afraid Chiyo thinks you have come for some amatory purpose,' he said, setting the tray on the floor.

Shizuka filled his cup and then he filled hers. 'In another life, maybe. There are many kinds of love,' she said almost flirtatiously. 'Let us drink to the love of friendship.'

He could not help but reflect on the strangeness of his life, that he should be sitting with this woman from the Tribe and pledging friendship with her. The wine was warm and fragrant, sending its cheerful message coursing through his body.

He poured the water into the fish-shaped dropper and prepared the ink. Then he took up the brush. 'Tell me about the Tribe.'

She took a deep breath. 'You must never utter a word of this to anyone. If the Tribe ever find out, they will kill me. I know my uncle has become a friend of yours. He above all must never know what I am doing.'

'You must realize that I can keep secrets,' Shigeru replied.

'I believe you to be the most devious person I know, outside the Tribe,' Shizuka said, laughing and adding quickly, 'It is a compliment!'

He poured more wine. It had cooled quickly.

'We work in groups and networks,' she said as he wrote down the details. 'Each member only communicates with his or her senior in the hierarchy – they are not allowed to speak of anything important among themselves. Our children are trained in this: it is second nature to us. Information only flows one way – upwards to the Master of the family.'

'Kikuta and Muto?'

'They are the leading families, supposedly equal, but the Kikuta are currently more powerful. I am from both families. My father was Muto – he passed away when I was a child – and my mother Kikuta.'

'Your mother was Kikuta? In what year was she born?'

'She turns forty this year.'

Forty years ago – could she have been his father's child? Only if either Shigemori or Shizuka had got the years wrong. It was entirely possible; most people had no very clear idea when they were born... names were frequently changed, dates altered.

'I can bring you copies of the genealogies,' Shizuka said. 'Blood ties are very important to the Tribe: we like to keep careful records of who marries whom and what skills each union produces in its offspring. Why are you particularly interested in the Kikuta?'

'I believe I may have a half-brother among them,' he said, and for the first time shared his father's secret with another person.

'It's extraordinary,' she said when he had finished. 'I have never heard even a rumour of this.'

'So you do not think there was a child born?'

'If there was its mother must have successfully hidden the fact that the father was not from the Tribe.'

'Is it something you can find out? Without revealing it to anyone else?'

'I will try.' She smiled. 'It's uncanny almost, that you should have a relative among the Kikuta!'

'And Bunta: is he a relation of yours?'

'No, he is from the Imai family. Most of the Imai men work as grooms and servants, as do the Kudo. The fifth family, the Kuroda, are somewhere in the middle: they have many of the special skills of the Tribe – I'm sure Kenji has demonstrated these to you – and a characteristic practicality which makes them superb assassins. The most sought after at the moment is Kuroda Shintaro, who currently is employed by the Tohan.'

'Someone tried to assassinate me three years ago,' Shigeru said. 'Were they from the Tribe?'

'One was; the others were Tohan, disguised as masterless warriors. In fact Iida paid the Kikuta family highly for this attempt and was furious when it failed. Since then Kenji has ordered the Muto to leave you alone; he has some influence with the other families, but not with the Kikuta.'

'Why has Kenji taken me under his wing? Sometimes I feel as if I am his tamed animal.'

Shizuka smiled. 'There is an element of that. Kenji is an unusual person: supremely talented, but a loner. He will become the Muto Master very soon: he is virtually head of the family already, for no one dares cross him. Your friendship intrigues and flatters him. He considers you belong to him; he says he saved your life, though he has never told me the full story. He admires you as much as he admires anyone. I believe he is genuinely fond of you. But I must warn you, his first loyalty will always be to the Muto family and to the Tribe.'

'Can you deliver messages to Maruyama?'

'I could take one for you now, but as I said before you and Lady Maruyama should not attempt to write to each other again.'

'This assassination attempt is a disaster for us,' he said, allowing himself now to express his feelings. 'We had hoped to seek permission to marry next year.'

'Do not even consider it,' Shizuka said. 'It will enrage Iida, and arouse his suspicions further.'

He seemed to have gained one advantage only to lose what he most desired, taken one step forward only to be thrown back two. 'What can I write?' he said. 'All I can say is farewell for ever.'

'Don't despair,' she said. 'Continue to be patient. I know it is your greatest strength. Iida will be overthrown; we will continue our struggle against him.'

'It's getting late; where will you sleep tonight?'

'I will go to the Muto house, where the brewery is.'

'Come here tomorrow; I will have a letter ready for you.'

'Lord Otori.'

They walked out together into the silent garden. Starlight glimmered faintly on the rocks around the pools, where ice was already forming. He was going to call for the guards to open the gates, but she forestalled him. She motioned him to be silent and leaped into the air, vanishing on the tiled roof of the wall.

He spent most of the night writing to Naomi, telling her what had transpired with Muto Shizuka, expressing his sorrow at her daughter's fate, and his deep love for her, warning her that it might be years before he was able to write again, telling her on no account to write to him. He ended echoing Shizuka's words: Do not despair. We must be patient.

A week later snow began to fall heavily, to Shigeru's relief, for he had feared that after the assassination attempt Iida would renew his demands for Takeshi to be sent to Inuyama. Now this would be put off until spring at least. It did not matter that the snow also closed the roads to messengers for he knew he would not hear from Naomi again.

In the fourth month of the following year, news came of Mori Yusuke's death on the mainland. It was brought by a ship's captain, who also delivered Yusuke's last gift to Shigeru: a stallion from the steppes of the East. The horse arrived thin and dispirited, exhausted from the journey; however, Shigeru and Takeshi both saw something in it, and Takeshi made arrangements for it to be well fed, and when it had recovered some of its energy put it out in the water meadows with the mares. Despite its thinness it was well put together, taller and longer of leg than the Otori horses, with flowing tail and long mane once the tangles had been unknotted. The old stallion had died the previous winter, and the new one quickly took the mares as his herd, nipping at them, bossing them, getting all of them with foal. Shigeru entrusted the handling of the horses to Takeshi.

The only surviving son of the horsebreaker's family, Hiroki, was occupied with his shrine duties, but he often discussed horses with Takeshi, for he had still retained the family interest in them, and he and Takeshi were the same age. It was ten years since the stone fight in which Hiroki's older brother, Yuta, had died, ten years since Hiroki had been dedicated to the shrine of the river god.

When the foals were born the following spring, one of them promised to be the pale grey black-maned sort so prized by the Otori. Takeshi named it Raku. Another was a black very like Shigeru's stallions Karasu and Kyu, the third a less handsome dull-coloured bay who turned out to be the most intelligent and tractable horse Takeshi had ever known.

CHAPTER FORTY-THREE

Isamu's widow was six months pregnant when her husband's body was found. She had hoped all winter that he would reappear in the spring as suddenly as he had done before; her disappointment and grief were only made bearable by the fact that he had obviously been murdered, unarmed. His repentence for his past life had been sincere; his conversion had not been a sham. He had not sinned; they would meet again in Heaven, as the old teachings said, in the presence of the Secret One.

She married her brother's oldest friend, Shimon, a boy she had grown up with, whose hopes had been destroyed by the stranger's arrival, and he became a father to the boy born in the seventh month, to whom they gave a name common among the Hidden: Tomasu.

The child had been unusually active in the womb and continued to be so after his birth. He rarely slept, walked at nine months, and from then on seemed intent on escaping into the forest. At first he seemed destined to die from some accident, drown in the flooded spring river, fall from the crest of a pine tree, or simply get lost on the mountain. His stepfather predicted all these ends for him, in between trying to control him with scoldings, punishments and rare beatings. His mother, Sara, swung between terror that they would lose him, and pride at his quickness, agility and affectionate nature.

Tomasu was in his fifth year when word came to the remote village of Mino of the persecution of the Hidden throughout the East, and his childhood was darkened by the shadow of Iida Sadamu, who, it was said, hunted down children like himself and killed them with his own hands. But two years later the Battle of Yaegahara seemed to divert Lord Iida's attention away from undesirable elements within his own domain. It was known that the losses on both sides had been huge; the villagers gave thanks, not for the deaths, but because they thought Iida's warriors would have more urgent concerns in the years to come than combing this distant forest for members of the Hidden.

Iida became something of an ogre, used by mothers to scare children into obedience. They both believed in his dark power and giggled at it.

The years passed. The Hidden continued their peaceful life, revering all living things, sharing their weekly ritual meal, rarely speaking of their beliefs, merely living them. Tomasu survived his childhood despite his stepfather's gloomy predictions; though he did not often show it Shimon loved the boy almost as much as Sara did and certainly equally with his own children, the two girls, Maruta and Madaren.

Shimon and Sara did not speak of Tomasu's real father, the stranger who was murdered, and Tomasu did not grow up to look like how they remembered him. He did not really resemble anyone they knew, but had a look all his own, thin and fine-featured. The only similarity his mother noticed was in the curious lines across his palms: she knew his father had had the same hands.

Tomasu was not exactly unpopular with the other boys of the village; they sought him out for his skill in games and for his knowledge of the forest, but he seemed always to be fighting with them.

'What happened to you this time?' his mother wailed when he came home late one afternoon in his eleventh year, dripping blood from a head wound. 'Come here, let me do that.'

Tomasu was trying to wash the blood from his eyes and staunch the flow. 'Just a stone I got in the way of,' he replied.

'But why were you fighting?'

'I don't know,' he said cheerfully. 'It was a stone fight. No particular reason.'

Sara had moistened an old rag and pressed it firmly against his temple. He rested against her for a moment, wincing slightly. Usually he wrestled with her embraces and struggled away from her.

'My wild boy,' she murmured. 'My little hawk. What will become of you?'

'Were the other boys teasing you?' Shimon asked. It was well known that Tomasu lost his temper easily and the other boys revelled in provoking him.

'Maybe. A bit. They say I have sorcerer's hands.' Tomasu looked at his long-fingered hands, marked by the straight line. 'I was just showing them how a sorcerer throws stones!'

'You must not fight back,' Shimon said quietly.

'They always start it,' Tomasu retorted.

'What they start is not up to you to finish. Leave it to the Secret One to defend you.'

The suggestion of sorcery disturbed Shimon. He watched the boy carefully, alert to any sign of real difference in him or of demonic possession. He kept Tomasu near him as often as he could, forbade him to wander alone in the forest where strange beings might enchant him, prayed day and night that the Secret One might protect him, not only from all the perils of the world but also from his own strange inner nature.

The wound left a scar that faded to silver against the honey-coloured skin like a three-day moon.

One day in early spring a few years later they were working together by the river, cutting alder saplings whose bark would be stripped to make cloth. The river was swollen from the thaw; it swirled over the coppiced base of the alders and raced across the rocks in its bed, deafening them with a noise like many men shouting. Shimon had already had to speak severely to Tomasu; first the boy had wanted to pursue a fawn and its mother that had been drinking from the pool, then he had been distracted by a pair of kingfishers. Shimon bent to gather the saplings already cut, tied them into a bundle and carried them up the slope so they would not get washed away. He left Tomasu alone for only a moment but when he turned to look back he saw his stepson disappearing downstream in the direction of the village.

'You worthless boy,' he yelled futilely after him, torn between continuing the work and pursuing him to punish him. His rage got the better of him; he grabbed one of the saplings and set off downstream. 'I'll thrash him properly for once! We're too soft with him! It'll do him no good in the long run.'

He was still muttering to himself when he came round the bend in the river and saw his youngest daughter, Madaren, struggling in the muddy water. She must have tried to cross the river by the stepping stones, had slipped into one of the deep pools, and was trying to save herself by grasping at the exposed roots in the bank.

Tomasu had already reached her. The little girl was shrieking, but Shimon could barely hear her above the roar of the water. He dropped the stick he was carrying and saw the river whisk it away. Tomasu was only just able to stand in the spot where Madaren had fallen in. He peeled her fingers back from the root she was clutching and she threw herself at him, clinging like a baby monkey to its mother. He held her tightly against his shoulder and, half swimming, half scrambling, brought her to the shore, where Shimon took her from him.

Sara came running, giving thanks that the child was safe, scolding Maruta for not looking after her, praising Tomasu.

Shimon looked at his stepson as Tomasu leaped onto the bank, shaking the water from his hair like a dog. 'What made you take off like that? You got to her just in time!'

'I thought I heard her calling me,' Tomasu replied. He was frowning. 'But I couldn't have...' The noise of the river rose around them, drowning all other sound.

'The Secret One must have warned you,' Shimon said in awe, and taking the boy's hand traced the sign of the Hidden on his palm. He felt Tomasu had been chosen in some way, to become a leader of the Hidden, perhaps, to take over eventually from Isao. He began to speak more seriously to him at night about spiritual matters and to lead him more deeply into the beliefs of the Hidden. Despite Tomasu's hot temper and restlessness, Shimon thought the boy had a natural gentleness and an aversion to cruelty which both his parents did their best to foster.

It was rare for strangers or travellers to come to Mino. The village lay hidden in the mountains; no roads came near it, only the tracks over the mountain and along the river through the valley. Both were almost impassable, overgrown through lack of use. A landfall had all but blocked the valley path a few years previously. Occasionally one or other of the men crossed the pass to Hinode and returned with news and rumours. It was nearly sixteen years since the stranger came and disappeared again; well over fourteen since the birth of his son. Tomasu had grown into a striking-looking young man. No one teased him any more and he no longer got into fights. Both boys and girls, Shimon noticed, sought him out, and it made his stepfather start to ponder the question of marriage. He gave Tomasu more tasks to do, demanding he spend less time running wild on the mountain but work alongside the men of the village and prepare for adult life.

Mostly Tomasu obeyed him, but one evening early in the ninth month he disappeared into the forest, telling his mother he was going to look for mushrooms. Shimon, returning wearily from a distant field where they had been harvesting the last of the beans, heard his wife's voice echoing through the valley.

'Tomasu! Come home!'

He sat heavily on the board step of the house; he was stiff all over, his joints ached. The night air felt frosty; winter would come soon.

'I swear I'll tear him into eight pieces,' Sara grumbled as she brought water for her husband to wash.

'Unnh!' he grunted, amused, knowing she would never carry out that threat.

'He said he was going for mushrooms, but it's just an excuse!'

Their older daughter came running up to the house. Her eyes were bright with excitement, her cheeks glowing pink from the cold air. 'Father! Father! Tomasu is coming and there is someone with him!'

Shimon stood, startled. His wife stared towards the mountain, shading her eyes.

The light was fading into dusk. Tomasu appeared out of the darkness, leading a short, stocky man who carried a heavy pack in a bamboo frame on his back. As they crossed the last dike, Tomasu shouted, 'I found him on the mountain! He was lost!'

'No need to tell the whole world,' Shimon muttered, but already people were emerging from their houses to stare at the stranger. Shimon glanced at them; he had known them all his life; they were the only people he had known, apart from the last stranger who had come out of the forest and caused such grief. Shimon knew of course which families were Hidden and which were not but to an outsider they were indistinguishable.

Tomasu brought the man up to the step. 'I told him we would feed him; he can stay the night with us and tomorrow I'll show him the path to Hinode. He has come from Inuyama.'

The boy's face was alight with the thrill of it. 'I found mushrooms too,' he announced, handing the bundle over to his mother.

'I'm grateful to your son,' the man said, easing the pack from his back and setting it down on the step. 'I was heading for the village called Hinode, but I've never been this way before; I was completely lost.'

'No one ever comes here,' Shimon replied cautiously.

The stranger looked around. A small crowd had gathered in front of the house; they stared with deep and undisguised interest but kept their distance. Shimon saw them suddenly through the other man's eyes: their old, patched clothes, bare legs and feet, thin faces and lean bodies. 'You can understand why; life is harsh here.'

'But even the harshest life needs some relaxation, some adornment,' the man said, a wheedling note entering his voice. 'Let me show you what I carry in my pack. I'm a peddler; I have needles and knives, threads and cord, even a few pieces of cloth, new and not-so-new.' He turned and beckoned to the villagers. 'Come and look!'

He began to unwrap the bundles that filled the bamboo frame.

Shimon laughed. 'Don't waste your time! You don't give those things away surely? We have nothing to spare to give you in exchange.'

'No coins?' the man asked. 'No silver?'

'We have never seen either,' Shimon replied.

'Well, I'll take tea or rice.'

'We eat mainly millet and barley; our tea is made from twigs from the forest.'

The peddler stopped his unwrapping. 'You have nothing to barter? How about a night's lodging and a bowl of millet and a cup of twig tea?' He chuckled. 'It sounds like riches to a man who was facing a cold night on the hard ground.'

'Of course you are welcome to stay with us,' Shimon said, 'but we do not expect payment.' He addressed his daughter who had been staring at the peddler without moving. 'Maruta, bring more water for our guest. Tomasu, take our visitor's belongings inside. Wife, we will be one extra for the evening meal.'

He felt a moment of sorrow as his stomach reminded him what that one extra mouth to feed would mean, but he put the feeling from him. Wasn't one of the old teachings about welcoming strangers, who might be angels in disguise?

He shooed the rest of the villagers away, seemingly ignoring their murmured pleas to at least be allowed to look at the needles, the cloth, the knives, all precious items to them, but inwardly wondering if he might perhaps secure a few needles for the women, something pretty for the girls...

His wife was adding the mushrooms to the soup; the inside of the house was smoky and warm. Outside it was growing colder by the minute; he thought again they would have the first frost that night.

'You would indeed have been cold sleeping outside,' he remarked as his wife poured the soup into the old wooden bowls.

The youngest child, Madaren, innocently began to say the first prayer over the food. Sara put out a hand to hush her, but the peddler very quietly finished her words and then spoke the second prayer.

There was a long moment of silence, then Shimon whispered, 'You are one of us?'

The peddler nodded. 'I did not know there were any here; I had never heard of this village.' He drank his soup noisily. 'Be thankful no one else knows of your existence for Iida Sadamu hates us and many have died in Inuyama, even as far West as Noguchi and Yamagata in the Middle

Country. If Iida ever succeeds in conquering the Three Countries he will wipe us out.'

'We are no threat to Lord Iida or to anyone,' Sara said. 'And we are safe here. My husband and Isao, our leader, are respected; they help everyone. Everyone likes us; no one will harm us here.'

'I pray that He will protect you,' the peddler said.

Shimon noticed the puzzlement in his daughters' eyes. 'We are safe under His protection,' he said swiftly, dreading seeing that puzzlement turn to fear. 'Like the little chicks under the mother hen's wings.'

When the sparse meal was finished, the peddler insisted on showing them his wares, saying, 'You must choose something; it will be payment, as I said.'

'It is not necessary,' Shimon replied politely, but he was curious to see what else the man carried and he was still thinking about the needles; they were so useful, so easily lost or broken, so hard to replace.

Sara brought a lamp. They rarely lit them, usually going to bed as soon as darkness fell. The unusual light, the precious objects made them all excited. The little girls stared with shining eyes as the peddler unwrapped squares of woven cloth in pretty patterns, needles, a small doll carved from wood, spoons made of red lacquer, skeins of coloured thread, a bolt of indigo-dyed hemp cloth and several knives, one of which was more like a short sword, though it had a plain hilt and no scabbard.

Shimon could not help noticing that Tomasu's eyes were drawn to it and that, as the boy leaned forward into the light to look more closely, his right hand seemed to curve as though the sword were already settling against the line across his palm.

The peddler was watching him, a slight frown between his eyes. 'You like it? You should not!'

'Why do you carry such instruments of murder?' Sara said quietly.

'People offer me things in exchange,' he replied, lifting the sword carefully and rewrapping it. 'I'll sell it somewhere.'

'Why don't we have weapons?' Tomasu whispered. 'We would not be so defenceless then against those who seek to kill us.'

'The Secret One is our defence,' Shimon said.

'It is better to die ourselves than to take the life of another,' Sara added. 'We have taught you that all your life.'

The boy flushed a little under their rebukes and did not reply.

'Did that knife kill someone?' Maruta asked, recoiling slightly as if it were a snake.

'That is what it is made for,' Shimon told her.

'Or to kill yourself with,' the peddler said, and seeing the children's astonished eyes could not resist embellishing. 'Warriors think it is honourable in certain circumstances to take their own lives. They cut their bellies open with a sword like this one!'

'It is a terrible sin,' Sara murmured, and taking Maruta's hand she traced the sign of the Hidden on it. 'May he protect us not only from death but from the sin of killing!'

The men whispered their assent but Tomasu said, 'We are not likely to kill; we have no enemies here and no weapons.' Then he seemed to become aware of his mother's disapproval. 'I pray too that we may never have either,' he said seriously.

Sara poured tea for everyone and they ended the evening with a final prayer for the coming of the kingdom of peace. The peddler gave the doll to Madaren and to Maruta some red cords for her hair. Shimon asked for needles and received five.

The next morning before he left the peddler insisted on leaving the hemp cloth. 'Have your wife make you a new robe.'

'It is too valuable,' Shimon remonstrated. 'We have done so little for you.'

'It's heavy,' the man replied. 'You'll be saving me the trouble of carrying it further. I'm grateful to you, and we are fellow-believers, brethren.'

'Thank you,' Shimon said, taking it gratefully. He had never owned anything so costly. 'Will you return here? You are welcome to stay with us at any time.'

'I will try to come again but it won't be for months. Next year, or the year after.'

'Where will you go from here?' Shimon asked.

'I was going to try and get to Hinode, but I think I'll give up that plan. I want to be in the West next year. If your son can show me the way back to the river, the Inugawa, I can get to Hofu by ship before winter comes.'

'Do you travel throughout the Three Countries?'

'I have been all over; I have even been to Hagi.' The peddler picked up the frame and Shimon helped fix it on his back.

'I have never even heard of Hagi,' he admitted.

'It is the main city of the Otori, who were defeated by Iida at the battle of Yaegahara. You must have heard of that!'

'Yes, we heard of it,' Shimon said. 'How terrible the struggles between the clans are!'

'May He protect us from them,' the peddler said. He was silent for a moment, then seemed to shake himself. 'Well, I must go. Thank you again and take care of yourselves.'

Both men looked around for Tomasu. Shimon noted with approval that he was already at work, gathering fallen leaves to spread on the empty fields, which were white with frost. He was about to call him when the peddler remarked, 'He does not look like you. Is he your own son?'

'Yes,' Shimon heard himself say, and even added, 'He takes after my wife's father.' He was suddenly uneasy at the man's curiosity and garrulity. 'I will show you the way myself,' he said. He was afraid if Tomasu left with the peddler he might never come back.

CHAPTER FORTY-FOUR

After her daughter, Mariko, went to Inuyama as a hostage at the age of seven, Maruyama Naomi travelled twice yearly to Iida Sadamu's city, now recognized as the capital of the Three Countries. Sometimes when the weather was settled she overcame her fears of the sea and took a boat from Hofu; more often she went by way of Yamagata, frequently stopping for several days there in order to visit the temple at Terayama, and then followed the highway to Inuyama. She rode on horseback through her own domain to the Western border of the Middle Country, but from there on travelled in a palanquin, careful to present herself as a fragile woman, no threat to the warlord who now held her daughter and would use her in any way he could to gain control over her domain and over the West. Iida was arming and training more men, forcing more of the smaller families to submit to him or be annihilated. Mostly they submitted, but reluctantly; risings against Iida erupted frequently among both warriors and farmers, leading to increased suppression and persecution, and the Seishuu were increasingly concerned that he would take by force what he could see no way to gain through marriage.

Iida made a point of always receiving her himself when she came to Inuyama, of treating her with great courtesy, heaping gifts on her, flattering and praising her. She found his attentions distasteful yet could not avoid them without insulting him. Each time she saw her daughter, Mariko had grown; she took after her father, would not be called beautiful but had his kindness and intelligence, and did her utmost to spare her mother pain. She seemed resigned to her fate in company, but wept silently in private, struggling to control her feelings and begging her mother's forgiveness. She was homesick for Maruyama, for its gentler climate and for the freedom she had known in childhood. In Inuyama, though Lady Iida treated her kindly, she was, like all women in the deep interior, always afraid of the sudden rages of the warlord and the brutality of his retainers.

Naomi refined the art of hiding her feelings, of appearing to be pliable and submissive while retaining the independence and autonomy of her clan and her country. She would give no one any excuse to kill her or usurp her. Carefully and methodically she built up a network of support within her domain and throughout the West. She travelled a great deal, from one side of the Three Countries to the other, in spring and autumn, usually in some splendour with her senior retainer Sugita Haruki and at least twenty men at arms, as well as her companion, Sachie, and other women; occasionally less ostentatiously, with only Sachie and a handful of men. Often the demands of government meant Sugita could serve her best by staying in Maruyama.

Occasionally Naomi went by way of Shirakawa and Noguchi. Her mother's sister was married to Lord Shirakawa, and strong bonds of affection tied the two women: both of them had daughters who were hostages, for the Shirakawa's eldest daughter Kaede had been sent to Noguchi castle when she turned seven. There were fears that the girl was not well treated there: the Noguchi, as well as being traitors who had caused the downfall of the Otori, had the reputation of cruelty; Lord Noguchi, it was said, strove to impress Iida by equalling him in brutality. The year Mariko turned eleven and Kaede thirteen (and Tomasu in Mino fifteen), Lady Maruyama visited the castle and was disturbed to find there was no sign of the Shirakawa girl among the women of the deep interior. When she made enquiries, replies were evasive, even dismissive, and her fears intensified. She noticed Arai Daiichi among the castle guard – though his father was in ill health back in Kumamoto and he had three younger brothers ready to dispute the domain, he had not been allowed to return home: it seemed he would lose his inheritance by default, Iida's punishment for the approaches he had made to Otori Shigeru, before Yaegahara, nine years ago.

Naomi was staying in one of the mansions that belonged to Noguchi yet lay beyond the castle walls. The breeze was warm and soft, the cherry blossom in the gardens on the point of bursting into flower. She was restless and almost febrile. The onset of spring had unsettled her; her very existence seemed intolerable to her. She slept badly, tormented by desire, longing for Shigeru's presence, not knowing how long she could continue this half life: her entire womanhood seemed to have been spent in this semi-deprived state, neither married nor free, sustained by the barest grains of memories. Sometimes in her darkest moments she contemplated sacrificing her child for the chance of marrying Shigeru; they would retreat to Maruyama and prepare for open battle; then she would remember Mariko's sweetness and courage, and shame and remorse would swamp her. All these emotions were compounded by her anxiety for Shirakawa Kaede, not only for the girl's sake but also because, after Mariko, Kaede was her closest female relative – heir to Maruyama if she and her daughter were to die.

As she had hoped, Arai came that evening to call on her. The visit was made openly: they were both from the Seishuu; it was to be expected that they would meet. Muto Shizuka accompanied him. Naomi greeted her with mixed feelings. Shizuka had delivered Shigeru's farewell letter to Maruyama, and just to recall that time now filled Naomi with the same confusion of grief, jealousy and despair. Six years had passed but her emotions had become no less intense. Their paths had crossed from time to time and Shizuka had brought some news of Shigeru. Now Naomi waited with the same blend of feelings: she would hear news of him, but Shizuka had been with him, had heard his voice, knew all his secrets, perhaps even felt his touch. This last thought was unendurable to her. He had promised her he would lie with no one but her, but six years... surely no man could restrain himself for so long. And Shizuka was so attractive...

They exchanged courtesies, and Sachie brought tea. After she had served her guests, Naomi said, 'Lord Arai is now captain of the guard. I suppose you rarely see Lord Shirakawa's daughter.'

He drank and said, 'I would be happy if I only saw her rarely, for that would mean she was treated as she should be and welcomed into the Noguchi family. I see all too much of her, and so do all the guards!'

'At least she is alive,' Naomi exclaimed. 'I was afraid she had died and the Noguchi were concealing it.'

'They treat her like a servant,' Arai replied angrily. 'She lives with the maids and is expected to share their duties. Her father is not allowed to see her. She is just at the point of becoming a woman; she is a very beautiful girl. The guards lay bets on who will be the first to seduce her. I do my best to protect her. They know I'll kill anyone who lays a hand on her. But it is shameful to treat a girl from her family in such a way!' He broke off abruptly. 'I cannot say more; I've sworn allegiance to Lord Noguchi, for better or worse, and I must live with my fate.'

'But not forever,' Naomi said in a low voice. Arai glanced at Shizuka, who seemed to listen for a moment before nodding her head slightly to him.

He said in a whisper, 'Do you know what Lord Otori's intentions are? We hear little of him – men say he has gone soft and has abandoned honour for the sake of being allowed to live.'

'I believe he is very patient,' she said. 'As we all must be. But I am not in contact with him.' She looked at Shizuka, thinking she might speak, but Shizuka said nothing.

'I have had to learn patience here,' Arai replied bitterly. 'We are divided, and made helpless; we all sit separately in the dark regretting what might have been. Will anything ever change? I will lose Kumamoto altogether if my father dies and I am still festering here. Better to act and fail than to continue like this!'

Naomi could think of nothing to say in response other than to urge him to continue to be patient, but before she could say anything Shizuka made a sign to Arai and he began immediately to speak about the weather. Naomi replied with enquiries as to the health of his wife.

'She has recently had her first child – a son,' Arai said abruptly.

Naomi looked briefly towards Shizuka, but the girl's face gave nothing away. Naomi had often thought enviously how lucky she was, able to live openly with the man she loved and bear his children. Yet Shizuka must now feel jealousy towards her lover's wife and his legitimate son. And what would happen to the two older boys?

Her thoughts were interrupted by a voice outside; the maid slid the door open to reveal one of Arai's guards kneeling outside; he brought a message that the captain's presence was required back at the castle.

Arai left saying no more beyond formal words of parting. She was glad he would be watching over Kaede, yet his attitude worried her. He was so impatient: one small event would set him off and then suspicion would fall on her and her child. Shigeru's years of patient waiting would be undone. Shizuka stayed for a little longer, but the residence became more busy as the maids began to prepare the bath and the evening meal, and they spoke only of trivial things. However, before she left, Shizuka said, 'I am travelling to Yamagata tomorrow. I am taking my sons to stay with my family in the mountains. Perhaps we could be company for each other on the road?'

Naomi was immediately seized by a desire to go to Terayama and walk in the peaceful gardens where she had first met Shigeru and felt the shock of recognition and the conviction that they were bound together from a former life. She had planned to go to the port of Hofu, and travel by ship to the mouth of the Inugawa and from there along the river upstream to Inuyama, but the prospect of the sea voyage was already unsettling her; there was no reason why she should not change her plans and go by the high road by way of Yamagata with Shizuka.

She had ordered the palanquin for the journey, but as soon as they were beyond the outskirts of the town she got out and mounted her horse, which one of the men led alongside his own. Shizuka was also riding: her younger son, who was about seven years old, sat behind her, but the older one had his own small horse, which he handled confidently and skilfully.

The sight of the boys filled her with sorrow: for her own son who would have been about the same age as Zenko, had he lived, and for the unborn children that would never exist – Shigeru's sons. She wanted to bring them into being through the sheer force of her longing and her will: they would be like these boys, with strong limbs, thick glossy hair and fearless black eyes.

Zenko rode with the men ahead: they treated him with respect, but teased him affectionately. The laughter and jokes made the younger boy jealous, and at the first rest stop he begged to be allowed to ride with his brother. One of the guards good-naturedly took him on the back of his horse, and the two women found themselves virtually alone on the road as it wound along the banks of the river: the Western border of the Middle Country. Within every bend rice fields had been cultivated, and the seedlings were being planted out to the accompaniment of singing and drum beating. Herons and egrets stalked through the shallow water, and the bush warbler's song erupted in the forest. The trees all bore new leaves of brilliant green, and wildflowers spilled over the banks. Sweet chestnut catkins attracted hundreds of insects; the air was warm, but it was still chilly in the shade of the forest.

Naomi could control her impatience no longer. 'Have you seen Lord Otori?' she questioned.

'I see him from time to time,' Shizuka said, 'but I have not been to Hagi this year. Last year I saw him in the spring and in the autumn.'

Tears sprang into Naomi's eyes astonishing her. She said nothing, not trusting her voice. Even though she turned her head away as if she were taking in the beauty of the view, Shizuka must have noticed her distress for she went on to say, 'I am sorry, lady, that I see him and you do not. He does not forget you; he thinks of you all the time and longs for you.'

'He speaks to you of this?' Naomi said, outraged that he should share their secrets, bitterly jealous of this woman who saw him when she could not.

'He does not need to. We speak of other things that it is safest for all of us not to divulge. You were right when you told Arai that Lord Otori is patient. Moreover, he is devious and hides his true self from the world. But he never forgets his hidden ambition: to see Iida dead and to marry you.'

It thrilled her to hear it spoken of openly by another person. She looked directly at Shizuka and said, 'Will it happen?'

'I hope for it with all my heart,' Shizuka said.

'And Lord Otori is well?' She simply wanted to keep speaking his name, to keep talking about him.

'He is; he maintains his estates with great success, he travels a lot, sometimes with my uncle, Kenji. They have become good friends. Lord Takeshi is also very close to him and has grown into a fine young man. Lord Otori is admired by everyone.'

'There is no one like him,' Naomi said quietly.

'I do not believe there is,' Shizuka agreed.

They rode in silence for a while, Naomi brooding on Shigeru. It was eight years since she had met him at Seisenji, six years since she had last set eyes on him. Yet on this spring journey she felt like a girl again, her whole body longing to be touched, longing to be part of the lush and fertile landscape pulsating with the energy of life.

Finally she said, 'You will spend the summer with your family?'

'The boys will,' Shizuka replied. 'I will return to Noguchi, unless...'

'Unless what?' Naomi prompted.

Shizuka did not answer, but rode in silence for a while. Then she said quietly, 'How much do you really know about me?'

'In his letter Lord Otori told me that you had sworn to help him, that you are from the Tribe, and that I must tell no one. I know that you have lived with Lord Arai for many years; he seems to care deeply for you.'

'Then I can say this much: unless the Tribe issue me with other instructions, for the time being, they are happy for me to stay with Arai.'

'I thought you were free to make your own decisions,' Naomi said.

'Is any woman ever free? You and I, for different reasons, have more freedom than most, yet even we cannot act as we might wish. Men are brutal and ruthless: they act as if they love us, but our feelings do not matter to them. As you heard last night, Arai's wife has just had a child. She knows of my existence, and the boys'; Arai lives openly with me, and has done since I was fifteen years

old, but he has not acknowledged my sons, though he seems to love and be proud of them. Ten years is a long time in a man's life. I daresay one day he will tire of me and want to dispose of me. I have no illusions about the world, you will realize. Accidents happen to children...'
She glanced at Naomi's face. 'Forgive me, I did not mean to open old wounds. But I do not intend to leave my sons where harm can come to them. Besides, they bear the name of Muto: they are Tribe children. It is time for them to begin their training, as I did at their age.'

'What is that training?' Naomi asked curiously. 'What does it equip you for?'

'You must know of the activities of the Tribe, Lady Maruyama. Most rulers use them from time to time.'

'I do not know of any Tribe members in Maruyama, and I have never employed them,' Naomi exclaimed. After a moment she said, 'Maybe I should!'

'Did Lord Otori not tell you about your groom, Bunta?'

Naomi swung round in the saddle. Bunta rode some way behind them, alongside Sachie. 'Bunta is from the Tribe?'

'It was from him that I learned of your meetings with Lord Otori.'

'I will have him executed,' Naomi said in fury. 'Sachie said he would keep my secrets!'

'He kept them from everybody except me. Luckily he told me, for I've been able to protect you both. And I have told no one else. Say nothing, and do nothing about him. He is able to keep me informed of your whereabouts and your safety. If you ever need to get hold of me you can do it through him.'

Naomi struggled to contain her astonishment and anger. Shizuka had revealed all these things perfectly calmly and she was smiling now. Trying to match her composure, Naomi said, 'Lord Otori told me you had sworn allegiance to him. Does he hope to use the Tribe in some way? Against Iida, I mean?' And then she said, 'Would you be able to...?'

She stopped, unable to voice the idea out loud, afraid that even in this sunny landscape where they seemingly rode alone, spies would overhear them.

'Lord Otori is waiting for the right moment,' Shizuka murmured, so quietly Naomi could hardly hear her. 'And then he will act.'

Shizuka's company raised Naomi's spirits and made her hopeful, and her cheerful mood continued after they parted in Yamagata. Shizuka went, she said, to her uncle's house, and Naomi spent the night in an inn before travelling on the next day to the temple with Sachie, two guards and Bunta. The men stayed with the horses at the resting place at the foot of the temple, and Naomi and Sachie climbed the steep path alone.

They left early in the morning: dew edged the tips of the bamboo grass and turned spiders' webs into jewels. As always she felt the spiritual peace of the temple drawing her towards it, and as the two women walked in silence she felt the familiar sense of awe settle over her. Naomi's head was covered by a wide shawl and she wore simple clothes, like an ordinary pilgrim. She had not sent messengers ahead, and her arrival was unexpected.

In the main courtyard and around the women's guest room, the cherry blossom was already past its peak, and the pink and white petals lay thick on the ground. Scarlet azaleas and peonies, white with red tips, were just coming into bloom.

Naomi walked in the gardens, and sat for a long time by the pool, watching the red and gold carp milling below the surface of the water. She had begun to believe that she was indeed just a simple pilgrim, divested of all the cares and anxieties of her life, when her reverie was interrupted by the appearance of the Abbot, Matsuda Shingen.

He came quickly towards her.

'Lady Maruyama! I had no idea you were here. Forgive me for not welcoming you before.'

'Lord Abbot.' She bowed to the ground.

'This is unexpected – but of course we are always honoured by your presence...'

He seemed to finish on a questioning note. When she made no response, he said, very quietly, 'Lord Shigeru is here.'

The blood rushed through her body as though it would burst out. She felt her eyes widen like a madwoman's, and she struggled to control herself.

'I did not know,' she said calmly. 'I hope Lord Otori is in good health.' It was all she could manage. I should never have come: his presence must have drawn me here. I must leave at once. If I do not see him I will die.

'He is making a retreat in the mountains,' Matsuda replied. 'He comes here from time to time – though we have not seen him for many months. I thought perhaps an arrangement had been made – like the previous time.'

'No,' she replied hurriedly. 'It is a coincidence.'

'So I do not need to send a message to Lord Shigeru?'

'Certainly not. I must not intrude on his meditation – and in any case, it is better that we do not meet.'

He seemed to gaze searchingly at her, but he did not press the subject.

They went on to speak of other things: the situation at Maruyama, Naomi's daughter, the beauty of the spring weather. Then he excused himself, and she remained alone, while the day drew to its close, and a silver sickle moon rose above the mountains, accompanied by the evening star.

The chill air of night finally drove her inside. Sachie was even more attentive than usual. Naomi felt her companion's concern and longed to talk to her, but did not dare: once she began to unburden herself, she feared she would lose all control. She bathed in the hot springs beneath moon and starlight, aware of the whiteness of her skin through the steam and the water, ate a little and retired early, before the moon was even halfway across the heaven. She lay awake most of the night, thinking of the moon and how her body followed its cycle. As the moon began to increase, she knew she was at her most fertile: all the more reason not to see him, for to conceive a child now would be a disaster; yet her body, ignorant of all her fears, longed for him with its own animal innocence.

Towards dawn she slept a little, but was woken by the insistent cries of sparrows beneath the eaves, driven by spring to mate and nest. She rose quietly and put on a robe, but not quietly enough for Sachie, who woke and said, 'Lady? Can I fetch you anything?'

'No, I will walk a little outside before the sun is up. Then we will return to Yamagata.'

'I will come with you,' Sachie said, pushing aside the quilt.

Naomi heard herself say, 'I am not going far. I would rather be alone.'

'Very well,' Sachie replied, after a moment.

I am possessed, Naomi thought, and indeed she seemed to be moving without volition, as if drawn by spirits through the dew-soaked garden and up into the mountain.

The world had never seemed more beautiful as the mist that hung around the peaks gradually dissolved and the light turned from grey to gold. She had meant to return once the sun had cleared the steep range to the east, but even after that, when the air became warmer, she found reasons to keep walking – just around the next bend, just to look at the view over the valley – until the path levelled out into a small clearing where a huge oak rose from the spring grass.

Shigeru lay on his back, his arms behind his head. At first she thought he must be asleep, but as she approached she saw his eyes were wide open.

It must be a dream, she thought. I will awaken soon, and she did what she would have done in the dream, lay down next to him, taking him in her arms, laying her head on his chest, saying nothing.

She could feel his heart beating against the flesh and bones of her face. She breathed at the same time he did. He turned slightly and put his arms around her, burying his face in her hair.

The ache of separation dissolved. She felt the tension and fear of the last years drain from her. All she could think about was his breath, his heartbeat, the urgency and hardness of his body; her complete desire for him, and his for her.

Afterwards she thought, Now I will wake up, but the scene did not change suddenly. The air was warm on her face, the birds sang in the forest, the ground beneath her was hard, the grass damp.

Shigeru said, 'Why are you here?'

'I am on my way to Inuyama. I felt I wanted to see the gardens. I did not know you were here: Matsuda told me last night. I was going to leave at once, but this morning something drew me to walk this way.' She stopped and shivered. 'It was as if I was under a spell. You have bewitched me.'

'I could say the same. I could not sleep last night – I was to visit Matsuda today before I return to Hagi. I thought I would do it early, then go back to my mountain hut – I lived there with Matsuda when I was fifteen; I was his pupil. I was moved to rest beneath this tree. It has a special significance for me, for I once saw a houou there – the sacred bird of peace and justice. I hoped to see it again, but I am afraid it will not be found in the Three Countries while Iida lives.'

The mention of Iida's name reminded her of the fear that hovered all around, yet in this place, with him, she felt protected from it.

'I feel like a village girl,' she said wistfully. 'Sneaking away with my young man.'

'I will go and announce to your parents that we are betrothed,' he said. 'We will be married before the shrine, and the whole village will celebrate and drink too much!'

'Will I have to leave my family and move to your father's house?'

'Yes, of course, and my mother will order you around and make you cry, and I won't be able to stand up for you, or all the village men will laugh at me for being besotted with my wife! But at night I will make you happy and tell you how much I love you, and we will make lots of children together.'

She wished he had not said those words, even jokingly. It was as though he had spoken something into existence. She tried to put her fears from her.

'I came with Muto Shizuka as far as Yamagata, and before that I was in Noguchi, where I met Arai Daiichi. He asked about your intentions, having heard that you were interested only in farming.'

'What did you tell him?'

'Only that you were patient, which Arai is not. He is on the verge of rebelling, I think. It will only take one small incident or insult to set him off.'

'He must not act alone, or precipitously. It would be too easy now for Iida to crush him and eliminate him.'

'Shizuka and I talked about the Tribe. An idea came to me, that we might use them. Lord Shigeru, we cannot go on like this. We must act. We must kill Iida. Surely if we cannot confront him in battle, we can find someone to assassinate him!'

'I have thought the same. I have even spoken to Shizuka about it. She has indicated that she would not be unwilling, but I am reluctant to ask such a thing of her. She is a woman, she has children. I wish I could fight Iida man to man, but I fear if I go to Inuyama I will be simply putting myself into his hands.'

They were both silent for a moment, thinking of the young Yanagi warrior who had died on the castle wall.

Shigeru said, 'The Tribe do not want Iida removed: he employs many of them. So we could only work with someone in whom we had complete trust, otherwise we run the risk of simply revealing our plans to the Tribe in general, and to the Tohan. As far as I can see there is no one apart from Shizuka.'

Naomi whispered, 'I will be in Inuyama in a few weeks. I will be in his presence.'

'You must not even think of it!' Shigeru said in alarm. 'Whatever your fighting skills you will be no match for him, and he is surrounded at all times by warriors, hidden guards and members of the Tribe. You and your daughter would both die, and if you are dead my life becomes meaningless. We must continue to dissemble, to do nothing to arouse his suspicions, to wait for the right moment to reveal itself to us.'

'And the right assassin,' Naomi said.

'That too.'

'I must go back. Sachie will be worrying about me. I don't want anyone coming in search of me.'

'I will walk with you.'

'No! We must not be seen together. I will set out for Yamagata as soon as I get back to the temple. Do not come there today.'

'Very well,' he said. 'I suppose you are right. I will go back to my solitary hut for another night.'

She felt tears threaten suddenly, and stood to hide them. 'If only I were just a village girl! But I have heavy responsibilities – to my clan, to my daughter.'

'Lady Maruyama,' he said formally as he too got to his feet. 'Don't despair. It will not be for much longer.' She nodded, not daring to speak. Neither of them looked at each other again. He bent and gathered up his belongings, put the sword in his belt and walked away up the mountain path, while she went back the way she had come, her body still ecstatic from the encounter, her mind already skittering with fear.

She spent the days of the journey trying to compose herself, calling on all the methods she had been taught since childhood to bring mind and body under control. She told herself she must never have such a meeting again, that she must stop behaving like a foolish girl infatuated with a farmer. If there were to be a future for Shigeru and herself together, it could only come through their self-control and discretion in the present. But already she knew in the deepest parts of both body and mind that it was too late to be discreet. She knew she had already conceived a child, a child she longed to have but which must not be born.

She considered returning immediately to Maruyama, but such an action might offend Iida and increase his suspicions to the point of harming Mariko. She felt she must continue her journey: she was expected at Inuyama; messengers had already been sent. Iida would never be convinced by any excuses of sickness: he would only be insulted. She could do nothing other than complete the journey as planned – and continue to pretend.

Her journey led her through the heart of the Middle Country – the former Otori lands which had been ceded to the Tohan clan after Yaegahara. The local people had resisted becoming Tohan and had borne the brunt of the Eastern clan's cruelty and oppression. She overheard little on the road and in the overnight lodging places, for the formerly ebullient people had become taciturn and suspicious, and with good reason. She saw several signs of recent executions, and every village sported a notice board declaring penalties for breaking regulations – most of them involving torture and death. At the fork where the highway divided, the northern road leading to Chigawa, the eastern to Inuyama, the palanquin bearers stopped for a rest outside a small inn which served tea, bowls of rice and noodles, and dried fish. As Naomi alighted, her eyes fell on another notice board: here, from its roof, a large grey heron had been suspended by its feet. It was barely alive;

it flapped its wings sporadically and opened and closed its beak in weakened pain.

Naomi was deeply distressed by the sight, repelled by the unnecessary cruelty. She called to the men to cut the bird down. Their approach alarmed it, and it died struggling against their attempts to save it. As they laid it down on the ground before her, she knelt and touched the dulled plumage, saw its eyes film.

The old man who kept the inn hurried out and said in alarm, 'Lady, you should not touch it. We will all be punished.'

'It is insulting to Heaven to treat its creatures so,' she replied. 'It must surely bring bad luck to all travellers.'

'It is only a bird, and we are men,' he muttered.

'Why does anyone torture a bird? What does it mean?'

'It's a warning.' He would say no more, and she knew she should not insist for his own safety, but the memory continued to trouble her as she made the final stage of the journey through the mountains that surrounded Inuyama. The fair spring weather continued, but Naomi could not enjoy the blue sky, the soft southern breeze. Everything had been darkened by the dying heron.

She stayed for the last night, a few hours' distance from the capital, in a small village on the river, and while the meal was being prepared she asked Sachie to speak to Bunta; maybe he would be able to find out something in the village.

She and Sachie had finished eating by the time he returned.

'I met some men from Chigawa,' he said quietly, after he had knelt before her. 'No one wants to talk openly. The Tohan have spies everywhere. However, these men told me a little: the heron is a warning, as the innkeeper said. There is a group – a movement – throughout the Middle Country: Loyalty to the Heron, it's called. The Tohan are trying to eradicate it. There's been a lot of unrest lately in Chigawa and the surrounding districts. It's all to do with the silver mines. The movement is apparently very strong there: the lives of the miners have become more and more wretched; many abscond and escape to the mountains; young people, even children are forced to take their place. The men say it is slavery, and under the Otori they were never slaves.'

She thanked him, but did not ask any more. She felt she had heard too much already. 'Loyalty to the Heron' – they could only be supporters of Shigeru.

Naomi rose early the next morning and arrived in the capital shortly after midday. She had made this journey many times now, yet she could never quite dispel the feeling of dread that the sight of Iida's black-walled castle inspired in her. It dominated the town, the sheer walls rising from the moat, their reflection shimmering in the slow greenish water of the river. A narrow street led in a zigzag pattern to the main bridge. Here, even though she was a frequent visitor and already known to the guards, she and Sachie had to descend from the palanquins while they were thoroughly searched – though, Naomi thought resentfully, only the smallest and most loose-limbed assassin could have concealed himself there.

The search was insulting, yet Iida's suspicions were well founded: many longed to see him dead – indeed, as she had said to Shigeru, she would kill him herself if she could. But she put all such thoughts from her, and waited impassively and calmly until she was permitted to proceed.

She entered the palanquin again and the porters walked through the main bailey to the south bailey, where Iida's residence was built. Here she climbed out once more, to be met by two of Lady Iida's companions. The porters and her men returned over the bridge to the town, and she and Sachie and their two maids followed the women through the residence gate, down the angled steps into the gardens, which extended away for a considerable distance as far as the riverbank.

The fragrance of flowers was everywhere: the purple irises round the stream that flowed through the gardens were just beginning to bloom, and heavy blossoms of wisteria hung like icicles from the pavilion roof.

Naomi and Sachie waited while the maids undid their sandals and brought water to wash their feet, then stepped up onto the polished wood veranda. It was newly constructed and ran round the entire residence, and as their feet trod over it it responded with little cries like birds.

'What is it?' Sachie said in wonderment to one of the maids.

'Lord Iida had it constructed this year,' she whispered quietly. 'It is a marvel, isn't it? Not even a cat can cross it without setting it singing. We call it the nightingale floor.'

'I have never heard of such a thing before,' Naomi said, her heart sinking further. Surely Iida had made himself invulnerable.

The residence was decorated in a sumptuous style, gold leaf covering the beams of the ceiling and picking out the triple oak leaf on the bosses on the walls. The floors of the passages were all polished cypress, and the walls were decorated with flamboyant paintings of tigers, peacocks and other exotic animals and birds.

They progressed in silence into the deepest recesses of the residence, into the women's rooms. Here the decorations were more restrained, delicate flowers and fish replacing the animals. Naomi was shown to the room she usually occupied; the boxes and baskets which contained her clothes, gifts for Lady Iida, new robes and books for Mariko, were taken away to the storehouse, Sachie going with them to oversee the unpacking, and tea was brought in elegant pale green bowls.

Naomi drank it gladly, for the afternoon was becoming very warm, and sat trying to compose herself.

Sachie returned with Mariko. The girl greeted her mother formally, bowing deeply, then came closer into Naomi's arms. She felt as always the rush of relief, almost like the gush of milk into the breast, that her child was alive, safe, close enough for her to hold, stroke the hair back from her forehead, gaze into her eyes, smell her sweet breath.

'Let me look at you,' she exclaimed. 'You are growing up so fast. You look pale. Are you well?'

'I have been quite well; I had a cold last month and the cough persisted. I am better now winter is finally over. But Mother also looks a little pale; you have not been ill?'

'No, it is just that I am tired from the journey. And, of course, so moved by seeing you.'

Mariko smiled as her eyes brightened with tears.

'How long will Mother stay?'

'Not long, this time, I'm afraid.' She saw Mariko struggle to hide her disappointment. 'I have things to do back in Maruyama,' she explained, and felt her womb clench in fear.

'I hoped you would stay until the plum rains are over. It is so dreary here when it rains every day.'

'I must leave before they begin,' Naomi said. 'They must not delay me.'

For the plum rains might last five or six weeks, and she would have to spend that time among the household women, who knew every detail of each other's lives, and when each one had to be secluded because of her monthly bleeding, a custom practised by the Tohan. These women had so little to occupy them they would study her day and night; she feared their boredom and their malice.

'Sachie has brought more books for you,' she said briskly. 'You will have plenty to occupy yourself with while you are confined indoors by the rain. But tell me your news. How is Lady Iida?'

'She was very sick in the winter with an inflammation of the lungs. I was afraid for her.' Mariko's voice fell to a whisper. 'Her women say that if she were to die, Lord Iida would have to make up his mind between you and me.'

'But she is, thank Heaven, still alive, and we hope will have many years of health. How is her little boy? Her father must be proud of him.'

Mariko lowered her eyes. 'Unfortunately he is a delicate child. He does not take to the sword and is afraid of horses. He is six years old now. Other boys his age are already receiving warrior's training, but he clings to his mother and his nurse.'

'It's sad; I cannot imagine Lord Iida is patient with him.'

'No, the boy is more terrified of his father than of anything else.'

Naomi met the child, Katsu, later when she joined Lady Iida for the evening meal. His nurse brought the little boy in, but he cried and whined, and was soon taken away. He did not seem to be very intelligent, and certainly was neither confident nor courageous.

She pitied the child and his mother. All men expected their wives to give them sons, but how often were those sons a disappointment or a threat! Iida would make life a torment for them both. She tried not to think how this in turn affected her own situation. If only Iida were happily married with dozens of sons. His dissatisfaction led him to consider changing wives and directed his attention more intensely on her. But she did not want even to consider these matters, lest her own hopes and fears undermine her composure and give her away.

The next morning she was summoned to Iida's presence and met outside by a man who she knew to be one of his favourites.

'Lord Abe,' she greeted him, though she thought to call him 'lord' was flattering him, for Iida honoured him far above his family's rank.

His bow was perfunctory; she suspected that like most of the Eastern warriors he had little respect for the Maruyama tradition and saw her as an aberration that should be removed as speedily as possible.

How swift would be her fall, how great her humiliation if anyone knew about the child. She would have to take her own life; Iida would marry her daughter, and Maruyama would pass to the Tohan. But to kill myself would mean I had given up hope, she told herself, and I have not yet, not yet. I will do anything in my power to see Iida overthrown, Shigeru restored, and to live with him as his wife. And there will be no more cruelty, no more torture, no more hostages.

With renewed resolve to withstand his tyranny, she stepped into the receiving room and dropped to her knees, retreating into herself, hiding her hatred of him behind the graceful form and appealing demeanour of a beautiful woman.

Iida's eyes appraised her, and she sensed his interest and his desire.

'Please sit up, Lady Maruyama. I am so delighted to see you again.'

He was far more courteous than his underling: he was the eldest son of an ancient family, and had been trained in such things since childhood; furthermore he was acquainted with all the different forms of human interaction, and used courtesy as he used cruelty – to further his own ends, and for his own gratification. Yet the courteous words sounded incongruous in his harsh Eastern accent, and she was neither flattered nor disarmed.

'It is of course with the greatest pleasure that I come to Inuyama,' she replied. 'I am so grateful to Lord Iida and Lady Iida for their care of my daughter.'

'She seems to be a healthy girl; and growing up so fast, though she cannot compare to her mother in beauty.'

She made no response beyond bowing again to acknowledge the compliment.

Iida went on, 'I hope you will honour us with your presence for many weeks.'

'Lord Iida's kindness is extreme. However, I must return fairly soon to Maruyama, as I have matters to attend to there. The anniversary of my father's death is approaching, among other obligations.'

He said nothing, but continued to watch her with a look of veiled amusement.

He knows about Shigeru, she thought, and felt the blood drain from her face as her heart thumped. But she showed nothing of her fears, simply waited composedly for him to speak again, reminding herself that it was one of his strategies to pretend to know everything about people until they broke down and confessed to far more than he suspected, condemning themselves out of their own mouths.

He finally broke the silence. 'What news do you bring me from the West? I suppose you stopped at Noguchi. I hope Noguchi is keeping Arai under control.'

'Lord Arai is one of Lord Noguchi's most trusted retainers now,' she replied.

'And what do you hear of the Otori?'

'Very little. I have not even set foot in the domain for years.'

'Yet I hear you have a fondness for herons.'

'I saw one of Heaven's creatures suffering,' she replied quietly. 'I did not understand what it meant.'

'You understand now, though? "Loyalty to the Heron." It is almost laughable. These people do not know what Shigeru has become; I'll wager they would not rally under the banner "Loyalty to the Farmer"!'

He laughed and waited for her to smile. 'The Farmer is growing a fine crop of sesame, they tell me,' he sneered.

He does not know, she realized.

'I suppose sesame is a useful seed,' she said, pretending disdain.

'Shigeru is far more useful as a farmer than he ever was as a warrior,' Iida muttered. 'All the same, I would be a lot happier if he were dead.'

She could not bring herself to acquiesce, simply raised her eyebrows slightly and smiled.

'He had some reputation once as a swordsman,' Iida said. 'Now people speak of his integrity and honour. I would like to have him in my power: I would like to see his honour then. But he's too wily ever to leave the Middle Country.'

'No one is as great a warrior as Lord Iida,' she murmured, thinking how fortunate it was that he was a vain man and no flattery was ever too excessive for him.

'I suppose you have seen my nightingale floor?' he said. 'My skills as a warrior are not all that I have. I am also cunning and suspicious, never forget that!'

The audience came to an end and she returned to her rooms.

The days passed, long and tedious apart from the pleasure of being with her daughter. Her anxieties mounted. Her monthly bleeding was two days late, three days, then a week. She feared that the physical changes in her body, especially the onset of morning sickness, would be all too quickly observed, and knew that she must not delay her departure. She lay awake at night trying to plan what must take place as soon as she got back to Maruyama. Who would be able to help her? Her normal physicians were all men; she could not bear to disclose her secret to them. And she could not ask either Sachie or her sister, Eriko, to help her kill her child, even though both had a knowledge of herbs, medicine and healing. The only person she could think of was Shizuka. Surely Shizuka knew about such things? And she would understand and not judge...

The day before she left Inuyama she sent Bunta with a message, begging Shizuka to come to Maruyama at once.

Mariko was deeply disappointed at her leaving, and they parted with tears on both sides. The journey back was difficult: it seemed everything conspired to make her miserable. The weather became suddenly unseasonably hot; the rains began before she left Yamagata, but she insisted on returning home and not staying in the city, so the last week of travel was in constant rain. In Bunta's absence the horses were bad-tempered and difficult. Everything was soaked and smelled of mildew. Sachie caught a cold, which made her even more unhappy about Naomi's inexplicable urgency. But unpleasant as the journey was, what she feared at home was even more alarming. She did not know how she would find the strength to do what she knew she had to.

CHAPTER FORTY-FIVE

By the time Naomi had arrived home, her companion Sachie who knew her so intimately had begun to suspect what had happened. When they were alone inside the residence the two women stared at each other. Sachie's eyes held the question. Naomi could only nod.

'But how?' Sachie began.

'At Terayama. He was there. Don't say anything to me. I know what a fool I have been. Now I am going to get rid of it.'

She saw Sachie flinch and was unreasonably angry with her. 'I am not asking you to have anything to do with it. If it offends you then leave me. Someone is coming to help me.' She was silent for a moment, then said, her voice breaking, 'But she must come soon.'

'Lady Naomi!' Sachie reached out to her as if she would embrace her but Naomi stood rigid. 'I would never leave you at a time like this. But is there no alternative?'

'I cannot think of one,' Naomi said bitterly. 'If you can devise some way out, some way for me not to kill Lord Shigeru's child, then tell me. Otherwise don't pity me or you will weaken me. I will weep later when it is all over.'

Sachie bowed her head, tears in her eyes.

'In the meantime you may tell the household I have caught a severe cold. I will see no one, except the woman with whom we rode to Yamagata, Muto Shizuka. She must come soon,' she repeated, gazing into the garden where the rain fell steadily.

Two days later there was a brief break in the weather and in a patch of sunshine and blue skies Shizuka arrived with Bunta.

Alone in the room with Naomi, she listened in silence to the curt request, asked for no explanations and offered no sympathy.

'I will be back tonight,' she said. 'Eat and drink nothing. Try and rest. You will not sleep tonight and it will be painful.'

She returned with herbs from which she made a bitter infusion and helped Naomi drink it. Within hours the cramps began, followed by severe pain and heavy bleeding. Shizuka stayed with her throughout the night, wiping the sweat from her face, washing away the blood, reassuring her that it would soon pass.

'You will have other children,' she whispered. 'As I did.'

'You have been through this too,' Naomi said, letting the tears flow now as much for Shizuka as for herself.

'Yes, my first child. It did not suit the Tribe for me to have it at that time. My aunt gave me this same brew. I was very unhappy. But if the Tribe had not done that to me I would never have dared defy them to help Lord Shigeru and to keep your secret. Men cannot foresee what the results of their actions will be because they do not take account of the human heart.'

'Are you in love with Lord Shigeru?' Naomi heard herself asking. 'Is that why you do so much for us?' The darkness, the intimacy between them, made her dare to utter such words.

Shizuka replied with the same honesty. 'I love him deeply, but we will never be together in this life. That precious fate is yours.'

'It is a fate that has brought me little but sorrow,' Naomi said. 'But I would not choose any other.'

Towards dawn the pain eased and she slept a little; when she woke Sachie was in the room and Shizuka was preparing to leave. Naomi was filled with dread at the idea of her departure.

'Stay a little longer! Don't leave me yet!'

'Lady, I cannot stay. I should not be here. Someone will find out and it will bring us all into danger.'

'You will not tell Lord Shigeru?' Naomi began to weep at his name.

'Of course not! It may anyway be a long time till I am able to see him. You may see him yourself before then.

You must rest and recover your strength. You have many who love you and who will take care of you.'

When Naomi wept more despairingly Shizuka tried to comfort her. 'Next time I go to Hagi I will come here first. You may send a message to him then.'

It was nine weeks to the day when Naomi had lain down next to Shigeru as if in a dream.

The child's life had been extinguished swiftly and easily. She could not even pray openly for its soul, nor express her grief and her anger that she could not live freely with the man she loved. Her mood became very dark, as if a heavy spirit had possessed her, and she was given to outbursts of rage against her retainers and servants, which led the elders to express among themselves the opinion that she was showing all the irrationality of a woman and was maybe not fit to govern alone. They began to suggest marriage to Iida or to someone chosen by him, thus enraging her further.

When summer passed and the cooler autumn weather came, she had still not fully recovered, and she began to dread the coming of winter. She had meant to travel to Inuyama again but knew she was not well enough to face Iida and maintain her self-control. Yet she feared offending him and disappointing Mariko further.

'My life is hopeless,' she said in despair one night to Sachie and her sister Eriko. 'I should end it now.'

'Don't speak in this way,' Sachie pleaded. 'Things will get better. You will recover your strength.'

'There is nothing wrong with my health,' Naomi replied. 'But I cannot rid myself of this terrible darkness that lies on my spirit.' She whispered, 'If only I could acknowledge the – what happened – I feel I would be absolved. But I cannot, and while I cannot I will never have any peace.'

Eriko and Sachie exchanged a quick glance, and Sachie said equally quietly, 'My sister and I were unable to help you with what you needed before. But perhaps we can offer you healing now.'

'There are no herbs for this sort of ailing,' Naomi said.

'But there is one who can help you,' Eriko said hesitantly.

Naomi sat in silence for a while. She had told Shigeru that she was familiar with the teachings of the Hidden, and even held a great sympathy for the persecuted sect. But she had not told him – for the secret was not hers to give away – that both Sachie and Eriko were believers; that Mari, the niece of the tortured man whom Shigeru had rescued years ago near Chigawa, worked in the castle and kept the two women in touch with the Hidden throughout the West and with the former Otori warrior Harada Tomasu, who had become something of an itinerant priest after serving Nesutoro as disciple and servant. She had had many discussions with the two sisters about their faith, and had in the past often felt a yearning to abandon herself like them to the love and mercy of a Supreme Being who would accept her for what she was, an ordinary human being, no better and no worse than any other. But now she had taken life, had sinned beyond forgiveness – and she could not repent, for given the same choices she would take the same action again.

'I know what you mean,' she said finally. 'I would turn to any spiritual being who would give me relief. But I have offended deeply by killing my own child. I am unable to pray openly to the Enlightened One or go to the shrine. How can I turn to your god, to the Secret One, when your first commandment is not to kill?'

Eriko said, 'He knows everything in your heart. His first commandment is to love him; his second, to love all men and forgive those who hate us. It is because of love that we do not take life. That is for him alone to decide. We live in the midst of the world; if we repent I believe he understands and forgives us.'

'And will forgive you,' Sachie added, taking Naomi's hand.

Eriko took her other hand, and they sat with bowed heads. Naomi knew the other two women were praying, and she tried to still her heart and her thoughts.

They delude themselves, she thought. There is nothing there – and even if there were I would not be able to heed its voice, for I am a ruler, and must rule with power.

Yet as the silence deepened she was aware of something beyond herself, some greater presence that both towered above her and waited humbly for her to turn to it. She saw suddenly how this could be the highest allegiance anyone could make: one could kneel before this and genuinely submit one's body and soul. It was the opposite to the earthly power of warlords like Iida, and maybe the only power that could check such men.

She did turn and whispered, 'I am sorry,' and felt the lightest of touches, like a healing hand on her heart.

Throughout the winter she talked to Eriko and Sachie often, and prayed with them, and before the beginning of the new year she had been received into the community of the Hidden.

She realized there were many levels of belief, and many people held them whom she had not suspected of so doing. She became aware of the network they formed across her domain, throughout the West, indeed throughout the Three Countries, though in Tohan lands they were still persecuted. It was whispered that Iida himself took part in hunting them down, indulging his pleasure in killing.

In many ways Naomi struggled against belief. It was not an easy decision. Her pride in her position and her family made her recoil from putting herself on the same level as ordinary people. She believed she had always treated them fairly, but to see them as her equals was strange and affronting to her. Yet belief brought her a sense of forgiveness, and forgiveness brought her peace.

There were other conflicts within her that seemed impossible to resolve. The beliefs of the Hidden forbade the taking of life, yet the only way to set her daughter free and bring not only happiness to herself but peace and justice to the Three Countries was for Iida to die. She remembered the discussions she had had with Shigeru about assassination; must she now abandon all these plans and leave Iida's punishment to the Secret One, who saw everything and dealt with everyone after death?

Heaven's net is wide, but its mesh is fine, she said to herself.

She thought of Shigeru constantly, though she had little hope of meeting him or hearing from him. The narrow escape from discovery had alarmed and shocked her: she could not bear to take such a risk again. Yet she still longed for him, still loved him deeply, wanted now to tell him about the child and ask his forgiveness. She wrote letters to him all winter which she hoped to send with Shizuka, and then tore them into scraps and burned them.

Spring came; the snows had melted: messengers, travellers and peddlers once again began their journeys across the Three Countries. Naomi had little time to brood, luckily, for she was always busy. She had to resume the control and leadership of her clan, which had slipped from her a little while she was ill. Even when the weather was too bad to ride outside, there were many meetings held with the clan elders, many decisions that had to be made regarding trade, industry, mining and agriculture, military affairs and diplomacy.

When she had time, she liked to retreat in the afternoons with Sachie and Eriko, and prepare tea for them in the teahouse built by her grandmother. The ritual took on some of the holy qualities of the shared meal of the Hidden. The maid, Mari, usually waited on them, bringing hot water and little cakes of sweetened chestnut or bean paste, and often Harada Tomasu joined them to pray with them.

One day in the fifth month, to Naomi's delight, Shizuka's name was announced to her, and Mari brought her into the garden.

Shizuka stepped into the teahouse and knelt before Naomi, then sat up and studied her face. 'Lady Maruyama has recovered,' she said quietly. 'And regained all her beauty.'

'And you, Shizuka, have you been well? Where did you spend the winter?' Naomi thought Shizuka looked unusually pale and subdued.

'I have been in Noguchi all winter, with Lord Arai. I thought I would be able to go to Hagi now, but something just happened, here in Maruyama, that has alarmed me.'

'Can you tell me what it is?' Naomi said.

'It may be nothing. I am imagining things. I thought I saw my uncle Kenji in the street. Well, I didn't see him actually, I smelled him – he has quite a distinct smell – and then I realized there was someone using one of the Tribe skills to hide their presence. He was ahead of me, and upwind, so I don't think he saw me. But it worried me. Why would he be here? He rarely comes this far to the West. I am afraid he is watching me. I have aroused his suspicions in some way. I should not go to Hagi for I will give away my friendship with Lord Shigeru, and if the Tribe find out...'

'Please go!' Naomi begged her. 'I will write to him now; I will be quick; I won't delay you.'

'I should not carry letters,' Shizuka said. 'It is too dangerous. Tell me your message. If I think it is safe – not only for me but for us all – I will try to see Lord Shigeru before summer.'

'Sachie, prepare tea for Shizuka while I sit for a few moments and think of what I want to say,' Naomi requested, but before Sachie could move Mari called quietly from the doorway.

'Lady Maruyama, Harada Tomasu has something to tell you. May I bring him here?'

Shizuka had gone still. 'Who is Harada?' she whispered.

'He was one of Shigeru's retainers,' Naomi replied. 'You have nothing to fear from him.' Harada was the former Otori warrior who had once taken a message from her to Shigeru and had arranged their first meeting. She held him in great affection for that reason, and also because she had spoken to him many times about his beliefs. 'Can he have brought a message from Hagi?' Her hands were trembling against the delicate pottery of the tea bowl, sending tiny ripples across the surface of the tea.

She called to Mari. 'Yes, bring him at once.'

Mari bowed and left, and returned after a little while with Harada.

Naomi greeted the one-eyed man warmly. He looked thinner and more spare, as though the fire of his conviction was consuming him from within.

'Lady Maruyama, I feel I must go to Hagi and see Lord Otori.'

'What has happened?' she said, with some alarm.

'I have had no news of Lord Otori for months,' he replied. 'As far as I know, he is well. But I have a strong feeling I should take some information I've heard recently to him.'

'Can you tell me what it is?'

'There is a peddler who travels from Inuyama; he has been to Hagi often too. He is one of us and brings news of our people from the East and the Middle Country. The year before last, for the first time he went beyond the capital into the mountains – he will return there this summer. He let slip there is a boy there who looks like one of the Otori.'

She stared at him, puzzled. 'What do you mean?'

'It may be nothing important. An illegitimate son... ?'

'Lord Shigeru's?' she said in a forced voice.

'No, no, I would not suggest that. The boy must be fifteen or sixteen, nearly fully grown. But from the Otori, definitely.' His voice trailed away. 'I am making too much of it: I thought Lord Shigeru would like to know.'

Shizuka had been kneeling quietly to one side. Now she said, 'Lady Maruyama, may I ask this man a question?'

Naomi nodded, grateful for the interruption. He is too old to be Shigeru's son, she was thinking in a mixture of relief and disappointment. But maybe they are related in some way.

'Did he notice anything else?' Shizuka said, her voice compelling. 'He speaks of a facial likeness, no doubt. Did he see the boy's hands?'

Harada stared at her. 'As a matter of fact he did.' He glanced at Naomi and said, 'Lady Maruyama?'

'You may speak in front of her,' Naomi said.

'He noticed them because the boy is one of us, one of the Hidden,' Harada said quietly. 'But he wanted to hold the sword. And his hands were marked across the palm.'

'Like mine?' Shizuka said, holding out her hands palm upwards.

'I suppose so,' Harada said. 'The peddler took a liking to the family, and now he is worried about them. So many of us are dying in the East.'

They all stared at Shizuka's hands, at the straight line that almost seemed to cut the palm in half.

'What does it mean?' Naomi asked.

'It means I have to go to Hagi at once,' Shizuka replied. 'No matter how dangerous it is, and inform Lord Shigeru. You need not go,' she told Harada. 'I must go! I must tell him this!'

The idea came to Naomi that she would present him with this boy; it seemed like a gift, to replace the child she had had to kill. She saw the hand of God in it. This was the message Shizuka must take for her. Amazed and grateful, she rose to her feet.

'Yes, you must go to Hagi and tell Lord Otori. You must go at once.'

CHAPTER FORTY-SIX

Shigeru's days were spent in overseeing his estate – the sesame crop had indeed proved successful – and his nights in sorting out the information Shizuka brought him about the Tribe. Chiyo had long since decided she was a woman from the pleasure district and approved wholeheartedly, while at the same time appreciating the need for secrecy and for the visits to be kept from Shigeru's mother. She made sure they were left alone.

For years Shigeru had been leading many different lives, all separate from each other, all kept secret from each other. He developed a liking for deception, his whole life a series of pretences, a game that he knew he played with flair and skill. The tragedies of his life had hardened him – not to make him less compassionate towards others but certainly towards himself, leading him to a detachment from self-concern that gave him a sense of freedom.

There was no trace of self-pity in his nature. Many people wanted him dead, but he would not succumb to their malevolence, nor take on their hatred. He embraced life more wholeheartedly and took pleasure in all its joys. Fate could be said to have dealt with him harshly, but he did not feel like a victim of fate. Rather, he was grateful for his life and all that he had learned from it. He remembered what Matsuda had said to him after the defeat: You will learn what makes you a man.

It had been a harder battle than Yaegahara, but it had not ended in defeat.

'I think I have found your Kikuta nephew.' Shizuka hardly waited for him to greet her or to take her safely inside the house before she whispered the news. It was almost the end of the sixth month; he had not expected visitors during the plum rains but now they were nearly over he had been hoping daily that she would come.

'It has been such a long time!' he said, astonished by his pleasure in seeing her, astounded by her words. She herself was trembling with emotion.

'I had been worried about you,' he went on. 'I had heard nothing from you for so long and I have not seen Kenji this year.'

'Lord Shigeru, I don't think I will be able to come again. I am afraid I am being watched. I only came now because this news was so important. And because I have been in Maruyama.'

'Is she well?'

'She is now, but last year... after your meeting at Terayama...'

She did not need to explain it to him; it was what he had feared each time they met.

'No!' he said. He could feel sweat forming on his forehead. Small spots danced in front of his eyes. He heard Shizuka speak as if from a great distance.

'She asks you to forgive her.'

'I should be asking for her forgiveness! All the difficulty of choice, the suffering was hers! I did not even know about it!' He felt rage such as he had not felt in years sweep through him. 'I must kill Iida,' he said. 'Or die myself. We cannot continue living like this.'

'That is why I came to tell you about this boy. I think he is your nephew and Isamu's son.'

Shigeru said, 'Who is Isamu?'

'I have told you about him; his mother did work in Hagi castle when your father was young. She must have been your father's lover. She was married to a Kikuta cousin. Isamu, who was born in the first year of the marriage, turned out to have unbelievable Tribe skills, but he left the Tribe. No one ever does that. And then he died, but no one will say why. I think the Tribe killed him – that's the usual punishment for disobedience.'

'And would be for you,' Shigeru said, amazed again at her fearlessness.

'If they ever find out! That's why I can't come to you any more. I don't think there is much more I can tell you anyway. You have your records now. You know more about the Tribe than any outsider ever has. But now this boy has appeared, among the Hidden in the East. The village is called Mino. He has an Otori look and Kikuta hands: he can only be Isamu's son.'

'He is my nephew!' Shigeru said with a sort of wonderment. 'I can't leave him there!'

'No, you must go and get him. If the Tribe hear of him they will certainly try and claim him, and if they don't he may well be massacred by Iida, who is determined to eradicate the Hidden from all his domains.'

Shigeru remembered the tortured men and children he had seen with his own eyes and his skin crawled with horror.

'And who knows, he may have inherited his father's skills,' Shizuka said.

'He would become our assassin?'

She nodded and they gazed at each other with excited eyes. He wanted to take her in his arms; it was more than gratitude, he realized, as desire for her flooded through him. He saw something in her expression, and knew he had only to reach out to her and she would give herself to him; that they both desired it equally; that neither of them would ever mention it again and that it would be no betrayal, just a recognition of deep need. Lust engulfed him, for a woman's body, a woman's scent... her hands, her hair – she would rescue him from loneliness and grief. She would share his excitement and his hopes.

Neither of them moved.

The moment passed. Shizuka said, 'For this reason also I must not come again. We are becoming too close; you know what I mean.'

He nodded without speaking.

'Go to Mino,' she said. 'Go as soon as possible.'

'I can never thank you for all you have done for me,' Shigeru said, speaking formally to hide his emotions. 'I am in your debt forever.'

'I have risked my life for you,' Shizuka said. 'I only ask that you make good use of it.'

After she left, Shigeru went to sit for a while in the garden. The air was humid and hot: not a leaf moved. From time to time a fish splashed. Cicadas droned. He realized his heart was pounding with far more than the sudden and unfulfilled desire: with excitement and anticipation. The boy was the piece in the game that opened up the way for a new attack, the unforeseen move that led to the downfall of the enemy. But more than that: the boy was the link between each of the separate seams of his life, the catalyst that united them all and opened them one to another. He was Lord Shigemori's grandson, Shigeru's closest relative, after Takeshi, his heir. He was the Tribe assassin's son with the skills that would destroy Iida...

He could not sit still. He thought he would take one of the horses out; he needed to feel the animal's rhythm while he made his plans. He had to share this news with someone; he would tell Takeshi.

Takeshi was in the former Mori water meadows with the colts, who were now in their sixth summer. He had broken them in two years before; he was riding the bay, whom he had named Kuri.

Shigeru called to him and Takeshi rode over.

'This horse is so clever,' he said. 'I wish he were better looking.'

Kuri put his ears back and Takeshi laughed. 'See, he understands every word you say. He'll be a good warhorse – not that there's much chance of me ever fighting a battle!'

'Is he fast?'

'Raku's faster,' Takeshi replied, looking affectionately at the grey with the black mane and tail.

'Let's race Raku and Kyu,' Shigeru said. 'See if the new blood can beat the old.'

Takeshi smiled and his eyes gleamed as he transferred bridle and saddle to Raku. It was the sort of challenge he loved. They rode to the end of the meadow and turned the horses. Takeshi counted down from five to one and both horses sprang into a gallop, rejoicing in the loose rein and their riders' shouts of encouragement.

Shigeru did not care if he won or lost. All he cared about was the release the gallop brought and the tears the wind whipped from his eyes.

Raku won by a head, to Takeshi's pleasure. Kuri did not follow them, but seemed to watch the contest with interest.

Takeshi appeared to have put the turmoil of the past behind him, and Shigeru was proud of his brother, impressed by the good looks and manners of the horses. On an impulse he said, 'Come and eat at home tonight. It will make Mother happy and I have something to tell you.'

'I will,' Takeshi said, 'if I can slip away after dinner.'

Shigeru laughed. 'Who is she?'

'Tase – a very beautiful girl. A singer from Yamagata, home of beautiful women. She's got lots of nice friends, if you'd like to meet one!'

'You know so many beautiful women,' Shigeru teased him. 'I can't meet them all.'

'This one is different,' Takeshi said. 'I wish it were possible to marry her.'

'You should marry,' Shigeru replied. 'This girl is probably not suitable for your wife, but someone else could be found.'

'Yes, someone chosen by Iida Sadamu to strengthen our alliance with the Tohan! I prefer to stay single. I don't notice you hurrying to marry either.'

'For similar reasons,' Shigeru replied.

'Iida has far too much say in our lives,' Takeshi said quietly. 'Let's kill him!'

'That's what I want to talk to you about.'

Takeshi breathed out deeply. 'At last!'

They rode back to Hagi together, talking about horses, and parted at the stone bridge, Takeshi taking the horses back to the Mori stables before joining his mother and brother, Shigeru riding through the town towards his mother's house. The unrest of the previous years had largely settled down: the town had regained its prosperous and industrious nature, but he hardly noticed it, nor the greetings that were called to him. He was thinking about the boy in Mino.

He ate the evening meal distractedly, but his mother did not notice; her attention was entirely taken up by her younger son. Chiyo was also delighted to have Takeshi in the house again, and kept appearing with more bowls of his favourite food. There was a festive atmosphere, and everyone drank a great deal of wine. Finally Shigeru excused himself, saying he had pressing affairs to attend to; Ichiro and Takeshi immediately offered their help.

'I do have some things to discuss with my brother while he's here,' Shigeru said. Ichiro was happy enough to remain behind and take a few more cups of wine. Shigeru and Takeshi withdrew to the back room, where the scrolls and records were kept. Shigeru swiftly told Takeshi the news about their nephew while Takeshi listened with astonishment and mounting excitement.

'I'll come with you,' he said at once when he heard Shigeru's intention to find the boy and bring him home. 'You can't go alone.'

'I can leave the city alone and go travelling. Everyone's used to my eccentricities now…'

'You have been planning this for years,' Takeshi said with admiration. 'I am sorry I ever doubted you.'

'I have been planning something. But I did not know what until now! I had to convince everyone that I was powerless and harmless. It is my main defence. If we travel together it will make our uncles suspicious.'

'Then let us leave the city separately and meet somewhere. I will go to Tsuwano or Yamagata: I will pretend it is for some festival. Tase will be my excuse and my cover. Everyone knows I put pleasure above duty most of the time!'

Shigeru laughed. 'I am sorry I scolded you so often for it when it was no more than a pretence.'

'I forgive you,' Takeshi said. 'I forgive you everything because we will finally have our revenge. Where shall we meet? Where is this village anyway?'

Beyond Inuyama, Shizuka had said, in the mountains on the edge of the Three Countries. Shigeru had never been that far to the East. The brothers pored over such maps as they had, trying to make sense of their rivers, roads and mountain ranges. Mino was too insignificant to appear on them. Shigeru turned to the records he had compiled from Shizuka's information, but Mino and the surrounding areas must have had no Tribe families, for there was no mention of them.

'In the mountains behind Inuyama,' Takeshi mused. 'We used to know the area around Chigawa well. Why don't we meet there, near the cavern where Iida fell in? We can pray that the same gods who led him there will oblige us and enable us to finish their work.'

They arranged to meet there a few days after the Star Festival. Takeshi would ride from Yamagata, Shigeru would take the northern way across Yaegahara.

'Now I must go to my Tase and tell her the good news,' Takeshi said. 'She'll be happy if we go to Yamagata. She longs for me to meet her family. I'll see you at the Ogre's Storehouse.'

'Till then,' Shigeru replied and the brothers embraced.

Shigeru wanted to leave immediately but while he was making preparations for his departure his mother began to complain of feeling unwell. She was often affected by the summer heat and he thought little of it. Then Chiyo told him there was some virulent fever going around: many people were dying in Hagi.

'Almost from one day to the next,' she said with foreboding. 'They are well in the morning; in the evening
they are burning and by dawn they have passed on.'

She encouraged him to leave at once to protect himself.

'My brother has already gone away. I cannot leave
my mother to die with neither of her sons present,' he
replied, filled with concern for her and anguish at the
delay her sickness would cause him.

'Shall I send word to Lord Takeshi?' Chiyo asked.

'Insist he does not return home,' Shigeru said. 'There
is no point in him risking infection.'

That night two of the household servants died and the
following morning his mother's maid followed them into
that other world. When Shigeru went to his mother's room
he saw that she too was near death. He spoke to her and
she opened her eyes and seemed to recognize him. He
thought she might reply; she frowned slightly, then
murmured, 'Tell Takeshi...' but she did not go on. Two
days later, she was dead. The next day he felt a sense of
doom descend on him; his head ached fiercely and he
could eat nothing.

By the time his mother's funeral took place, Shigeru
was delirious, burning with fever, assailed by terrible hallu-
cinations, made worse by his sense of urgency that Takeshi
would go to the Ogre's Storehouse and Shigeru would not
be there.

Chiyo hardly left his side, tending him as she had
when he was a child. Sometimes priests came to the
doorway and chanted; Chiyo burned incense and brewed

bitter infusions, sent for a spirit girl, and muttered spells and incantations.

When he began to recover he remembered her weeping beside him, the tears falling, it seemed, throughout the night, when they were alone in the struggle against death and all formalities removed between them.

'You did not need to cry so much,' he said. 'Your spells worked. I have recovered.' He had felt well enough to bathe, and sat in a light cotton robe – for it was still very hot – on the veranda while the upstairs room where he had spent so many days of sickness was cleaned and purified.

Chiyo had brought tea and fruit; though she was delighted that he was well, her eyes were still puffy and red-rimmed. She looked at him and could not control herself. He saw the grief was for something else, and fear stabbed at him.

'What has happened?'

'Forgive me,' she said, her voice breaking with sobs. 'I will send Ichiro to you.'

Shigeru waited for his old teacher with mounting dread. The man's face did not reassure him: he was as grief-stricken as Chiyo. But his voice was firm, and he spoke with his usual self-control, without shrinking from the blow nor trying to soften it.

'Lord Takeshi is dead. A letter came from Matsuda Shingen. He died in Yamagata and is buried at Terayama.'

Shigeru thought stupidly, He will not be waiting for me. I don't have to worry about that. Then he could hear nothing but the sound of the river beyond the garden. Its waters seemed to rise around him. He had lost Takeshi in its murky depths after all. Now all he wanted was for the water to submerge and choke him.

He heard a harsh sobbing and realized it was himself, a terrible pain spreading through chest and throat.

'It was the fever? He did not escape it?'

Why now, just when they were about to act together? Why had the plague not taken him in his brother's place? He saw Takeshi on Raku's back, galloping through the water meadows, his look of delight when he won the race, his face bright, intensely alive, the emotion with which he spoke of the girl, Tase.

'I am afraid not,' Ichiro said bleakly. 'No one knows what happened. Matsuda says the body bore many wounds.'

'He was murdered?' Shigeru felt the sword cuts in his own flesh. 'In Yamagata? Did anyone know who he was? Has any reparation been made?'

'Believe me, I have tried to find out,' Ichiro said. 'But if anyone knows, they are not telling.'

'My uncles have been informed, presumably. What has their reaction been? Have they demanded apologies, explanations?'

'They have expressed their deep regret,' Ichiro said. 'I have letters from them.'

'I must go to them.' Shigeru tried to rise, but found his body would not obey him. He was trembling as if his fever had returned.

'You are still not well,' Ichiro said, with unusual gentleness. 'Do not confront them now. Wait a few days until you are fully recovered and have regained your self-control.'

Shigeru knew Ichiro was right, but the pain of waiting, while he did not know how Takeshi had died nor what the Otori clan's response would be, was intolerable to him. The days of grief and mourning dragged slowly by. He could not comprehend the cruelty of fate that had given him a nephew only to take his beloved brother.

Kenji will know, if anyone does, he thought, and wrote to his friend, sending the letter through Muto Yuzuru. He tried to heal grief with rage. If his uncles would do nothing, then he himself would have to avenge his brother against the men who had killed him, against their lord. But the lack of knowledge paralysed him, leaving him unable to act. He longed for the days of fever to return, for with all their torment they had been more bearable than this terrible helpless grief. He had thought himself not made for despair, but now its darkness closed around him. When he slept, he dreamed of Takeshi as a child in the river. He dived repeatedly, but his brother's pale limbs slipped from his grasp and his body disappeared with the flow of the tide.

Awake, he could not believe Takeshi was dead. He heard his footfall, his voice, and saw his shape everywhere. Takeshi seemed embodied in every object in the house. There he had sat, this bowl he had drunk from, this straw horse was one he played with years ago. Every corner of the garden bore his imprint – the street, the riverbank, the whole city.

Seeking some activity to distract him, he thought he should check on the horses now Takeshi was no longer there to care for them, and found Mori Hiroki had taken it upon himself to oversee them. They grazed unconcerned; he was relieved to see the black-maned grey still there, Raku, who would forever remind him of his brother, and the black colt from the same mare as his own horse, Kyu.

'Where is the bay?' he said to Hiroki.

'Takeshi took him,' Hiroki replied. 'He made a joke about it, saying Raku was too recognizable, and Kuri was a better disguise.'

'Then we will never see the horse again,' Shigeru said. 'If he survived, someone will have stolen him by now.'

'It's a shame. Such a clever horse! And Takeshi had taught him so much.' Hiroki continued to stare towards the horses while he said, 'His death is a terrible loss.'

'So many of us are gone,' Shigeru said. So many of the boys who fought each other with stones.

Two weeks later, when he was beginning to recover some of his physical strength, Chiyo came, saying a messenger had arrived from Yamagata.

'I told him to give me the letter, but he insists he'll put it into no one's hands but yours. I told him Lord Otori did not receive grooms, but he won't go away.'

'Did he give his name?'

'Kuroda, or something like that.'

'Send him to me,' Shigeru said. 'Bring wine and see no one disturbs us.'

The man came to the room, knelt before him and greeted him. His voice was uneducated, the accent that of Yamagata. Chiyo was right: he looked like a groom, possibly once a foot soldier, with an old scar across his left forearm, but Shigeru knew he was from the Tribe, knew he would be tattooed beneath the clothes in the Kuroda fashion, as Shizuka had told him, could no doubt dissemble his features and appear in many different disguises.

'Muto Kenji sends you his greetings,' Kuroda said. 'He has written to you.' He took the scroll from the breast of his jacket and gave it to Shigeru. Shigeru unrolled it and recognized the seal, the old way of writing 'fox'.

'He has also told me everything he could find out, and I myself already had some details,' Kuroda said, his face and voice expressionless. 'You may ask me any questions when you have finished reading.'

'Were you there?' Shigeru asked at once.

'I was in Yamagata. I knew of the incident as soon as it happened. But no one knew until some days later that the murdered man was Lord Takeshi. He was in travelling clothes; everyone else with him perished inside the house. It seems the Tohan surrounded it and set fire to it. Your brother escaped the flames but was cut down outside.'

Shigeru read the letter, his face muscles clenched, saving other questions for afterwards, when he might be able to speak without weeping. When he had finished reading, silence fell on the room. The cicadas droned, the river ebbed.

Finally Shigeru said, calmly, detachedly, 'Kenji writes that there was a fight earlier, outside an inn?'

'Lord Takeshi was provoked and insulted by a group of low-rank Tohan warriors. He was not drunk, but everyone else had been drinking heavily. The Tohan often act in this way in Yamagata: they swagger around like conquerors and always end up insulting the Otori, and – forgive me – Lord Shigeru in particular. Lord Takeshi bore it as long as was humanly possible, but inevitably a fight broke out – six or seven of them against one. After Lord Takeshi had killed two of them, the rest ran away.' He was silent for a moment. 'It seems he was an excellent swordsman.'

'Yes,' Shigeru said briefly, remembering the strength and grace of the young man.

'He returned to the house where he was staying: he was with a young woman, a very beautiful girl, only seventeen years old, a singer.'

'I suppose she is dead too?'

'Yes, and her entire family. The Tohan said they were Hidden, but everyone in Yamagata knows they were not.'

'The men were definitely Tohan?'

'They wore the triple oak leaf and came from Inuyama. They forbade anyone to move Lord Takeshi's body – no one knew who he was, but a merchant from Hagi who was visiting Yamagata recognized him. He spread the word, went to the castle himself and demanded the body be released to him. It has been very hot, this summer. Lord Takeshi needed to be buried. The merchant took the body immediately to Terayama. The murderers of course were aghast: they had had no idea they had killed Lord Otori's brother. They surrendered themselves to the lord at the castle, pleading only to be allowed to kill themselves honourably, but the lord advised them to return to Inuyama and inform Iida themselves.'

'Iida has punished them?'

'Far from it. He is reported to have received the news with pleasure.' Kuroda hesitated. 'I don't want to offend Lord Otori...'

'Tell me what he said.'

'His exact words were, "One less of those Otori to worry about. Too bad it wasn't the brother." Far from punishing them, he rewarded them and now looks on them with favour.' Kuroda pressed his lips firmly together and stared at the floor.

Rage seemed to lick his gut with its molten tongue. He welcomed it, for it dried up grief and tears instantaneously. Rage would sustain him now, rage and his craving for revenge.

His uncles' behaviour did nothing to dull his rage. They expressed their profound regret for Takeshi's death, and for his mother's, as well as their deep concern for his health. When Shigeru demanded to know what their response would be and when they would seek apologies and recompense from Iida, they were first evasive and finally adamant. No demands would be made. Takeshi's death was an unfortunate accident. Lord Iida could not be held responsible.

'We do not need to remind you of your brother's recklessness in the past. He has been involved in many brawls,' Shoichi said.

'When he was younger,' Shigeru said. 'Most young men make similar mistakes.' Indeed, Masahiro's oldest son, Yoshitomi, had only recently been involved in an ugly fight in the town in which two boys had died. 'I believe Takeshi was settling down.'

'Maybe you are right,' Masahiro said with palpable insincerity. 'Alas, we will never know. Let the dead rest in peace.'

'To tell you the truth, Shigeru,' Shoichi said, watching his nephew carefully, 'negotiations are under way for a formal alliance with the Tohan. We would agree to establish legally the current borders, and support the Tohan in their expansion into the West.'

'We should never make such an alliance,' Shigeru said immediately. 'If the Tohan move into the West they will encircle us completely. Next they will absorb what's left of the Middle Country. The Seishuu are our defence against that.'

'Iida plans to deal with the Seishuu – by marriage if possible, and if not, by war.' Masahiro laughed as if with pleasure at the prospect.

'Who in the West threatens war against him? He imagines enemies everywhere!'

'You have been ill: you are not completely informed about recent events,' Shoichi replied blandly.

'Lord Shigeru should think about marrying again,' Masahiro remarked, apparently changing the subject. 'Since you have retired from the political stage, you should enjoy your simple life to the full. Let us find you a wife.'

'I have no desire to marry again,' Shigeru replied.

'My brother is right, though,' Shoichi said. 'You must enjoy life and regain your health. Take a trip, look at some mountain scenery, visit a shrine, collect some more ancient tales.' He smiled at his brother, and Shigeru saw their mockery.

'I will go to Terayama to my brother's grave.'

'It is a little early for that,' Shoichi said. 'You will not go there. But you may travel to the East.'

CHAPTER FORTY-SEVEN

Very well, Shigeru thought. I will obey my uncles. I will travel to the East.

He set out the next day telling Chiyo and Ichiro he would visit the temple of Shokoji and spend a few days in retreat there, praying for the dead. For the first part of the journey he rode, taking Kyu and several retainers with him as companions. He left men and horses at the last small town before the border, Susamura, and went on alone on foot, like a pilgrim. He stayed for two nights at the temple, Shokoji, and on the third morning rose before dawn under the full moon and walked through the mountain pass, directly east, following the twin stars called the Cat's Eyes until the sky paled and he was walking directly towards the rising sun. Its light fell across the browning grass of the plain; there was little sign now of the ten thousand who had died there, though occasionally bones of horses and men lay in the dust where foxes and wolves had been scavenging. He could not help recalling how he had ridden here with Kiyoshige, how the young horses had galloped eagerly across the plain – and the scenes of torture they had found on the other side in the border village. Now all this country belonged to the Tohan: would any Hidden have survived here?

He saw nobody on the plain, only pheasants and hares. He stopped to drink at the spring where he had rested with Kiyoshige, remembering how the tortured man Tomasu had come crawling towards them, wordlessly imploring them to help him. It was past midday by then, and very hot. He rested for a while beneath the shade of the pines, trying to keep from his mind images of a boy with Takeshi's face dying slowly above a fire, until the sense of urgency drove him on. He followed a fox track that went almost straight across the tawny surface towards the mountains that lay to the north of Chigawa. Mostly, he slept outside, only for the hours between moonset and dawn while it was too dark to see the path in front of him. He followed mountain tracks, frequently getting lost, having to retrace his steps, occasionally wondering if he would ever return to the Middle Country, or if he would perish here in the impenetrable forest and no one would ever know what had become of him.

He avoided Chigawa itself, taking the track to the north, and then turning south again. He met few people on the path, but as it bent back around Chigawa there were signs that a large group of men had recently travelled along it. Branches were broken back; the ground was smoothed out by their feet. Shigeru did not want to meet whoever they were coming back; he was looking for a way to strike out to the east but the terrain was very wild, with many jagged outcrops of rocks, steep ravines and thick forest. It seemed he had no alternative but to follow the track all the way to the pass.

He turned a corner to see something pale in the undergrowth. A dead man lay there, his throat recently cut, his barely clothed, emaciated body still warm. Shigeru knelt by him, saw the rope marks on wrist and neck, the calluses on his knees, the broken nails and scarred hands, and realized who was ahead of him: this man had been a miner, one of those forced to work in the silver and copper mines that riddled the district around Chigawa. Part of a group being moved from one mine to another, he must have collapsed from exhaustion and been cold-bloodedly dispatched and left unburied.

He was Otori once, Shigeru thought, one of the thousands who looked to me for protection, and I failed them.

He dragged the body further up the hill, found a crevice and buried it there, piling the entrance with rocks and praying before it. Then he went in search of water, both to ease his thirst and to cleanse himself. He found a pool where water had oozed between rocks, and decided to sleep for a while to give the mining party time to outpace him. There was no wind, no sound at all other than the mewing of kites and the clamour of cicadas.

He woke to the same sounds, drank again, and went back to the track. As he came to the pass he could see all the way back across Yaegahara and as far as the sea to the north. The sun was well over to the west; he thought it would be two hours or so before sunset – but anyway he planned to walk all night, south to the mountains behind Inuyama.

He made the descent quickly in the cooler air, always listening for the sounds of human activity on the track ahead, but he was almost in the valley and the light was fading before he came suddenly on the mining party.

They had stopped to rest by a small pool, presumably for the night. The miners, men and women tied together, some hardly out of childhood, had fallen to the ground where they had halted, and slept as if already dead, like grotesque heaps of corpses. No one had made fire: a group of armed men – five by his swift count – squatted at the head of the line, eating cold food from a shared box and passing a bamboo flask around. They ate in complete silence.

Their hands went to their swords when they saw Shigeru: he greeted them briefly and walked on past them, ready at any moment to turn to meet their attack with Jato. Their glances were suspicious; they did not jump on him, possibly deterred by his sword, but one of them called to him, 'Sir, just a moment, please.'

He turned: the man who had spoken stepped towards him, a large soldier with an air of authority, not the sort of person he would have expected to find guarding what was little more than a bunch of slaves. Shigeru felt he knew him, might have seen him once years ago when Iida had ridden away from Chigawa. He stood and waited impassively.

The soldier peered up into his face. Recognition flickered into his eyes.

'Is it you?' he began, but got no further, as a disturbance erupted behind him among the prostrate bodies. One of the miners was screaming, thrashing against his bonds, tossing those tied to him from side to side, their bony arms rising and falling as though thrown up by the sea.

Shigeru saw Komori, the man who had saved Iida's life: the Underground Emperor. He realized that Komori knew him, that this was a ploy to save Shigeru's life, and, in the instant it took to draw Jato, that he would die here rather than abandon him.

The large man screamed to the others, 'It is Otori! Don't kill him! He must be taken alive.' Shigeru struck him from behind, in the neck, severing the spinal cord. Two others had seized a net, with which they trapped villagers to abduct them into the mines. He evaded their first throw, ducking under it and cutting one of them upwards deep into the thigh, opening the main artery of the leg. As the wounded man fell, his net descended over him, enmeshing him. Shigeru rolled backwards, using his left shoulder to propel himself out of the reach of the fourth man. He landed on his feet, and in the same movement went forward and brought Jato down on this man's right arm, severing it. The fifth man rushed at him, but the roped miners rose like one shuffling beast and wound themselves around him. He cut vainly at them, but they overpowered him and brought him down.

Shigeru ended the lives of the three who still breathed; then, taking out his short sword, cut the bonds of the prisoners, starting with Komori.

Many of them were wailing with distress and fear: most of them, as soon as they were released, ran to the pool to slake their thirst, and then disappeared into the forest.

Komori was bleeding from a cut under his armpit. It was impossible to tell in the fading light how deep it was. Shigeru washed it as best he could and packed it with moss from around the tree roots. Neither of them spoke at first: Komori's eyes glittered; he was so thin his bones seemed to glimmer palely through his taut skin.

'We have a few hours' start,' he said, getting to his feet and wincing. 'We are not expected at the mine until tomorrow midday. Lord Otori must be on the other side of Yaegahara by then.' He looked at the dead men, kicked their leader and spat on him. 'None of them will talk!'

'What about the prisoners?'

'They will go home – until they are kidnapped again. This is what life is like for us under the Tohan. They will not want to betray you, but no one knows what he will blab out under torture. That's why you must go now, as fast as you can.'

'I would take you with me,' Shigeru said. 'But I am not going back. I am going on.'

'They will come after you. Moreover you are heading straight towards Iida himself. He is combing that whole area,' he jerked his head towards the southeast. 'Searching for those poor wretches they call the Hidden.'

'That's why I must get to a place called Mino. There is someone there I have to save from Iida.'

'Then while I can walk, I will come with you. I think you will go faster with me to guide you. I've never been to Mino but I know Hinode: there's an old mine there. Mino is not far away. Loyalty to the Heron! It will be my last act of service to you.'

Komori muttered one last curse as they left the bodies. 'How I've longed for this day, to see that brute dead. Iida gave us to each other. He has a flair for matching people up like that. He never forgot me, how I made him strip naked and leave his swords behind, and saved his life. This was my reward: to be kept alive in the mines with my own personal jailer and torturer. Never fall into his hands, Lord Otori. Never come into the East again. Unless you come at the head of an army,' he added bitterly. 'We should have left Iida in the Ogre's Storehouse. If you meet him again make sure you kill him.'

'I intend to,' Shigeru said. 'I'm only sorry you have suffered so, through my decision and my defeat.'

Night fell, and for a while they walked as if blind, yet Komori knew the path and did not falter. By the time the moon rose, they had crossed the valley, the pale light casting shadows on the summer grass, picking out the young seed heads. Now and then a fox barked, its mate screamed, and an owl floated suddenly out of the darkness.

Komori started with the same energy Shigeru remembered, and they travelled at some speed, saying little; but as the night wore on, and the half-moon traversed the sky, Komori began to waver; his feet strayed from the path, and several times Shigeru had to take him by the arm and guide him back. He began to babble, believing himself first to be in the mine, and then in Inuyama.

'Across the nightingale floor,' he mumbled. Shigeru did not understand him and Komori seemed gripped by a desperate desire to explain. 'That is where you will find Iida, but no one can reach him because no one can cross it.'

Shigeru made him lean on his shoulder, putting his arm round him to support him and feeling the man's flesh begin to burn as the fever mounted and the blood soaked away. Day was breaking as they reached the next pass. They stopped to rest for a few moments. At their feet lay a steep valley, followed by the next range: he did not think Komori could manage the climb, and wondered how far he would be able to carry him.

'I'm thirsty,' Komori said suddenly, and Shigeru lifted him and carried him down to the river. He set the man down in the shallow water on the nearer bank.

'Ah, that feels good,' Komori sighed, but within moments he was shivering violently. Shigeru cupped his hands and helped him to drink, then drew him up onto the rocky bank, into the morning sun.

'Go, Lord Shigeru, leave me here,' Komori pleaded in moments of lucidity, in between trying to impress on Shigeru the path he must take to reach Mino, but Shigeru could not bring himself to abandon him to die alone, so he sat with him, bathing the sweat away and moistening his parched mouth.

Komori said suddenly, 'When you come out from underground, the world always looks so bright and fresh, as if it had just been created!'

He spoke so clearly Shigeru imagined he was recovering, but he did not speak again; and before midday he was dead.

There was nowhere to bury him. Shigeru piled rocks over the body as best he could, and said the necessary prayers for the dead; he resumed his journey sick at heart with sorrow and rage for Komori's terrible punishment, for the sufferings of his people. Komori had said he should return at the head of an army – but he had no men, no influence, no power. All he had was his sword and the boy who waited somewhere ahead of him. Now he let his rage give him the strength to walk day and night towards him.

Finally he came to the small village, Hinode, a few houses and an inn around a series of hot springs. The air smelled of sulphur, and the village itself was shabby and dirty. He asked about the surrounding district, and was told that the only other village nearby was the tiny one of Mino, not much more than a hamlet, on the other side of the mountain, a day's walk away, where no one ever went and the people were considered strange. The woman who ran the inn would not say more, though Shigeru pressed her, and though she was quite happy to take his coins and knew very well what silver was.

He slept for a few hours and set out before daybreak, following the track she had told him about. It was steep and narrow, a hard climb up to the top of the pass, and then an awkward scramble down. The path did not seem much used – the two villages obviously had little contact with each other – except by adders who as the day grew hotter basked on the warm surface and shot away into the undergrowth at his approach.

When he reached the pass it was mid-afternoon. He realized the weather was changing, dark clouds moving in from the southwest. He was about halfway down towards the valley when it began to rain. As the light faded, a renewed sense of urgency gripped him. He thought he could smell smoke and hear shouts and screams. What if Iida were there? What if he were able finally to confront his enemy? He found his hand straying to Jato's hilt and felt the sword's longing to be released. He plunged downwards, leaping from rock to rock, ignoring the path, taking the most direct route, until his rushing descent was halted by a huge cedar that rose beside the path on the edge of the bamboo grove, next to a small stone shrine. The straw rope round the trunk gleamed in the dusk.

There was no doubt about the smell of smoke. It filled his nostrils and made his mouth dry. Ahead of him he could even see the glow of flames. An ominous silence had fallen; apart from the hiss of the rain there was no sound at all. No screaming, no clash of swords, no dogs barking, no birds singing. However, as Shigeru caught his breath he heard footsteps. Someone was running up the path towards him, running for his life, pursued, he thought, by at least three men.

Shigeru stepped out from behind the tree and the boy ran straight into him. Shigeru caught him by the shoulders, peered into the terrified face and saw the image of Takeshi.

He gripped him as if he would never let him go. The boy twisted and struggled, then went still and Shigeru saw his lips move as if he were praying.

He thinks he is going to die. He thinks I will be the one to kill him. But I have found him! I will save him!

He was laughing with joy and relief. The blood seemed to resound between them. Then he readied himself to fight for his life, for both their lives, as three Tohan warriors rounded the curve and halted in surprise in front of them.

None of the three was in armour nor did they carry swords. They were not expecting to fight, but to slaughter. Their leader approached Shigeru, his hand on the hilt of the knife he wore in his belt.

'Excuse me, sir,' the man said. 'You have apprehended the criminal we were chasing. Thank you.'

Shigeru did not reply immediately. He wanted the three of them to come closer so he could deal with them all at once. He was assessing their build, their weapons. He could see the knife; the other two had poles.

'What has this criminal done?' he said, turning the boy a little so he could push him aside out of harm's way in an instant, all the while studying the man in front of him. He was fairly sure he had never seen him before.

'Excuse me, that is no concern of yours. It is purely the business of Iida Sadamu and the Tohan clan.'

'Unnh, is that so?' Shigeru replied with deliberate insolence. 'And who might you be to tell me what is and what is not my concern?' He wanted to enrage them, and, as the leader snarled, 'Just hand him over,' pushed the boy behind him and drew his sword all in one movement.

The closer of the two men carrying poles took a swing at him. Shigeru ducked under the blow, stood and let Jato strike at the man's neck, severing the head; he turned immediately and met the leader's attack, his sword connecting with the outstretched arm and slicing through it as though through bean curd. The man fell to his knees, his left hand grasping at the stump and the spurting blood. He did not make a sound.

The third man dropped his pole and ran back down the path, shouting for help. In the distance someone called back.

'Come on,' Shigeru said to the boy who was standing trembling with shock. Shigeru's voice seemed to rouse him; he fell to his knees.

'Get up!'

The boy protested that he must find his mother, but Shigeru pulled him to his feet. He did not think that anyone would remain alive in the village, and he was not going to risk the boy's life in finding out. He hurried him up the slope. The rain was falling heavily and it was almost dark. He doubted they would be pursued once night had fallen.

As they ran the boy told him in brief shocked words about the soldiers and the attack, and then said, 'But that wasn't only why they were after me. I caused Lord Iida to fall from his horse.'

It made Shigeru burst out laughing. It seemed like a sign: a sign of Iida's downfall at this boy's hands.

'You saved my life,' the boy said. 'It belongs to you from this day on.'

Shigeru laughed again with mixed feelings of delight and pride. He had courage and fine instincts; he was a true Otori.

'What's your name, boy?' he asked.

'Tomasu,' the boy replied.

Tomasu!

'That's a common name among the Hidden,' Shigeru said. 'Better get rid of it.'

An idea suddenly came to him and he said, 'You can be called Takeo.'

He had already decided he would adopt this boy and make him his son. Otori Takeo: his son. And together they would destroy Iida Sadamu.

ACKNOWLEDGMENTS

I would like to thank:

Asialink for the fellowship that enabled me to go to Japan for twelve weeks in 1999–2000; the Australia Council and the Department of Foreign Affairs and Trade for supporting the Asialink program; the Australian Embassy in Tokyo; Akiyoshidai International Arts Village, Yamaguchi Prefecture, for sponsoring me for that time; Shuho-cho International Cultural Exchange House program for inviting me for a further three months in 2002; ArtsSA, the South Australian Department for the Arts, for a mid-career fellowship that gave me time to write; Urinko Gekidan in Nagoya for inviting me to work with them in 2003.

My husband and children who have supported and encouraged me in so many ways.

In Japan, Kimura Miyo, Mogi Masaru, Mogi Akiko, Tokuriki Masako, Tokuriki Miki, Santo Yuko, Mark Brachmann, Maxine McArthur, Kori Manami, Yamaguchi Hiroi, Hosokawa Fumimasa, Imahori Goro, Imahori Yoko and all the other people who have helped me with research and travel.

Christopher E. West and Forest W. Seal at www.samurai-archives.com

All the publishers and agents who are now part of the Otori clan round the world, especially Jenny Darling, Donica Bettanin, Sarah Lutyens and Joe Regal. My editors Bernadette Foley (Hachette Livre Australia) and Harriet Wilson (Pan Macmillan), and Christine Baker from Gallimard.

And my most profound thanks to Sugiyama Eiichi, brother of my former calligrapher Sugiyama Kazuko who passed away in 2006, for the calligraphy for *Heaven's Net is Wide*.

SET 300 YEARS BEFORE OTORI . . .

The Tale of Shikanoko

is the brand-new series by Lian Hearn